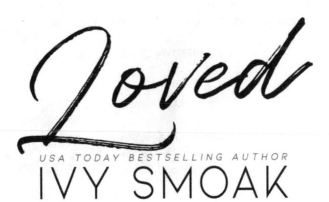

Loved

USA TODAY BESTSELLING AUTHOR

IVY SMOAK

This book is a work of fiction. Names, characters, places, and incidents are fictitious. Any resemblance to actual persons, living or dead, events, or locales is purely coincidental.

ISBN: 978-1-942381-58-7

2024 First Edition

To everyone who loves James as much as I do.

Chapter 1

Tuesday

My heart was hammering against my ribcage. I didn't know what Isabella had done. But I knew it was bad.

I looked down at the invitation in my hand. I'd thought it was from my friends. But…what if it wasn't? What if it was some twisted game Isabella was playing?

She'd hurt people before. My crazy ex-wife had a penchant for ruining lives. I was pretty sure that was her vice. Hell, I'd even let her ruin mine for a few years.

My vices were usually alcohol and drugs. I thought about Penny lying naked in my bed. And sex. Definitely sex. But if Isabella had hurt one of my friends…I wasn't letting this go. Maybe my new vice would be ruining Isabella's life for a fucking change.

"Ian," I said into my phone. "Just tell me what Isabella has done."

"I tried everything to stop…"

"Tell me."

Ian sighed. "She leaked the story to the press."

I looked up from the invitation. "Wait. What?"

"Her version of events of what happened between you and Penny. It's bad, James."

It took me a second to process his words. This wasn't about my friends? I set the invitation down. I'd been thinking about college, reminiscing with my therapist. I was thinking about trying to mend my relationships with my friends. But Isabella didn't know that. Isabella had no reason to lash out at Mason, Matt, or Rob. She had no reason to lash out at me either. But…it was Isabella.

"So my friends are okay?" I asked.

"What does that have to do with anything?" Ian asked. "James, the story is being printed as we speak."

I set the invitation down as the repercussion of what Isabella had done finally hit me. She'd gone to the press. With *her* version of what happened between us. Which meant she'd left out a lot of details. Like that fact that she'd cheated on me. *Ah, fuck me.*

"Then stop the story," I said.

"We're in the middle of nowhere. We don't have connections to the press here."

I'd hardly classify Delaware as the middle of nowhere. But he was right. I didn't have the same connections here as I did in New York. "What paper is it? Surely we can hand someone some cash to make this disappear."

"I already tried everything. It's a huge story, James. Especially for a small town like this to break."

I leaned back in my chair and stared at the ceiling. "How bad is it?"

"Isabella told the press that Penny was a minor."

Jesus. "Surely they'll do their due-diligence."

"I don't know," Ian said. "Like I said…small town. Not many resources. And it's already being picked up by national media."

For fuck's sake. "Give me the name of the paper. I'll handle it."

"It's the Delaware Post."

I hung up the phone and called them. But it went straight to voicemail. What kind of shit press was this?

I called one news outlet after the next. I reached out to all my connections in New York City. But everyone just told me the same thing. That stopping the story there wouldn't help. Everyone was reporting it. Since when had the news turned into a gossip column?

LOVED

Around 2 a.m. a news van pulled up outside my apartment building.

Ian was right. There was no stopping this.

I pushed away from my desk and walked into the hall. The only thing I could do was get some sleep before all hell broke loose in the morning. I went into my bedroom and stared down at Penny sleeping peacefully in my bed.

I'd wanted to talk to her about our future. I wanted it to be us to decide together what our next steps were.

But Isabella had stolen that from us.

I got ready for bed and climbed under the sheets next to Penny. I breathed in her cherry perfume and tried to sleep.

But I'd never been good at lying still.

I pushed the covers off of me and wandered back into my office. I'd really wanted to talk to Penny about this. I did want to. But we didn't have that luxury now. I needed to get ahead of this situation.

I pulled out a piece of paper and started to write my resignation letter. My fresh start in Delaware was dead. But this was the last thing I'd let Isabella rob me of.

I shot an email to the dean scheduling a meeting for the morning. Even before the news story, my lawyer thought I'd be fired. There was no real choice here. And there was nothing Penny and I could discuss now either. There was no way to keep our relationship a secret until after the semester. I had to get control of this scandal in my own way. I slipped my resignation letter into an envelope. It was done.

But Penny and I would get through this. We had to. Because I knew what the alternative was. I knew what I was capable of and what I wasn't. And I had to make this work. Because if I didn't...

I sighed. I was tired. Just so fucking tired of ruining everything around me. If I lost Penny I wouldn't be able to make it through that. I'd slip. And there'd be no point in coming up for air this time.

***

Even though I knew what Isabella had done, I still couldn't shake away my thoughts about the weird invitation I'd gotten. I'd looked up the address and it was just a normal bar. Nothing odd about it. But I'd still texted Mason, asking how he was. I just needed to know that everything was fine so I could put my mind at ease.

Mason liked to party, but it was almost 3 a.m. on a weeknight. I'd have to wait until the morning to hear from him.

So instead I just stared at the Delaware Post website, waiting for it to refresh. My hands were buried in my hair as I stared down at my cell phone. The news would drop online any minute. *Any fucking minute.*

"James?"

I looked up. Penny was standing in the doorway of my office in one of my t-shirts. She was so beautiful. And I'd just ruined her life. I couldn't help but think that. I was trying to be better for her. But trying was a lot different than actually being better.

The news wasn't just ruining my fresh start. It was ruining her college experience. And she'd already told me once that I'd ruined her.

"Why didn't you come to bed?" she asked.

"I did." I sighed. "I couldn't sleep."

She walked over to me. "We'll figure it out. Just like you said." She leaned against my desk.

I shook my head. "I was so busy thinking about my feelings for you that I didn't think about all the repercussions..."

"You did think everything through. We talked about that on our first date."

I shook my head again. Loving her had consequences. But I thought I was the one jeopardizing everything. I was selfish. This story was going to throw her in the lime light, and I knew she didn't like being there. "I never thought that the dean would find out before I talked to him, though."

Her eyes grew round. "Has he?"

I'm so sorry, baby. But for some reason I couldn't say it out loud. I wished that this wasn't my fault. I wished we could just keep going the way we had been. I stood up and walked over to the window. I pulled the curtains to the side and looked down at the street.

Penny stepped up beside me and looked down at the shit show below.

There were three news trucks down there now. More would be arriving at dawn.

"Maybe it's for something else?" she said.

I shook my head. "No. The story is being printed in the Delaware Post in the morning." And a million other places. "I've tried everything." I let go of the curtain and raked my fingers through my hair. "I fucked up, Penny. I should have thought about what Isabella would do if..."

She grabbed my arm to stop me from pulling my hair out. "James, you couldn't possibly know what Isabella would do."

"I should have. It's my job to protect you." And Isabella had done shit like this before. I should have known. I fucking should have.

"It isn't. I made my own choices. I knew I was breaking the rules. I kept pursuing you. I wanted to be with you. I knew there might be consequences. I can face them."

"It *is* my job to protect you." Didn't she see that? I wrapped my arms around her and rested my chin on top of her head. She was the only good thing in my life now. For so long I'd thought of teaching as my fresh start. But I didn't really feel better until I'd met her. She was my fresh start. And I should have done more to prevent her from getting hurt by all this.

She sighed and leaned into my chest. "The worst that can happen is that you get fired and I get expelled."

It sounded like she was okay with all of that. How was she so clam right now? "I don't care if I get fired. I just don't want you to get expelled."

"I have good grades. I can get into a different school."

This was what I'd wanted to talk to her about last night. But the conversation was different now. Because we didn't have a choice. And I wasn't sure if she was saying this because she had no other options now or because she really didn't care. Either way, it wasn't that easy.

"It's a scandal, Penny. Other universities may not see your grades as valid." And if Penny was allowed to stay at the University of New Castle…things wouldn't be easy for her. I knew how fast rumors spread better than anyone. And I knew how people would perceive Penny if they believed Isabella's side of events. They'd think Penny broke up a happy marriage. They wouldn't care about the facts, only the idea of a scandal.

"James," Penny said. She leaned back so she could look up at me. "If I could go back, I'd do it all over again."

There was a lump in my throat that I couldn't get rid of.

"Even if I knew I'd be expelled," she said. "You make me so happy. I want to be with you. That's all that matters."

I didn't deserve her. I didn't. But I was never letting go.

She scrunched her mouth to the side in that adorable way I loved. "If anything, I should be apologizing to you. You told me to forget about you. On multiple occasions. I didn't listen..."

"Stop, Penny." This wasn't on her. It was on me. "I couldn't leave you alone either. And I didn't want you to leave me alone. I never meant it. I can't even imagine not being with you."

She took a deep breath. "So we'll face it together."

"Mhm." I smiled down at her. Even though the conversation was different than what I'd wanted, we'd still kind of had it. Maybe we would have come to the same conclusion. Maybe we wouldn't have. But all that really mattered was that we were facing this together like she'd said. "I'm not used to having a partner in crime."

"Well get used to it. You're getting me kicked out of school, so you should probably stick with me for a while. It's the right thing to do."

I laughed. "You should probably call your parents." Hearing this from her would be better than reading about it in the paper.

She finally looked as horrified as I thought she'd be about all of this.

"I'm sorry, Penny."

"I think I'm dreading that discussion more than talking to the dean."

"I'm sorry," I said again.

"Please stop apologizing. James." She put her hands on the sides of my face. "I love you. That's all that matters."

I smiled down at her. I hoped that was enough. I hoped we'd be able to make it through this. I was used to the press, but Penny wasn't. All I could do was try to be her rock through this. "I love you too."

"So will you please come to bed now?"

"Mhm." I leaned down and kissed her.

She laughed as I scooped her up into my arms.

Chapter 2

Wednesday

The alarm started beeping at 6 a.m. I winced. We had a meeting with the dean in an hour and I wasn't ready to face all this.

Penny had been so positive last night. I'd been spiraling and she'd pulled me out of it. But it had been a lot easier when she was wrapped in my arms in the comfort of my bed.

This morning I was a professor.

But in a few hours, I probably wouldn't be.

My pestering thoughts didn't stop the incessant beeping of the alarm though. I turned it off and rolled over to look at Penny. Part of me was surprised she was still here. It would have been a hell of a lot easier for her to come away from this unscathed if she changed her story. She could tell the dean I forced the situation. That I pressured her. That I was a fucking pervert. Disgusting. Violent. That I used my title to take advantage of her. She could throw me under the bus. But she wasn't Isabella.

Still. She could have saved herself. And I wouldn't have blamed her one bit. "You're still here."

Penny smiled. "Of course I'm still here." She propped her head up on her hand.

All I wanted to do was sink my fingers into her hair.

"I need you to promise me something," she said.

"Name it."

She pressed her lips together as she stared at me.

That was more like how I'd been expecting her to look last night. Unsure. I just wanted to pull her into my arms and ignore the world. When we'd gone to New York for the day, I'd wanted to be out of our bubble. But now I just wanted to stay in it forever.

She took a deep breath. "No matter what happens...please don't resent me."

How could she think that? "Penny..."

"Promise me."

"I don't resent you. Please don't think that I'm mad at you about any of this. This is everything I ever wanted. Actually, it is tempting to just run away with you. For you, I'd leave it all. I need you to know that." And I was prepared to. I'd already written my resignation letter. I'd go anywhere with her. As long as we were together, I didn't care where we were.

"I'd leave it all for you too. But I'd be uneducated."

I laughed. "You're very intelligent. A diploma doesn't change that."

"I forgot that you just want me to be a housewife anyway."

Was there really something so wrong with that? I smiled and ran my fingers through her hair like I'd wanted to. "Well today can't go all that poorly because you just told me you want to be my wife. I'm certainly in a good mood."

"I..." her voice trailed off and her cheeks flushed.

God I loved when she blushed. But she had no reason to be embarrassed. "Don't be flustered." I moved my hand to her cheek. "I'm 27 years old. You're the love of my life. I know you feel the same way. You risked everything to be with me. So you must realize that I have every intention of marrying you, Penny Taylor."

Her throat made that adorable squeaking noise. "But we..."

LOVED

"Are you going to fight me on this too?" I flashed her a smile.

"No."

I smiled and climbed out of bed. I knew this conversation was a lot. She was only 20. I was her first real boyfriend. But…everything felt right. And I knew she felt it too. This was how love was supposed to feel. And as long as we had that, how bad could today really be?

I quickly pulled on a pair of navy blue dress pants and buttoned up a grey dress shirt. I rolled the sleeves up my forearms as I walked out of the closet.

Penny was standing there in just one of my t-shirts.

I smiled and glanced at my watch as I finished rolling up my sleeves. "Ellen's already here. So unfortunately you'll need to get dressed."

Penny nodded and disappeared into the closet.

I finished getting ready while she was changing. And then I walked over to the window in my bedroom. The were more news trucks outside my apartment building and there were dozens of people standing outside. A combination of reporters and paparazzi. Probably a few nosey students too. My chest felt tight as I stared at the chaos. *Fuck*. I raked my fingers through my hair.

"Do you think this is okay?" Penny asked.

I turned around. The tightness in my chest immediately eased. It was hard to be stressed out when she was smiling up at me. She'd changed into a pair of jeans, a tank top, and a cardigan. She looked like a student that wouldn't fuck her professor.

"I'm not sure if he's going to be paying attention to what you're wearing," I said. "But you look beautiful."

She looked so nervous despite my words.

I gave her a quick kiss. *It's going to be okay.* We just had to take today one step at a time. I grabbed her hand and led her out to the kitchen to meet Ellen.

Ellen was standing at the stove. As soon as she heard the door open, she turned toward us. She had a huge smile on her face. I knew she'd been looking forward to this.

"You must be Penny," she said. "Oh dear, aren't you pretty. James didn't exaggerate."

Penny blushed again.

"Penny, this is Ellen," I said. It was weird, but now I suddenly felt nervous. I wanted them to get along. Ellen was the closest thing I had to a loving mother. But she'd like Penny. Honestly, she'd probably love anyone who wasn't Isabella.

Penny smiled. "It's so nice to meet you."

"I've heard so much about you, dear."

Why did she keep saying stuff like that? *Stop it, Ellen. Be cool.*

Penny smiled up at me.

Well...Ellen wasn't lying. I talked about Penny all the time. I just never expected Ellen to talk about that fact so much. All I could do was shrug.

"And how do you prefer your eggs?" Ellen asked and turned back to the stove.

"Scrambled," Penny said. "Do you need help with anything?"

Ellen laughed. "I like you already. But no. Sit, sit."

Penny and I both sat down at the kitchen island. There were two newspapers on the counter. The Wall Street Journal and the Delaware Post. I always got the Wall Street Journal, but I'd requested for Ian to grab me this shit local paper too because of the article it contained.

I put my elbow on the counter and rested my chin in my palm. And then I turned my attention to Penny. Because I'd much rather look at her than read those papers.

"You look sexy in glasses," she whispered to me.

"Is that why you're looking at me like that?" I whispered back.

"Like what?"

She knew exactly *like what*. I leaned forward until my lips were against her ear. "Like you want me right here, right now."

Her body tensed.

As much fun as the distraction would be...I knew Penny liked the idea of almost being caught. Not the idea of actually fucking in front of someone else.

I really did need to tell her about the security cameras. And Ian...

But that could wait. I turned back to the papers on the counter. "Have you read it?" I asked Ellen.

Ellen sighed. "The things people say. If they could see how happy you are, you'd think they'd leave well enough alone. My husband is ten years older than me and no one ever gave me a hard time for it. Love is love. Circumstances be damned."

What she'd said was really sweet. But my mind stuck on that one line. My husband *is*.

Ellen's face fell, realizing her slip up too.

I knew she missed her husband. And I knew it was hardest when she slipped up and used the present tense. I forced a laugh, knowing she'd just want to move past it. "I'm guessing it's bad then?"

Ellen looked relieved. "It's not good." She turned back to the stove.

I picked up the paper and unfolded it. At the bottom of the first page there was an article titled, "University of

New Castle Conceals Student, Professor Affair. See more page B9."

I mean...the university didn't conceal it. They didn't fucking know. I sighed and turned to B9. I put my hand on Penny's knee and we both began reading.

Student-Professor Affair Uncovered at the University of New Castle

Bill Raffer, The Delaware Post 10:12 p.m. EST October 21, 2015

An investigation is underway involving adjunct professor, James Hunter, and a student from one of his classes at the University of New Castle.

Hunter, Blive Tech International founder and board member, started teaching at the university last semester. Although Hunter does not have a PhD, he was given a teaching position due to his experience starting Blive Tech International. His loose credentials have led him to a loose interpretation of the University of New Castle's code of ethics. Two months ago he began engaging in a sexual relationship with Penny Taylor, a sophomore in his communications class. Taylor, age 19, is an exemplary student on a First State scholarship. Although there have been no sexual harassment complaints as of yet, Taylor is unavailable for comment. Allegations of sexual harassment as well as other instances of sexual misconduct are imminent.

Hunter was fired from his last teaching position in New York City for physically threatening the dean of admissions, Jared Halloway. All charges were dropped in the matter, but Halloway commented that, "Hunter attacked him, completely unprovoked." Dean of students at the University of New Castle, Joseph Vespelli, hired Hunter despite known allegations of violence and Hunter's lack of credentials.

Hunter has also engaged in misconduct during his own days in college at Harvard University. He was arrested for underage drinking as well as vandalism.

The University of New Castle has never needed explicit rules against student-professor relationships. An unnamed source from the university says that their code of ethics skirts around the idea of something happening because it shouldn't have to state common morals, but that these events will make the university reevaluate the core values of the institution.

Hunter's wife, Isabella, was distraught when she found out about the affair. She filed for divorce as soon as she uncovered the truth, but their marriage had already begun to unravel before that when Hunter had sold his shares of Blive Tech International and declared he wanted to become a professor. "I should have realized his motivations," said Mrs. Hunter. "I should have warned the college. I feel like part of the blame should be on me. I can only imagine what this poor girl is going through."

Mrs. Hunter was almost in tears during her interview. The separation only became final yesterday afternoon. She went to the press and to the college immediately to request that Hunter resign from his teaching position. She believed he was doing more harm than good in the classroom, emphasizing that there needs to be a mutual trust between students and their professors.

In response to the allegations of having a sexual relationship with a student eight years younger than him, Professor James Hunter said, "Our relationship was completely consensual. There is no explicit rule that states such a relationship is against the code of ethics of this university." And when asked if he would end the relationship, he said, "I can't deny that I am in love with her. Nor do I have any intention of ending my relationship with her." In response to his wife's allegations, Hunter said, "My wife and I have been separated since last December, when I filed for divorce after I found out she was cheating on me. The documents are public and can be acquired from the New York City court." Said documents have not yet been released from the court.

The University of New Castle's dean of students, Joseph Vespelli, was contacted but declined to comment. His offices have informed us that an official statement will be released shortly.

Contact senior investigative reporter Bill Raffer at (302) 150-4527, braffer@delawarepost.com, on Facebook or Twitter @braffer

"Shit," I said. *Senior investigative reporter my ass.* Bill Fuckface Raffer didn't even reach out to me. My quotes were from when I'd contacted one of my New York City acquaintances in the press last night. I hadn't been on the fucking record. *Traitor.* I didn't want to be quoted in this mess. But at least it showed a little of my side. Not all Isabella's.

And Penny was 20, not 19. At least they hadn't called her a minor though. And what was all that stuff about my past? Penny probably had a million questions about all that. But I wasn't really concerned about how I came off. I was only worried about one thing. One thing that I'd tried endlessly to control last night. Just one fucking detail. I'd thought I'd at least accomplished that. But I was wrong.

I folded the paper and threw it down on the counter. "I didn't think they were going to release your name."

"I'm going to lose my scholarship," Penny said. She was staring at the papers in horror.

"What?"

"There were all these rules when I got it. I don't remember what they were. I'm sure being in the paper about sleeping with my professor broke at least one of them. James..."

"Don't get upset before we know, okay?" The scholarship wasn't really the main concern here... She was probably going to be expelled.

"Isn't this slander? How could they possibly print this? There isn't any proof. Can't we do something?"

"It doesn't matter. It's Isabella's word against mine." I needed to fix this as best I could. If Penny was upset about the scholarship, that meant she wanted to keep going to this school. I needed to figure out a way to make that happen. "Stay here today. Let me go to the meeting alone. Let me handle this."

"No. I'm not letting you take all the blame for this. It's my fault too."

"I don't want you to get..."

"James. No. I'm coming with you."

Ellen walked over and set our plates down in front of us. She gave us a sympathetic look. When she walked away Penny looked back up at me. "And it does matter. Can't you sue them for printing this nonsense? They didn't even check any of their facts. It's a joke of a news report."

I sighed. "I just want this to blow over as fast as possible. A lawsuit will make it worse. It'll draw it out. I don't want to drag you into this. I'll be fine."

Penny looked angry yet defeated at the same time.

I squeezed her knee. "Really, it's fine."

But she didn't look fine. And that made me feel...

My hand shook and I let it fall from her knee. I took a deep breath. *Get a grip.* I couldn't have a panic attack right now. Penny was relying on me.

Breathe.

All I could do was fall on my sword and try not to drag Penny down with me. And I could do this. I took another deep breath. I was good at negotiating. I rarely lost. And I'd already lost when it came to this article. Today would be a win.

I grabbed my hand so Penny couldn't see it shaking. *Breathe.*

I always got what I fucking wanted.

Chapter 3

Wednesday

Penny was staring at me like I'd lost my mind. And hell, maybe I had

"I'm coming," she said firmly.

And I could hear my therapist's voice in the back of my head, telling me that Penny and I needed to be a team. To work through things together. Dr. Clark was right. And so was Penny.

I nodded. "Well, we need to get going soon if you insist on coming, so eat."

She picked up her fork and took a bite of the eggs.

I swallowed hard as I watched her. There was just something about the way she wrapped her lips around a fork that did something to me.

"Ellen, these are fantastic," she said.

Ellen smiled over at us. "I'm glad that you like them. Eat, James."

I hadn't realized that I was just sitting there.

"Are you okay?" Penny asked.

"Yeah." I smiled at her and began to eat too. We ate in silence. And it felt so…normal. Like we'd done it a million times before. Like we'd do it a million times more.

When Penny finished, I stood up and stared down at her. It was time to leave our bubble. But I still wanted to protect her from all this. "Do you want to wear a hoodie or something?" I asked. "I don't want..."

"I want to be with you. No more hiding. Besides, everyone already knows."

Fair point. But she wasn't used to being photographed leaving her home. This wasn't going to be easy. I knew we were a team, but I still wanted to take care of her. "I'd really prefer if you let me do this by myself, Penny. There's no reason why you should be there."

"I'm going to get in trouble too. I have to be there."

I lowered my eyebrows. "You won't." I wasn't going to let her get expelled. "But if you insist, let's go do it then." I held out my hand for her and she immediately grabbed it.

"Good luck," Ellen said to us as we stepped onto the elevator.

When the doors closed Penny looked up at me. "I like her. She seems really nice."

"She is."

Penny looked down at her shoes. "Are you nervous?"

I took a deep breath. I already knew how this morning was going to go. And I was calmer than I thought I'd be. I was happy with my decision to resign. I knew it was the only way. I wanted a future with Penny more than I wanted to keep teaching. It was going to be fine. "Not really. I have everything that I want. Teaching doesn't define me. Like I told you on our first date, I don't think we're doing anything wrong. This feels right to me."

"It feels right to me too. It's weird, you know. I never in a million years thought I'd be in this situation. I didn't even have my first kiss until last semester. And now I'm embarking on this big scandalous affair with my professor. I'm not even sure my parents will believe me."

I laughed. "You should have called them already. This is just going to get worse as the day goes on."

"I'll call them later. I need to know what the dean says first." She squeezed my hand.

She was procrastinating. She was dreading telling her parents. I got that. I did. But I didn't want her to be embarrassed by our relationship. I didn't want her to suddenly change her mind about us. What if they told her she had to break up with me? What would she choose to do then? *Breathe.*

"What did you vandalize?" she asked.

I laughed, relieved at the change of subject. I couldn't believe the paper put shit about my past in the article though. "There was this professor I hated. I had him for an 8 a.m. The night before one of his classes my friends and I broke into the classroom and drew...vulgar things all over the chalkboard." Mason, Matt, Rob, and I had each been trying to draw the biggest dick. We couldn't stop laughing. I'd also been very, very high. All of us were. Or else we wouldn't have been drawing dicks on my professor's chalkboard.

"With chalk?"

"Yeah."

"Is that really vandalism?"

I shrugged. "I didn't think so. And I didn't get arrested for it either. It was a harmless prank. Hilarious, but harmless."

"So another lie."

"Mhm." Senior investigative reporter Bill Fuckface Raffer was supreme at his job.

"And were you arrested for underage drinking?"

"I got a warning. They had a three strikes policy like they do here. I only had two strikes, one for that and one for the chalkboard thing. I was never arrested while I was in Harvard." Although, I probably should have been for that other thing. I smiled, remembering the four of us running from the cops.

The elevator doors opened and we walked over to my cars. Part of me wanted for us to climb into my convertible and just get the fuck out of here. But if Penny wanted to keep going here, we had to face the dean. I opened up the door of my Audi for her.

I closed the door behind her and took another deep breath. This would all be over soon. I climbed into the car and started the engine.

"Well, you're lucky I don't hate you," Penny said. "Or maybe I would have pulled a prank like that on you. I wonder what you would have done if you came into class and there were obscene things all over your chalkboard?"

"I probably would have thought you were giving me suggestions of what I should do to you next." I raised my eyebrow at her and she laughed. That was one of the many things that made this all worth it. I was pretty sure I was obsessed with the sound of her laughter.

I pulled the car out of the parking spot and exited the parking garage. As soon as my car emerged on the street, cameras started flashing.

Penny held her hand up in front of her face. "So are they here because you're a rich, eligible bachelor or would this really normally be that big of a deal?"

"I don't know. I'm sure my name doesn't help the situation." I maneuvered around the chaos and sped off down Main Street. It was early and there was barely anyone out. But soon the campus would be filled with gossiping students. "I want you to let me do the talking, okay? I'm going to fix this for you. That's my top priority." I pulled into a spot outside the dean's office. There weren't any news vans outside. If the reporters actually cared about the story, they'd be here too. This wasn't about a breaking story. It was about me. And I hated that I'd dragged Penny into this shit.

"I wish you had just been a student," she said.

I laughed, even though it was forced. "I think you love that you're dating your professor."

"I do. Let's get this over with." She reached for the door handle.

"Hey." I grabbed her chin in my hand. "We got this, okay?" I pressed my lips against hers. It really was going to be okay. As long as the two of us were okay.

I stared to pull away, but Penny grabbed a fistful of my hair and deepened the kiss. She needed reassurance. That this was real. I'd give her all the reassurance she needed.

God, but the way she was kissing me... I groaned and pulled back. "We need to stop or I won't be able to go in there. Having an erection during our meeting with the dean would probably be frowned upon."

She laughed and kissed my cheek. "I love you."

"I love you." And that's all that mattered. That's why we were going to get through today. I climbed out of the car and walked around to her side. I put my hand out for her and she grabbed it. We continued to hold hands as we went into the building. It was the first time we'd done something like this on campus. We were done hiding now.

We entered through the side door and made our way through the lobby and down the hallway. I dropped her hand, opened a door, and gestured for her to walk through. Joe's receptionist looked up at us. She smiled at me, but then her face fell when Penny grabbed my hand again. Like she'd just remembered why I was there.

I cleared my throat. "Hi, Becca. We have a meeting with Joe."

"Yes. Joe is expecting you." She picked up a phone on the desk and punched in a few numbers. "Your 7 a.m. is here." She looked over at Penny. "Yes, she's here too." She paused again. "Okay," she said and hung up the receiver. "He'll be right out." She stared at us for another second before her eyes drifted back to her computer screen.

I escorted Penny to some chairs and we sat down. As each second passed, Penny squeezed my hand tighter and tighter. I was pretty sure I was about to lose circulation. I leaned toward her and whispered in her ear, "Penny, you're hurting me."

"Oh, geez, sorry." She stopped gripping my hand so tightly.

I rubbed my thumb along her palm and leaned toward her. "Don't worry," I whispered. "The dean likes me. I think everything's going to be fine." Joe didn't like me *that* much. But he'd been thrilled when I asked him if I could work here. And he'd be thrilled now when I gave him my letter of resignation.

"Why didn't you tell me that in the first place?"

"Because I didn't want you to get your hopes up."

"And now?"

"And now I need to believe it's true too." I squeezed her hand. It was going to be a tough sell to keep Penny enrolled here.

Joe stepped out of his office. Normally his salt and pepper hair made him look distinguished. But today he just looked…tired. Tired of me. Tired of being the dean. Tired of all of it. He took one look at us holding hands and shook his head. He turned and walked back into his office.

Well that wasn't a good start. I sighed and stood up. But I kept my fingers intertwined with Penny's. We were done hiding this. And Penny needed my hand. I knew how nervous she was. We walked together into Joe's office.

Joe was sitting behind his desk. He looked up at us. "Close the door, James." He sounded as tired as he looked.

And I wondered if he'd been up all night trying to squash the story too.

I closed the door and we both sat down across the desk from him.

Joe sighed deeply and leaned forward in his chair. "Excuse my bluntness, but this is a fucking mess."

Yeah, that sounded about right. "Joe, it was never my intention for this to happen."

"What, you didn't intend to sleep with your students when you accepted this position? Or you didn't intend for anyone to ever find out?"

For fuck's sake. "I never intended to sleep with *a* student. Singular, not plural. And I was going to tell you. I didn't want you to find out this way."

"And we met before I knew he was my professor," Penny said. "And he made it clear that we couldn't fraternize. I refused to listen. It was my fault."

Jesus, Penny. Stop talking. I was trying to keep her enrolled here and she was throwing herself under the bus. I squeezed her hand hard, hoping she'd get the hint. "I take full responsibility for this, Joe."

He pinched the bridge of his nose and shook his head. He looked like he was in pain. "Sorry, what is your name?" he asked and stared at Penny.

"Penny Taylor."

"Well, Penny, this is not your fault. James is an acting professor at this university. It's his responsibility to uphold the rules." He turned back to me. "We have a code of ethics, which I know you're aware of. Although not explicitly stated, dating a student violates the core values of this institution. What the hell were you thinking? And not only did you fail to disclose this relationship to me, but I had to find out in the damn newspaper." He slammed his fist down on top of his desk where today's newspaper was sitting. "Your ex-wife has made it a point not only to disgrace you but this entire university. It's like a fucking reality T.V. show."

"Joe..."

"I don't want to hear your excuses. You should have told me, James." He sighed and leaned back in his chair. "I know all that stuff your wife said is a lie. But it's going to be hard to convince other professors as well as your students' parents otherwise. They made it seem like you molested her or something." He paused and sighed. "It's a mess. They're pulling me down with you. I've already given my okay to launch an investigation. All your students will have to be interviewed because of the press's allegations, even though no one has openly come forward. And if you're lying about it just being her...if you laid a finger on any other girl...then I recommend you just resign right now, because..."

"It's just Penny." Joe had every right to question my character. But not on this. I hadn't gone anywhere near any of my students. Even though several of them blatantly flirted with me. I hadn't even asked for his help when that student was practically stalking me last year. Not that I could really judge. I'd stalked Penny when we were on a break. I knew I was a mess. And I knew this situation was a mess. But it was only ever Penny. This wasn't just some dumb fling. I was in love with her.

Joe sighed again. "Well the board has already decided to suspend you during the investigation. That decision is over my head, but I completely agree with them. We may be able to lift your suspension if everything comes back clean after that. But my recommendation is that you two terminate your relationship immediately. This can't go on if you intend to keep working here."

"We're not doing that." *No way in hell.*

"Well I don't have any other ideas. We've already had dozens of calls this morning from concerned parents. I have to act or I'll probably be fired next. Stop seeing her and if the interviews with other students show no other instances of misconduct you can keep teaching at this university under a probationary period. If there are no more violations we'll lift the probationary period in six months. And continuing to screw one of your students counts as a violation. So it needs to end. Otherwise we have to let you go."

Yeah. I figured that was the case. I glanced at Penny. She looked so young and naïve. And it was possible that I was about to make the biggest mistake of my life.

Chapter 4

Wednesday

Breathe. No, I wasn't about to make a mistake. It didn't matter that Penny was young. She was old enough to know that she fucking loved me back. I had a hard time trusting people. But I trusted her. I trusted what we had. And we'd get through this together. We had to. Because I wasn't going to let myself slip again.

"Then I guess I resign," I said. I pulled an envelope out of my pocket and put it down on top of the desk. "Here's my letter of resignation." I slid it toward Joe. And for just a second, I couldn't breathe.

"James?" Penny sounded panicked.

I'd wanted to talk to her about all this last night. I'd wanted to make this decision together. But I didn't have a fucking choice here. Didn't she see that? I was doing this for her. I was giving up everything for her.

I swallowed hard. *No.* That wasn't true. This job didn't matter. I had to believe that. Yes, I loved teaching. But I loved her more. She was all I needed.

"That makes you look guilty of everything people are saying," Joe said. "You'll never get another teaching job."

I know. I expected to feel as panicked as Penny looked. But I was eerily calm. "I only see two possibilities. I do everything your way, except I keep seeing her in secret, or I quit. And since continuing to work here and keep seeing her seems to be out of the question, I quit."

"Is this really worth ruining your reputation over? The press is already jumping to conclusions. If you resign it'll basically be a confession that you slept with all your female students. It'll look bad on the school too. I need you to say you made a mistake and stop seeing her. Stay out of the news during the investigation. Keep quiet for your six months of probation. That's it. I need this to disappear as soon as possible. Don't screw me on this."

"I don't know what to tell you, Joe. I love her. I'm not doing that."

"You've got to be shitting me."

"I'll have an interview with the press," Penny interjected.

"Penny," I said. "Please let me handle this." This wasn't a discussion. I'd already made the decision. It was done.

"I'll tell them that it was completely consensual," she said. "And that I love him. Everyone will calm down. Maybe they won't care if we date then. And you can still conduct the interviews with other students. Everything will come back clean. It will all blow over."

Joe eyed Penny again. He looked mad at her too. But I could see his mind working. And I didn't like that one bit. Under no circumstances was Penny talking to any of those idiots in news vans.

I shook my head. "No. I don't want her talking to the press. I'm not dragging this out longer than necessary."

"James, let me help you keep your job," she said.

"Enough," I said. I stared into her eyes. *Please, Penny. I'm doing this for you.*

She turned back to Joe. "Do you think it will help?"

"Several news stations have already called me. It'll be national news by the end of the day. I don't know if it'll matter at this point. It's just a matter of public opinion. They've already labeled him. And in my opinion the only way to change their opinion is for you to terminate your relationship."

What the fuck? Why were we still talking about this?

"Can't we at least try my idea?" she asked.

I knew she was trying to help, but this was ridiculous. "Penny and I need to talk in private for a second." I stood up.

"Nothing about your relationship is going to be private now." Joe stared at us. "Sit down, James. Let's just get this over with." He looked down at a paper on his desk.

I slowly sat back down. I knew that Penny and I should have talked about all this. But we had talked about some of this already. Some very important details and I thought we were on the same page. I leaned toward her. "Penny, we've already talked about this," I whispered.

"No we haven't. You never said you were going to re-sign..."

"I mean about waiting until you graduate. I'm not doing it. We've had this discussion. If I stay we won't be able to be together. I'm not waiting to be with you. I've already made my decision. And it was the easiest decision I've ever made. Please just let me handle this. I'm not changing my mind."

Joe cleared his throat. "Midterm grades are due at the end of this week. You'll still need to submit those. I've already gotten other professors to cover your classes during the investigation."

I wondered who he'd gotten to teach my class that Penny was in.

"They can just continue doing it until the end of the semester," Joe said. "You two have one class together. The validity of your grades is in question, Penny. You'll have to re-present your speeches to your new professor so he can sign off on them. This way you won't have to completely retake the course. Or you can stop taking the class. That's up to you. But the drop/add window has passed, so you'll have to withdraw and pay the fee for changes in registration. It'll appear as a W on your transcript, but it won't hurt your G.P.A. You'll have to let me know by next Tuesday before the window closes.

"So I'm not being expelled?" she asked.

"No," Joe said. "I'm giving you two strikes which will go on your record. You broke the rules too, but the blame for this lies on James. It has to. The university has standards for their professors. I don't know how your relationship started and I don't want to know. Don't give me reason to make your punishment harsher."

Penny pressed her lips together. It looked like she wanted to say more, but she was finally staying quiet. And she looked a little relieved.

She'd gotten a slap on the wrist. Which was all she deserved. This was all on me. And it was a good thing Joe did like me. Or I think all of this would have been much worse.

I ran my thumb along her palm. She was going to be okay. And so would I. Eventually.

"So I'll talk to the press today and let them know about your resignation," Joe said. "Unless there is any way I can change your mind?"

"I'm sorry, Joe." If I could help him out, I would. But I wasn't walking away from the first good thing that had happened to me in years. I needed Penny. And I knew how fucked up that sounded. But I did. I needed her.

"I'd prefer if you didn't flaunt your relationship around the school. I know I can't tell you what to do anymore, James. But I'm asking this as a favor. Let things settle down. We're still running the investigation. The university has to come out looking like we did everything we could do. Especially now that you're resigning. It makes you look guilty."

Yeah. I know. Isabella had gotten exactly what she wanted. And that was the only part of this I wasn't okay with.

"I believe that it's just her, but this is only just the start. It's going to get worse before it gets better." He grabbed the newspaper off his desk and tossed it in the trash. "And I have to ask, under the circumstances. What happened to your eye?" He stared at my black eye. It was fading, but it was still visible.

"Just a misunderstanding," I said.

"Good." Joe sighed. "I thought the next thing you were going to tell me is that you got in a fist fight with a student."

Well... technically I had. But Joe didn't need to know that.

Joe laughed and shook his head. "That's the last thing this school needs right now. And I didn't want to have to talk about that in the interview."

I shifted in my chair. Tyler wasn't going to tell anyone about that. He was a piece of shit, but he did care about Penny. And he was at least smart enough to know that telling anyone about our fight would hurt her. Honestly it was probably a good thing I wasn't a professor anymore. Because there was a pretty high chance I was going to fail that kid for just being an asshole.

"Penny, do you mind if I have a word alone with James?" Joe asked. "We need to discuss a few more things."

"No, that's fine," she said.

"Go to class. And be prepared for most of the student body to already know."

Penny glanced up at me. She looked so...defeated. And hurt. All I wanted to do was pull her into my arms and kiss her. But I had a feeling that Joe would really be pissed if I did that. So I just nodded at her and let go of her hand.

She stood up. "Thank you for being so understanding, Mr. Vespelli. And I'm sorry about all of this."

"Well you really should have thought about that beforehand, shouldn't you have? One more strike and you'll be expelled. Don't let me see you in here again."

She gulped and looked once more at me before turning her attention back to Joe. "Thanks," she said quietly and walked out, closing the door behind her.

As soon as the door closed, Joe put his hands behind his head and leaned back in his chair with a heavy sigh. "Seriously, James? You couldn't keep it in your pants until at least the end of the semester? Winter break would have been a lot better for me."

I laughed. "Sorry, Joe."

He finally smiled. "You're going to get me fired you know."

"I think you'll be fine. They're not going to find anything else in the investigation. And I'll say anything you want to the press about it."

"But you won't stop seeing her?"

I shook my head. "No. I won't."

"So it's true what the paper said? You're in love with her?"

"Yeah. I am."

"She's 19, James."

"Well, the papers weren't right about that. She's 20. Her birthday was last week."

He stared at me like he didn't think that made much of a difference. And honestly it didn't. Because I'd been with her longer when she was 19 than since she'd turned 20. And I would have pursued her either way. I couldn't stay away from her. I knew how fucked up all of it was, but I couldn't stop myself.

"Fucking Isabella, man," Joe said.

I nodded. "Fucking Isabella." Joe knew all about my past. He'd been a good boss. This had been a great job. And I was really going to miss it.

"Just lie low. Please."

"I'll do my best. Who do you have teaching my Comm class?"

Joe glanced down at a piece of paper. "Professor Nolan. I figured it would be better to get someone who you got along with. For Penny's sake."

"Thanks for that. Well, if there's nothing more...I should get going." I needed to make a call to Professor Nolan.

"Nothing more?" Joe cursed under his breath. "Sure, nothing more for you to do. I'm going to be cleaning up this mess for weeks."

"Will a donation to the university help smooth things over a bit?" I asked and stood up.

"Yeah, I'm sure a Hunter Hall will be really well received right now."

"It was just an idea," I said.

"Well. Hold on a sec. Of course I want that. Just wait a bit, okay?"

"You got it, Joe. Have a good rest of your morning," I said, holding back a smile.

"Oh, fuck you." But he laughed too. "Ah, wait, I almost forgot. Sign these real quick." He handed me a few papers.

"And what are these?"

He waved his hand through the air. "You quit. You don't get severance. All that stuff. Not that you're worried about severance. I promise I'm not fucking you over like you fucked me over."

He was right. I didn't care about a severance package. And I knew he wouldn't screw me over, even if he was a little pissed at me. I signed the papers.

Joe gave me the finger.

And I waved goodbye and walked out of his office. It felt like a weight was lifted from my shoulders. I wasn't a professor anymore. I smiled. I wasn't dating a student. I was no longer breaking any rules. But I had a lot of damage control to do.

I immediately called Professor Nolan.

He answered in two rings. "Hey, James. Joe already sent me over all the information. I'm heading over to your class now."

There was an awkward pause. "Just ask it," I said.

"Is it true? About you sleeping with students?"

"It's just Penny."

He whistled. "Have you seen Joe yet?"

"Yeah. I just resigned."

"Damn. I'm really sorry, James. If there's anything you need from me, just let me know, okay?"

"Well, that's why I'm calling. I'm going to try to get Penny to skip class today. But in case she shows up...can you look out for her today? I'm worried about how the other students are going to react."

"Yeah, this is going to be a shit show. What does she look like?"

"She has red hair and she sits in the back row. You can't miss her." That was the whole problem I had when I was trying to be a good professor and keep my distance. My eyes were always drawn to her.

"I'll do my best to look after her," he said.

"It is probably best if she drops the class though, don't you think?" I asked. There were a few reasons why I wanted her to drop the class. But there was one beyond the obvious of other students being assholes to her once they found out. I hated the idea of her sitting with Tyler without me there. And there was that dick in the front row that would probably give her a hard time. Raymond Asher. He was always joking around, but he was going to jump all over this. I hated that kid.

"Let's see how today goes. But I promise I'll look after her."

"Thanks, man. I appreciate it."

"No problem."

I ended the call and texted Penny: "I hope that you're holding up okay. Can I convince you to come back to the apartment instead of listening to speeches?" She really didn't need to be there today.

My phone immediately buzzed with her reply. "I want to face this. Waiting will make it worse. How did the rest of your conversation with the dean go?"

I really hated that she wouldn't listen to me. Going to class was a mistake. But I couldn't force her to skip it. "I just had to sign a few papers. Can we at least meet for lunch? We really need to talk." I wanted to at least try to convince her to not go to the rest of her classes in the afternoon.

"Okay."

I took a deep breath. *Good.* I slid my phone back into my pocket. There were students walking around campus now. I was used to the stares. But there were definitely more today. And lots more whispering too.

I tried to keep my head down as I made my way to my car.

"Professor Hunter!" someone yelled.

LOVED

I turned around. *Oh, fuck me.*

Chapter 5

Wednesday

Kristen ran over, stopping way too close to me. She was wearing a sports bra that was definitely a size too small, because her breasts were practically pouring out. She wiped some sweat off her forehead with the back of her hand.

I silently cursed in my head. I'd been thinking about my stalker earlier and it was like I'd just willed her into existence again.

She gave me a sad smile. "I heard what happened. I can't believe it. Are you alright?"

Am *I* alright? I wasn't the one she should be worried about. *I'd* broken the rules. *I'd* slept with a student. *I* was the monster in this situation. It didn't matter whether I was alright or not. I just stared at her.

"Some women, am I right?" She touched my shoulder.

I wasn't sure if she was talking about Isabella or Penny. And I didn't really care. I shifted my shoulder back so Kristen's hand would drop. The last thing I needed was for there to be a picture circulating of me talking to Kristen. I looked around at the other students staring at us.

And no one looked mad at me. They looked more like Kristen. Sympathetic. And I had a sinking feeling in my stomach. They weren't blaming me for this. They thought this was Penny's fault. *For fuck's sake.*

The article was pretty damning against me. And yet...I'd been worried about this. That some people would blame Penny. People really were ridiculous.

"I'm good, Kristen. If you'll excuse me."

"Well if you need anything." She placed her hand on the center of my chest. "Anything at all. Even just a workout buddy to get rid of some of the stress of all this."

Did she mean an actual workout buddy? Or like a…workout by having wild sex? By the way she was staring at me, it was definitely a sex thing. I'd slept with a student, yes. But it was singular. Why did everyone just assume that I'd slept with a ton of them?

Kristen had been pursuing me ever since I'd stepped foot on campus. She was probably shocked that I'd slept with a student that wasn't her. But she just wasn't my type. Her hair and figure reminded me too much of Isabella. I preferred the shy girl in the back row.

"I'm good," I said again.

"Okay, *Professor Hunter*." She said it in such a sultry way.

But it wasn't the way Penny said it. God, I really loved the way Penny said it. Had Kristen missed the part of the article where I also said I was in love with Penny? She really needed to move on from this crush. "I'm not a professor here anymore."

"Wait, what?" Her eyes grew round.

"Now if you'll excuse me." I walked past her and climbed into my car.

I was half expecting her to force herself into my passenger seat. But I was glad that she turned around and continued on her run. Hopefully she'd find someone more suited for her soon so that I could stop worrying about her popping up all the time.

I took a deep breath before pulling my car out of the parking lot. I wished Penny had skipped class. I hated picturing her in class all alone. Or in class next to Tyler. My fingers tightened around the wheel.

There were more news vans and paparazzi outside my apartment building now. But I somehow managed to evade them and pull in the parking garage. I shot Ian a text to meet me in my apartment. When I walked in, he was already helping himself to something from the fridge.

"What a mess," I said with a sigh and tossed my keys onto the kitchen counter.

Ian put some leftovers in the microwave and turned around. "A lot of people are trying to reach you for a comment."

"It's still a no. I just want this whole thing to blow over." I sat down and stared at him.

"At least they didn't print that she was a minor."

I nodded. Yeah, that was the one win. Ian though they were going to say that in the story.

"So…are you going to tell me how your meeting went? I thought you'd be with Penny the rest of the day."

"She wanted to go to class."

"Really? Why?" The microwave beeped and Ian pulled out his plate. "Want some of this?"

"I just ate breakfast."

"But it's lasagna." He sat down and started eating.

"You're ridiculous."

He laughed. "You didn't answer my question. Why did Penny go to class? Isn't that going to be…well…the worst?"

I pressed my lips together. "I think she was probably mad at me. Maybe. Actually, no. She was definitely mad at me."

"Why?"

"Because I resigned."

Ian just stared at me.

"I don't think she was mad that I resigned. More so that I didn't tell her I was going to before the meeting. I already had my resignation letter ready. And she was trying to figure out solutions for me to keep teaching and I kept shutting them down in the meeting."

"So you left her in the dark?"

"She had to have known that's where this was leading. And Joe didn't give me much of a choice. Either I could keep my job and stop seeing Penny. Or quit and keep seeing her. It was an easy decision."

"But you didn't talk to Penny about it."

I shook my head.

"Well no wonder she's pissed at you. She liked banging her professor, and now you're not her professor anymore."

I glared at him.

"I'm joking. But in all seriousness...you gotta talk to her about this stuff, James. She's not your employee. She's your girlfriend."

"What is that supposed to mean?"

"Which part?" Ian asked and took another bite of lasagna.

"Do I do stuff all the time without explaining it to you first? You're acting like I'm a bad boss."

"You are a bad boss."

"What? No I'm not." Where was this coming from?

"You threw a bottle of scotch at me once."

"One time. Years ago."

Ian shrugged. "Fine. Whatever. You're a great boss. I just meant that you can't just tell her how things are. You're a team."

Had he been talking to Dr. Clark too? "I was going to talk to her. About everything."

"Even the cameras?"

God the fucking cameras were going to get me in trouble at some point. "Mhm."

"That was very unbelievable."

I laughed. "I'm going to tell her. It's for her own safety. Speaking of which…how is the new addition to the security system going?"

"I already installed it. No more surprise Isabella visits. I promise."

I nodded. I thought about his comment about my being a not-so-great boss. "I am sorry about last night, Ian. I didn't mean to take it out on you. Of course it wasn't your fault that the story got leaked to the press."

"But Isabella was only here because…"

"Because the security system wasn't perfect yet. Which is on me. I was just upset and I took it out on you."

Ian smiled. "Like when you threw that bottle of scotch at me."

"That was one time!"

He laughed. "Well, I am sorry you lost your job. I know how much you loved being a professor. Do you think you'll be able to find a new teaching position somewhere else?"

Penny was here. I wasn't going anywhere else. Besides… "Resigning pretty much put a nail in the coffin on that. I look guilty. No one's hiring me again. I was lucky enough that Joe gave me a second chance here."

"Sorry, man."

"It's fine." I actually did feel okay. Calm. In control. It was going to be okay.

Ian didn't look like he believed me.

"Really, I'm good. I thought I'd have to spend the rest of the day with Dr. Clark, but I'm okay."

"If you say so."

My phone buzzed in my pocket and I pulled it out. I was hoping it was a text from Penny telling me she was coming home.

LOVED

But it was from Mason: "I'm good, man. Excited to see you in a couple weeks."

I breathed a sigh of relief. So the strange invitation *was* from him. I held up my phone for Ian to see. "The invitation was from Mason after all."

"I thought you already knew that?"

"Last night when you called, I couldn't get the invitation out of my head. I thought Isabella had maybe sent it. That she was fucking with my friends or something."

"Ah. That explains why you asked me if your friends were okay. I would have asked you more about that last night but…I was preoccupied with the imminent shit show."

"Well, one less thing to worry about." I slid my phone back into my pocket. "I'm excited to catch up with them."

"So will you just go to New York for the day?"

"Probably. Penny still wants to go to school here I think."

"You think?"

"She was freaking out about possibly losing her scholarship this morning. She was happy she just got two strikes on her record instead of being expelled. And she seemed eager to get back to class and out of that meeting."

"James Hunter," Ellen said firmly as she walked out of my bedroom with a load of laundry. "What on earth are you doing?"

I glanced at Ian.

"You're in so much trouble," he said.

I turned back to Ellen. "What do you mean?" I asked.

"You're bulldozing that girl. You're not putting her feelings first. You're making all the decisions without consulting her."

"That's what I was saying," Ian said.

Jesus, why were my employees acting like my therapist right now? One therapist was plenty. "I resigned *for* her. That is putting her feelings first."

"How was it for her if she didn't tell you she wanted that?"

"Because it was the only way for us to stay together. And I was going to talk to her about all this. There wasn't time. But we'll talk about it all now."

"When?" Ellen set the laundry basket down and put her hands on her hips. "Tell me when."

"Penny's coming back for lunch."

"She's in the lion's den and you're planning lunch? And you didn't even tell me! What am I supposed to make? I might need to head to the store because Ian's just finished the lasagna." She gestured angrily to Ian.

"Sorry," Ian said around his last forkful.

"We need a team meeting," Ellen said. She walked over to us and sat down at the kitchen counter too. "Penny is the best thing that's happened to you in a long time, and you're going to ruin it. And of course she went to class this morning because she was mad at you. Obviously."

"So you were eavesdropping on the whole conversation then?"

"Yes," she said. "Grabbing laundry isn't loud. But you two are with your gabbing."

Ian laughed.

"And what is this about cameras?"

Ian's laughter died in his throat.

"It's…security," I said.

"Are you filming Penny without her consent?" Ellen raised her eyebrow at me.

"It's not like that." But honestly…it was a little like that. Because I'd saved some of the footage and watched it. I'd watched it a whole lot while Penny and I were on a break. It was some seriously hot footage.

"It's kind of like that," Ian said.

I glared at him.

"You made me save…"

"Enough," I said. "I'm going to fix this. You two have nothing to worry about."

Ellen just stared at me. "You still haven't told me when."

"At lunch…"

"No, not lunch. She's in your class without you. Can you imagine what people are whispering or saying to her face? The women are always the ones to blame. You need to go to her. Right now. And talk all of this out before you do irreparable damage."

I glanced down at my watch.

"Now, James."

"Okay, okay. She's in class right now, but…I'll catch her when she's leaving."

"Good. Go."

"But class doesn't end until…"

"Now," she said again more firmly. "You're acting like you've never been in a relationship before. Pull it together."

Well, I'd never been in a healthy relationship before. "You know, I planned out this morning perfectly. I came appropriately prepared. And Penny should have let me handle it."

"Get out of here with that," Ellen said.

I glanced at Ian.

"I'm siding with Ellen," he said.

Of course you are. "Okay. But just for the record, Ellen, the cameras aren't any worse than you eavesdropping."

She opened her mouth and closed it again. "I beg to differ."

I smiled. She knew it was the same. "Okay, I'm going."

"Don't bulldoze Penny again. She's soft spoken. Take a deep breath and hear her out."

That was where I knew for sure I could handle this situation without the help of Ellen's meddling. Yes, Penny was soft spoken. But not around me. She was feisty and passionate. And had no problem speaking her mind. Hopefully she'd be easier on me than Ellen had been.

"And now I'm actually going," I said. Even though I'd told Joe I'd lay low on campus, I did need to go to Penny. She had no idea what she was walking into. But she'd know now. After facing Comm, the worst was probably over. But I needed to be there for her.

Chapter 6

Wednesday

I kept my head down as I walked up the stairs to my old Comm class. The campus was pretty empty right now since 8 a.m. classes weren't over for a few more minutes. But I still didn't want to draw attention to myself.

I wasn't exactly sure what my plan was. I just needed to be alone with Penny to talk all this out. To figure out what our next steps were. To make sure she was okay. To make sure *we* were okay.

The back door to my Comm class opened. *Shit.* I couldn't let any of them see me. Joe would have a field day. I grabbed the doorknob of an empty classroom, but it was locked. I tried another door and breathed a sigh of relief when it opened. I ducked inside and hit my foot against a bucket. It was dark, but the bucket and the lemon scent told me I was in a custodial closet. I opened the door a crack to peer down the hall.

The class was quickly emptying out. Everyone was whispering and I didn't need to hear it to know what they were talking about. But Penny was nowhere in sight. I frowned and stared at the door until she finally emerged. It looked like she was seconds away from bursting into tears.

Fuck. Her arms were wrapped around herself like she was trying to make herself smaller. The whispering grew louder. People were staring.

I waited until she was a step away from the closet before I opened the door. I grabbed her arm and pulled her into the closet next to me. The door closed and it was pitch-black, but I'd already seen how she was feeling.

IVY SMOAK

"Are you okay?" I asked as my eyes slowly adjusted.

She immediately burst into tears.

"Penny?" I pulled her face against my chest and ran my fingers through her hair. I didn't know what to do to make this better other than holding her. "I don't like seeing you cry. Tell me what you need."

She didn't respond. She just continued to cry.

"Penny, please talk to me," I said.

"I told you I'd give up everything for you," she sobbed. "I said I didn't care about finishing school here. I said we could run away together. I'll do whatever you want. Please don't do this."

I put my hands on her shoulders. "Do what? What are you talking about?" I'd already resigned. I couldn't just undo that.

"Please. I can't lose you. I know what living is like when we aren't together. I don't want to feel that way again. I can't feel that way again."

"You're not losing me. Hey." I grabbed her chin and tilted her head up so that I could see her eyes. "I love you. Where is this coming from?"

"You're not breaking up with me?"

"No." I laughed. I couldn't help it. The thought was preposterous. What had even given her that idea? I'd just quit my job to ensure that we could stay together. "Penny, no."

"Well don't say things like we need to talk then," she said through her tears. "When people say that, it means they want to break up."

I pressed my lips together so I wouldn't laugh again. "You really do watch too much T.V." I wiped her tears away with my thumbs. "Please stop crying."

She took a deep breath. There were still tears on her cheeks, but she looked a little pissed off now. "We're supposed to be a team."

"We are a team."

"No, we're not. You made the decision to quit without even discussing it with me first."

"I listened to what Joe had to say. There wasn't even a decision that needed to be made. There was only one option."

"But you had already decided," she said. "You had a resignation letter with you."

"I like to be prepared..."

"You knew what you were going to do."

Yeah, fair. I didn't really know what to say. I'd wanted to talk to her about it. We didn't get a chance. But I did all this to protect her. I did it for her. For us.

"You knew and you didn't tell me. I felt blindsided in there."

"I told you to let me go alone. I asked you to let me handle it. And it was my choice to make. Not yours."

"What? It was a decision that affects both of us. Why do you want to do everything alone? I gave up everything to be with you. Stop pushing me away."

"Please stop crying. I don't know what you want me to do." I couldn't take back what had happened this morning. It was done. And I just wanted to move past it. "I want to give you what you need. Please just tell me what you want. Let me reassure you about how I feel." I wiped away more of her tears with my thumbs.

She grabbed the back of my neck and kissed me hard.

I had not been expecting that. But I liked this turn of events. I grabbed her waist and pulled her against me. My hands slid to her ass. Yeah, I definitely liked this turn of events. If there was one thing I knew we were good at, it was makeup sex. But I didn't want to do it in this lemon scented closet.

"Let's go back to the apartment," I said as I traced kisses down the side of her neck.

"No." She unbuttoned and unzipped my pants.

I usually liked being the one in control. But her flipping the script already had me rock hard.

"This is what I need." She wrapped her hand around my cock.

If my dick deep inside of her was the reassurance she needed, I'd give it to her. I grabbed her thighs and lifted her legs up around me. I stepped toward the wall, but tripped over a bucket.

She slid down my torso and her feet hit the ground again.

"Shit. Sorry, Penny."

She silenced me with another kiss.

I'd had so many dreams of fucking her in my classroom. I had two favorites. Taking her right against the chalkboard was one. And I was especially fond of this one dream where she was at the podium trying to give her speech while I ate her out. We'd never have sex in my classroom now. This janitor's closet was probably the closest we'd ever get to that. But just thinking about my fantasies while her lips were against mine was driving me crazy.

I heard the zip of her jeans. I pushed my body against hers, pressing her back against the wall. I slid her pants the rest of the way down. She held on to me as she stepped out of them and her shoes.

"I think this will reassure you," I said and knelt in front of her. No, she wasn't in the middle of giving a speech like in my fantasy. But I could still make her scream.

She probably expected me to kiss the inside of her thigh, or gently brush my fingers against her clit to tease her. But just the scent of her had me undone. And I was suddenly starving. I thrust my tongue deep inside her wetness.

"Fuck," she moaned as her hands fell to my shoulders.

Her pussy was as greedy for my tongue as I was for her. I swear the taste of her was the only sustenance I needed. I thrust my tongue even deeper inside of her as I rubbed my nose against her clit.

"James," she panted.

I lifted her thighs over my shoulders so that I was supporting all her weight. I slid one of my hands underneath her tank top and beneath her bra. I groaned against her swollen clit. I loved every inch of her. But the weight of her breast in my hand did something to me.

I reached down with my other hand and grabbed my cock. Fuck, I needed a release. I needed it to be my cock inside her tight pussy instead of my tongue.

I thrust my tongue deeper and rubbed my nose against her clit again. *Come for me, baby. Come and then let me fuck you so hard.* I ran my hand up and down my shaft faster.

She moaned as her pussy clenched around my tongue. God, she was so sweet. I lapped up all her juices as her body shuddered.

"Do you feel better now?" Because it was my turn. I placed another long stroke against her wetness as I reached up and moved her thighs off my shoulders.

She was too breathless to respond. She just stared at me as her back slid down the wall.

"Because your cunt is delicious. I could do that forever." I leaned forward and kissed her stomach. I needed my cock deep inside of her, but I always did my best negotiating with her when she was perfectly sated from an orgasm.

I needed to hear her say that she trusted me. I needed to know that we were okay.

I stayed on my knees and stared up at her. "I told you everything would be okay and it will be. I need you to trust me. I need you to trust my judgment."

"I do trust you."

"Then we should be celebrating today, not fighting." I sunk one of my fingers into her wetness.

She moaned.

"I'm divorced." I thrust my finger deeper.

She was still soaked.

"I'm not your professor anymore." I slid another finger inside of her. How was she still so tight?

"James," she moaned.

I slowly moved my fingers in and out of her, stretching her wide for my cock. "We can finally be together, just like you wanted. So tell me, how else can I reassure you?"

She moaned again.

I stood up and hooked my fingers, hitting her in that spot she loved.

Her body shuddered again.

"Do you need me to take you home and make love to you?" I kissed her neck. "Or do you want me to fuck you in this closet? Because I need my cock inside of you. I need reassurance too." I pressed my thumb against her clit.

"Fuck me. Oh God, please fuck me."

Good, girl. "I was hoping you'd say that," I said and bit down on her earlobe. I grabbed her thighs, lifted her legs around my waist, and sunk my cock deep inside of her tight pussy. *Fucking heaven.* I slammed her back against the shelves on the side of the closet.

Penny buried her fingers in my hair as I started moving my hips.

God, every thrust was perfection. The way she gripped me drove me fucking crazy.

Bottles toppled to the ground from the shelves behind her. The fake lemon scent filled the room even more. But I didn't care that we were making a mess.

Her fingers tangled in my hair even more as she deepened the kiss.

I began to thrust faster. Harder. She tilted her hips to meet me. I groaned into her mouth. It was like her body had been created to please me and only me. I dug my fingers into her hips to try to calm down.

"Harder," she moaned.

My girl was a greedy little slut. Desperate for my cock. Desperate for my cum to fill her. I slammed into her harder, almost knocking the shelves over.

"If you want it harder, I'll give it to you harder." I carried her over to a table and pushed some of the contents to the ground. They must have been paper products, because they barely made a sound. I laid her down on the table and leaned over her.

She reached out and unbuttoned my shirt, sliding her hands down my six pack. "I'll never get enough of you," she whispered.

I had said those words to her before. It was different for me though. Twisted. I was an addict. But it was like she was saying she was addicted to me too. She was trying to put us on an even playing field. And that's what I wanted. I wasn't her professor anymore. We were just...us.

"Good," I said. "Because I'm never letting you go." I grabbed the edge of the table near her head and slid my hard cock back inside of her. *Fuck*.

She tilted her head to the side, trying her best not to make a sound.

But I wanted her to look at me. I grabbed her chin and turned her head back toward me. "Look at me when you orgasm, Penny. I want to see your face." I let go of her chin, wrapped my hand around her thigh, and moved my hips faster. The angle let me go even deeper. It was rough and intimate at the same time. Just the way she liked it. This was what she needed. "Come for me, Penny."

It only took a moment before I felt her pussy clenching around my cock. Fuck. I groaned as shot after shot of cum filled her.

Penny closed her eyes, but I grabbed her chin again. She stared up at me as she milked every last drop of cum out of my cock. I loved the way she was staring up at me. Like I was a fucking god. I'd thought that would change when she found out all my problems. But she still looked at me the same. She still loved me. And I knew I'd made the right choice by stepping away from my job. Nothing else in the world mattered when we were together.

I slowly pulled out of her. We were good. But there was still something we needed to do today. And I hoped we weren't too late.

Chapter 7

Wednesday

I started buttoning my shirt as I turned toward Penny. "I know that you're worried that I'm going to resent you because I had to stop teaching. But it's the complete opposite. For the first time ever, I feel like I'm exactly where I should be. Life is good here, with you. I'm in love with you." I paused. The words didn't seem like they were enough to convey how I felt. "I love you so much. I never knew what I was missing."

"I'm so in love with you, James Hunter."

I leaned forward and ran the tip of my nose down the length of hers. "Now, we're going back to the apartment. You don't need to face everyone today alone. We'll deal with this together. We'll make our decisions together. Well...except for this one. Because I really want to take you home right now."

Penny laughed. "I'm sorry. I just lost it today. Everyone..."

"Don't. Don't apologize. I know you needed me. That's why I was hiding in this closet in the first place." I smiled at her and pushed a strand of red hair behind her ear. "I was prepared to resign today. I should have told you before we went into the meeting. I wasn't going to stop seeing you. It was out of the question."

"I know. I think you made the right choice."

I made a pretend shocked face. "I'm right? What?"

She nudged my shoulder. "So if you didn't want to break up with me, what did you want to talk to me about?"

"Nothing." I picked her pants up off the ground and handed them to her. "We're okay."

"No, what was it?" She quickly got dressed as I stared at her.

I'd wanted to talk to her about a lot of things. Skipping classes for the rest of the day. Making sure she was okay. But... "Honestly, I was really mad at you. I'm still mad at you. I told you to let me handle the situation this morning. You shouldn't have interfered." I could hear Ellen's voice in the back of my head reprimanding me for saying this. But I was trying this whole telling the truth thing for once in my life.

"I know, but you also didn't tell me that you were planning to resign. How was I supposed to know what to do? If you don't talk to me, I can't know what you're thinking. I thought I was helping. Actually, I was mad at you too."

"I know. I'm still getting used to this." I reached out and cradled her cheek in my hand. "I'm not used to having someone on my side."

"Well maybe you should get used to it. Because I love you. I'm not going to run off. I want to be with you."

"It's hard for me to believe that."

"Why?" She put her hands on the sides of my face. "Why don't you feel worthy of love? Why don't you trust me?"

"I didn't mean that. I do trust you. I'm just not used to being...I don't know how to explain it..."

"Vulnerable?"

I frowned. "Vulnerable? I'm not sure if that's the word I was looking for."

"I just mean that you don't have to be strong around me all the time. I just want you to be you."

"This is me." I wasn't vulnerable. I stared at her. But maybe she wanted me to try to be. I was always prepared. I always knew what I wanted. I was always in control. And that wasn't necessarily a good thing for a relationship.

"I know. I just mean, you don't have to be scared of showing me every side of you."

"The only thing I'm scared of is losing you." But I'd try my best to be more open with her.

"You're not going to lose me. I'm sorry. I was upset that you made the decision to quit without me. And then I thought you were going to break up with me. And it was hard being in class without you. I don't know if I can do it."

I know, baby. "Let's forget all the noise for right now, okay? Let's just enjoy us. We finally get to be together, Penny." I found the light switch and flicked it so that I could see her better.

She had that ruffled sex hair that I loved so much. I finished buttoning my shirt as I stared down at her.

She looked around at the mess we'd made in the closet. A few bottles of cleaner had spilled from the shelves and I'd knocked a bunch of other stuff over too. "James, do you think maybe we should pick some of this up?"

"Eh, I don't work here anymore. Let's get the hell out of here before someone finds us." I grabbed her hand and opened the door a crack. The next classes for the day were already in session and the coast was clear. I pulled Penny out after me and we ran hand-in-hand through the hallway. It was strange holding her hand in the middle of this building. And I couldn't hide the smile on my face if I even tried.

A few students walking along the green turned to look at us as we ran to my car. I opened the door for Penny and she quickly got in. I closed her door and ran around to my side. I turned my key in the ignition and leaned over and kissed her.

This was what I'd been waiting for. There had been so much stress in our relationship. It finally felt like we were allowed to be happy. We were acting like two teenagers in love. And that's how I felt. When I was next to her, I felt like anything was possible.

I looked over at her. "Truth or dare?" I asked. There was something we still needed to do before we could shut the world out for the rest of the day. We needed to tell her parents about us.

Her eyes met mine. She bit her lip as she pondered which to choose. "Dare."

That's what I was hoping she would choose. This would be better to do in person than over the phone. Besides, I wanted to get as far away from here as possible.

Every mile we drove away from the University of New Castle, the more relaxed I felt. Part of it was the scenery. The colorful autumn trees blurred together as we sped by. But the better view was the smile on Penny's face. It was hard not to be relaxed when she looked so damn happy. I kept stealing glances at her as I drove down the highway. Each time I looked, she was already staring at me. And I couldn't wipe the smile off my face. We were...free.

"What are you staring at?" I finally asked.

"You."

I rubbed my thumb against her palm.

"What now?" she asked.

I was waiting for her to ask where the hell we were going. "Well, do you have a passport?" I think we both needed a trip after this day was over.

"No. I've never needed one."

"You've never left the country?" I glanced at her again. Was she joking?

"I have. I've been to Canada. But I didn't need a passport."

"That's because going to Canada doesn't really count as leaving the country. So where have you been? I want to take you somewhere new."

She turned and looked out the window. "I haven't really been that many places." She stared at the colorful trees for a moment before turning back to me. "I've pretty much stayed on the east coast. Pennsylvania, Virginia, and Maryland. Oh, I've been to North and South Carolina. And New York of course." She squeezed my hand. "And Florida a few times to go to Disneyworld."

"Disneyworld?" Was that her idea of an exotic vacation?

"Yeah, I love Disneyworld. Everyone loves Disneyworld. Don't look at me like that."

I laughed and turned my attention back to the road. "I wouldn't know. I've never been."

"You've never been to Disneyworld?"

"No." I pressed my lips together. I hadn't exactly had a normal childhood. Penny knew that and she was looking at me like she felt sad for me. But there wasn't anything I could do about my past. And my future looked pretty damn bright with her next to me.

"Well, maybe you should let me take you to Disneyworld."

I laughed. Unless we were allowed to fuck in front of Mickey Mouse, that was a terrible idea. "This is my dare. I'm taking you somewhere. Not the other way around."

"So, where are we going then?"

In a few minutes, Penny was going to wish we were anywhere else in the world. But we needed to do this in person. Instead of responding to her, I put on my turn signal and took an exit off I-95.

"Aren't we going to the airport?" she asked.

"We are. I just wanted to make a quick stop first." I'd take her anywhere she wanted to go after we did this.

"I don't know. I haven't decided if I want to make that speech on Friday yet. So we can't go anywhere that far I guess. And I forgot that I really should be studying for my Stat test. You know what? Let's just turn around. Let's spend the day in your apartment. Don't we have to get stuff ready for your brother anyway?"

I was pretty sure she knew exactly where we were going. And she was trying to get out of it. "Ellen will get everything ready for Rob's visit."

"I forgot, I think I have a psychology test tomorrow too. Oh geez, we better get back."

"You chose dare, Penny. Who backs down from a dare?" I drove down Concord Pike and put my turn signal on again.

Penny looked completely panicked now. "You know what? I actually think I've been around here before. There's this cute little diner right down the street. I'm starving. Do you want to stop and eat?"

I think I've been around here before? I lowered my eyebrows. "Penny, you're a terrible liar."

"What? Psh. Professor Hunter..."

"You really should stop calling me that." I turned into Windy Park. It was a cute little neighborhood, a perfect display of suburbia.

Penny took a deep breath. "How do you know where I live?"

"Oh, is this your neighborhood?" I looked over at her and raised my left eyebrow.

"James, pull over."

Nope. I continued to drive down the street and stopped at the stop sign before turning onto Smith Lane.

"James!"

I turned the corner and pulled to a stop at the bottom of her street. "Penny, you'll be lucky if your parents don't already know. It'll be better if they hear it from you. You said you'd call them..."

"And I will call them. I can't do this in person."

"You can."

"James, I can't." She dropped her head back on the headrest in total despair.

She was being adorable. This wasn't going to be so bad. I tried to hide my smile. "We need to do this. Today."

She didn't respond.

"You don't have to do it alone. I'm going to be with you. I'll even do most of the talking if you want."

"I feel like that'll make it worse. I need some air." She opened up the car door and stepped out into the sunshine.

I knew Penny didn't like to run. But I was a little worried she was getting ready to sprint away from me. I climbed out of the car and walked over to her. She wasn't fleeing, so that was good. I knew she just needed a moment. I leaned against the car and stared at the manicured lawn in front of us.

Penny sighed and leaned against the car too. "Who uses a dare to make their girlfriend disclose their illicit affair to her parents? You're super lame. How about you dare me to give you head at that diner I told you about a minute ago? Or maybe we can join the mile high club on an airplane?"

I pressed my lips together. Did she honestly think I wasn't already part of that club? She knew my issues. But her offer was certainly tempting. Wasn't it kind of a mile high club member's duty to initiate new members? I tried to shake away the thought. This was important. I wanted her parents to like me. And I'd already made a pretty bad first impression.

"Please don't tell me that you're already part of the mile high club."

"Stop trying to change the subject." I put my arm around her shoulders. "I'm not going to force you to tell them. If you really don't want to, that's your decision. It would make me feel a lot better about everything though."

"Unless my dad punches you in the face."

I laughed and looked down at her. But she looked dead serious. I frowned. "Wait, do you seriously think that's going to happen?" Her dad was not a big man. I was almost a foot taller than him. But he wasn't super thin or anything. He might have a secret mean right hook or something.

"I have no idea. I usually don't upset my parents. Disappointing them isn't exactly something I do all the time. I'm a little out of my element. And I've never even brought a boy home."

"Luckily I have tons of practice with disappointing parents. I'm not even sure if my parents love me."

Penny winced. "That can't possibly be true."

"I don't think it's far from the truth." I looked down at her. "I'd really prefer if your parents didn't hate me. That's probably asking too much given the situation. The sooner we tell them, the sooner they might be willing to forgive me though."

"They won't even be home for several hours," I said.

"Okay. How about you give me a tour of your hometown? Unlike you, I've really never been here before." I smiled at her. "And if you still don't feel like telling them in person by the time they're supposed to come home from work, we'll leave. They won't even know we were here."

"Oh, Penny! Is that you?" someone said.

We both turned around. An older woman with a huge smile was walking over to us.

"Hi, Mrs. Bennett," Penny said with zero thrill in her voice.

Mrs. Bennett gave Penny a hug and then looked over at me. "And you must be the new boyfriend I've heard so much about?"

Maybe we were too late. Whoever Mrs. Bennett was already knew about me from the papers. Or…maybe Penny's parents had told her about me? After we met at the hospital? She wasn't staring at me with disdain or anything. I cleared my throat. "Hi, I'm James." I put my hand out for her to shake.

She took my hand and didn't let go. "Pulling Penny away from her classes, are you? Her parents won't be pleased to hear about that. But your secret is safe with me." She finally let go of my hand.

Ditching classes with me was going to be the least of Penny's parents' worries.

"So what are you two kids doing here?" Mrs. Bennett asked.

Kids? Okay, so she definitely didn't know about the article. Or else she'd know I was a grown ass man. I looked down at my outfit. I didn't think I looked like a kid either way though.

"I was just showing James where I grew up," Penny said. "A little tour of town."

"Well that's fun. Your parents are going to be so thrilled that you're visiting. I think having an empty nest doesn't suit them very well. I was thinking about giving them one of my cats. I know you already have a cat, but trust me, two is better than one."

Penny laughed. "I'm sure they'd really appreciate that."

"Did you know that I used to babysit Penny when she was a wee little thing?" Mrs. Bennett asked. "The thing that stands out the most was that it was almost impossible to ever get her in the tub. She was always so feisty. I always thought it was the red hair."

Penny's face was completely red.

I laughed. "She's still pretty feisty."

It was Mrs. Bennett's turn to blush. "Oh my." She lightly touched my arm. "Well I don't want to interfere with the tour. I'll let you two kids get to it." She waved and walked off.

I waited till she was out of earshot to turn back to Penny. "Not a fan of baths, huh? I never would have guessed that. We always have so much fun in the shower."

Penny did not seem pleased by my comment. She grabbed my car keys out of my hand and walked past me.

Where the hell did she think she was going with my car?

Chapter 8

Wednesday

Penny started to walk toward the driver's side door.

"Hey."

She didn't turn her head.

Before she took another step, I grabbed her wrist. "What are you doing?"

"You wanted a tour."

I was relieved that she wasn't trying to run away from me. "I'll drive." I held out my hand for the keys.

"You won't be able to see anything I show you then. Can't you give up control for just a few minutes? I want to show you something."

Was this one of those instances where she wanted me to be vulnerable or something? I didn't love it. But I could tell she really wanted to drive. And I was curious to see where she'd take me. I took a deep breath and dropped her wrist.

She smiled and walked around the car. She opened up the driver's door and climbed in.

I reluctantly sat down in the passenger's seat.

Penny was so far away from the wheel, I wasn't sure she could even reach it. She looked around for how to adjust the seat. She pressed a button and the seat got even lower. Her head was beneath the top of the steering wheel now. Even if she could reach the wheel, she wouldn't be able to see a damn thing.

I laughed. "Here." I leaned over her and pressed a few buttons. As the seat rose, I placed a kiss against her lips.

She grabbed my chin. "You should probably put your seatbelt on, James."

I lowered my eyebrows. I really hoped she wasn't planning on speeding. I'd never seen her drive, but based on how she was trying to adjust the seat...I wasn't expecting much. I sat back in my seat. As soon as my buckle clicked into place, Penny put her foot down on the gas hard.

The car jolted forward.

Jesus. She was going to kill us. I gripped the handle on the door, holding on for dear life.

She did a very jerky U-turn.

"Maybe I should drive," I said.

"I got this."

It took her a little bit, but she did start to adjust to the sensitivity of the gas and brake pedals. She looked very confident as she drove out of neighborhood and back onto Concord Pike. Overly confident, really. Because the car was still weirdly jerky under her control.

I kept holding on to the handle on the door. I was starting to wonder if Penny even had her driver's license.

I needed a distraction from her terrible driving. "So is Wilmington one of those small towns where everyone knows each other?" I asked. I'd always been so curious about Delaware. Ever since high school when I was told that people were nicer here. And I'd only ever been in Newark and to the beach.

"If you haven't noticed, all of Delaware is like that."

I smiled. "I have kind of noticed that. It's very different from New York."

She laughed and turned into a parking lot next to a beautiful park. She pulled into an empty spot and miraculously didn't hit the tree that she seemed dead set on hitting.

Thank fuck. I was never letting her drive again.

"Well you should be comfortable today then," Penny said. "No one ever really notices me. So today we can pretend like we're in New York."

It wasn't just the way she said it that made me frown. It was the fact that she really believed that was true. That she was invisible. She couldn't be farther from the truth.

She handed me my keys back before stepping out of the car.

I climbed out after her. I closed the distance between us and immediately wrapped my arms around her. *You're not invisible, Penny.*

She hugged me back.

And we stood like that for a long time. I felt so...calm. I closed my eyes and took a deep breath. Her cherry perfume mixed with the smell of the autumn leaves. No, Penny definitely wasn't invisible. She was home to me. She was all I ever saw.

She slowly pulled back. "Let me call my mom. I'll tell her we're here and that she should come home for lunch. You're right, the sooner the better."

I stared into her blue eyes. "Are you sure?"

"I'm sure."

***

Penny had said she was sure. But...she still hadn't called her mom. And the longer we walked on the path through the woods, the less sure she looked. We'd been walking on the trail for a good half hour. It was the most amazing fall afternoon. But it was a little hard to enjoy it when Penny was a ball of stress.

"Enough," I said and dropped her hand. We were on an adorable little bridge. A perfect place to steal a kiss. But she looked like she was going to throw up. "Just do it."

She groaned.

"Penny, the longer you wait, the more likely it is that your mother will find out." I glanced at my watch. "And it's almost 11:30. If you want to do it over lunch, you need to give them at least a little heads up."

"You're right. I know you're right."

"But?" I said and raised my eyebrow.

"What if they're really mad, James?"

I smiled. "It'll be fine. You know how charming I can be." But I was worried about the same thing. What if her dad tried to slug me or something? Was it okay to knock him out? Or was that poor etiquette when meeting the parents? *Screw me.*

Penny nodded.

"And we'll get through it together," I said. "No matter what. Besides, it's much more likely that they're going to be mad at me, not you." The first time I'd met them had been in a hospital and I'd blatantly lied about who I was. I was the one in the firing line, not her.

"You're right. I've got this." She laughed awkwardly and pulled out her phone. She tapped on her screen and put the phone to her ear. She turned away from me as it rang.

I leaned against the railing on the small bridge and stared at her.

"Hi, Mom," she said and turned away from me.

I really hoped for both our sakes that her mother didn't know yet.

"Yeah, everything's great!" Penny said. "Nothing weird or out of the ordinary going on at all."

What is she saying right now? I held back a laugh.

"I just wanted to show James around," she said. "He was curious about where I grew up." She glanced over her shoulder at me.

I gave her an encouraging smile.

She turned back away from me and listened to something her mom was saying.

I leaned over the railing of the bridge and stared at the water. Yeah, this would have been the perfect fall afternoon if we didn't have this cloud over our heads.

"Actually, Mom, I was hoping you and Dad could come home for lunch? James and I have to get back soon and I want to make sure I get to see both of you."

Another long pause.

I wondered if Penny's father would off me and throw me into this river tonight...

"James actually needs to get back soon," Penny said.

I turned back toward her. *I do, do I?*

"I'm feeling a lot better," Penny said and touched her forehead. "You have absolutely nothing to worry about."

Nothing? She was doing a terrible job prepping her mom for this. Piling lies on top of lies was more my speed than Penny's. But it was better to do this in person.

"Really, Mom, I'm good. Text me about lunch, okay?" Penny nodded to herself. "Great. See you later." She hung up and sighed.

"I need to get back soon, huh?"

"I didn't want to commit to dinner in case, well, everyone's freaking out."

I nodded. "Probably a good idea." I put my elbows back on the railing.

She leaned on the ledge beside me. "I used to run on these paths in high school."

"I didn't know that you liked to run." I thought she'd told me she didn't.

"I don't," she laughed. "I made myself. I wanted to make sure I was in good shape for volleyball. I actually hate running."

"You played volleyball?"

"Why do you always seem surprised when I tell you about my athletic abilities? I'm an only child. I used to play stuff with my dad all the time. He never had a son." She shrugged her shoulders. "I was actually pretty awesome at volleyball."

"You're probably awesome at everything you do." I put my arm around her shoulders and pulled her in to my side.

"I used to dream of having a boyfriend to walk with back here. I even used to dream about sneaking out of my house and coming over here for secret rendezvous."

"Hmm." I leaned down and kissed her. "You were always quite scandalous. The news of you dating your professor shouldn't shock your parents at all then."

She laughed uneasily.

I needed to change the topic. We'd deal with her parents soon enough. "What were you like in high school?"

"What do you mean? Like I am now. Or, like I was before I met you, I guess. Shy and quiet. Completely invisible. I don't feel invisible anymore." Her phone buzzed and she pulled it out of her pocket. "They will both be home in an hour." She took a deep breath. "What's the plan exactly? How do you think we should bring it up? We already told them that you were a student. And you look young, James. I feel like they're going to think I'm joking."

I pulled her against my chest. "I don't think there is any right way. Let's just try not to think about it."

"How can I possibly not think about it? I want them to love you as much as I do."

I ran my fingers through her hair. "I think it's more likely that your dad will punch me in the face than love me." *And then toss me in that river.* Although, it was a terrible place to hide a body. It didn't look deep at all.

Penny laughed. "He's not going to do that."

She didn't expect him to do it. But she didn't know for sure. We were in uncharted territory here. Penny had never had a boyfriend before. She had no idea how her dad was going to react to her dating a professor that was quite a bit older than her. He was definitely going to fucking kill me.

I tried to shake away the thought. "I'd love a tour of your house. So I can plan my escape route and everything before they get there. Just in case."

"If you need to make an emergency escape, please don't leave me in the crossfire."

"I would never." I had every intention of throwing her over my shoulder and escaping with her. Part of me wanted to follow her lead from earlier and just get the hell out of the country. But this was the last hurdle we needed to face today. Everything would be easier after we came clean to her parents. I hoped.

"Can I drive again?" Penny asked.

God no. Was she trying to give me a heart attack before her dad tried to murder me? It was like the Taylors were out to get me.

"What is with that face? I'm a good driver."

According to who? "I'm driving."

"We'll see about that." She laughed and grabbed my hand. Our feet crunched in the leaves as she pulled me back in the direction we'd come from. Her red hair blew in the wind and I just wanted to freeze time.

I enjoyed the walk back to the car a lot more than the walk away from it. Her laughter was contagious. And when she stopped on the pavement and looked up at me, I already knew I was going to cave.

"Please?" she said and put out her hand. She bit her lip as she looked up at me.

How was I supposed to say no to her when she was biting her lip like that? I knew I was going to regret it, put I placed the keys back into her hand. *Please don't kill us.*

Chapter 9

Wednesday

Penny opened the front door of her house and flicked on the lights. I closed the door behind us and looked around. Penny twisted her hands nervously in front of her. She looked like she did when she was about to give a speech in my class. But I had no idea why she was nervous. No, I didn't grow up in a house like this. But I knew what a normal colonial house in the suburbs looked like. From pictures, that is. I'd never been in one before. But it was classically homey. The exact opposite of my home growing up in every way. And I meant that as a compliment.

An orange cat came running into the foyer meowing.

Penny laughed and picked the furball up in her arms.

"This is Teddy," she said.

"I didn't realize you were a...cat person." The cat's fur and Penny's hair were almost an identical color. I wasn't exactly sure what I was looking at right now. Had she picked the cat because it had the same hair color as her? Or had her parents gotten it because they missed her or something? Or was it just a really weird coincidence?

"I wouldn't classify myself as a cat person."

So maybe it was just a coincidence that she matched the cat. *Good.* I was not a pet person.

Penny held it out to me.

What was she expecting me to do? Pet it? Hold it?

She held Teddy out further.

"Oh, um, okay." I grabbed Teddy and held him out in front of me. Was I doing this right? I was pretty sure I was about to squish him. Teddy began to squirm in my hands.

"Oh God." I tossed the little orange beast onto the floor, and he immediately darted out of the room.

Penny started laughing. "So, I'm guessing you aren't an animal person?"

"Was it that obvious? I just never had a pet growing up. Now cats and dogs just kind of freak me out."

She laughed again and grabbed my hand. "Well, I just have the one cat. So you don't need to worry about running into any more. And I'm pretty sure Teddy is going to stay away from you the rest of the afternoon."

"I hope that's not a bad omen." I wanted her parents to like me more than Teddy did.

"Don't be ridiculous." But she didn't look like she believed what she was saying.

Yeah, me neither.

"Okay, well, this is the dining room," she said, changing the subject. She walked through the archway into the dining room. It was simple, just a table and chairs and some pictures on the walls. *Ohhhh, pictures.* Now that was something I was excited to see.

I walked over to the wall and looked at a picture of a very young Penny hugging a tree with bright red leaves. What on earth was she doing hugging a tree trunk? She had the biggest smile on her face though. And her smile made me smile. "You're so adorable."

Penny laughed. "I'm really glad there aren't any pictures of my awkward stage in here. I begged my mom to stop putting them all over the house. Maybe she finally listened." She glanced over at the China cabinet and then snapped her head back toward me. She looked absolutely horrified.

Bingo. I walked over to the China cabinet to see what had her so flustered.

"Don't you want to see the kitchen?" she asked.

I leaned down and stared at a picture of Penny smiling with braces. Okay, yeah, that was not the best picture. I wondered what made her choose to smile so hard in it. So hard that the tendons in her neck were showing. Maybe she was trying to make people not notice her braces? I stifled a laugh.

Penny groaned.

I looked over at her and smiled. "Super adorable. I have no idea why you've never had a boyfriend before."

"Oh shut up." She grabbed my arm and pulled me away from the dining room.

"Seriously, Penny." I pushed her back against the doorframe between the kitchen and dining room. "You're beautiful." And sexy. Who cared about one bad school portrait? But I did love how flushed her cheeks were over the whole ordeal of me seeing it.

"Not in that picture."

I placed a soft kiss against her lips. "Well you should have seen me in junior high."

"You were probably always sexy."

I laughed. "I'm sure Rob will love showing you picture evidence of how that is so not true." I was a little lanky before I started working out in high school. But no, I didn't have any pictures like I'd just witnessed of Penny. I don't think I'd ever smiled quite as hard as she had in that photo. The thought made me frown. That wasn't true. I used to smile all the time with my friends. Before senior year of high school, anyway. I tried to push the thought away. But it just stuck there. And I couldn't help it.

I thought about the girl who'd first told me that the people were nicer in Delaware. Had she lived in a house like this before she moved to New York? I didn't think so. She wasn't as well off as Penny's family. Her house was probably smaller. Even homier. I pressed my lips together.

I wondered if she'd still be alive if she'd gotten to stay in Delaware, far away from me and my friends.

"I'm excited to meet him," Penny said, pulling me back into the present.

I took a deep breath. I needed to stop thinking about what ifs. I was allowed to be happy now. I was allowed to move on. So why was there a lump in my throat?

"It'll be fun having him around," I said as I stared down at Penny. And I knew why there was a lump in my throat. I'd been so worried about ruining her life. What if I already had? What if her parents wouldn't forgive her? What if she moved to New York with me and...I lost her.

Breathe. I released Penny from my embrace and walked into the kitchen. *Breathe.* I exhaled slowly, this time pushing my plaguing thoughts away better. I looked around the kitchen. "I like your house. It's...warm." I smiled at her.

"Warm. I like that." She led me into the family room.

This room was carpeted and looked even homier than the rest of the house. I could tell Penny spent a lot of time with her family in this room. And best of all, there were two exits in here just in case I needed to flee lunch. "Garage and back door. Noted."

"James, you're not going to have to make an escape. It's not like you're my super old professor. You're not even that much older than me. Plus you aren't even my professor anymore. It could be so much worse. And I think they just want me to be happy. You make me so happy."

"Hmm." I tried my best to give her an encouraging smile. But I still heard that voice in the back of my head. *You ruined her.*

"Come on, we haven't finished the tour." She showed me the living room, the office, and a bathroom. "And that's the basement," she said, pointing to a door. "And the laundry room." She pointed to a different door. "And that's it."

That definitely wasn't it. I wanted to see her bedroom. I looked over at the stairs. "Well, what's up there?"

"My parents' room, two guest rooms, and two more bathrooms. Oh, and my room."

"I think I'd like to see that."

"You want to see my room? I'm not allowed to bring boys upstairs." She gave me a very innocent smile.

"Is that so? Maybe I can convince you to bend the rules just this once?" I raised my left eyebrow.

"How much time do we have before they come home?"

I glanced at my watch. "Half an hour."

"Okay. But really quick. I do not want our discussion to start out that way. Absolutely no funny business."

I lifted my hands to either side, acknowledging that I'd behave. *Maybe.*

She bit her lip and turned toward the stairs. She made her hips sway more than usual as she walked up the stairs.

It was like she was hoping I'd abandon my resolve. Penny had never had a boyfriend. Which meant she'd never had a boy in her room before. How many times had she imagined it? Had she wanted someone sneak in her window and climb into her bed? Had she ever spread her legs beneath her covers at night, touching herself where she'd dreamed her boyfriend would?

I could feel myself growing hard.

But that ended as soon as I almost tripped over clothes strewn all over her bedroom floor. "You're kind of a slob." I laughed and stepped over more clothes. It was a good thing I had Ellen, because I wasn't sure I couldn't handle a mess like this in my bedroom. I smiled to myself.

I really loved the idea of sharing a bedroom with Penny permanently.

"I'm a lot better when I have a roommate," she said. "A lot of it was from when I was packing. It's hard to know what to bring to school when you only have so much space." She picked up some of the clothes and put them into a hamper in the corner.

I walked over to her bookshelf and looked at the titles. "Jane Eyre? Are you a fan of all the classic romances?"

She laughed. "No, actually. I read it for my senior thesis. Jane and Mr. Rochester drove me crazy. Clearly they should have been together the whole time. It made me so mad." She tossed some more clothes into her hamper.

I smiled at her. She did see the irony in her words, right? She had told me she wanted to wait to be with me until she graduated. But she'd caved a lot quicker than the characters from Jane Eyre. I took another deep breath. I was so happy to be right here right now with her. "I couldn't agree more."

"Honestly, I think I'm done reading classics as soon as I'm done with school. I prefer reading books like Harry Potter."

"I prefer books like Harry Potter too." I shoved my hands in my pockets. I'd read those books so many times. I'd wanted nothing more in the world than for someone to appear and whisk me away far far away from my parents.

"Really? You've read Harry Potter?"

"Why is that so surprising? I'm pretty sure that Harry Potter was actually my generation's thing, not yours. And who doesn't love the concept of magic? Besides, there was this cute little red headed girl in it that I loved reading about." I smiled at her.

"I was Ginny Weasley for Halloween last year."

Damn, I wish I could have seen that. The pictures were probably as cute as the one of her hugging a tree. "Quite the leap from Ginny to sexy Poison Ivy."

"Yeah, well I started dating this sophisticated, older gentleman. I was trying to impress him."

"You don't need to change for me. I love you just the way you are." I looked over at her bed that was completely covered in stuffed animals. "Stuffed animals and all. Geez, that's a lot of stuffed animals."

She laughed. "Yeah, well, I didn't have my boyfriend's sweater to snuggle up to at night. Or the man himself."

So she'd snuggled with stuffed animals? I smiled and walked over to her bed. I sat down on the edge so that I wouldn't disturb the assortment and stared around her room some more. "The Beatles?" I asked, and nodded my head toward a poster on her wall.

"I'm an old soul."

"You're full of surprises, Penny Taylor."

"I hope that's a good thing."

I smiled. "What is the wildest fantasy you had in this room?"

"Honestly, nothing that risqué. I just had tons of dreams about getting my first kiss."

"Was your actual first kiss everything you dreamed it would be?"

"No. The first kiss we had was much more like my dreams." She closed the distance between us, stopping right in front of me.

I lightly brushed my fingertips against her thigh. "And why is that?"

"It was sexy and romantic." Her cheeks flushed.

She was right. That kiss was what dreams were made of. Sinful dreams anyway. God, I'd thought I'd have one taste of her and it would be enough. I should have known better. One taste was never enough.

"Until you told me I had to stop thinking about you, of course."

I was such a fool. I grabbed her hand and she laughed as I pulled her on top of me. She straddled me on the bed and smiled down at me.

I put my hands on her waist. I loved this part of her. The tiny dip right above her perfect ass. "It's good that all you dreamed about was kissing. Because I want to make all your fantasies come true. And if it was something else, I'd be obliged to comply. Even though your parents are going to be home any minute."

I didn't think her childhood bedroom would have turned me on so much. But there was something about taking her on this bed that had me growing hard. She'd been waiting for me and only me. And I could give her every single thing she ever wanted.

She ran her hand along the scruff on my jaw line. "James, I'm so nervous."

"I know. I'm nervous too."

"What if they freak out?"

"We'll figure it out together."

She glanced at the window. "We should probably go downstairs."

"We *probably* should." But instead of getting up to go downstairs, I leaned forward and kissed her. What we needed was a distraction. And it was easy to get lost in her kiss. Just as easy as it was to imagine her dreaming of a first kiss in this bed.

But I believed she did more than dream about a kiss. She was just too shy to tell me. Did she have any idea when her fingers had been buried in her pussy back then that my tongue would feel a million times better? I could so easily picture her writhing in her bed with her legs wrapped around my head, begging me for more. She'd whimper, trying not to be caught. But I knew exactly how to make her scream my name.

She smiled and pulled back. "You're good at distracting me."

I ran the tip of my nose down the length of hers. I could distract her a lot more with my cock down her throat…

It was like she knew what I was thinking because she sighed and climbed off my lap. "Okay, let's go downstairs." She smoothed her shirt down.

"Penny, it's going to be okay." I waited a moment before standing up so that she couldn't see the tent in my pants.

"How can you be so sure?"

"As long as I have you, everything will be okay."

She looked like she was going to throw up.

But I knew she felt the same way I did. She was just nervous. And fuck, so was I. I'd much rather stay up here and drench her pretty little face in my cum.

Stop. I took a deep breath. I needed to calm down. I was about to re-meet her parents, for fuck's sake.

She grabbed my hand and led me out of her room and down the stairs. I looked down at the front of my pants. My dick was trying to break through the zipper. Hopefully that would go away before her parents got back.

Chapter 10

Wednesday

"What's the game plan?" Penny asked. "Should I just tell them everything real quick? Just throw it all out there?"

She was adorable when she was nervous. And for some reason, her being nervous made me less nervous. I could be the one in control of this situation. It was going to be fine. I rubbed my thumb against her palm.

"So, slow then? Just let it all unravel?" She bit her lip.

Please stop doing that. I wanted to be the one to bite her lip for her. "Take a deep breath, Penny." I heard a car door slam outside.

"Oh God," Penny said with a groan. She squeezed my hand as tightly as she had this morning in Joe's office. "Try to look natural, okay?"

"Natural." I smiled. "Got it."

"You're dressed really professorly today by the way. I don't know whether that's a good or bad thing."

"Professorly?" I laughed. "Yeah, that's not a word."

"Now I'm making up words. How am I going to tell them that I'm dating my professor when I can't even talk?!"

I held back my laugh this time because I knew she wouldn't appreciate it when she was spiraling. "Luckily I'm not your professor anymore. Does that make it any better?"

"Not really."

"I think maybe it makes it a little better." I raised my eyebrow.

Her face flushed. "Okay, maybe a little better."

I squeezed her hand. "Thanks for doing this. It means a lot to me. More than you know." I really did want her parents to like me.

"Sometimes it still feels like I made you up. Maybe this will make it feel more real."

"It *is* real."

She looked up at me and took a deep breath. "I love you, James."

"I love you." And we were going to get through this awkward conversation together. I squeezed her hand again as the front door opened. Coming clean to her parents was the final thing we needed to do in order to move forward. And that made it worth all the awkwardness. I just needed Penny's parents to realize how much I loved their daughter. How serious I was about this relationship. That's all that parents wanted, right? For their kids to be happy? For just a second I thought about my parents. I pressed my lips together. They certainly didn't give a shit about my happiness. Fuck, what if I had it all wrong? What if Penny's parents were actually monsters like mine?

"Penny?" Mrs. Taylor called from the hallway.

"Hi, Mom!" Penny dropped my hand and hugged her mom as soon as she walked into the kitchen.

"It's so good to see you, sweetie." Her mom pulled back. "And James!" She put down some paper bags from the grocery store and hugged me too.

I was surprised by the embrace. I took a deep breath and patted her back. I had nothing to worry about. Penny's parents were nothing like mine. And her mom seemed to really like me. I smiled over at Penny.

It looked like she was trying not to laugh.

Was I doing this wrong? I patted her mom's back again. I was pretty sure this was right. But I couldn't remember the last time my own mother had hugged me.

And I didn't really know what to do with my hands. "It's great to see you again, Mrs. Taylor."

"I hope sandwiches are okay." She looked over at Penny. "I stopped by that little French bistro on the way home that you like so much. La Patisserie."

"That sounds fantastic," Penny said.

"If I wasn't so happy to see you both, I'd reprimand you for skipping classes today. Why the sudden urge to come home?" Mrs. Taylor opened up the fridge.

Technically I wasn't skipping classes. I'd been fired. But I knew what she meant. The first time we'd met I'd told her I was a student. Which meant I shouldn't be here in the middle of the day on a Wednesday.

"We both didn't have anything important going on today," Penny said. "I thought it might be fun to show James where I grew up."

I heard the front door open again. And it was like some of Penny's nervous energy transferred to me. It was her dad that I was really worried about talking to.

"Hey, Pen." Mr. Taylor opened his arms the second he entered the kitchen.

Penny quickly gave him a hug.

I stared at them hugging. He probably still saw Penny as his little girl. And I had no idea how he was going to feel when we disclosed our relationship. I didn't want Penny's parents to view her any differently. Or think she made a mistake. Penny was a good girl. Well, until she met me. No, she was still good. She was just bad around me. And I had a feeling her father would really hate that.

Mrs. Taylor set the table, poured us each a glass of lemonade from a pitcher, and gestured for us all to sit.

I sat down next to Penny and put my hand on her knee. I wanted her to go at her own pace with this. But I

LOVED

was kind of hoping she'd just rip the Band-Aid off and tell them.

"So, what's up with you two?" Penny asked. "Do you have anything new and exciting going on?" She took a huge bite of her sandwich.

Okay, so delaying it was the game plan then…

I kept my hand on her knee.

"Just the usual," her mom said. "What about you two? How's Comm going?" She started to eat her sandwich too.

The food looked great. But it would be easier for me to run away from her father on an empty stomach.

"Comm has been...interesting," Penny said. "Actually, the real reason that I'm here is that I have something I need to tell you." Penny took a huge sip of lemonade to stall.

That was good thinking. Running was easier when you were properly hydrated. I took a sip too.

"Actually, that *we* need to tell you." She looked over at me.

Was she waiting for me to cut in here? I couldn't read her face.

"Oh my God." Her mom slowly placed her sandwich down on her plate. "Oh my God, you're pregnant?!"

I choked on my lemonade. What the fuck kind of conclusion was that?

"What?!" her dad practically shouted.

I winced.

"No," Penny said. "No! I'm not pregnant." She laughed awkwardly. "I couldn't possibly be..." her voice trailed off.

Well, I wasn't sure that was entirely true. Yes, she was on birth control, but it was still *possible*. Especially since I really liked not using a condom.

I pressed my lips together. I was pretty sure she was just trying to say she wasn't sexual active, though, which was hilarious. Did she seriously think her parents didn't know we were fucking? And why the hell were we even talking about this right now? Penny wasn't pregnant. But just the idea had made me start sweating. I'd be a shit father. Just like mine had been. *Fuck. What if she is pregnant/?*

Her parents were just staring at us in silence.

Penny stole a sideways glance at me.

I had no idea what to say. This conversation had taken a very weird turn. Could she tell how uncomfortable I was talking about her being pregnant? *Breathe.*

"Definitely not pregnant," she added, staring at me. And I knew she was saying it more for me than her parents at this point.

I knew I was probably pale. We'd barely talked about kids. My heart was beating funny in my chest and I had no idea why. Maybe because now I was picturing having a daughter one day. And her sitting across from me telling me she was fucking her professor. Penny's dad was going to kill me. *I'd* kill me.

"Actually, what I needed to tell you is that James isn't a student at the University of New Castle."

Her mom started laughing and put her hand on her husband's shoulder. "That's it? You scared me half to death."

Me too. I took another deep breath. Penny wasn't pregnant. I needed to calm down. Penny needed me right now. Because her parents were probably going to be just as upset about our actual news.

"So what do you do, James?" Mr. Taylor asked. "Are you in vocational school or something?"

Vocational school? The only thing I knew how to fix was computers.

"He's actually done school, Dad. He graduated a few years ago. Several actually. He's 27."

"Oh?" her mom said. She glanced at her husband and then back at us. "Well, that's quite an age difference."

I swallowed hard. It wasn't *that* big of an age difference. We were all silent for a second. The disapproval almost seemed palpable. Most of the professors at the University of New Castle were well into their 50s. This could have been a hell of a lot worse.

Penny's father was frowning. "So that brings me back to my original question. If you're no longer a student, what is it that you do for a living, James? And why on earth are you dating a teenager?"

Because I'm a sick fuck.

"Dad, I just turned 20."

Her parents did not seem to care about that rebuttal.

"Well." I shifted in my seat. *Fuck, what the hell do I say to him?* He'd already made up his mind about me. I was pretty sure he had when we first met and he kept giving the Eagles' players weird names. He'd already been fucking with me then.

Breathe. Well, her father didn't look like he could hate me any more than he already did. And if Penny wasn't going to tell them I was her professor, I just needed to do it. As fast as possible. "This is not going to sound great. But I want you both to know that I love your daughter very much."

Shit, now I was stalling. I shifted in my seat again. "I actually resigned from my current position this morning," I continued. "But before that, I had a job at the University of New Castle." I paused and stared at them. They understood, right? Her father was staring at me like he understood. Or did he just look confused? *Fuck me.* I was usually good under pressure. But it was different when I wanted them to like me. And there was no way they'd like me once I said the words out loud.

"He's my professor," Penny finally blurted out.

I froze.

Penny's parents froze.

And then her mom burst out laughing.

Her dad quickly started laughing too.

What was happening right now?

I turned to Penny. She looked just as confused as me. I shrugged. I'd expected cursing and for her father to throw a punch. Definitely not laughter.

"I don't know what you've done to Penny," her mom said between bouts of laughter. "Because she never pulls pranks on us. Well done. You both had us going."

I clenched my jaw. They thought we were joking?

"She can't even pull an April Fool's Day prank," her dad added. "That was hilarious!"

I never in a million years expected them to have this reaction. But I guess it made sense that they thought we were joking. Penny had never even had a boyfriend before. Jumping from no boyfriend to fucking her professor was a big leap for someone who didn't usually break the rules.

"Mom, Dad." Penny's voice caught in her throat. "We're not joking. You said it yourself, I don't know how to play pranks. It's not even April Fool's Day."

"Of course you're joking," her mom quickly said. "The age difference? Your professor? It's not even believable. It's ridiculous. It's absolutely ridiculous."

It wasn't *that* ridiculous. I clenched my jaw even harder. No, I didn't expect this reaction at all. And I really didn't like it. My profession or my age didn't matter. All that mattered was that I loved Penny. And it was like they were laughing at our relationship.

"James is my Comm professor," Penny said. "*Was* my Comm professor, I mean."

"You're joking. You are, right?" Her mom suddenly looked pale. She looked over at me and frowned, as if seeing me for the first time.

I was clearly older than her daughter. And like Penny said...I was dressed professorly today. I wanted to laugh at the made-up word, but I just clenched my jaw even tighter as Mrs. Taylor stared at me. So much for Penny's mom liking me.

"We met before I knew he was a professor," Penny said.

"And you..." her mom's voice faded. "And he..." She closed her mouth again.

Stunned silence. I could work with stunned silence. "Mr. and Mrs. Taylor, I know how this might sound, but..."

"She's a sophomore," her dad said calmly. "She's only a sophomore." He was staring at me like I was some kind of pervert.

Penny was 20 years old. It was only a seven-year difference. Seven years was nothing.

But hadn't I thought of myself the same way? I'd tried so hard to stay away from her. I really had. And yes, I was fucked up in the head. But... Penny belonged with me. I truly did believe that. "I thought she was a senior," I said, as if that would help.

"You thought she was a senior? So you only hook up with seniors, is that it?"

Oh fuck you. I took a deep breath. The last thing I needed to do was say that to him.

"Dad, it wasn't like that at all," Penny said.

"I think you should probably leave, James. We need to have a conversation with Penny in private."

"I really think we should talk about this," I said as calmly as I could. "I am in love with your daughter. I'm not going anywhere."

"You're a 27-year-old man. She's a sophomore," her dad said again.

"I'm 20 years old, Dad. It's not that big of an age difference."

"Seven years? You need to focus on school, Penny. You're not ready for the same things that *he's* ready for." He pointed at me as if I was an object instead of a person.

I really did not like that. I glared at him. And what kind of things was he referring to exactly? Sex? Because I was fucking his daughter so hard every night. And most mornings too. Penny was not the good little girl he thought she was. Not when she was crawling to me and begging for my cock. A good little slut would be a much better description of her. I smiled to myself.

"I am ready for those things. I love him, Dad."

"You're ready for marriage? And children? And responsibilities? You have no idea what it's like to be an adult. You don't even know how to write a check. You're just a child. He's an adult. You're too young to date him."

Well, that was a leap. We'd only said we were dating. And Penny didn't need to write any checks. That was all online now. For some reason picturing Penny's dad writing checks instead of paying bills online made me smile.

This whole conversation was ridiculous. "I'm not even ready to get married again..." I instantly closed my mouth. *Oh fuck.* I hadn't meant to say that. I was hoping that could be a discussion for a different day. Dating her professor was one thing. Dating her recently divorced professor sounded way worse.

"You were already married?" Penny's mom finally broke her silence.

"I'm recently divorced, yes."

"How recently?" she asked.

"I filed for a divorce last year."

Penny's parents just stared at me.

Shit. I cleared my throat. "It became official yesterday, but..."

"You got divorced yesterday?" her mom asked incredulously. "You started a relationship with my 20-year-old daughter while you were still married?" She didn't hide the disgust in her voice.

I definitely preferred stunned silence.

Chapter 11

Wednesday

I wasn't even sure why I'd said it. Mentioning not being ready to get married again? Seriously? What the hell was I thinking? Yes, I wanted to marry Penny. One day. But not today. Why hadn't I kept my mouth shut? I needed to get control of this conversation.

"Mr. and Mrs. Taylor, please just let me explain. I would never put your daughter in a position like that. As far as I'm concerned, my relationship with my ex-wife was terminated as soon as I filed..."

"You put her in a terrible situation," her dad cut in. "You're her professor. You were her *married* professor."

"Yes, I was Penny's communications professor. And I realize that I crossed the line. I completely understand why you're upset. But my marriage really has nothing to do with this."

"I was the one that crossed the line," Penny said.

I was not expecting her to say that.

"You shouldn't be mad at him, you should be mad at me." Her phone started to make a buzzing noise, but she ignored it.

"We *are* mad at you," her dad said. "But we will deal with you later."

This was ridiculous, she wasn't a kid anymore. What were they planning on doing? Grounding her? Banning her from seeing me? She was practically living with me.

"It was my fault," Penny said. "I fell in love with my professor and he told me to stay away from him."

Oh, Penny.

"I didn't listen. You two met and fell in love in college. This isn't any different than that. You were my age when you met. You should understand better than anyone."

"Those were completely different circumstances," her dad said.

"Were they that different?" asked Penny. "Yes, you were the same age, but you were both as young as me. You have to at least accept the fact that I'm in love with him. And he resigned for me. So that we could be together."

"Did he get divorced for you too? Was he cheating on his wife with..."

"It wasn't like that," I said. "I would never cheat on someone." I thought back to high school and my first girlfriend. Rachel had kissed one of my best friends. Maybe they'd done more. I never really found out the truth. I knew I could be distant. I knew when I was spiraling I was hard to be around. But I'd never cheat because I knew how it felt to be cheated on. Like being held down in the water when you were already drowning. And yeah, maybe I was sick in the head, but I wasn't a dick.

"You have a very strange sense of morals, James," her dad said.

I clenched my jaw again. It was like he was asking for me to punch him instead of the other way around. He didn't know me. He didn't know what I'd been through. And he certainly didn't know how much I loved getting into fights.

Breathe. "I would never do anything to hurt Penny," I said, as calmly as I could. And that meant I also wouldn't punch her dad in the face. Even if he fucking deserved it.

"You already have," her dad said. "What's going to happen when other professors find out? And students? Can't she be expelled for this?"

"We talked to the dean this morning when I resigned,"
I said. "Penny got two strikes on her record, but other
than that, nothing. The news is circulating fast and I assume most of the college already knows. That's why we're
here. We wanted to tell you before you found out from
someone else. Despite my *loose* morals, I respected you
both enough to want to tell you the truth in person."

Mr. Taylor didn't seem at all placated by my words.
"And what now? You just quit your job. You're divorced.
You probably have alimony to pay. And you're dating a
college student. What kind of future could you possibly
have? You're just going to drag her down with you."

I lowered my eyebrows. "I'm starting a tech company."

Penny's phone kept buzzing incessantly, but she still
ignored it.

"A tech company?" He laughed. "And where are you
going to get the startup money for such a venture? I was
wrong about you. You're not an adult. You're just as immature as any college student."

"Dad!" Penny looked horrified.

Did her father not usually make rude, snap judgements
about strangers? *Just me then? Great.*

"He's probably here to ask us for money," her dad
huffed.

What the actual fuck? I didn't need their money. I didn't
need anything from them. I came here out of respect for
their daughter. But I could only take so much. "I have the
necessary funds to start the company," I said through gritted teeth.

The house phone started ringing. When no one answered, it automatically switched onto the voicemail
recorder.

"Hi, I'm trying to reach Penny Taylor or the parents of
Penny Taylor. This is Ellen Fitzgerald with..."

Penny stood up so fast, her chair almost toppled over behind her.

I grabbed her arm. "Penny, don't. It could be the media."

"It's not." She looked like she wanted to throw up. She went to grab the phone, but her dad beat her to it.

"Hello, Ellen. This is Penny's father speaking."

"Who is it?" I whispered to Penny.

"She works for the First State scholarship committee."

Oh shit. There was only one reason for her to be calling. Penny was going to lose her scholarship. I knew she'd been worried about that. Her dad was already upset. This was going to make it so much worse.

"Allegations?" her father asked.

This was really fucking bad.

"There are no allegations..." he went silent and looked over at Penny in me. "The Delaware Post? I don't even know what you're referring to."

Silence.

"Penny has successfully maintained the 3.5 average."

Silence.

"I don't see how this is a behavioral issue. Her professor clearly..."

Silence.

"Ellen, I really don't see why..."

Silence

"How dare you insult my daughter?!"

Silence.

"You'll be hearing from my lawyer." He slammed down the phone. His face was visibly red.

"Peter?" Penny's mom said. "Peter, take a deep breath."

Instead of acknowledging her, he turned toward me. "Get out of my house!" he yelled.

I quickly stood up. "Mr. Taylor, I don't know what you just heard on the phone, but..."

"There's an article in the Delaware Post about this mess? Why didn't you two start with that?!"

Fair point. I probably would have remembered to mention it if he hadn't been throwing insults at me though.

"Dad, what did Mrs. Fitzgerald say?" Penny asked. Even though it seemed pretty obvious.

"She said you lost your scholarship because you're sleeping with your professor." He pointed at me. "Didn't you think about that, Penny? Did either of you think of any of the consequences?!"

"I can get a job, Dad. I can pay the difference. I'll figure it out. Please just calm down."

"You know how we feel about you working during school. It's out of the question. You need to focus on your grades. Something that you've clearly put on the back burner recently."

Penny looked like she was about to cry. And I really hated when she cried.

"Mr. Taylor, the scholarship isn't an issue," I said. "I can pay the difference. I'd like to pay the difference."

"So you're going to start a thriving tech company and pay for my daughter's education? Do you have the necessary *funds* for all that? What, do you have a wealthy family to fall back on?"

It felt like he'd slapped me. My whole life people had assumed I was handed everything. They had no fucking idea how hard I worked. I didn't take a cent from my parents. I didn't even want to ever fucking see my parents again. And I didn't need to be reminded of a past that Penny's father knew nothing about.

I pictured standing in the kitchen of my childhood home, asking my mother if I could play football with Matt and Mason. How unkind she'd been. How judgmental. This conversation today wasn't the first time I'd been made to feel like I was nothing. Like I had no future. Like I was the scum of the earth. Like I couldn't have what I wanted. But I was no longer a kid wanting my mom's approval. I got what I fucking wanted now. And I wanted Penny.

Penny's dad glared at me. "Are you just some rich, entitled kid that never grew up? That goes around screwing students because you think there are never any consequences? Well, we don't want your money. We don't want anything from you. Haven't you done enough?! Get the hell out of my house!"

"Dad!" Penny stood up beside me. She looked truly horrified by her father's words.

I knew being defensive was the wrong move. But something inside of me snapped. It wasn't just Mr. Taylor's words to me. It was how they were affecting Penny. I hated seeing her upset. Penny was the love of my life and I was the one taking care of her now. Not him.

"Mr. Taylor, you don't know anything about me. And it does not appear that you want to. Yes, I was your daughter's professor. Yes, I got divorced yesterday. Yes, I am not ready to get married today or tomorrow. But I have every intention of marrying your daughter. And I will provide for her. I want to provide for her. You don't have anything to worry about. Her future is secure. That is all you need to know."

Every word out of my mouth made Mr. Taylor's face even redder.

I was done with this conversation. I needed to get out of this house. But it wasn't as simple as that. Because Penny had to come with me. And I didn't know if she would walk away from her parents.

"How could it possibly be secure?" her dad pressed. "You just ruined her education. And you ruined your own career. This is a scandal. No one's ever going to want to hire you or her."

For Christ's sake. "I don't need anyone to hire me. I told you, I'm starting my own company."

"You have no tech background. You're a communications professor."

"Working at the University of New Castle was not my career. I wanted to give back. It was never a permanent situation. I just needed a break. I needed to start over. I was doing a good thing there."

"A good thing?" her dad scoffed.

You pompous ass. "Yes, a good thing," I said firmly. "I founded my first tech company when I was 22 years old. Right after I graduated with honors from Harvard University. Blive Tech International. Maybe you've heard of it? It's a publicly traded Fortune 500 company. Well, I sold it last year for 2.8 billion dollars. I don't need to work another day in my life. Your daughter, our future children, and our grandchildren won't need to work a day in their lives if they don't want to." *I can't breathe.* I pushed my chair back under the table and looked down at Penny. *Please can we leave?* I couldn't be here anymore. I felt like it was my mother sitting across the table from me seething. *I can't breathe.*

Penny grabbed my hand and the air filled my lungs again. She nodded at me. "I think we should probably go."

She was choosing me. She was the only person in my life who'd ever chosen me. I'd always felt…abandoned. And a piece of me hadn't expected her to do it. A part of me still had trouble trusting anyone. But now? I didn't have a single doubt in my mind. Penny meant everything to me. And I'd do my best to be everything for her.

"Wait," her mom said, breaking her silence. "A break from what, James? Why did you need to start over?"

Because I wanted to kill myself. I took another deep breath. I didn't think adding suicidal thoughts to my list of qualities was a good idea right now. "I felt empty in New York. I needed a fresh start. Teaching helped with that. I wish that the circumstances had been different. But Penny is my fresh start. She made me feel whole again."

"I do understand," her mom said. She looked at her husband. "Penny was right. We were her age when we fell in love. I'd like to think that if the circumstances were different for us, we'd still be together. Please don't go, Penny." She gave her husband a pleading look. "Peter, say something."

"So that means your last name is Hunter?" her dad asked.

So he did know about me? "Yes."

He sighed and sat down. "James Hunter, the founder of Blive Tech International. I didn't realize you had taken a sudden career change into teaching."

"I needed the change."

"You know, I actually own stock in your company."

"You do?" I remembered him talking about stocks the first time we'd met. He'd called Tesla Tesller. I wondered how he was going to start butchering the name of Blive Tech...

Her father nodded. He put his hands together on the table and looked down at them for a second. "I'm sorry. It's just...Penny's our baby." He didn't look angry anymore. He just seemed...sad.

"I know," I said. "I understand that you're just trying to protect her. And I truly am sorry about how this happened."

"You can't really understand until you've had children of your own."

We were both silent for a second. I could accept his apology. And it seemed like he accepted mine too. The tension was slowly seeping out of the room. I was really glad I hadn't said the thing about Penny being a good little slut for me out loud earlier. Or we probably wouldn't have reached this moment.

"So, your relationship was written about in the paper?" her mom asked.

"Yes, there was an article in the paper this morning," I said. "If you read it, you should know that it is not accurate."

"What do you mean?"

"It's mostly from my ex-wife's point of view. And it implies that there will be charges of sexual misconduct from other students I've had. And from Penny. That's not the case."

"Okay." Mrs. Taylor took a deep breath. "What happens now?"

I ran my hand through my hair. "It's really up to Penny. I've advised her to drop Comm. Unfortunately, the way that the information was leaked about our relationship does not make it easy going forward."

"I think it'll all die down if I ignore it," Penny said. "I just want things to go back to normal."

Normal? She really had no idea how hard this was going to get. The camera crew outside my apartment wasn't going away anytime soon. Neither were the rumors spreading around campus.

"This whole thing has been blown out of proportion because of my name," I said. "Under other circumstances, it would not have gotten as much press as it has already. Normalcy is a long way off."

"So you resigned because of the allegations?" Mr. Taylor asked.

"They gave me the option to stay if I was willing to terminate my relationship with Penny. I wasn't willing to do that. Resigning was the only option."

"That's very romantic," her mom said.

I smiled. I wasn't sure if it was romantic. It was just what needed to be done. Because there was no way I was walking away from this girl. I squeezed Penny's hand and then pulled her chair back out for her. Now that everyone had calmed down, we needed to stay and answer any more questions they had. Her parents understood. Love was love. All the messy details didn't really matter. And I felt so relieved, like a huge weight had been lifted off my chest. We both sat back down.

"And if things can't proceed as normal, what then?" her dad asked.

"Honestly, I'm not sure what the backlash is going to be like," I said. "The blame for this lies on me, not Penny. It is my understanding that the University of New Castle will make that clear. If things don't go smoothly, she can always apply for different schools next semester."

"Mom, Dad, it's going to be fine. I went to class this morning and it wasn't even that bad."

I glanced down at her. Not that bad? She'd practically been in tears. I didn't know what exactly had happened in class, but it certainly hadn't been good. That was Comm though. Hopefully her other classes would be better.

"Unfortunately we both need to get to work," her mother said. "Are you sure we can't get you to stay for dinner?"

"No, we need to get back," Penny said.

"Okay." Mrs. Taylor looked over at her husband.

"Do you mind if we talk to Penny alone for a second?" her dad asked.

"Of course." I stood up. Honestly, I was relieved to be excused. "I'll be outside." I put my hand on Penny's shoulder for a second and then walked out of the kitchen. I closed the front door behind me and took a deep breath.

That could have gone worse. *I guess.* I took another deep breath and sat down on the front step. I was glad it was done.

I pulled out my phone. I had a million missed calls from Ian. *Fuck, what now?*

Chapter 12

Wednesday

"Where the hell are you?" Ian asked after one ring.

"You know where I am. There's a tracking device on my car."

"You know what I meant! Seriously, you can't just drive off on a whim. You have to tell me. I though Isabella kidnapped you or something."

"Honestly that might have been equally as terrible as the conversation I just had with Penny's parents."

There was an awkward pause. "So you told her parents?"

"Mhm."

"And how did that go?"

"Bad. Really fucking bad." Now that I was outside by myself, I felt worse about snapping. The outcome had been...decent. But getting there had been pretty messy. And I was still pissed about all that shit Penny's dad had said about me.

I was more concerned about what they were saying about me right now behind my back though. They were obviously talking about me in there. Or else they wouldn't have asked me to leave...

"Was it the age thing or the professor thing that really ticked them off?"

"Both," I said with a sigh. "And the fact that I just got divorced."

"Why the hell did you even talk about that?"

I groaned. "I don't know. It just slipped out. It was probably good it did though. I'm sure they'll read the article in the Delaware Post after this, and it's better that they heard it from me."

"True." There was some noise on the other end. "Ellen says you should have told her you were visiting Penny's parents and she would have sent you some brownies or something."

"Yeah, that probably would have been a good gesture. But it was a spur of the moment trip."

Ian relayed the information to Ellen.

"Does Ellen want to talk to me?"

"No, she's cleaning. Ow!" Ian said.

Ellen must have hit him.

I laughed.

And then I must have made some kind of strange noise when Penny's cat ran over to me, because Ian said: "You okay, man?"

"Yeah. Penny has this cat." *That looks exactly like her.* "It just surprised me is all." I petted the top of Teddy's head.

He meowed.

"I don't think I've ever seen you around an animal before," Ian said.

"I really don't like pets."

"What if Penny wants to bring him home with you?"

"No."

Ian laughed. "Really? You'd just tell her no?"

I stared at Teddy. He rubbed against my leg. Maybe he wasn't *that* bad. "I'd probably say yes, but I really hate the idea of this furball being in my apartment."

Ian laughed again. "Fair."

"Can you buy me a T.V.?"

"That was a weird segue," Ian said.

I shook my head. "Yeah. Sorry. I was just thinking about the fact that Penny likes to watch T.V. And maybe if

I buy her a nice one she'll be entertained and not want to take this creature home with us." Besides, classes were going to be hard the next few days. She needed an escape. And as much as I wished I could have sex with her for hours every night...my dick wouldn't be able to handle that. This was how she liked to relax.

Plus when Penny and I were on a break, I'd measured one of my walls one night, thinking that if I bought her a big T.V. she'd forgive me. I'd been really drunk. And I think I'd dropped a hammer on my foot. I had no idea why I'd even had a hammer out. But Ian didn't need to hear all that.

Ian laughed. "One T.V. Got it. Wait, what size?"

"I'll email you the one I want. Hold on a sec." I quickly found the link and shot him the email.

"Got it."

"Thank you. Oh and there's a wrapped box in the drawer of my nightstand. Can you put that and the T.V. in the living room?" It was another thing I'd done when I was drunk and missing Penny. But sometimes drunken actions were useful later.

"It's not like...a dildo or something, right?"

"Why would I have a dildo in my nightstand?"

"I don't know what you're into."

Lies. He knew everything I was into because there were security cameras in my bedroom. "It's not a dildo."

"Great. I'll put that with the T.V. Okay, so you're going to start watching T.V. You quit your job. Came clean to her parents. What's next? Are you going to tell her about the cameras?"

"I think that's enough excitement for one day."

"Agreed."

"Tell her about the cameras, James!" Ellen yelled in the background.

I'd tell her. *Eventually.* I heard the front door start to open. "I gotta go."

"Later," Ian said.

I hung up and petted the top of Teddy's head again.

"I see you two are getting along now," Penny said and smiled down at me sitting on the steps

"Yeah, I think he actually likes me." *Unlike your parents.* I turned around. I saw her parents standing next to her. I was really glad I hadn't said that last thing out loud. I quickly stood up.

"I'm really sorry that you two can't stay," Mrs. Taylor said. "I hope you come visit us again soon. I promise that we're not usually this hostile."

I'd hope not.

She leaned in and hugged me.

"Thank you for being so understanding," I said.

Her mom laughed. "Were we? I feel like we weren't. But I do understand. And I'm so glad that you make our daughter happy."

She pulled away and gave Penny a quick hug too.

"James." Mr. Taylor stuck out his hand.

"Mr. Taylor." I shook his hand.

"You can call me Peter." Her dad nodded at me and then walked over to Penny. He gave her a big hug. "Don't you ever think that you've disappointed us, Pen. We love you so much." He kissed the top of her head and released her from his hug.

I had no idea what it would feel like to be told that. I was the epitome of a disappointment to my parents. My mother had said those exact words to me once.

"Thanks, Dad." Penny teared up at her father's words.

Actually, I knew how I'd react if my parents had ever said that to me. I'd laugh. Because *that* would have been an April Fool's Day prank. I wondered how they'd react to the news about me dating Penny. But I'd never find out. Because I had no intention of telling either of them. They could read about it in the tabloids like every other stranger.

Penny and I climbed back into my car. We waved to Penny's parents as they drove off back to work. And for some reason, I didn't start the car. I just stared out the windshield.

Penny turned toward me. "That went well, right?"

"In the end, yeah. Your dad...well, he surprised me."

"I'm sorry about what he said. I've never seen him make snap judgments like that before. He's usually really nice. He didn't mean any of that. He was just upset."

"At least he didn't try to punch me in the face." I smiled at her. "What did your parents say to you after I left?"

"They grounded me."

"Wait, what?" I lowered my eyebrows. When I thought they'd do that, I'd been half joking. How could they ground her when she wasn't living under their roof? But if they required her to be spanked, I could definitely arrange that...

"I'm just kidding. They can't ground me, I'm an adult."

"So if they didn't ground you, what did they say?"

"They just wanted to make sure you didn't sexually harass me or anything."

"Oh God." I put my forehead down on the top of the steering wheel and started laughing. *What a fucking day.* All you could do was laugh it off.

Penny started laughing too.

I sighed and lifted my head back up. "That must have been awkward."

"Well, they didn't actually put it like that." She put her hand on my knee. "I think they phrased it by asking how rapey you were on a scale of one to Michael Jackson."

"What?!"

"Just kidding. They said something like pressuring me, or something."

I put my hand on top of hers and ran my thumb across her knuckles. I mean...I was older than her by several years. I was her professor. And I could be pretty demanding. "I haven't, have I? Pressured you?"

"No. James, I love you. I want to be with you. I'm not sure what else I can do to make you believe me."

I lifted up her hand and kissed her palm. "I do believe you. I'm sorry that I lost it in there. It almost felt like I was lecturing your father. I didn't mean to do that."

"Well, you were a professor." She shrugged. "It kind of goes with the territory I think."

"Yeah. I just feel like I kind of threw my money in his face. And that wasn't what I meant to do at all. I feel like a dick." Dr. Clark was not going to be impressed when he heard about this. I was supposed to be able to control my anger now. And...clearly I couldn't.

"He certainly pushed enough of your buttons. James, I don't think my dad is mad at you. He seemed embarrassed about how he acted. Please don't over think this. We told them. It's over. Let's just be happy."

I smiled. That sounded like a good plan. And I'd promised her a trip. I'd have to text Ian when I got to the airport though, because he was definitely going to freak out when he saw my car parked there. And he'd want to tag along. "Just tell me where you want to go." I put my key into the ignition.

"Actually, I think I just want to go home."

"Home?" I raised my eyebrow. God, I really loved the sound of that.

"Mhm."

"Penny Taylor, are you referring to my apartment as home?" I couldn't stop smiling.

"It's where I feel most comfortable. And of course, it's where you are. So, yes, I consider it home." She smiled back at me.

"You know, I'll take you wherever you want to go. Well, anywhere in the U.S. We really need to get you a passport."

"All I want to do is snuggle up in your bed with you."

"Okay. Home it is." *Home.* I pulled the car away from the curb. I think it had been a long time since anywhere had felt like home. But I was pretty sure that anywhere we went would feel like home. As long as she was beside me.

***

When we pulled up to my apartment building, there were even more news vans parked outside. My hands tightened on the wheel. Why couldn't they just leave us in peace?

People with microphones jumped out of the vans as I turned into the parking garage. I sped up to the third floor and pulled my car into an empty spot.

"Maybe we should've gone somewhere else," I said. I really didn't want her to be subjected to all this. But we'd be recognized together anywhere now.

"It's fine. They'll probably leave soon. Aren't celebrities always doing weird stuff? Kanye West and T-Swizzle will get into a knife fight or something and the paparazzi will move on. Especially if you don't give them anything good to talk about."

I laughed and stepped out of the car. I opened her door and grabbed her hand, escorting her to the elevator. "You do know that I'm not a celebrity, right?"

"Right. You're just a super sexy, eligible bachelor worth 2.8 billion dollars. You're not a celebrity at all."

We stepped into the elevator.

"Yeah, I'm not worth 2.8 billion dollars." I pressed the button for my floor.

"Oh, right." She said it in a way that made it seem like she thought I had a lot less than that. Maybe because of the divorce? But that wasn't the case at all. I was really good at investing. And I owed some credit to Mason and Matt's father too. Mr. Caldwell handled most of that for me with his firm.

I smiled down at her. "I'm worth way more than that." I slid my card into the reader and stepped into the apartment.

"You have more than 2.8 billion dollars? That's insane, James. What on earth are you going to do with all that..." She stopped talking when she saw a huge box in the middle of the living room floor.

I smiled. The new T.V. I'd had Ian grab was wrapped in blue wrapping paper with a huge bow on top. There was a small box sitting on top of it, also in blue wrapping paper with a matching blue bow.

"Oh." I smiled. "I almost forgot about that. Apparently I'm going to buy you gifts with it." I walked into the living room. But Penny just stood in the foyer.

"James, you already got me a birthday gift. I don't need anything."

"It's not for your birthday. Besides, it's kind of for both of us." I smiled at her.

"But..."

She was terrible at receiving gifts. "Oh come on. You don't even know what it is yet. If you don't like it, I'll take it back. Just open it."

She walked over to me. "I don't want you to spend your money on me. I just want to spend time with you." She stood on her tiptoes and ran her hands through my hair.

"I know." I placed a soft kiss against her lips. It was one of the many reasons why I'd fallen in love with her. I picked up the small present and tapped my hand on the large box. "Please just open it." I really wanted her to like it. And she'd just told me she wanted to snuggle up for the rest of the night. We could do that on the couch instead of the bed. This was going to be fun.

She finally looked excited too as she grabbed one of the folds in the wrapping paper and pulled it down. She pulled the paper as she walked from one side of the present to the other, and then pushed the paper out of the way.

"Is this a T.V.?" She smiled up at me.

"Well, after this morning I wasn't really sure if you'd want to go to classes the next few days. So if we're camped out here, I thought you'd like to have a T.V. to watch. You seem to love T.V." *And I don't want a cat.*

She laughed. "That's incredibly sweet. But you know, I have a T.V. already. I can just bring it here. Melissa won't mind. She's always at Josh's anyway."

"Yeah, but it's tiny."

"There's nothing wrong with my T.V." She laughed.

Yes there was. The people on it were the size of my pinky finger. "I was going to hang it over there." I pointed to the wall across from my sofa. "And I measured and this T.V. is the perfect size for the distance between the couch and the wall. And since Rob is coming, I wanted something to watch the Giants games on. So..."

"You're adorable," said Penny. "I'm definitely not going to make you take back that T.V. Clearly you want it."

"But do you like it?"

"Of course I like it. It's going to be like we're in a movie theater. Thank you."

I laughed and smiled down at her. "And there's one more thing." I held out the small box. "Now, before you start protesting, it didn't even cost me anything. It's just something that I really want you to have. And after today, I think maybe now's the best time ever." I tucked a loose strand of hair behind her ear.

Penny's eyes grew round.

I looked back down at the box. It was a really small box. I looked back at her and realized what she was probably thinking. It was a ring sized box. I really wasn't ready to get married any time soon. But being engaged? That sounded pretty good to me. I wanted my ring on her finger so everyone knew she was mine. But she was clearly panicking at the thought. I lowered my eyebrows. "Are you okay?"

"What? Yeah."

I grabbed her hand and put the box in her palm. "Open it, Penny." *One step at a time.*

She took off the bow, slowly unwrapped the box, and lifted the lid. There were two plastic cards inside with her name on them. She looked up at me.

"Welcome home," I said.

"Are these access cards to get into your apartment?"

"*Our* apartment, yes."

She ran her finger along her embossed name as a smile spread across her face.

"I find it incredibly hard to fall asleep when you're not beside me. I'd like you to move in." *Officially.* "If that's what you want too."

She looked up at me.

We had talked about this before. Before our fight. This was a big step. Not as big as an engagement, but still big. And she looked so damn excited.

I wrapped my arms around her. "So what do you say?"

"Yes. Absolutely yes." She hugged me, pressing the side of her face against my chest.

I wondered if she could tell how fast my heart was racing. Because now that I was thinking about giving her a ring…I really wanted to do it. I wanted her in my arms like this forever. It finally felt like I was exactly where I was supposed to be. I just hoped when I proposed she wouldn't look so panicked.

Chapter 13

Thursday

"Close," I said and sat down next to Penny on the sofa. I scanned the math she'd done to solve the equation. She'd gone wrong somewhere… "Okay, there. You forgot to transform the random variable into a z-score."

"Oh. Oops. I knew to do that too." She bit her lip as she fixed the equation.

I loved watching her when she was concentrating. I liked it even better when she got the equations correct, because I'd been rewarding her with kisses. And I really liked rewarding her when she was good.

She lifted her pencil, stared at the equation for another second, and then handed the paper back to me. "How's this, *Professor* Hunter?"

Fucking hell. I wasn't sure how I'd ever taught in a room with her. She smiled at me and I laughed. She really was distracting. I looked down at the sheet of paper. "Much better." I leaned down and kissed her.

My phone started buzzing again. It had been buzzing nonstop all morning.

"Are you sure you don't want to answer that?" she asked. "Maybe it would be best to just get it over with."

It was never a good idea to talk to paparazzi. "Talking to them will make it worse. If I ignore them, they'll get bored and move on to the next thing." I stood up and walked back over to the T.V. mount I was screwing into the wall. It had been a long time since I'd done something like this myself. I was sure Ian was laughing at the camera footage right now. But it was good to be using my hands. I lifted the power drill. When it stopped whirring, Penny filled the silence.

"But you don't even know who it is. You haven't listened to any of your messages. You could always answer and hang up."

"Which means I refused to comment. Which looks bad."

"Oh."

"Besides, if it's someone I know, it'll ring." And I didn't have many contacts in my phone anymore. I'd gone through and deleted a bunch of people with Dr. Clark's help. It started with my dealer and went on from there. I turned back to the T.V. and grabbed a screwdriver.

"Speaking of people we know..." Penny's voice trailed off.

I turned around to look at her.

"I was wondering if I could hang out with Melissa tonight?"

We had gone to Penny's dorm room this morning and grabbed a few things. But Melissa had been in class. I was pretty sure they'd been texting, but it was different hearing about all this in person. Like the fact that Penny was moving out of their shared dorm and into my apartment.

I set the screwdriver down. "You know that you don't have to ask me permission." But maybe she thought she did. Because I hadn't let her go to classes today, despite her saying she wanted to. I was trying to protect her. But there was a difference between protecting her and controlling her.

"I know. I just wanted to make sure it was okay." She glanced toward the window.

Yeah, I was protecting her from the shit show outside. Penny wasn't used to reporters following her around, demanding to talk to her. Even though she said she wanted to go to class this morning, I knew she was nervous about all of this. And if she didn't feel comfortable leaving the apartment, there was no reason for her to.

I cleared my throat. "Well, how about you just invite her over here?"

"Are you sure that's okay?" She looked relieved.

"Of course." I smiled and turned back to the T.V. mount. Now how the fuck did this thing attach to the T.V.?

"Do you want my help with that?" she asked.

"I'm pretty sure I can figure it out." I picked up the instruction booklet off the floor and turned the page.

My phone started to ring.

I glanced down at the screen. "It's just the front desk," I said to Penny and then quickly answered. "Hunter."

"Mr. Hunter," Ben said. "There are two men here who say they were sent by Joe Vespelli."

"Regarding what?"

There was an awkward pause. "I made sure they weren't with the media. They say they're detectives. They're here to see Penny Taylor. For an interview?"

I tried my best not to stare at Penny. "Do you mind putting them on the phone for a second?" I shoved my free hand into my pocket, turned away from Penny, and walked toward the kitchen.

"Hello, James, this is Detective Tim Reed. I'm here to speak to Penny Taylor regarding what happened in your class."

"It was my understanding that she wouldn't be included in this."

"Well, then you must have understood wrong."

"We've already disclosed our relationship to Joe. If you have any other questions then I'd recommend discussing them with..."

"My instructions have come straight from Joe."

What the fuck, Joe? I removed my hand from my pocket and ran my fingers through my hair. I wanted to tell him to get the hell out of my apartment building. But I knew that would just make things worse. It was better to get this over with. "Fine. Please put Ben back on the phone."

"Do you want me to send them up?" Ben asked.

"Yes, go ahead and let them up. For future visitors please tell them I am out of town until further notice."

"Of course."

I hung up the phone and tossed it onto the kitchen counter. Seriously, what the fuck? Penny didn't need to be part of the investigation. We'd already told Joe everything. *Unless...* I sighed. Unless someone had told them something during another interview that had them questioning what we'd already disclosed. The first person that popped into my head was Tyler. It was a shame that I'd only broken his nose and not his jaw. I heard Penny's footsteps behind me.

"James?" she said quietly.

I sighed and turned around. "Apparently the people they hired for the investigation need to talk to you."

"Why would they need to talk to me? We already told everything to the dean."

"I don't know. But it probably isn't good."

"That's not necessarily true."

I pressed my lips together. "Well, I guess we'll find out."

"How do you think they knew I was here?"

"Maybe they already tried your dorm room. It doesn't exactly take a great investigator to assume you'd be here."

A dinging noise sounded through the apartment. I walked over to the elevator door and gave a subtle nod toward the small camera mounted above it to let Ian know everything was fine. I pressed the button and the doors slid open.

Two men in suits stepped out. One looked about my age and the other was probably 20 years older or so.

The older one put his hand out to me. "James Hunter, I'm Detective Tim Reed. And this is my partner, Scott Turner.

I shook Detective Reed's hand and then Detective Turner's. "I still don't see why this is necessary. Penny has already talked to Joe."

"It's a formality, really. We just have a few questions."

I hoped that was true.

Detective Reed peered around my shoulder. "You must be Penny."

I hadn't even realized I was standing in front of her. I couldn't protect her from this. I'd *caused* this. I stepped to the side.

"Yes, hi." She didn't offer them her hand. Instead she crossed her arms in front of her chest. "You said you have some questions for me?"

I smiled. Maybe she could handle the paparazzi after all. Because it looked like she was ready to take zero shit.

"Right. Well, we're actually going to need to talk to you in private, Penny." Detective Reed turned to me.

Oh fuck off. I'm not messing with her mind. Penny was with me because she wanted to be. Not because I pressured her. And I didn't like the insinuation. "I really don't see why that's necessary." I didn't bother to hide my chilly tone.

"Something has come up in our investigation. And we need Penny to be able to talk freely about your relationship."

For Fuck's sake. I lowered my eyebrows. I was going to kill Tyler Stevens. "What has come up in the investigation?"

"We can't really discuss that with you right now. I'm sure Joe will be in contact with you shortly."

"I think that you both should leave," I said.

"James, it's fine," Penny said. "I'll talk to them."

"You don't have to answer their questions, Penny. Let me call my lawyer. He'll handle this."

"It's fine. I really don't mind." She gave me a stern look that I'd never seen her give before. It was fucking sexy. I knew she wanted to get this over with. And if she thought she could handle this…then I should let her. They'd never believe me. Besides, if I stayed in this room much longer, I'd probably end up punching a detective. And that wasn't good for anyone.

I nodded. "I guess I'll be in my office then." I put my hand on her shoulder for a second and then walked away. I went into my office and closed the door behind me.

My phone immediately started ringing.

"Hey, Ian," I said. "We have a camera in the living room, right?"

"Already adjusting the angles for you," he said. "What do you think came up in the investigation?"

I sat down behind my computer and opened up the feed of my living room. "Probably something to do with Penny's *friend* Tyler."

"I thought the investigation was about sexual misconduct? Did you spank Tyler after you broke his nose?"

I knew he was trying to lighten the mood, but this shit wasn't funny. I ignored him and turned the volume on my computer up a bit.

Detective Reed was smiling at Penny. "You know, when people act defensive, it usually means that they have something to defend."

She glared at him. "I don't have anything to hide."

"It looks like she's got this covered," Ian said.

"Yeah." I smiled. I really loved when she was feisty. I kept watching the screen.

"Good," Detective Reed said. "I expected as much. You're an open book, Penny. Straight As in high school. Same here except for the occasional B. You're a good girl. Respectable. A First State scholarship winner even. That must have made your parents proud."

"Yes, it did." She straightened her shoulders a bit.

"So the question is, what made you risk all that? What made you decide to sleep with your professor? Were you worried about…losing your scholarship?"

He thinks she slept with me for a grade? He'd just said that Penny was smart and had good grades. She didn't need to do that. What kind of shit detective was this guy?

"What? No," Penny said firmly.

"What kind of arrangement did you two have exactly?"

"I have no idea what you're talking about."

"Was it for the presents? Or maybe you weren't doing as well this semester. You have a C average in your statistics class right now."

That was because I was distracting her. Not the other way around.

"Did you do it for the grades?" he pushed.

"Do *what* exactly?" she said.

"Did he, or did he not, agree to give you an A in his class if you gave him sexual favors?"

She stood up. "I think you should go."

"So it's true, is it?"

"You have no idea what you're talking about. We never did anything that we didn't both want to do. James is a good guy."

"Good professors don't sleep with their students."

"Tim." Detective Turner had finally spoken. He put his hand on Detective Reed's chest, as if holding him back.

"Why don't you let me take it from here." Detective Turner gestured toward the couch.

Detective Reed nodded and sat down on the sofa. I stared at Detective Turner, who was now smiling. I was a little surprised by the sudden change. Were they seriously trying to good cop, bad cop Penny?

"Amateur move," Ian said.

I nodded. "Agreed." They knew that Penny got good grades. But they hadn't done enough research to know that she loved T.V. She knew this move and she wasn't going to fall for this shit.

"Please, Penny, take a seat," Detective Turner said. "I'm sorry about my partner's outburst."

Penny sighed and sat down as far away from Detective Reed as possible.

I smiled to myself.

"You said you have nothing to hide," Detective Turner said.

"I don't."

"Would it surprise you, then, if James was hiding something from you?"

"Do you think he knows about the cameras?" Ian said. Something started crunching on his end.

"No. He's just making something up to push on her nerves. And are you eating popcorn right now?"

"Shh," he said. "I'm enjoying the show."

I knew he ate popcorn while he watched us!

Penny just glared at the detective.

He put his hands in his pockets as he studied her face. "It wouldn't, would it? I've heard that James is quite a complicated man."

"And who did you hear that from? His ex-wife?"

Detective Turner smiled again. "It's not too late, you know. If you're willing to cooperate with us, we can give the First State scholarship committee a call. Maybe we can get them to reissue that scholarship of yours."

"If I cooperate?"

"Yes. You see, we are building a case against James regarding sexual misconduct."

"I'm not going to lie in order to get my scholarship back. Like you said, I'm a good girl. Besides for that fact, you have it all wrong."

"Unfortunately we don't. We do want to help you, Penny. But we don't actually need your statement. Yes, it'll help, but I think we already have everything we need."

"What do you mean?"

"Two girls have already come forward saying that James agreed to give them As for sexual favors."

What? Who the fuck said that?!

"They're lying," Penny said firmly.

"And how sure are you of that? Because Tim and I are trained to tell if suspects are lying. These girls didn't seem like they were lying. Actually, they were both in tears. They were embarrassed and ashamed because of the position that their trusted professor put them in."

Go eat each other's nuts.

"I don't believe you," Penny said.

"And their stories lined up. They both said that James lured them into his office to dispute a poor grade. And that he agreed to change it only if they agreed to have sex with him."

Penny didn't respond.

Because…isn't that what I'd done to her? Kind of? *What the fuck?* How could these detectives possibly know that? And how had the two girls that lied found out about it?

"Does that sound familiar, Penny? Did he do that to you too?"

"No. It wasn't like that."

"How about you tell us what really happened. And we'll get that scholarship back for you. Your life will go back to normal. All of this will disappear."

"I think this discussion is over." She stood up again.

"Don't you want your old life back? We can give you back what you lost. Stop defending him. Can't you see what he's taken from you?"

"I'm not defending him, I'm telling you the truth."

"He's not who you think he is."

"Yes he is." Her face was flushed. And for the first time it wasn't because she was embarrassed or turned on. She was…angry. She was losing her temper.

"He's a predator, Penny. And you're the prey. Don't you see that? Those two other girls were his prey too. Who knows how many others didn't come forward? You're probably one of a dozen. You can't hide from the truth. He seduces students. He's not a good man."

I'd thought that before. That I was the hunter and she was my prey. But only with *her*. Only ever her. I knew I'd crossed the line as her professor. I knew I was fucked up in the head. But it was only ever her.

"Get out of my apartment," Penny said.

I wanted to go out there and hug her. She'd called this apartment ours. And she was defending me. Even though part of what they were saying was true.

"Your apartment? Is that the deal then? The gifts, the apartment? Is that to keep you quiet?"

"You're terrible detectives," she snapped.

"We're trying to protect you."

"Protect me? I don't need your protection. I wanted this relationship just as much as he did. I love him." She put her hand on the center of her chest. As if they should be able to so clearly see her heart. Too bad they were blind.

"He doesn't love you."

"Yes he does."

"Arrogant assholes," Ian said through a mouthful of popcorn. "It's obvious that the two of you are in love if they spend two minutes watching you."

I tried to focus on the screen.

"Do you even know anything about him?" the detective said. "Do you know that he has a criminal record? Do you know that he's spent time in jail? This is the kind of thing he does. This is the kind of thing that a bored man with too much money and no sense of morals does."

"If you both don't leave right now, some of your detective buddies will actually have a crime to solve."

Oh, fuck. Penny. Don't threaten them.

Ian coughed on his popcorn. "She's as bad as you."

Yeah. Penny looked so pissed. I smiled at the screen. *That's my girl.*

"Did you just threaten us?" Detective Reed stood up. "You do know that it's illegal to threaten a police officer?"

"Oh, I didn't realize you were police officers. I really couldn't tell. All you're doing is throwing out accusations without any evidence."

Ian and I both laughed.

"Consider this a warning, Miss Taylor. We will be in contact again. This is far from over."

She didn't respond. She just watched them walk over to the elevator, step in, and disappear.

"That was kind of amazing to watch," Ian said. "Uh oh."

"What?"

"She's heading to the freezer. Women going to the freezer means ice cream. Which means she's upset."

Yeah. I wasn't sure what the hell was going on. How did the detectives know about Penny coming to my office? And who the hell were the other girls that came forward with those lies?

"Nope," Ian said. "She's more upset than ice cream. That's not good."

I stared at the screen. Penny had grabbed a bottle of vodka that I'd hidden from Ellen in the back of the freezer. What was she doing?

Chapter 14

Thursday

"She's going to be the death of me," I said.

Ian laughed.

"I'm sure you'll have lots of fun watching this conversation." I watched Penny down a shot.

"Absolutely."

I ended the call and hurried out into the hall. There'd just been detectives in here and Penny was drinking underage? Serving alcohol to minors didn't exactly paint me as the good guy she claimed I was. And yes, I'd let her drink in front of me before. But I hadn't known her age back then.

She downed a second shot as I walked into the kitchen.

"I see you've found the liquor," I said.

She looked up at me.

I was pretty sure she was waiting for me to reprimand her. But no one was coming into this apartment without my knowledge after the security updates. And it wasn't like I'd been sober when I was 20, so I wasn't one to talk. If she was going to drink, I preferred if she did it around me. And I needed a drink too. I hadn't had a sip of alcohol since we'd gotten back together. Because I didn't need it. I also knew I wouldn't lose control if I had some. All I truly needed was her. And right now, she needed us to be on the same page. So I grabbed a shot glass for myself and slid it toward her.

She poured some vodka into the glass.

"You know, I could get in trouble for this," I said and held up the glass.

"Is that the only thing you're worried about getting in trouble for?"

I lowered my eyebrows. "What, did they tell you what supposedly came up during their investigation?" I already knew. But Penny was upset about the allegations from these two girls. The last thing she needed right now was to know I was lying about cameras all around the apartment. I could hear Ellen yelling at me in the back of my head. But I was right about this. *One hiccup at a time.*

Penny shrugged. "They knew you lured me into your office so you could seduce me."

"That's not exactly how I'd put that." I downed my shot.

"Then how would you put it?"

"That I was mad at you. And I wanted to see you." I ran my hand through my hair. "I didn't want to have to share you with Tyler. I wanted more. I wanted you to want more too." I hesitated for a second. "And at the same time I didn't. I wanted to get over you. I wasn't really thinking clearly. I couldn't get you out of my head."

"But how did they know that? How did they know about the fake grade? And me going into your office?"

I have no idea. No one had seen us. I was sure about that. I'd locked the door. And yet...the detectives knew. "I'm sure there's a logical explanation for that."

"Right. I'm waiting for the explanation. What is it?"

"I don't know. That's their job. They're the investigators. They must have pieced something together."

She looked down at her empty shot glass. "They didn't actually know if that had happened. They just inferred it."

"Inferred it? From what?" I poured myself another shot and downed it. Because I already knew what they'd inferred it from.

"From what two other girls said during their interviews. Apparently both of them said that you lured them into your office to seduce them under that pretense of a poor grade."

"Penny, you know I didn't do that. That's ridiculous." I stared at her. She'd told the detectives off. But...I saw the doubt in her eyes.

"Is it that ridiculous? You kind of did that to me."

"And I just told you that was different. I've said it a million times, Penny. It's only ever been you. You know that. You know how I feel about you."

"But why would those girls lie? Why would they say you did that?"

"I don't know." *Probably because the detectives were pushy and promised them an A in the class like they'd promised you your scholarship back.*

"And in the exact same way? How would they have known that if it wasn't something that you just do to tons of students?"

"Is that really what you think?" This conversation wasn't going well. And I had the vague thought that I probably shouldn't be drinking.

"I don't want to think that. But..."

"But you do?"

She didn't respond. She just stared at me.

Breathe. But it was a lot easier to lash out than breathe slowly. Especially when she was accusing me of this stupid shit when I'd made my feelings for her perfectly clear. "You think I gave my prettiest female students bad grades in hopes that they'd come to my office hours? So that I could get them alone and then what? Bargain with them to improve their grades? I didn't bargain with you, Penny. *You* kissed me. *You* asked me to punish you. I can get any girl I want. I don't need to make deals with immature college students to suck me off. I'm not desperate." *Yeah, I really shouldn't be drinking.*

"Then why are you dating me?" she asked.

"Because I love you."

"You can have any girl you want, James. Maybe you should go try to find someone a little more mature. You know, someone who isn't a college student."

For fuck's sake. "That's not what I meant." My hands were gripping the countertop so hard that my knuckles were turning white. I liked her anger better when it had been directed at the detectives.

"It's what you said, James."

I took a deep breath and ran my hand through my hair. "I don't understand why you believe them over me. I just need you to believe me. I need to know that you trust me." Why did our fights always seem to come back to the issue of trust? Why did she always purposely push my buttons? If she wanted angry makeup sex, we could have stopped this conversation five minutes ago and just jumped to the good part.

"I do trust you," she said.

"Okay."

She glanced down at my shot glass and then back at me. "Should you really be drinking that?"

I raised my eyebrow. "Should you?"

"No, probably not." She gave me a small smile.

Yeah, me either. I leaned against the counter and looked down at her. "You shouldn't believe everything you hear. The tabloid you read that interviewed my ex-wife, these detectives...they have other motives. I don't want to fight with you every time something like this happens. And it happens more than I'd like. It comes with the territory."

"The rich, successful, eligible bachelor territory?"

"Minus the eligible bachelor." I tucked a loose strand of hair behind her ear. "I'm taken."

She smiled at me. "I'm sorry. The detectives just made it seem like they were so sure that you had done it."

"I mean, if you were told you had to make up a story about your male professor doing inappropriate things, wouldn't you just automatically go to sexual favors in exchange for good grades? It's not even clever."

"Right. So they're lying. But why?"

"Maybe they hated me? I could be rather distracted in class. Sometimes I was so focused on you that I'm pretty sure I was an awful professor." Half my classes in Comm deviated from my lesson plans because I'd get so focused on the beautiful redhead in the back row making sex eyes at me.

"I don't think anyone hated you. Especially in Comm. At least all the girls loved you. Oh." She looked up at me. "Maybe they're just jealous you didn't choose them. Maybe they think you'll notice them now?"

"By dragging my name through the mud? Smart."

"Well, I don't know. I'm not them." She closed the distance between us and put her hands on either side of my face. "I'm sorry I doubted you."

I slid my hands to the small of her back and pulled her even closer. "If a bunch of pricks in suits told me that you had been doing stuff behind my back, I think my reaction would have been a lot worse than yours."

"My reaction was bad with the detectives too. I'm pretty sure I threatened to kill them."

I laughed. "Wait, really?" I said, even though I'd seen the whole thing. "You can't threaten a cop, Penny." *But I'm damn proud of you.* My hands slid up her waist, pushing up the hem of her shirt a bit. I loved the feeling of her skin beneath my fingers. And I was ready for my makeup sex now. I was thinking right on this counter.

"I know that now."

I laughed again. "You're full of surprises."

"Am I?"

"Mhm." I placed a soft kiss against her lips. My hands slowly pushed her shirt up even more. Yes, I loved the feeling of her skin pressed against my palms. But I loved her breasts filling my hands the most.

"Would it surprise you if I told you that alcohol tends to make me incredibly horny?" she said.

"Incredibly horny? That's quite the predicament." I grabbed her ass and lifted her up, setting her down on the kitchen counter. I wanted nothing more than to partake in my new favorite dessert. But... I put my hands on either side of the counter and stared at her. Everything about her was a contradiction. I knew her. And yet...she never ceased to surprise me.

"What's wrong?" she asked.

"You defended me to the detectives even though you doubted me."

"Of course."

"But why?"

"I'll always defend you. I love you."

I lowered my eyebrows. I think that was the whole problem. I was still getting used to feeling loved. Because I'd never felt it before. She was choosing me. Always.

Like when she'd grabbed my hand at her parents' house. And when I woke up yesterday before our meeting with dean and she was still lying next to me. She had my back. And I wasn't used to it. The only person I could ever really count on before was Rob. And half the time he wasn't in the country.

"I swear to you that I didn't do what they said. I've been completely consumed by you. All I ever do is think about you."

"I know," she said with a smile. "I've been completely consumed by you too."

I smiled too. "I can't believe how lucky I am." I leaned closer to her, my lips stopping a fraction of an inch from hers. "Now, about that predicament. I think I can probably assist you with that." I grabbed my t-shirt by the nape of the neck and pulled it off.

She ran her fingers down the line of my abs.

I still felt that spark of electricity run through me every time we touched. I thought it might go away once we didn't have to hide our relationship anymore. The sneaking around, the excitement, the forbidden dynamic. But it was still there. And I wasn't sure that I wanted it to ever disappear. I knew for sure that I'd never grow tired of her calling me professor in that sexy way she always did.

I leaned forward and kissed her. Softly at first and then more passionately. She clasped her hands behind my neck as I pulled her ass to the edge of the counter. Now it was time for dessert. She'd been so good with those detectives. And now I was going to reward her. Well, reward both of us. Because I couldn't stop thinking about her delicious cunt.

Her phone started vibrating in her pocket.

She unwound her hands from my neck and grabbed her cell.

"Don't answer it." My lips drifted to her neck. I wanted to bruise her skin again. I wanted her to go to class and for people to finally know it was me that had marked her. I pressed my lips against her neck harder.

"But it's probably Melissa." She turned her head away from me so she could see her screen. "She's here."

"Maybe you should tell her to come back." I kissed down her neck and across her clavicle.

"James, she walked here." She put her hand on my chest.

I sighed. "Her timing is impeccable." I leaned down and grabbed my shirt as Penny slid off the counter.

Her phone buzzed again. "She's at the front desk. They told her we weren't here."

I laughed. "Oh, right." I pulled my phone out of my pocket and called down to the front desk. "Is there a Melissa down there asking to come up?" I put my hand over the receiver. "Is her last name Monroe?" I asked. I was pretty sure Ian had mentioned Melissa's last name to me once. I was a pretty good stalker, but Ian was much better.

"Yes."

"Yes, please let Melissa Monroe up. Thanks, Ben." I put my cell phone back in my pocket. "So, what can I expect today?"

"What do you mean?"

"Well," I said as I wrapped my arms around her, "every time she's seen me, she's been mad at me."

"No she hasn't."

"Yes, she has. She hates me."

"She doesn't hate you. She doesn't even know you. Maybe tonight she can finally get to know you better. I want you two to be friends too."

"I'll try to be super charming." I flashed her a smile.

"Yeah, I don't think you need to try to be charming. It comes quite naturally to you."

A dinging noise sounded through the apartment. I nodded toward the elevator doors and released her from my embrace. "I'm probably going to need another shot." I grabbed the bottle off the counter and poured vodka into my glass.

Penny laughed and went to go let Melissa in.

As soon as the doors opened, Melissa ran out of the elevator and gave Penny a big hug. "Where the hell have you been? How are you feeling? How's your head? I can't believe everything that's been going on..." her voice trailed off as she released Penny from her hug. "Oh my God. This place is amazing." Melissa walked past Penny and toward the windows all along the back of the apartment. She folded her arms across her chest as she looked out at Main Street below.

"It's pretty awesome, right?" Penny asked as she walked up next to her.

"I didn't even know Main Street could look this pretty." Melissa turned toward Penny. "No wonder you're never at our dorm anymore. This place is amaze-balls. I might never leave either."

"Amaze-balls, huh?" I said as I walked up behind them. "Hi, Melissa, how are you?"

Melissa rolled her eyes as she turned to look at me. "I've been better, James."

"Oh. I'm sorry..."

"You're sorry? Yeah, you should be. You know what? You and I need to talk."

I lowered my eyebrows. "About what?"

"You know what."

"Hey, Melissa." Penny put her hand on Melissa's arm. "Maybe you and I can talk real quick? I feel like I haven't seen you in forever."

"Yeah, which is another thing I want to talk about. But first I need to talk to your boyfriend."

Geez. Why did it always seem like Melissa wanted a fight? Penny just needed a fun night in with her friend. Couldn't Melissa see that? I glanced at Penny. *Told you she hated me.*

Penny shrugged. But she looked as confused as me about what Melissa was upset about now.

"If something is bothering you..." I started.

"Bothering me? Of course something is bothering me. Don't you remember our conversation the first time we met?"

"I remember that it was rather one sided."

"Very funny. But you promised me that you wouldn't hurt her. And do you know what you did that very night? You broke up with her. So yeah, you could say that's been bothering me. You lied to me."

I didn't break up with her. We were just on a little break while I sorted out my shit. "I don't think you understand the circumstances."

"Oh, no, I do. Penny told me that she didn't tell you she was a sophomore. Which doesn't seem nearly as bad as having a secret wife."

For fuck's sake, this girl was something else. "I know I messed up. But Penny has forgiven me for that. For both things. And I was just..."

"Right," Melissa said, cutting me off again. "You were trying to protect her or some crap like that? Well I don't buy it. Because this whole thing," she said, pointing down to the news vans. "That doesn't protect her at all."

"Penny and I both want this. The way people are reacting is not my fault."

"Yes it is. Of course it's your fault. You can't cheat on your crazy ex-wife with a student and not expect things to blow up. You're like a celebrity."

Wow. Okay then. I didn't cheat on my ex-wife, she cheated on me. Why did everyone believe what they read in tabloids? "I'm not a celebrity."

Penny started laughing. And it was like once she started she couldn't stop. For some reason that made me start laughing too.

"What is wrong with you guys?" Melissa asked.

We both continued to laugh. The last few days had been so fucking stressful.

"Oh my God. You're drunk, aren't you? That's your drunk laugh." Melissa turned toward the kitchen. The bottle of vodka was still open on the counter. "Is that what you've been doing holed up in here?"

I couldn't seem to stop laughing.

"Stop laughing at me," Melissa said.

"I'm not laughing at you. I'm sorry," Penny said, still giggling.

"Whatever, I can't even judge you for this whole underage drinking mess you have going on. Josh gets me alcohol all the time. One of the many perks of dating an older man. Or super old," she said and looked at me.

"I'm not super old. I'm only 27."

"27 is the new 20," Penny said.

"Okay. I need a drink too because you're both being ridiculous. I'm glad this is going to be fun. Because I passed on a very sexy date with Josh to hang out with you guys." Melissa walked over to the kitchen.

"See, she's always mad at me," I whispered.

"Well maybe you shouldn't have broken up with me," replied Penny.

"I didn't break up with you. I just said I needed some time." I smiled at her. "I really wish we were alone right now." I put my hand on her waist and let it slowly slide down to her ass.

"Oh my God, James." She grabbed my hand and moved it off her ass. "Apparently you get horny when you're drunk too?"

"No, I just always want you."

"You know, you're supposed to be charming Melissa, not me. I mean, not like that obviously. In a gentlemanly way."

I laughed. "Don't worry. The only ass I want to touch is yours." I slapped her ass and walked toward the kitchen. It was time to win over Penny's best friend.

Chapter 15

Thursday

"Were you guys just drinking straight vodka?" Melissa asked. "No chaser or anything?"

"We both just really needed a drink," I said and sat down in one of the stools at the counter.

"Gross." Melissa opened up the fridge like she'd been here a hundred times.

She was very different from Penny. I stared at her as she poured a can of cherry coke into a glass, topped it off with some vodka, and leaned against the counter. Actually, she was pretty much the opposite of Penny. I wondered what they had in common. Or maybe it was something about them not having anything in common that made them friends?

"Why did you both need a drink so badly?" Melissa asked.

"The cops showed up," Penny said and shrugged.

"Wait, what?"

"To interview me for that stupid investigation they're doing."

"Did they tell you how the investigation was going?"

Penny looked at me.

"Apparently two of my former students said I was asking for sexual favors in exchange for giving them better grades. Or something along those lines."

Melissa already hated me. This wasn't going to help.

"And..." she said.

"And nothing. It isn't true. Either the girls made it up, or the detectives did to try to get information from Penny."

"You have a history of lying."

Yes, Melissa hated me. And I was starting to hate her too. But I knew I needed to squash this nonsense. If I could get Penny's parents to like me, I could get her supposed best friend to like me too. "Here." I pulled out my phone and set it on the kitchen counter. I pushed it and it slid across the counter to her. "Check my phone. I'm telling the truth."

"So I can just look at your phone?" Melissa asked. "At your texts? And contacts? And emails? And pictures?"

"Suit yourself."

Melissa swiped her finger across the screen. "What's your password?"

"Oh." I laughed and raked my fingers through my hair. "Actually it's Penny." I couldn't get her out of my head while we were on a break. Every time I grabbed my phone, I'd hoped there'd be a text from her. I was trying to be strong and I'd thought if I could type her name when I unlocked my phone, I could resist actually typing anything *to* her. And I hadn't changed it back. Because I liked thinking about her all the time.

"I'm your password?" Penny slid into the seat next to mine.

"Yeah, I happen to like thinking about you." I put my arm around her.

Melissa tried to hide her smile as she started to scroll through my phone. "I hate that I'm mad at you right now, James. Because you two really are adorable."

Penny leaned her head against my shoulder. The scent of her cherry perfume affected me even more when alcohol was coursing through my veins. I really wished we were alone.

She put her hand on my thigh. Apparently she was thinking the same thing.

"Insatiable," I whispered.

Penny's throat made that adorable squeaking noise I loved.

"Who's Jennifer?" Melissa asked.

"My sister." That made sense that she was checking my female contacts. If I had access to Penny's phone, I'd definitely look at her male contacts. And immediately delete Tyler freaking Stevens. And Brendan whatever face. Fuck those guys.

"Oh." She looked back down at my phone. "What about Ellen?"

"That would be my housekeeper."

Melissa wasn't going to find anything incriminating. Because there was nothing incriminating to find. The worst thing that I had was X-rated footage of Penny. And that was on my computer. And Ian's. I frowned. I needed to make sure he wiped those recordings from his computer.

"Okay, fine, there's nothing on here." She placed my phone back down on the counter. "Actually there's barely anything on here. Which is suspicious all by itself."

"Sorry to disappoint you."

"Well I'm adding myself into your phone. Because if Penny winds up in the hospital again, I want to know."

"You'll be the first person I call," I said. I had her number written down somewhere. But I hadn't added it to my phone. Because I didn't particularly like her. I'd thought she was a bad influence on Penny and honestly not a great friend. But...I could admit when I was wrong.

She clearly did have Penny's back even if she was rather abrasive about it.

"I'd better be. And her parents. Have you talked to them yet, by the way?"

"We did," Penny said and lifted her head off my shoulder. "It went pretty well actually. My dad was not thrilled about me losing my scholarship, but other than that...it was good."

"Oh crap, Penny. I didn't realize you lost your scholarship. What are you going to do?"

"I don't know why everyone is making such a big deal out of this," I said. "You know I have the money to pay for it."

"The perks of having a loaded boyfriend." Melissa smiled. "Speaking of which, I'd love a tour."

Melissa was finally smiling. Which meant this was probably a good time for me to bow out and let the two of them talk. Besides, I needed to get to the bottom of what the hell was going on with those detective. And the girls that were lying about me. "I will let you handle the tour, Penny. I need to get some work done." I stood up.

"But you're not a professor anymore," Melissa said.

"I'm working on some other stuff." I kissed Penny's cheek. "I'll be in my office." I walked out of the room and into the hall.

Behind me I heard Melissa say: "Oh my God, this place is so cool! Show me everything!"

I smiled. She'd come around eventually. If I stopped fucking things up with Penny. And I was definitely done doing that. I was all in here. I walked into my office and closed the door behind me.

I hit Ian's name in my phone. He answered in one ring.

"I can't wait to listen in on this," Ian said.

"We're not listening to their conversation." I sat down at my desk.

"Wait, what? Why?"

"Because it's an invasion of their privacy."

Ian laughed. "*This* is but watching Penny with those detectives earlier wasn't?"

I pressed my lips together. *I don't know. Apparently my morals are all messed up.* But that situation was different. I was trying to protect her. I didn't need to protect her from Melissa. *I think.* Unless Melissa was whispering poison about me to Penny… *Stop.* "We have something else we need to do. We need to get the bottom of who the two girls lying about me are. And why they're doing it."

"I'm already on it," Ian said. "I'll figure it out soon enough. But I want to take a break and see what Penny and Melissa are saying."

"No."

"But they're obviously talking about you. Don't you want to know what they're saying?"

"Of course I want to know," I said and eyed the black screen on my computer. I could easily just…switch it on. And see what Penny was saying about me in private with her best friend. But that was the whole problem. It was supposed to be private. And as inappropriate as me filming Penny with me was, it was a shared moment between us. For some reason I could rationalize that better.

"So we can watch?" Ian asked.

"Ian, when did you become such a voyeur?"

"I don't know," he said very seriously.

"I was kidding, Ian."

He laughed. "I know. Me too."

Was he though? When was the last time Ian had mentioned going on a date? I pressed my lips together. Wait, had I ever heard him talk about a date before? I didn't think so. The only girl I ever heard him talk about was my sister. And I didn't think that was sexual. At least, I really hoped it wasn't. Because that would fucking suck if he moved to California with Jen and left me without a security detail. Also…I'd miss him. He'd somehow become my best friend since he moved into the building.

I cleared my throat. "We're not watching."

Ian groaned. "Fine. Whatever. I'll turn it off."

"Wait, you were already watching?"

"Yes."

"Well…what are they saying?"

Ian laughed. "They're in your closet talking about clothes. They're not even naked. And there's no pillows or anything. Lame."

I shook my head. "You thought they were going to have a naked pillow fight?"

"I don't know. Isn't that what college girls do?"

I laughed. "I mean…sometimes."

"Well, they're not doing it. Maybe we should send Ellen in with some extra fluffy pillows…"

"Now you want to see Ellen naked?" I asked with a laugh.

"No. She'll put the pillows on the bed and leave. I'll give her very specific instructions about that."

I laughed. "Speaking of naked pillow fights, I need you to delete that video footage of Penny from your computer."

"Which video footage?"

I pictured my favorite one. With Penny on her knees worshipping my cock at the country club. "All of it."

"If I delete it from the server I'll be deleting it from your computer too."

"I know," I said.

There was a long pause. "You already saved it somewhere else, didn't you?" asked Ian.

"No," I lied. But I didn't even believe me.

"*Sure.*"

I sighed. "How the hell do you know that I already have a backup?"

He laughed. "You back up everything. But I know the footage is on your external hard drive. Top right drawer of your desk. Because I saw you do it."

"You're out of control, Ian. Stop watching every single thing I do."

"It's literally my job."

"You need to get out of the apartment more."

"You need to get out of the apartment more," he mimicked back at me.

I laughed. "Whatever."

"Besides, last time I was out of town, Isabella broke into the apartment. And you freaked the fuck out. I won't be doing that again for a long time."

"Good." I really didn't love the fact that he'd lost track of time talking to my sister.

"Good," he agreed.

Well, that was settled then. He'd keep watching and… *Wait.* That wasn't what I wanted. I shook my head. It was fine. He was right, I felt more comfortable knowing he was on the other side of the security cameras.

We were both silent for a few seconds.

"You want to know what they're saying, don't you?" Ian asked.

"Fuck yes."

"They're just talking about Rob visiting this weekend. Speaking of which, is he coming tomorrow or Saturday? Or is it Sunday? Ellen wants to know."

"I don't know, he just said this weekend. Actually he said this weekend-ish. So who knows. Let me text him."

I stayed on the call with Ian and sent Rob a text.

He responded right away: "I'm banking on the fact that you're willing to break your co-ed rule for one night to celebrate my homecoming. So I'll be there early enough for you to take me to the best party on campus tomorrow night."

Well that's not happening. I read it out loud to Ian.

He laughed. "You haven't told him about Penny yet? Or anything that's going on?"

"Nope. I thought it would be a fun surprise."

"Absolutely. I can't wait to watch the whole thing."

Of course.

There was a knock on my door.

"I gotta go, Ian."

"I'll text you if there's a naked pillow fight."

I laughed.

"Oh wait. It's actually Melissa at your door."

"Thanks for the heads up." I hung up just as Melissa poked her head in.

"I just wanted to say goodnight," she said. "And to thank you for having me over."

"Of course."

She looked over her shoulder and then back at me. "And thanks for making her happy," she said a little quieter, so Penny wouldn't overhear.

Yeah, maybe Melissa really was a good friend. "That's my job." Actually, it was my only job. And I was going to take it very seriously.

She smiled. "I guess so. Goodnight, James." She closed the door behind her.

That felt like progress to me. I stared at the top right drawer of my desk. If I destroyed the hard drive, that would be progress too. I opened the drawer and stared down at it.

But Penny on her knees... Oh, and when she crawled to me? How was I supposed to permanently delete that? It was fucking art.

And I could feel myself getting hard just thinking about those videos. I kind of wanted to make a new one right now.

I slammed the drawer shut. Making another video sounded a hell of a lot better than deleting the others.

Chapter 16

Thursday

"There you are." I wrapped my arms around Penny and kissed the back of her neck. I'd been looking all over the apartment for her. She'd wandered into the billiards room and was staring at the only picture I had hanging up in the whole apartment.

"When was this picture taken?"

"When I was in college." I kissed the back of her neck again.

"You look so happy."

"I'm happier now."

"I recognize Mason. Who are the other guys?"

I looked up at the picture. "They're my frat brothers." It was taken my senior year. A rare picture of me smiling. Mason, Matt, and Rob were in it, along with a few of my other friends.

"You were in a frat?"

Technically it was a final club. It was more prestigious than a frat, but no one ever knew what I was talking about when I mentioned final clubs. "Why do you seem so surprised?"

"I don't know. I usually consider frat guys to be immature. But maybe you were immature back in college."

"Hmm." I traced my lips down the back of her neck again. Her skin pebbled beneath my lips. "Is thinking about getting laid all the time immature?"

She laughed. "Yes."

"I was definitely immature then. And I guess I'm still immature. Because all I could think about all night was fucking you." All the naked pillow fight talk hadn't helped the situation.

Her quick intake of breath made me even harder. I loved the way she reacted to my dirty words.

I pushed her forward slightly so that her hips were pressed against the pool table. "Are you good at pool, Penny?" My fingers dipped beneath the hem of her shirt, pushing it up the sides of her torso.

"I'm okay. I haven't really played that much."

Her throat made a weird noise when my hands fell from her waist.

She wanted me as desperately as I wanted her. But first...I had an idea. I placed the cue ball down on the table and racked up the other balls. "Show me what you got." I handed her a pool stick.

She stared at my hands instead, like she wanted them back on her. But she reluctantly grabbed the pool stick. "Am I stripes or solids?"

"Whichever you hit in first." I smiled at her. "And let's make things interesting." I leaned against the pool table. "Whenever one of us gets a ball in, we get to choose one thing for the other person to do."

"One thing for the other person to do?"

"Mhm. So if I get a ball in, I could say I wanted your lips around my cock." Because I really fucking did.

Her teeth sunk into her lip like she was starving for me.

Jesus. This is going to be fun. "You're up, Penny."

She bent low and arched her back. I loved that she was shy for everyone but me. My eyes fell to her ass.

She looked over her shoulder at me, catching me staring. She smiled and then hit the cue ball. It slammed into the rest of the balls, but none of them went in.

"That's a shame. I really wanted to see what you'd make me do." I grabbed another stick off the wall and lined up my shot. "I'll be solids." I easily hit one in and turned toward her. "Take off your shirt, Penny. And you might as well take off your bra too." I leaned over and sunk my next shot, which actually included two more balls. I raised my eyebrow at her.

She slowly peeled off her shirt and unhooked her bra. She dropped both items to the floor.

God, her tits were perfect.

"James, this isn't even fair."

Had I said it was going to be fair? I was really fucking good at pool. And I wanted her naked in the middle of the table with her legs spread. But I was curious about what she'd make me do too. "How about a maximum of two balls in a row?" I said as I tore my eyes off her breasts and back to her face. "Which means you're up."

She leaned down and my eyes went straight back to her tits. I wanted to lick every inch of her skin.

I forced myself to stand still. Because if I closed the distance between us, there was no way we'd finish the game. I'd left her an easy shot. The only thing she had to do was make sure she didn't hit the cue ball in.

Her back arched even more as she hit in her first striped ball.

Damn, I hadn't realized how distracting she'd be.

She smiled and stood up. "I think you should take your shirt off too."

Is that all you got? I locked eyes with her, grabbed my shirt by the nape of the collar, and quickly pulled it off.

Her eyes drifted down my six pack. But then she abruptly turned around and lined up her next shot.

It was another easy one. The cueball had almost rolled in after her last shot though...

"And, Penny," I said and walked over to her. I put my hand on the arch of her back. "I forgot to mention, if you hit the cue ball in, that results in a punishment."

Her eyes locked with mine. "A punishment?"

I lowered my mouth to her shoulder. "But I happen to know you like being punished." I nipped at her shoulder blade. The taste of her skin was almost as distracting as the sight of her tits.

"James, stop trying to distract me."

My fingers fell from her back, but I stayed right next to her. I loved the way my gaze made her blush. Or maybe it was my touch that had her cheeks flushing. Or my words. Penny loved being punished. And I really fucking loved punishing her.

She hit her second shot. But I'd successfully distracted her enough that she hit it too hard in her excitement. The striped ball and the cue ball dropped into the pocket.

Fuck yes. I grabbed her waist and lifted her onto the edge of the pool table. "If you weren't pouting, I would have thought you had done that on purpose." I sunk my teeth into her earlobe. One taste and I couldn't get enough.

She moaned and tilted her head to the side. I kissed down her neck and slowly traced kisses across her clavicle. My mouth stopped between her breasts. There was nothing better than burying my face between her tits.

I ran my fingers up the insides of her thighs, took one of her nipples in my mouth, and lightly tugged.

"James," she moaned. She tilted her hips, desperate for some friction.

Not yet, baby. This wasn't a reward. This was a punishment. She hadn't earned my cock yet. I pushed down on her thighs, pressing her ass back down against the table. My tongue swirled around her nipple and I squeezed her other breast. I'd never get over how perfectly they fit in my hands. I mimicked the movement of my tongue with my fingers on her other nipple.

My free hand traced up her leg and along the top of her thigh. Her skin pebbled under my touch. It wasn't just her body that had me hard. It was the way her body responded to me that I loved the most. Like she needed me. I didn't have to feel her thong to know that she was soaking wet right now. I tugged harder on her nipple with my teeth.

"James, please," she panted.

I wondered if she realized what her punishment was yet. I had no plans to give her what she really wanted for a long time. I was just teasing her. Torturing her. Punishing her.

I lifted my head from her tits. "I want you," I said. I hooked my thumbs in the waistband of her leggings.

"I want you too." She lifted her hips slightly, waiting for me to peel off her leggings.

She needed my hands, my tongue, my cock. Anything. But she hadn't earned it yet.

"Then you'll have to play better than that." I let her waistband slap back against her skin.

She gaped at me.

I picked up my pool stick and easily hit another solid ball in. "Get on your knees, Penny."

She immediately slid off the pool table and got down on her knees.

Good girl. I slowly unbuttoned and unzipped my jeans as I walked over to her. I ran my thumb along her plump bottom lip. I wanted those lips wrapped around me. "Make me cum in your mouth."

She reached up and pulled my boxers down.

My erection sprung free. Take all of it, Penny.

She looked up at me as she wrapped her hand around my base. She looked shy. But I knew she wasn't. *Suck me off, my little slut.*

She ran her tongue from my base to my tip and then locked eyes with me as she gently kissed my tip.

The vixen inside of her was coming out to play. I loved this side of her.

She wrapped her soft lips around me and slowly slid down my length.

I groaned. *Just like that, baby.*

She tightened her lips around me in response. And then she began to slide my cock in and out of her mouth, slowly at first, but then picking up speed. She reached up and gently cupped my balls in her hand.

I groaned again and buried my fingers in her hair. Normally this was where I'd start guiding her. Fucking her pretty little mouth. But I'd asked her to make me cum. I wanted her to do it without my guidance. *Give me what I like.*

She tightened her lips even more and did something I'd never felt before with her tongue.

"Fuck."

She bobbed her head up and down faster. And then she did that thing with her tongue again.

Jesus. Where had she been hiding that trick?

She paused at my tip, swirling her tongue around me.

"Don't stop, baby," I groaned. *Don't ever stop.* I fisted my hand in her hair, but still resisted guiding her.

She quickened her pace and my tip hit the back of her throat.

I expected her to gag, but she didn't.

Instead, she dropped her hand from my base, grabbed my ass, and pushed my cock all the way into the back of her tight throat.

Fucking hell, Penny. I felt that familiar pull in my stomach and began to pulse in her mouth.

Her mouth slid to the end of my cock just in time, letting my hot cum shoot into her mouth instead of directly down her throat.

Shot after shot into her mouth.

And she didn't stop. She kept bobbing her head. Sucking every last drop from me like the greedy little slut she was.

I slowly pulled out of her mouth and zipped up my pants. "Maybe now I can focus," I said and turned back to the table.

"You're already winning," she said with a laugh.

I wasn't winning until she was in the middle of the table begging for my cock. I hit another shot and a solid ball sunk perfectly into one of the corners of the pool table. "But I don't even have you naked yet." I turned around and Penny was still on her knees. I put my hand out for her.

She grabbed my hand and I pulled her to her feet.

"Now take off your pants," I said.

She pushed her leggings down her thighs, stepped out of them, and threw them at me.

I smiled and caught them in my hand. She really was begging to be spanked.

She grabbed her stick and walked around the table, trying to find the easiest shot.

I walked up behind her. I let my fingers wander down her back. "I like this." I touched her lacy red thong. I loved this color on her.

She looked over her shoulder at me. "Well, you should. You're the one who bought it for me."

Hmm. "How about you let me help you with this shot. I'd really like to see what you want me to do next."

She smiled. "Okay."

I leaned forward, pressing my naked torso against her back. I did want her to get her next shot. Almost as much as I wanted her to turn around and kiss me.

I put my left hand on top of hers, pressing her fingers down on the felt of the pool table. I grabbed the pool stick and pulled it back. I pictured my dick sliding through her fingers instead of the wood. I blinked, trying to focus. But it was hard when her ass was pressed against me.

"Okay," I whispered into her ear as I wrapped my right hand around hers too. I pushed her forward slightly, so that her hips were digging into the side of the pool table.

A sharp exhale escaped her lips.

I know, baby. Get this shot and I'll give you whatever you ask. "Let's hit the nine into the left pocket." I moved my right hand back, pulling the stick back farther, and pushing her hips even harder against the pool table.

She'd just made me cum, but I was already growing hard again. My erection pressed against her ass. I really did love the red lace.

"Gently, Penny." I kissed the side of her neck. "I can't wait to see what you want me to do." I hoped it involved my tongue in her delicious cunt. I kissed her neck again.

"I think you're just trying to distract me even more." Her voice was light and airy. Like she was living in a dream.

She'd be dreaming in a minute when my face was buried in her pussy. "No. I want you to make it. I haven't tasted you since yesterday."

She didn't respond. But I knew she was already picturing it too.

I lightly slid the pool stick forward, guiding her hand, and hit the cue ball. The nine ball went right into the left pocket. "See...gentle." I kissed her neck again.

"I want you to lick me," she blurted out.

Lick her? That wasn't very specific. I smiled and let my hands fall from hers. I grabbed her shoulders and pulled her back against my torso.

"You want me to lick you?" I whispered into her ear. I gently slid my tongue along the back of her ear.

"Not there." Her voice sounded so needy. So desperate.

And yet...she couldn't say the words. I raised my eyebrow at her. I wanted her to say it. I wanted her to beg me to eat her out.

She looked down at her thong and then back up at me.

I wanted her to say the words. But I loved how innocent she was too. It was my job to teach her. After all, I was her professor. I grabbed the sides of her thong and slid them over her hips. "You want me to lick your pussy?"

She gulped. "Yes."

"You shouldn't be embarrassed to ask me for that." I grabbed her waist and lifted her onto the side of the pool table. I pushed on the insides of her thighs, spreading her legs for me. "You know that I love the taste of you." I knelt down in front of her and massaged the insides of her thighs. Her pussy lips were glistening for me. She was as soaked as I expected. Just waiting for my tongue. "So ask me, Penny. Tell me exactly what you want me to do."

"I want you to lick my pussy."

Fuck. If I wasn't already hard, the way she said pussy would have done it. "It's sexy when you say it." I leaned forward and placed a slow stroke against her wetness. *So fucking sweet.*

"Oh God."

This is what you get when you ask for what you want. I swirled my tongue inside of her, pressing against all her walls, as my nose rubbed against her clit. I breathed in her scent. Her pussy lips were so soft. So wet. I pulled back to stare at her swollen lips. So inviting.

I pushed her thighs even farther apart and held them down firmly. A tiny drop of her pleasure landed on the wooden edge of the pool table. She'd swallowed down every drop of my cum. And I was going to do the same for her. I licked the edge of the table and then shoved my tongue even deeper, pressing my nose firmly against her clit.

"James!" She grabbed the back of my head to hold me in place.

I continued to swirl my tongue inside of her for a few more seconds. I wanted nothing more than to make her come. But...she hadn't asked me to do that. She'd asked me to lick her. I'd given her another chance and she'd told me to lick her pussy. If she wanted more...I wanted her to ask. I wanted to hear her say those dirty words. Hearing her say it made me so fucking hard. I grabbed her hand, removed it from the back of my head, and pulled away from her.

"No, James. Please don't stop."

"Baby." I kissed the inside of her thigh. "I like pleasing you." I kissed her opposite thigh. "And I like when you tell me what you want." I stood up and pulled her off the table. "But you didn't ask me to make you come. I wish you had. I love making you come with just my tongue. It's your shot, though. Get your next ball in and tell me what you want."

Chapter 17

Thursday

Penny pressed her thighs together as she stared at me.

But I doubted that extra friction helped her predicament. She really should have asked me to make her come.

She tried to make her next shot, but the cue ball bounced off the wall and didn't hit anything.

I picked her thong up off the ground and tossed it at her. "I believe I have to earn this. But don't bother putting it back on." I easily sunk my next ball.

She threw her thong back at me.

I laughed.

"If I had known how good you were at this, I wouldn't have agreed to this game."

She was frustrated. I got it. She'd teased me for weeks before I'd finally gotten to fuck her. But she should have asked me to make her come if that's what she wanted. "I'm not sure if that's true," I said and hit another solid ball easily into one of the pockets. "Besides, you must have known I wasn't terrible if I owned a pool table."

She put her hand on the edge of the table. "Well, if I had been thinking clearly, I would have just asked you to fuck me on it."

I lowered my eyebrows. "Unbutton my jeans, Penny."

She looked down at the bulge pressing against my jeans. "That's what you want me to do to you?"

"I need to be ready when I get my next shot in." I grabbed her hand and placed it on the waistline of my jeans.

She ran the back of her hand down my happy trail and slowly unbuttoned and unzipped my pants. She pushed my jeans down, put her hands on the waistband of my boxers, and looked up at me.

I nodded my head.

She pushed my boxers down, freeing my cock again. She wrapped her hand around my length.

I cleared my throat and handed her the pool stick.

She batted her eyelashes at me. "Sorry, wrong stick."

I pressed my lips together and watched her walk back to the table. She bent over again, arched her back, and spread her legs.

My eyes fell to her ass. She was trying to tempt me. But all she needed to do was sink this shot and ask. Actually ask. But I only had so much control. I walked up behind her and trailed my fingers up the backs of her thighs.

She arched her back even more.

"I think maybe you should try to make your next shot like this." I slipped a finger inside of her.

She froze.

I slipped another finger inside of her greedy pussy, slowly stretching her out. "Take your shot, Penny."

She hit the cue ball. It went straight into the far right pocket.

I laughed and pulled my fingers out of her.

She turned around. "You cheated."

Did I? I slid my fingers into my mouth, licking off her juices, as I rounded the table. I don't think Penny and I had ever been naked in the same room without fucking. And my cock knew it. I was having a hard time concentrating too. But I loved games. Especially this one. Penny had just earned another punishment. I grabbed the cue ball, tossed the ball up in the air, and caught it as I walked back over to her.

"Put your hands on the table, Penny."

"James, you cheated. You distracted me."

"If I recall, I also helped you with one of your shots earlier. I think it evens out. Hands on the table. Now."

She bit her lip then slowly turned around. She placed her hands on the wooden edge of the pool table and arched her back again.

I knew how she wanted me to punish her. By fucking her hard against the side of the pool table. But that sounded a lot more like a reward. Instead, I rolled the cold cue ball roll up the back of her right leg. It shouldn't have been sexy. But everything about Penny's body was sexy. Her whole body shivered with desire.

"James." Her voice sounded needy.

I silenced her by spanking her ass hard.

She moaned.

I knew how she liked being punished. She wanted my handprint on her ass and her wetness dripping down her thigh. I rolled the cold ball over the spot I had just spanked, soothing the skin.

"Penny, I'm going to give you one last shot." I moved the ball to the back of her other leg and slowly rolled it up to her ass.

"One shot won't help. You're going to win next time you have..."

I spanked her again. "I like that you're full of surprises. Surprise me, and I'll give you exactly what you want. I'll fuck you as hard as you want. For as long as you want." I kissed the side of her neck. "I'll do whatever you want me to." I massaged the cue ball over my handprint. Fuck, I just needed to be inside of her. *For the love of God, make the shot, Penny.*

"Give me the ball," she said.

I tossed it over her shoulder. She moved it a little to the right. Instead of aiming for one of her striped balls, she shot the cue ball into the eight ball. Both balls went into the pocket.

And she thought I was a cheater? I grabbed her waist. "The eight ball and the cue ball?"

She just smiled.

I pushed on her back so that her torso was flush against the pool table. "Ending the game and ensuring that I'd punish you even more? That'll do." I would have spanked her again, but I'd been staring at her curves for what felt like hours. I felt like I was starving. I thrust deep inside of her, all the way to my hilt. *Fuck.* It was everything I wanted and more.

She moaned.

"Tell me what you want," I said as I thrust in and out of her, faster and faster.

"Please," she panted. "Please, James."

She couldn't say it. But I knew what she wanted. I'd tortured her enough.

"Okay," I conceded. I pulled her up so that her back was pressed against my torso. "Okay." I kissed her neck gently and began to massage her clit. *You were such a good girl.* "You can come now." I had plenty of time to corrupt her. Right now she just needed a release.

She immediately shattered around me, her pussy pulsing around my cock.

God, the way she gripped my cock.

"Professor Hunter," she moaned and collapsed back down on the table. Her pussy kept clenching me.

I gritted my teeth. I didn't want to cum again. Not yet. I'd had a picture in my head of how I wanted her as soon as I saw her in this room. I waited for her orgasm to subside before slowly pulling out of her.

LOVED

She turned around and looked up at me. There was that innocent look again. Like she hadn't just come around her professor's cock.

I grabbed her chin in my hand. "I still like when you call me that."

"Professor Hunter?"

My Adam's apple rose and then fell. "Yes."

"Then why did you tell me to stop?"

"I want us to just be us. Besides, I'm not even a professor anymore."

"I like calling you Professor Hunter."

I lowered my eyebrows. Every time she said it, I wanted to fuck her. I liked that she was my student and that I was her professor. It was dirty. And wrong. And forbidden. I knew I was fucked up in the head. Hell, I wasn't even a professor anymore. But I never actually wanted her to stop calling me that.

"You'll always be Professor Hunter to me," she said.

I grabbed her waist and set her down on the edge of the pool table. "I don't know why I find it so sexy when you call me that."

"Professor Hunter." She ran her hands down my six pack.

I leaned forward and kissed her hard.

She grabbed my hair and pulled me back. "I want you to fuck me in the middle of the pool table, Professor Hunter."

I thought you'd never ask. "Then get in the middle and spread your legs, Miss Taylor." I flashed her a smile. And I swear her pupils dilated. She liked when I called her that. Maybe we were both fucked up in the head. A perfect match.

She pushed some of the balls out of her way and scooted into the center of the table.

I climbed onto the table after her, stalking toward her on all fours. I leaned over her and pushed more balls out of our way. They clanged together as I pressed down on the center of her chest, shoving her back onto the table.

I couldn't wait any longer. I needed to feel her grip me. I wanted her to milk my cock with her pussy like she had with her mouth.

I grabbed her thighs and thrust deep inside of her.

"Professor Hunter," she moaned.

I kept one hand on her thigh and grabbed the edge of the table with my other hand for leverage. "I've missed hearing you say that." I wanted her to say it a million times. I loved that she wasn't ashamed of how we met. She was proud to be mine. I kissed her hard as I continued to slide my length in and out of her. She was still so fucking wet. So tight. So perfect.

We were so much more than professor and student now. But this was so incredibly hot. It brought me right back to our very first time in my office. When I first tasted her on my desk.

"Harder, Professor Hunter," she moaned.

I loved how bad she was for me. I grabbed both of her hands and lifted them above her head, knocking more balls out of the way. "Fuck, Penny." I moved my hips faster. "I'll never get enough of you."

"I'll never get enough of you either."

I leaned down and kissed her again as I moved my hips faster. I loved how rough I could be with her. How wet she always was for me. How greedy she was for my cock.

She moaned again.

I knew she was close. "Say my name when you come, Penny. I want to hear you say it when you clench around my cock." I tilted my hips, hitting her in that spot that always made her lose control.

"Professor Hunter!" she screamed as she came again, pulsing around me.

And I lost control too. Shot after shot of cum filling her aching pussy. I kept sliding in and out of her warmth as my heart rate slowed.

Yes, I'd been her professor. And she'd been my student. I loved that. But we were more than that now. She was...everything to me. Every single thing. I slowly pulled out of her and collapsed beside her. I pulled her head onto my chest.

Her cherry perfume mixed with sweat was my favorite smell in the world. I don't think I had ever felt so relaxed and happy.

Penny sighed and nuzzled against my chest.

"I love you, Penny." I ran my fingers through her hair. "I love you more than I even knew I could." I just wanted to stay here all night, tangled up in her.

She tilted her head and kissed my chest. "I love you."

I stared down at her.

She kissed my chest again. "James."

I swallowed hard.

She kissed my collar bone. "Professor Hunter."

I stifled my groan.

She kissed the scruff under my chin. "C.E.O."

C.E.O. I was going to have to get used to that again. Maybe I could get her to come work for me. I did love fucking her against my desk...

She kissed my lips.

I grabbed the side of her face and deepened the kiss.

"Whatever you want to be," she said. "You're mine." She smiled down at me.

I ran my palm along her cheek. "Yours." How the fuck did I get this lucky? I was hers and she was mine. Nothing else mattered. No matter what I did, she'd be beside me. And I wouldn't be able to keep my hands to myself.

Chapter 18

Friday

Sweat dripped down my back as I increased the speed on the treadmill. I hated running indoors. But going outside right now wasn't exactly a great option either. And I just needed this tension out of my body.

I rarely had nightmares since I rarely ever slept. But it was easy to fall asleep when Penny's head was on my chest. Her light exhales soothed something inside of me. She didn't follow me into my dreams last night though.

I'd felt Isabella's fake nails digging into my back. I'd felt her pulling me closer. I'd woken up sweatier than I was right now, gasping for air.

I still didn't know what had happened that night she drugged me. I didn't know if the dream was a memory. Maybe I was finally getting pieces of that night back. But I didn't believe I'd slept with her. I wouldn't have. Or…had I? I cringed. No. It was just some new fucked up thing playing in my brain. Or the truth. *Fucking hell.* I had no idea what was real.

I shook my head. That wasn't true. I knew what was real. Penny.

But I needed to get my shit together. I thought I was over this. What happened with Isabella didn't matter. I already came clean to Penny about what possibly occurred. I just needed to put that night behind me. Penny needed me right now. I needed to be my best self for her. I could hide out in the gym all day, but she had to go to class. She had to face all this without me.

I'd left her a note asking her to text me so we could meet up for lunch. And telling her not to fall in love with her new Comm professor. But I hadn't wanted her to see me after my nightmare. I never wanted her to see me like that. Weak.

I went to increase the speed again when my phone started buzzing.

I grabbed it and kept running. "What's up, Ian?" I said.

"You have an appointment with Dr. Clark in an hour. Want me to drive you?"

"No, I'm good."

"You sure? You sounded pretty shaky this morning."

"I'm good," I said again and started to decrease my pace. But he had a right to be worried. Calling him at 6 a.m. asking him to schedule an emergency session with Dr. Clark wasn't exactly screaming that I was fine.

"If you say so."

I kept slowing down until I was walking. I took a deep breath. "The workout helped actually."

"So do you want me to cancel your appointment?"

"No, I should go." I wanted to be a better man for Penny. And that meant seeing Dr. Clark on a regular basis. I wouldn't be able to go on Sunday because Rob was visiting. So I needed to go talk to him now.

"You're sure everything's okay, James? You know I'm here if you want to talk."

"Thanks, Ian," I said and wiped my face off with a towel. "But if I talked to you about all my shit, you might quit on me."

"Nah. No one will pay me as good."

I laughed. *Fair.* "I should go. Thank you for making the appointment."

"Any time." He cleared his throat. "One more thing. You should probably check your email."

I sighed. "Just tell me what it says."

"The investigation isn't going in the direction Joe hoped. Another girl came forward."

"What the fuck?"

"All your classes are being cancelled. They're just handing out As to everyone."

"Well at least Penny got an A."

"Actually she's getting an incomplete. Joe's pissed that she isn't cooperating in the investigation."

I ran my fingers through my wet hair. "And he sent all this via email?"

"Yeah."

He didn't even have the balls to call me? *What an asshole.* No one seemed to care about finding out the truth in this so-called investigation. They were making me out to be a monster.

I took a deep breath. But…wasn't I?

***

"I thought you'd have a little more to say after Ian called my office ten times to get you this appointment."

I stared at the newspaper on the coffee table between us. A copy of the Delaware Post. I knew there'd been more articles written since that first one. One announcing my resignation and the investigation. For all I knew, the investigative findings were in that paper there. "You already know what happened."

"I read the articles. But we both know that wasn't the truth."

"At least you believe me."

"Does Penny not?"

"Honestly? I don't know. I hope she does. But I wouldn't blame her if she didn't. The dean is running this sham of an investigation and three girls have said I seduced them too."

Dr. Clark nodded. "And how does that make you feel?"

"Pissed." I shook my head. "Confused. The detectives knew Penny came to my office hours. They seemed to know everything that happened. But I don't care what people think about me. I just want Penny to trust me."

"You don't care what anyone else says about you?"

"No."

He adjusted his glasses. "Not even a little?"

"The article is all lies. But they painted me just right, don't you think? So who cares how they got to that conclusion?"

"And what do you think the article painted you as?"

"The villain."

"Is that how you think of yourself?"

I shrugged.

"James, you're the author of your own story. You can be whoever you want to be."

"Sure," I said with a laugh. That sounded like a line ripped straight out some bullshit self-help book.

He leaned back in his chair. "Do you think Penny sees you as a villain?"

"No." *More like a sex god.* I smiled to myself.

"Why are you smirking?"

"Do you not want me to smile?"

"Of course I want you to smile. James, you're not a villain. You're not the man they've portrayed in the article. Not unless you believe you are. And I don't think you do."

He didn't know about the mantra I'd said while I'd been trying to stay away from Penny. I did believe I was a sick fuck. I did believe I was a monster. But…I didn't want to believe that. "I actually didn't ask for this appointment because of the article."

"No? Well, how about you tell me about that conversation you had the other night after we got off the phone. You were going to talk to Penny about what she wanted. What did the two of you decide?"

"We didn't get a chance to talk about what she wanted from her college experience. I found out the article was coming out and I was trying to do damage control."

"What kind of damage control?"

"Writing my resignation letter…"

"You decided to resign without discussing it with her?"

"Before you jump down my throat, Penny already gave me hell about this. And I know I should have spoken to her about it ahead of time. But I was just trying to get ahead of everything. And there was only one option. I had to resign."

"James, we talked about how important it is to be a team…"

"Yeah, yeah. I know. Penny and I are a team. But she still should have trusted my judgement and let me handle it."

"Why? Because you're older than her? That doesn't sound like the two of you are on equal footing at all."

"But I *am* older than her."

"Being significantly older clearly doesn't make you wiser."

I glared at him. "Touché."

"So you resigned without discussing it with her. So…now what?"

"She wants to keep going to classes." At least the ones that hadn't been cancelled because of me.

"So the two of you are staying in town?"

"That's what she wants."

"But what do *you* want, James?"

"I want to be with her. Wherever she is."

He smiled. "Interesting."

"Interesting?"

"You're putting her thoughts and feelings above your own. That's very mature of you."

"You're acting like I'm usually a selfish immature prick."

"I've never once said that."

I took a deep breath. "So you think that's a good idea then? To stay in town? Even though everyone here is a lying asshole?"

Dr. Clark cleared his throat.

"Sorry," I quickly added. He hated when I cursed.

"Everyone?" he asked. "Really? Including me?"

"I meant most people."

"If Penny did decide to drop out of classes, where would you like to move?"

"Is this a trick question? You want me to say that I'd talk to her about it, right?"

Dr. Clark smiled. "No, I'm just genuinely asking where you'd like to be if you weren't in Delaware."

"I'd like to go back to New York." I didn't even hesitate. My friends were there. I thought I'd never want to go back. I found the city to be suffocating. But…when Penny and I had visited for a day together? I'd felt like myself again. In my element. I was happy there with her.

"Have you told Penny that?"

"She wants to stay."

"Have you told Penny that?" he repeated.

"No. I'm being the mature adult you know I am and I'm putting her wants first."

"But your happiness is important too. I think it's a discussion the two of you need to have. An *actual* discussion."

"Hmm an actual discussion? So you're saying I should just whisk her away to New York this weekend and buy an apartment?"

"What, no, I..." his voice trailed off and he laughed when he saw that I was smiling. "Hilarious. But no. Tell her that you're excited about maybe starting fresh somewhere new with her. See what her ideas are of a new location. And you can tell her yours. Open communication."

Yeah. But Penny wanted to stay here. And I'd do anything for her. "Maybe once she graduates," I said.

"So you plan to stay here for another two and a half years doing what exactly? Talking to me?"

I laughed. *God I hope not.* "I've been working on this new security system."

"Right, right, I remember. And you'll feel fulfilled doing that here?"

"Really, as long as I'm with Penny I feel plenty fulfilled. She's everything to me."

"Everything is a very scary term to use, James. She's an important part of your life. But she can't be everything. You know that's a slippery slope."

Dr. Clark was wrong this time. Penny could be everything to me. She was everything to me. I took another deep breath. "I gave up my whole life to be with her. She is everything."

"So you're all in?"

I nodded. "I'm all in." I'd come here to tell Dr. Clark about my nightmare. Or memory. Or whatever the fuck it was. But I was done thinking about Isabella. I was done with all of it. Isabella had taken her last shot at me. It was done. I doubted I'd ever hear from her again. I was ready to move past this. I was ready for whatever was next with Penny. Here, New York City, somewhere across the Atlantic Ocean. It didn't matter where. Because I was all fucking in.

"I'm happy for you, James."

I smiled. I was happy for myself too. My phone started buzzing in my pocket and I pulled it out.

There was a text from Penny: "Can you come get me? I'm at my dorm."

What was she doing at her dorm? I quickly texted her back. "Why aren't you in Stat? Are you okay?"

"I'm okay. Please can you come?"

"I'll be right there." I looked back up at Dr. Clark. "I gotta go."

"You still have 30 minutes left of your session."

"Penny needs me."

He frowned. "Is everything alright?"

"I…I don't know. She should be in class right now. Something must have happened." I stood up.

"James?"

"Yeah?"

"Remember that taking care of her and being in a relationship with her are two different things."

I wasn't so sure about that. At least, they weren't two different things for me. If someone messed with my girl, you better believe I'd fuck someone up so it would never happen again.

Chapter 19

Friday

I walked out to my car. I had a feeling I knew why Penny was upset. She'd probably gotten an email from Joe similar to the one I'd received. I hit the button to unlock my car as I called Joe. He couldn't hide behind his computer forever.

"What now, James?" he said after only one ring.

"An incomplete? Really?" I started my car and pulled out of the parking lot.

"That's all you have to say about the matter?"

"What do you want me to say? I told you those girls were lying. Anyone else coming forward is lying too."

He sighed.

"You're giving everyone else an A who doesn't deserve it. Including the girls that are lying. At least let Penny withdraw from the class instead of giving her an incomplete on her transcript. That's bullshit and we both know it."

"And we also both know that it's past the window to withdraw from…"

"Joe. Don't make me give you hell." We both knew I would.

He sighed again. "As if you haven't already?"

True. "What if I double that donation I discussed in our meeting the other day?" I was starting to like the idea of a Hunter Hall.

"Fine. I just want this all to go away."

"Thank you."

"You really owe me one, James. I can't believe you were so careless leaving that note in your desk. It was just waiting there for the detectives to find."

Shit. "Note?" But I already knew what note. *Fucking hell.*

"You had a paper with a bad grade you gave Penny just sitting in your desk. With a saucy little note that she wrote to you underneath. Ring any bells?"

Yeah. I'd lured Penny to my office with a bad grade. She'd crumpled up the paper and threw it at me. And then she'd left me a cute note after we had sex for the first time in my office. I'd uncrumpled her grade and saved both it and her note. Because I was obsessed with her. And the two things together were pretty damning.

So...that was how the detectives knew what happened. And how the narratives of the girls that came forward were all so similar. Because those shit detectives fed it to them. It all made sense now.

I breathed a sigh of relief. I was starting to worry that they'd bugged me or something. I'd never once thought about my office... "Wait, didn't they need a search warrant to search my office?"

"It's university property, James. I gave them permission. I didn't think you were dumb enough to leave evidence all over the place."

Fair. I sighed. "Well it's pretty obvious what happened now. The detectives must have pressured those girls into agreeing with their theory. They promised Penny she could get her scholarship back if she went along with it. Did you know that? They must have done something similar with those three girls. They probably just offered them As. Joe, we can clear all this up..."

LOVED

"I just want it to go away," Joe said with a groan. "And if you didn't want this to happen, you shouldn't have left those papers in your desk."

"Sorry about that." I knew the detectives were in the wrong here, but I just wanted this to go away too. For Penny's sake. *Shit, is this what she's upset about?*

"Please tell me you're in your apartment lying low like I requested?"

I pulled up outside Penny's dorm. Joe did not want to hear about this. "Yup," I lied.

"Great. Keep doing that. I have to go." He hung up the phone.

I really hadn't meant to create a shitstorm for Joe. But honestly, it could be worse. After all, I'd beaten the shit out of the last dean I'd worked for. *Hmm.* Maybe that was why he'd sent an email instead of calling.

I parked my car and shot Penny a text: "I'm here. Do you want me to come up?"

My phone buzzed with her response. "I'll come let you in."

I slammed my car door closed and kept my head down as I walked up to the back of Penny's dorm. It was between classes so no one was around. But I'd try my best to be discreet for Joe's sake, even if he had pissed me off this morning with that idiotic email and the sham investigation.

Penny opened the door. Her eyes were pink and her nose was swollen from crying.

Screw discreet. I took the stairs two at a time and wrapped my arms around her. "Penny, what's wrong?"

She immediately burst into tears.

"It's okay," I said and kissed the top of her head. "It's okay, I'm here." I lifted her into my arms and carried her through the hallway of her dorm and up the stairs. She melted into my chest. I was glad that she felt safe in my arms. But I had a sinking feeling that her tears weren't about a withdrawal from class versus an incomplete. I would have guessed she was pissed at me about keeping that note. But wouldn't she be pushing me away instead of clinging to me? Something else must have happened.

I opened the door to her room, kicked it closed with my foot, and then set her down on her bed. I put my hands on the bed on either side of her so that I could stare right at her.

She just blinked and stared at me.

"Penny." I grabbed her chin in my hand. "Talk to me."

"I just wanted to see you. Can you hold me?"

I smiled. "I'm all sweaty." I'd been freaking out this morning and had gone straight to see Dr. Clark after my workout. I was still in my athletic shorts and a hoodie.

"I like when you're sweaty."

My smile grew. "Okay, move over." I kicked off my sneakers and climbed into her bed next to her, wrapping my arms around her.

She sighed and pressed the side of her face against my chest.

"If you're upset about your conversation with Joe, I convinced him to change the incomplete to a withdrawal. It looks better on your transcript."

"But Mr. Vespelli said you couldn't withdraw from a class that was canceled."

"Yeah, well Joe was being an asshole."

"Thank you," she said. But she still seemed tense.

"If that isn't what's bothering you, what is it?"

"It's nothing important."

Anything that had upset her was important to me. But I could wait for her to tell me. I ran my fingers through her hair and looked around the dorm. "Why did you come

LOVED

here?" If she was upset, she could have come...*home. To me.*

"I don't know. It's cozy."

Which meant *our* apartment was not cozy. I swallowed hard. But we could fix that. Together. "Okay." I tilted her head up to look into her eyes and pushed a strand of hair out of her face. *Tell me what's going on. Let me in.*

"I'm sorry. Your apartment is so big and it's always cold. And it was farther away and I was crying."

"Why were you crying?"

"It doesn't matter."

"Penny, no more secrets. Just tell me."

She put her hand under her head to prop herself up. "It's harder than I thought it would be. I don't know if I can do it, James."

I could hear Dr. Clark's voice in the back of my head. Telling me to tell her that I didn't want to be in this town anymore. That I wanted to go back to New York. And maybe Penny might want that too. But this didn't feel like the best moment. Not until I knew why she was having a change of heart. "Tell me what happened today."

"It wasn't just one thing. It was everything. It was awful."

"Tell me." I put my hand on her cheek. "Please tell me."

"On my way to class I got a text from Professor Nolan telling me not to come to class. And that the investigation went south or something. He said Mr. Vespelli would be calling me with details."

"Well, it's good he told you not to come. I'm sure everyone had a lot of questions. You didn't need to be there for that."

"Yeah. And I ran into Tyler. He took me to breakfast."

Tyler fucking Stevens. He was like a gnat that I couldn't swat away. What the hell was that kid's problem?

I must have made a face, because Penny said, "Stop. As friends. He was being nice. He knew I was upset."

"Okay. I'm glad that he was there for you." I really fucking wasn't, but what else could I say? "You could have come home though. I want to be the one that's there for you." I never wanted her to feel the need to run to someone else. Especially Tyler.

"You are that person. That's why I asked you to come."

After talking to Tyler. I clenched my jaw. I needed to drop this. She was with me now, that's all that mattered. I pushed another strand of hair out of her face. Penny couldn't help who she ran into on campus.

"And at breakfast I talked to Mr. Vespelli. He told me that there were now three girls who accused you of..."

"I know. I talked to him too. Penny, if that's why you're upset, we've talked about this. You know me. You know how I feel about you."

"It did upset me. How could it not upset me? But I know it isn't true. And it was more upsetting that Mr. Vespelli was just going to give up the investigation. I don't understand why they don't want to find the truth. They're going to put it in the paper, James. They're going to tell everyone, and then people will think it's true even though it's not."

"Penny, I want them to stop the investigation. It's fine. It'll make the news vans go away."

"But those girls lied. Clearly they just wanted to get As. Mr. Vespelli even said that they all had bad grades in your classes. It's ridiculous."

Yeah. It was a sham of an investigation. But I'd already resigned. I already looked guilty. And I didn't care what anyone said about me. "It's fine. The sooner it's over, the sooner things will go back to normal. Isn't that what you want?"

"I'm not sure anything will ever go back to normal."

I sighed. "I know. I told you to take the rest of the semester off. You can switch schools, Penny. You can pick up where you left off somewhere new in the spring. It's okay. We can go wherever you want." I stared at her. That's what I wanted. To go somewhere and have a fresh start. I'd put it out there.

"That isn't why I don't think things can go back to normal. At breakfast, Tyler warned me that it was going to be bad. Apparently everyone loves you. Which makes sense. You're very loveable."

I lowered my eyebrows. Did that mean people were upset with Penny? *Ah, fuck.* I wanted all the blame to be put on me. But I was worried about how other students would react to Penny, especially when the article said I was still married.

"Everyone's mad at me. I was hiding in the bathroom before Psych and I overheard these girls talking. People are upset that your classes are canceled. And it's because of me. Because I'm a slut and a whore. I ruined your career. I ruined your life."

She couldn't be more wrong. "You saved me. Penny, I was drowning. Don't you see that? I'm not a professor. I was never meant to be a professor. It was an escape from my life back in New York. It was just like everything else I've ever done. It was just another escape."

"But you loved teaching. You were a great professor."

I was a pretty shitty professor. "I didn't love teaching." I liked it, yeah. It made me happy for a time. I needed it when I was going through a hard time. But I didn't love it. "The only thing I think I've ever truly loved is you."

"I don't want to hold you back from..."

"Stop. Please stop. I don't understand why you won't accept what I'm telling you. You're all I want. You're all I care about." She was everything to me. Dr. Clark thought that was a slippery slope. But I didn't. There was nothing wrong with being obsessed with something that was good for me. It was being obsessed with things that were bad for me that got me in trouble.

"I just feel so selfish," Penny said.

I rubbed her tears away with my thumb. "You're it for me. I don't know how else I can tell you." I ran the tip of my nose down the length of hers.

She sighed like the action was the most comforting thing in the world.

"If you're going to keep going to class, you need to ignore what other people say. Because I don't like seeing you cry." *Or we could just move...*

"That wasn't it. That wasn't what made me cry. It just got worse from there."

Fuck. Whatever it was...it was bad. I just wanted to take her pain away. I could take it. I was used to living in pain.

"I got to Psych late because I was upset about what I heard in the bathroom. The professor called me out and asked me to talk to her after class. No one wanted me to sit with them. Luckily Tyler had called one of his frat brothers who had saved me a seat."

That was actually really nice of that shit head. "I'll have to thank him for that," I said calmly.

"After class I went to talk to the professor. She told me my grades were slipping. Which I already knew. But she implied that she thought I had been getting perks in my other classes because of our relationship."

I sighed. *Seriously?* I barely even spoke to any other professors. What did her Psych professor think was going on? That I called all of my professor bros, told them I was hooking up with a student, and they were like cool, I'll give her an A too? *Fuck off.*

"I told her I had gotten to class early, but had been hiding in the bathroom because I was trying to avoid hearing what everyone was saying about me. And she basically said that she wasn't sympathetic and wasn't friends with you, so that she would have no problem failing me."

"What is your professor's name?" I needed to have a talk with this idiot. She clearly wasn't very good at psychology, because she had no idea what the hell was going on around her.

"I don't want you to talk to her. I feel like that will just make it worse."

"You know that I can find out without you telling me."

Penny sighed. "Professor Thornton. But please don't talk to her. I'm going to get my grades back up. When you weren't talking to me I just fell apart. But I have the rest of the semester to fix it."

Right. The rest of the semester. I wanted to do that thing I'd just joked about in my session. I wanted to just buy an apartment in New York City tonight and whisk her away to it. But that wasn't exactly putting her needs first. Or being a team. I'd mentioned leaving town several times now. Penny wasn't biting. I had to just face the fact that we were staying here.

I nodded. "Okay. I won't talk to her. Honestly, I don't even recognize her name. I don't think I've met her. There probably isn't anything I could do anyway. I don't know that many professors outside of the business school."

She just stared at me. And she still looked upset. She hadn't told me the worst thing yet.

So I didn't say a word, waiting for her to continue telling me about her day.

She sighed. "My intro to marketing class was the worst. It's what made me cry. I didn't expect anything like this to happen. I didn't expect any professors to even talk to me. And I was already upset about everything else. I got a paper back in that class. I got a C-. So when Professor McCarty mentioned an extra credit assignment, I wanted to do it. But apparently he had already explained it in the class I missed on Wednesday. And I hate raising my hand in class. It makes me all nervous and..."

"I know." I picked up her hand and kissed her palm. "You ramble when you're nervous too. It's incredibly cute." I kissed her palm again.

Penny looked like she was going to start crying again.

I looked down at her hand. My heart was racing so fast. She was about to tell me why she was crying earlier. And I could only think of one thing. She got nervous in class. So...she talked to Professor McCarty after class was dismissed. When the two of them were alone. And I knew what I always wanted to do when I was alone with Penny. She was beautiful. Alluring. Sweet. So fucking sweet. I clenched my jaw.

"It's okay," I said. "I want you to tell me." I needed to know what that old prick had done. If he had touched one hair on her body, I was going to fucking kill him.

Chapter 20

Friday

Penny blinked fast, holding back her tears.

It felt like there was a knife in my chest, slowly twisting. *Tell me what happened. Put me out of my misery.*

"So, I waited till class was over and went up to ask him what the assignment was. He pulled out the paper that it was on and asked me to come behind his desk so he could explain it to me."

I couldn't breathe.

"I had never really talked to him before. I sit in the back row. I usually get As on all my papers and tests. I never had any reason to talk to him."

I know, baby. Fucking hell, just tell me. I ran my thumb up and down each of her fingers, trying to distract myself from my racing heart.

"He put his hand on my back when I went behind his desk. I didn't know what to do. I thought he was just being nice. I felt kind of frozen."

Breathe.

"I thanked him for the extra credit assignment and told him I had another class to get to."

I felt like I was slowly dying. I could picture the scene so easily in my head. *Breathe.*

"But he said he thought we might be able to work out some kind of arrangement that would be better."

Breathe.

"And he put his hand on my ass."

All I could see was red. I was going to fucking kill him.

"And I didn't know what to do. I told him to stop. I eventually slapped him. But he grabbed my wrist. He said he had more connections than you at the university, so it would be more worth my time."

He was a dead man. Did I look like a guy who needed to prey on students getting bad grades? He'd leapt to the wrong conclusion about Penny. And now he'd never get another chance to jump to a conclusion again.

"I told him that I was going to report him to the dean. But he said that if I told Mr. Vespelli, he'd say I had come on to him. Somehow he knew I had two strikes. He knew I'd be expelled if I got in trouble again."

I dropped Penny's hand and sat up. "Did you want to stay here or do you want me to drop you off at the apartment?" I got off her bed and pulled on my shoes.

"What are you doing?"

"I'm going to go pay your professor a visit." *Don't you remember when Tyler touched you? I really enjoyed breaking his nose.* I couldn't wait to rearrange Professor McCarty's ugly old mug.

"James, I don't want you to do anything to Professor McCarty. That wasn't why I told you about it. I need to know what to do. I can't go back to that class."

"He touched you," I seethed. This wasn't up for negotiation.

"And I slapped him."

I shook my head. *That's not good enough.* "I'm going to kill him."

"James!"

"He shouldn't have touched you!"

Penny glanced nervously at the walls. I knew people in the rooms next door could probably hear me, but I didn't fucking care. What were they going to do…report me to the dean? I didn't work here anymore. And I could do whatever the fuck I wanted. Including killing Professor McCarty.

"No, he shouldn't have," Penny said. "But that doesn't mean you should kill him! He didn't even know that we were dating. I just want you to help me switch classes. I just don't want to see him. And I don't want to be expelled. I don't want you to hurt him. The last thing I want is for you to do something that'll get you in more trouble. I just don't know what to do."

I looked down at her left hand. "Marry me." The words just tumbled out of me. That predatory asshole hit on her because he didn't realize she was with me. And I wasn't going to let that happen again. Everyone needed to know that she belonged to me and only me.

"What?"

"Let's get married." I ran my hand through my hair. "And move somewhere where no one knows either one of us. We can start over together." *Please, Penny. I can't breathe here.*

"James, you just told my parents a few days ago that you weren't ready to get married. You just got divorced. This isn't what you really want. You're just upset."

"I don't want anyone else to touch you ever again. I don't want anyone else to flirt with you. I want everyone to know that you're mine."

"I am yours."

"Then marry me. We can go to Vegas right now."

"James, I can't just marry you. I want my parents to be there. I want my friends to be there. And what about your family? I haven't even gotten to meet any of them yet. I want them to be there too."

"I don't want a big wedding. I've already done that." *I just want you.*

"That's not what I said. I don't care about having a big wedding. I just want a few people besides us to be there." She was staring at me like I'd lost my mind.

And fuck, maybe I had. Or maybe I was finally seeing everything clearly. But this wasn't what she wanted. She was telling me no. *Breathe.* "So that's a definite no?" I put my hands on her knees.

"No. I want to marry you. Just not...today. This was hardly a romantic proposal, Professor Hunter."

I looked down at her left hand again. I ran my thumb along her ring finger. She needed a ring. As soon as possible. No other guy would ever touch her again. "Romance, got it. Next time I ask, you'll definitely say yes." I met her gaze and smiled. She probably didn't realize how serious I was about this. But I was damn serious.

"If you hadn't said we should go to Vegas right now I probably would have said yes."

Really? I pushed some of her hair behind her ear. "I wish I hadn't mentioned Vegas then." I smiled at her.

"Maybe we should just go somewhere that no one knows us, though," she said.

Yeah?

She wrapped her hands around the back of my neck. "I was prepared for other students being mean. I never expected my professors to..." she let her voice trail off.

"You won't be going back to his class. We can transfer you into a different one. Or you can withdraw from that too. I'll call Joe now."

"He's not going to let me do that. He's going to expel me."

"He's not going to expel you." I moved my hand to the side of her neck. "And if that creep wasn't on tenure, I'm sure I could get him fired."

LOVED

"But are you sure you even want to stay here?" she asked.

No. I wanted to be anywhere but here. "If this is where you want to be, then yes."

She pressed her lips together.

I want to be in New York City again. Let me take you there. But for some reason, I didn't say the words out loud. She'd already denied my proposal. I didn't want another no right now.

"Can you wait to call Joe?" she asked. "Maybe we can see how we feel on Monday?"

"Okay." I stared into her eyes that were still a little red. "Penny, I'm so sorry."

"You like to apologize when you've done nothing wrong."

I laughed. "I guess you're rubbing off on me."

My phone started buzzing in my pocket. *God, what now?* I kissed Penny's forehead before pulling my phone out of my pocket. "It's Rob," I said. "He's here early." When was he ever early? I figured he'd come on Sunday even though he said he was coming tonight. This couldn't be worse timing.

"We should probably go then," Penny said.

"Are you sure you're okay? Are you sure *we're* okay? I thought you might be mad at me."

She just stared at me.

"I can't believe I gave them the fuel they needed for the investigation. I never even thought about them searching my office. I can't believe how careless I was."

"Wait, what? What are you talking about?"

I lowered my eyebrows. "Joe didn't tell you?"

"Tell me what?"

"About the paper with the bad grade on it that I gave you? The one that you crumpled up and threw at me in my office. I kept it. It was in my desk. With the cute note you left me after we had sex."

"Oh." The recollection flashed across her face. "Why did you keep that?"

"I just...I didn't want to forget. I thought it was just going to be a one time thing. And it killed me that it had to be a one time thing. I thought it was the only thing I could hold on to."

She looked up into my eyes. "That's so sweet."

"And stupid."

"No, it's sweet. Wait, didn't they need a search warrant to go into your office?"

"I would have thought so too. But the university gave them permission. My office at the school is technically their property."

"So that's how the detectives knew?"

"I think it was easy to figure out what happened after seeing those two pieces of paper. Especially since the white out on the paper with your grade on it wasn't even well done." I frowned. "And if they did a black light test..."

"That's embarrassing."

I laughed. "Yeah, it is. But it all makes sense now. I think I know what happened with the other girls too. Did the detectives promise you anything if you cooperated with them?" I already knew the answer to that. Because I'd watched the whole thing. I still needed to tell Penny about the security cameras...

"Yes, they did. They said they could get my scholarship back."

"I think the detectives did something similar with the girls they interviewed. I think they told the girls they would get As in the class if they agreed with their story. I'm not sure if the detectives knew about the school's policy or not, or maybe they were just bluffing. But I think they pressured those girls into agreeing with the story that they told them. A story they inferred from your grade and the note you left in my office. All those girls had to do was say yes."

"That makes sense. The detectives told me what had happened with the other girls and were just trying to pressure me into agreeing it was the same way you seduced me. Those assholes. We have to tell the dean."

"I already told Joe that. He just wants this to disappear, Penny. And so do I. I don't want you to keep having days like this. I want it to get better, not worse."

"Are you sure we shouldn't..."

"I'm sure."

"I'm not mad at you for saving the note I left you. It's ridiculous that you think I'd be mad about that." She smiled up at me.

"So we're okay?"

"Yes." She kissed me and slid off the bed. "I love you so much, Professor Hunter."

God, I loved when she said my name like that.

She let her hand run down between the zipper of my hoodie. I'd been in too much of a hurry to grab a shirt earlier and I loved the way her fingers felt pressed against my skin.

I smiled. "Try to remember to call me James in front of my brother, please." Because Rob would definitely give me hell. I lightly slapped Penny's ass.

"I'll see what I can do. I'm so excited to meet him. Give me a second though, I'm sure I look like a hot mess."

"Just hot."

She laughed and walked over to the mirror on the wall. She wiped away the smudge marks from her mascara and added some more makeup that she definitely didn't need.

She turned back to me. "I'm kind of nervous."

Nervous around Rob? Definitely not necessary. "You don't have anything to be nervous about. He's going to love you." I wrapped my arms back around her. I wanted to be excited for this moment. This was the first time Penny was meeting anyone from my family. But I couldn't erase the image of Professor McCarty's hand on Penny's ass from my head. I knew she didn't want me to do anything. But…I'd never promised I wouldn't. Someone needed to teach that old prick a lesson.

"Are you sure you're okay?" I asked.

"I'm fine."

"James."

"I don't know what you want me to tell you. Of course I'm upset. I'm pissed. I won't feel better until I've punched him in the face."

"Please, please don't do that."

"Penny, he touched you."

"Can we please just focus on your brother visiting? Just forget about it for now. I don't want to think about it anymore. Let's just have a fun weekend."

"I'll try." It would be a fun weekend. Especially after I beat the shit out of a certain handsy professor.

Chapter 21

Friday

"What's Rob like?" Penny asked as I led her out of her dorm room.

What was the best way to describe my brother? "He's...fun."

"You mean like funny?"

"No, I wouldn't say funny." He'd been hilarious when we were kids. But after I'd married Isabella his jokes had become more annoying than funny. "He likes to have a good time. I invited him to stay with me when I didn't have you." And because he had nowhere else to go. "He's good at distracting me." I stared down at her as we walked outside. I didn't like talking about the time we weren't together. Going on a break with her had been a terrible mistake.

Penny laughed, but there was something else in her eyes. She looked...sad. She was probably remembering our time apart too. She hadn't fared much better than me.

She cleared her throat. "Is he like you at all?"

"Like me? He looks a little like me, I guess."

"Yeah, I've seen his picture. I mean, is he like you personality wise?"

Huh. That was a good question. I opened up the car door for her.

She climbed in and I walked over to the driver's side.

Was Rob like me? Even a little? Rob was fun and carefree and always smiling. He traveled all the time. He hadn't accomplished much of anything since graduating college. "No," I said as I climbed into the car and buckled my seatbelt. "He's not really like me at all. He's kind of the opposite of me." But I guess I did smile more now. Because of her.

"What do you mean?"

"He's not independent."

"What does that mean exactly?"

"He lives off my parents' money. He's never held a job for more than a few weeks." I pulled out of the parking lot.

"Oh. So is he close with your parents?"

Closer than I am, that's for sure. "It's funny. I felt like I was the only one of my siblings who ever listened to them. And they like me the least."

"I'm sure that isn't true."

No, it was true. My parents hated me for selling my company. For leaving Isabella. For living my life the way I wanted. Yet, Jen and Rob could do whatever they wanted and my parents didn't say a word.

"Do your parents know about me?" Penny asked. "Do they know about your divorce?"

"They know I filed for divorce. I told them about it before I did it. They tried to talk me out of it." My mother thought I was an idiot. Her exact words. And I thought she was an over-botoxed bitch. I was pretty sure I'd said those exact words to her face.

"And what about me?"

"I haven't talked to them since I left New York."

"They haven't tried to talk to you at all? That was almost a year ago."

I glanced at her for a second before turning my attention back to the road. "I didn't say that." My mother had reached out. A few times. She'd left voicemails about how divorcing Isabella would be the biggest mistake of my life. I'd deleted them instead of calling her back. My mother preferred when I was numb to the world. When she could control me. But I was done living my life that way.

"So they have tried to talk to you? And you haven't taken their calls or something? James, maybe..."

"Penny. It's better this way."

"I'll have to meet them eventually."

Unfortunately. "I know. How about you meet Rob first. Then you can decide if you want to meet the rest of my family." That was actually a terrible way to decide. Penny would love Rob. And she'd get the wrong impression and want to meet my parents too. My parents couldn't be more different than Rob though.

"I think Rob sounds great. Does he know about me?"

"No, actually. He doesn't even know that my divorce is final." I wanted to surprise him.

"So he thinks that it's just going to be two single rich bachelors in a college town? He's going to hate me."

I laughed. "He's not going to hate you."

"He probably thinks you're going to go out every night and pick up girls."

"I'm sure he wishes that's what we would be doing. But he knows I wouldn't have done that whether I had a girlfriend or not."

"Why wouldn't you if you were single? Wasn't that kind of the point of inviting Rob to live with you in the first place? To get over me?"

"I don't go to bars and pick up women. I like to practice self-control, Penny." It was weird being so open with her about my issues. But also...good. Yeah, it was good. But my hands were gripping the steering wheel a little tighter. I didn't like talking about my addiction problems with her. But I knew it was important. She needed to know every side of me. Even the bad.

"So what made you give in to temptation with me?"

That was an easier question. "You. I've never been so instantly attracted to someone in my life. You're different than other girls I've met. You chose option two."

She laughed. "Our day in New York was perfect. I'll always choose option two."

"I know. And I couldn't seem to control myself around you." I glanced at her again. "Not because I'm addicted to you." I'd been over and over that issue with Dr. Clark. And I wanted to believe that he was right about this.

"I don't care if you're addicted to me, you know. I'm addicted to you."

I pulled to a stop at a light. "That's different, Penny." It was cute when she said she was addicted to something. It was a lot more sinister when I said it.

"Is it that different?"

"When I'm low I feel like I can't breathe. Even when I indulge in whatever it is I'm addicted to. It's just an escape. But with you, I feel like I can finally breathe for the first time. You're not an escape. You're a new way of living that I didn't even know was possible." It was a fine line. A very fine line.

But she wasn't staring at me like she thought I was a monster.

I turned back toward the road. "Shit." I pulled the car to a stop outside my apartment building. The reporters were blocking the entrance to the parking garage. Penny had dealt with enough today. This whole thing was ridiculous. How long could they sit out here in their vans? The investigation was done. I was about to press on the horn when Penny unbuckled her seatbelt.

"Penny, stay in the car."

She opened the door, ignoring me.

"Damn it, Penny!" The last thing we needed was a scene. It just fueled them.

She slammed the car door.

Fuck. I put the car in park and flung open my door.

"What do you want to know?!" she yelled. "Why are you standing out here? Don't you have anything else to report on? This isn't news."

"Penny! How do you feel about the recent findings in the investigation?" One of the news reporters approached her, quickly followed by her cameraman. "Did you know that James was..."

"He wasn't. He hasn't done anything wrong. What is wrong with you people?"

I ran up to her and grabbed her arm. "Penny, get in the car now."

"Is that how this started?" the reporter asked. "Him telling you what to do? Did he force you..."

Fuck off. I put my hand in front of the video camera lens that was in our faces. "Penny," I said sternly. Why the hell was she engaging with these people?

"He didn't force me to do anything," Penny said. "Haven't any of you been in love? James is kind, and caring, and wonderful."

I stared down at her. I hadn't expected her to say that.

The reporter stepped closer. "He cheated on his wife in order to be with you."

"He didn't," Penny said. "Stop standing out here harassing us and go do your job. You're just spreading rumors. This isn't news!"

It was sweet of her to try to defend me. But I didn't mind taking the heat here. I wanted to. For her. "We don't have any other comments at this time," I said and stepped in front of her.

Penny climbed back into the car.

I knew why she was upset. Her fellow classmates were assholes. Girls were lying to get As. Joe was just accepting crappy detectives' theories in order to sweep this whole mess under the rug. And these reporters had chosen us to harass. It was ridiculous. But engaging with them just made everything worse. And for once in Penny's life, I just wanted her to listen to me. To let me handle this the way it needed to be handled.

I climbed back into the car, slammed the door, and laid my hand down on the horn. The reporters didn't back away so I just started slowing driving forward until they had to move.

What a fucking shit show. The investigation was done. They were probably getting ready to pack up and go on to the next thing. But after finally getting a word from Penny? They were going to stay even longer after that. My hands gripped the steering wheel even harder than they had when we were talking about my addiction problems. Really, why couldn't Penny just for once listen to my advice? I knew how to handle these people. I'd been in the limelight for years. You had to ignore them or they'd never stop.

I pulled into my parking spot and got out of the car. I needed a second to calm down. I couldn't protect Penny in her classes. And apparently I couldn't even protect her when she was right next to me. I was used to being in control of all aspects of my life. And I felt very out of control right now.

I heard her chasing after me as the elevator doors slid open.

I stepped on.

She hurried inside before the doors closed. "James, I'm sorry. But this needs to stop. They can't stay out there forever."

I shook my head and hit the emergency button on the elevator. The elevator came to an abrupt stop. "What the hell is wrong with you?" Wasn't today bad enough? Why make it a thousand times worse?

"It doesn't make any sense that they're out there. They're being relentless."

"And you just made it worse. I specifically asked you not to talk to them."

"James. Doesn't it make you mad? Why won't you defend yourself?"

"I know you've had a bad day. But I'm trying very hard to remain calm right now. I need to know that you'll listen to me when I ask you not to do something."

"If you won't defend yourself, I'll defend you. Everyone at this school already hates me. I don't care anymore."

"What you just did is going to make it worse. Not better. That's going to be all over the news tonight."

"Good. I want everyone to know that you're not a bad person. It sucks walking around campus hearing people say bad things about me. But I can deal with that. What I can't handle is people saying bad things about you."

"And I can't stand that you have to hear bad things about you. I'm used to getting my way. I don't know how to fix this. I never expected this to happen." I sighed and leaned against one of the walls in the elevator. *I never meant for any of this to happen.*

"I know. You're used to being in control. And I'm infuriating." She shrugged.

An exasperated laugh fell from my lips. "I can't think straight when I'm with you. I'm so unbelievably mad at you right now. But all I want to do is fuck you in this elevator."

Her throat made that adorable squeaking noise. "I'm sorry."

"I'm sorry too." I looked down for a second, took a deep breath, and then looked back up at her. We were supposed to be a team. And me yelling at her to listen to me didn't exactly scream team. She wanted me to talk to them. So...maybe I was the one that needed to give here. "If you think it will help, I'll talk to them. It might help around campus."

"Not if you're going to take all the blame."

She was impossible. I closed the distance between us in the elevator, pressing her back against the cold steel. "You really are infuriating." I leaned down and kissed her hard. I didn't like when she was mad at me. But I liked this. We'd always been really good at makeup sex. I could make love to Penny for hours. But sometimes I just really liked spanking her.

Her fingers slipped beneath the back of my hoodie and cascaded up my back.

I grabbed her hands and pushed them against the side of the elevator. "There are cameras in here." I stared at her face. It was the first time I'd ever mentioned the cameras. But she didn't look like she had any intention of backing down.

Instead her eyes darted to my lips.

Holy hell, Penny. I knew the cameras would turn her on. *So fucking kinky.* I'd give anything to turn her around right now and teach her a lesson about defying me, but...

"Rob is waiting for us upstairs," I said. "I had the front desk let him up." Actually Ian would have let him up. But that was a whole other discussion.

"Okay."

"To be continued?" I ran the tip of my nose down the length of hers.

"I kind of wish Rob hadn't come early."

I laughed and let go of her hands. *That makes two of us.* I stared down at her rosy cheeks. "Your face is flushed." I rubbed my hand along her cheek.

"No kidding."

I smiled. Making her incredibly horny before meeting my brother was kind of an odd choice. But I loved her just like this. "Ready to meet my little brother?"

"Absolutely."

I hit the emergency button again.

Penny pressed her thighs together and leaned against the side of the elevator.

The doors of the elevator slowly opened.

"Finally, man!" Rob's voice sounded from the kitchen.

I walked into the kitchen. Rob was sitting at the island eating straight out of a pizza box. It had been a while since I'd seen him. He looked tanner and his hair was shaggy and in need of a cut. I guess that's what happened when you were on a perpetual vacation.

He tossed a piece of crust back in the box and walked over to me. Instead of hugging me like a normal person would, Rob wrapped his arms around me and lifted me slightly off the floor. What was he doing? I was still taller than him.

"It's so good to see you!" he said really loudly, like we were outside.

Why was he yelling? And why hadn't he let me go yet?

I heard Penny laugh.

I smiled. Rob's good mood had always been contagious.

Rob set me back down and leaned in close. "Dude, is this seriously Ellen? You didn't tell me she was super hot. Please tell me you're tapping that?"

He knew this wasn't Ellen. He knew Ellen. He loved Ellen. What kind of game was he playing? And why had he said that so loudly?

Penny's face turned even more red.

"No." I said. "That's not Ellen." *Which you damn well know, you crazy person.* "That's..."

"Shit, are you serious? I get my own housekeeper? I should have come here ages ago." He patted me on the chest and walked over to Penny.

What the fuck is he doing right now?

"I'm Rob." He put his hand out for Penny to shake.

"Penny." She looked confused but also ready to burst out laughing again.

"So tell me about yourself, Penny." Rob leaned against the counter and locked eyes with her.

Great, now he's actually hitting on her.

"For starters, I'm not a housekeeper," she said.

His smile got even bigger and he looked over his shoulder at me. "I knew it! You're the best brother ever." He winked at me.

Oh. He... I laughed. *Well, fuck.* I'd told him I had a surprise for him when he visited. And I guess *this* was the surprise he'd wanted. He just assumed we were on the same page. He was playing along with it, flirting like always. Pretending to be surprised. Sliding in smooth compliments, the way *I'd* taught him.

Rob winked at me again.

Yup, he definitely thought Penny was a prostitute.

Chapter 22

Friday

It honestly wasn't that big of a leap to think that Penny was a high-end prostitute, because she was fucking gorgeous. I mean…she'd be a great surprise for him if she wasn't *mine*. It was a hilarious mix-up. One that could be kind of fun to go along with…

Rob winked at me again.

Nope. I needed to put an end to it before my brother kissed my girlfriend. "Jesus, stop talking, Rob." I walked over and wrapped my arm around Penny's shoulders.

"So…" Rob looked back and forth between us. "You are fucking then?"

"No, Rob. Or, well, yes actually." I smiled at the flush crossing Penny's cheeks. "This is my girlfriend." I squeezed her shoulder.

"Wait, what?" Rob looked back and forth between us. "What about the troll?"

"We're divorced." God that felt good to say.

"Seriously?!"

I don't think I'd ever seen Rob look so excited. Well, except for when he was playing a prank on someone.

"I didn't really think you had the balls to cut that cord."

I laughed. *Yeah, me too.* Apparently I just needed to sober up to grow a pair.

"Okay, wow. So, we should probably start over," Rob said to Penny.

"Yeah." Penny smiled and stuck her hand back out to Rob. "Let's just pretend that didn't happen."

Rob laughed. "No, actually that's a great story. I can't wait to tell people I thought my brother's new girlfriend was a prostitute. And it's a compliment really. You're hot. I'm sure you get that all the time."

Her cheeks flushed even more. "Only recently."

I tightened my grip on her shoulder. Rob was an incorrigible flirt, I knew that. But I wasn't loving him flirting with Penny. What was he doing? I hadn't liked anyone in a really long time. And I couldn't remember if he'd always flirted with girls I'd liked or if this was a new annoying trait he'd developed overseas.

Rob laughed again. "She's funny. And young." He looked her up and down. "You look really young. How old are you?"

Oh screw me. He was going to give me so much shit about this. I'd been so adamant about the fact that I hadn't started teaching to hook up with hot students.

"Twenty," Penny said.

Rob stared at her for a second and then looked back at me.

I shrugged. What else could I do? It wasn't like I was going to be able to keep it a secret from him that Penny was my student.

"Oh shit! Don't even say it. She's your student, isn't she? Oh my God, this is golden. The perfect son is fucking one of his students? I love it. Do Mom and Dad know?"

"Okay, we need to talk for a second," I said and let go of Penny's shoulder. I walked toward the living room, grabbing Rob's arm on the way.

"Does he get mad at you a lot too?" Rob yelled over his shoulder. "I bet that makes things exciting in bed."

"Shut up," I said and pulled him out of earshot of Penny.

"I'm so confused. I thought you weren't going to hook up with any of your sexy students."

"I didn't plan to. And I met her before classes started."

"You've talked to me since classes started." He gave me a very stern look. Which was just funny because he was never stern.

"Trust me, when she showed up in one of my classes, I tried to be on my best behavior."

"And clearly failed."

Yeah, I had nothing to say to that.

"You told me you had a surprise for me, though," Rob said. "Where is it?"

"Penny was the surprise."

"But Penny's not a prostitute. So...that's hardly a surprise for *me*."

I laughed. "I thought you'd be happy for me."

"I'd be happier if I was getting head from a prostitute right now."

"Fair. By the way, Ellen's going to be annoyed that you pretended you didn't know who she was."

Rob laughed. "Ellen would never be mad at me. I'm her favorite."

"Her favorite what? You can't be her favorite. She's my employee."

"Her favorite Hunter brother."

"You're ridiculous." But I couldn't stop smiling.

"You missed me."

I nodded. "I did."

Rob rubbed his hands together. "So does this mean you're not going to be upset if I hook up with a hot student too? Because I was definitely planning on doing that. Wait, how does the school feel about your relationship with Penny?"

"Not great. Isabella broke the story before I could talk to the dean. Did you see all those news vans out there? Some of my other female students claimed I hit on them too after the story broke. Just so they could get As. It's all such a mess. I had to resign."

"Shit, really? I'm sorry, man. I know you really liked this job."

I shrugged. "I like her more."

"Yeah, no wonder." He tried to peer around my shoulder to check Penny out so I hit him in the back of the head.

"Ow." He rubbed his head. "What was that for?"

"You know what it's for. Why are you flirting with her?"

"I always flirt with whoever you're dating. It's my thing."

Was it though? "You never flirted with Isabella."

He pretended to throw up. "Clarification. I flirt with your *hot* girlfriends. And Isabella is a troll. But Penny's gorgeous. High-five, man." He lifted his hand.

I couldn't *not* high-five him. I felt like I'd won the lottery with Penny.

Rob stared at me. "It's weird." He cocked his head to the side.

"What's weird?" *Stop looking at me like that.*

"I almost forgot what you looked like when you smiled."

I swallowed hard. *Yeah. Me too.* I looked back over at Penny. She was taking a huge bite of pizza. And something about it made me laugh.

"You've got it bad," Rob said.

"Yeah. I really do." I turned back to him. "Did Ian tell you anything when he let you in?"

"Nope. He asked me a lot of questions about Jen though. Is there something going on between them?"

"I don't think so." Honestly I had no idea though. And I wanted to talk more about that. But there were more pressing matters. "Penny doesn't know about Ian. Or any of the cameras installed around the apartment." *Except the one in the elevator now.* And I was pretty sure she'd assumed that had been installed by the building manager, not me. "So please don't mention anything about it to her."

"You have cameras all over the apartment? Okay, psycho."

"It's a security system."

"Sure it is."

"It is," I said.

"So you don't rewatch footage of the two of you hooking up on the couch?" He gestured to the couch we were standing next to.

"No."

"You're lying," Rob said.

"I'm not lying."

"Yes you are. I know all your tells. That's why I always beat you at poker."

"You don't always beat me at poker."

"I do. And you film Penny and jerk off to the footage. Fucking amazing. Can I see it?"

What the fuck? He was as bad as Ian. "No you can't see it."

"Fine. I'll keep your dirty little secret footage and bodyguard a secret and I'll keep flirting with Penny. Deal? Deal." He patted my chest.

Wow. That was not the deal at all. "No deal. Stop flirting with her. And stop being so brazen, man."

"Eh. We'll see what happens. I don't really believe in filters."

Of course he didn't. "Just be on your best behavior."

"I don't even know what that is," he said with a laugh. He slapped my back and started walking back into the kitchen.

I had no idea if he was going to stop flirting with Penny or not. But at least he'd give me time to tell Penny about the cameras and Ian. She'd been really turned on by the ones in the elevator. She wasn't going to care. But it was still better to tell her myself. I followed Rob back into the kitchen.

"Ugh, I have to share my pizza with her too? This is the worst." Rob laughed and sat down next to Penny. "Just kidding. Have all the pizza that you want. James caught me up on the whole illicit student professor affair thing. So apparently now I won't say anything that will embarrass him. And I'm sorry that I thought you were a prostitute."

"It's fine," Penny said with a laugh.

"Thanks for helping get the troll back under her bridge. I owe you one. I tried to get rid of her for years. But I just made fun of her all the time. She was so stuck up. She always had the craziest reactions to stuff. If I had mistaken her for a hooker, I'm pretty sure she would have had a heart attack. I always thought I'd be the one to make her run screaming. I'm sure sucking her husband's cock made it easier for you to be victorious, though."

"What did we just talk about?" I said.

"Dude, chill. I'm sure Penny and I are on the same page here."

Penny started laughing.

"See, she thinks I'm funny." He grabbed another slice of pizza. "So what do you two usually do on a Friday night?"

"Last Friday night we went to a Halloween party," Penny said. "And James ended up punching one of my friends in the face."

I pressed my lips together. Penny told it like it was a fun story. But it absolutely was not. *Fucking Tyler.*

Rob laughed. "Sounds fun. I bet we could find a good Halloween party to go to tonight."

"Or we can stay in," I said. "Penny and I have been practicing what it would be like if we were under house arrest."

"That sounds awful. Did you say you were only 20, Penny?"

"Yeah."

"So a bar is out. Crashing a college party it is." He rubbed his hands together.

"I think it's probably best if I stay away from college parties for a while," I said. For Joe's sake. I was already making his job hard enough.

"Oh, because of the whole rapey thing?"

What the fuck? "I need to go shower. Maybe you can give him a tour, Penny?" I wouldn't have wanted to leave Rob alone with her, but I was still dirty from my workout. Besides, if Rob actually did anything terrible, Ian was watching. And Penny giving Rob a tour meant they'd stumble upon the pool room where we'd left our clothes scattered all over last night. That would scream that Penny was off-limits.

"Sure," Penny said.

"And stop saying inappropriate stuff to my girlfriend, Rob."

Rob shrugged. "I don't think I've even said anything that inappropriate."

Seriously? I kissed Penny's cheek and at the same time I shoved Rob's shoulder.

Rob laughed as I walked into the bedroom.

Part of me wanted to hop onto my phone and watch the security feed to see what they were talking about. But Ian would tell me if something weird happened. And I was trying to be better. I took a deep breath and forced myself to step into the shower.

***

I ran my fingers through my wet hair as I followed Rob and Penny's voices. They were chatting by the pool table. I glanced down at the clothes on the ground that Penny and I had left there last night and smiled. "Oops," I said and wrapped my arms around Penny.

She looked up at me and laughed.

"Your girlfriend and I had lots of fun while you were in the shower," Rob said.

"What was so much fun?" I asked.

"Well, let's see. All sorts of stuff. I think we really hit it off. Especially after I gave her a proper spanking. Oh, and here's your girlfriend's bra back." Rob pulled Penny's bra out from behind the bar and tossed it at me.

I lowered my eyebrows. *I really wish I'd been watching the video footage.* I knew all of that was bullshit. But Penny had probably told him she liked being spanked. And I didn't love them talking about stuff like that together. "I guess you decided to keep being inappropriate?"

"Absolutely. Besides, if I recall correctly, you've stolen a few girlfriends from me."

Had I?

He gave me a hard stare.

I honestly didn't remember. I shrugged. "That was a long time ago. And you weren't in love with them."

"Love? Really?" asked Rob. "I just assumed it was about the great sex. I thought that was all you really cared about?"

My whole body seemed to stiffen. Penny knew about my addiction problems, but it never made talking about stuff like this any easier. "That was also a long time ago."

"So Penny's bad in bed? I find that very hard to believe."

I laughed. "No. I'd be lying if I said that wasn't part of the reason I fell in love with her."

"James." Penny lightly pushed on my chest.

"What, it's true." I put my lips up to her ear. "You're also amazing on the pool table."

Her cheeks flushed again. "You guys are super immature."

"Said the hot 20-year-old." Rob put down his empty beer bottle. "Okay, come on, James. I need to get laid before I steal your girlfriend."

"I'd really rather stay in," I said.

"You're my wingman."

"You two should go." Penny smiled up at me. "You'll have fun."

"Yeah, I don't know." I stared down at her. I mean, yes Rob and I would have fun. But I didn't want to leave Penny here all alone. She'd just been crying because of her pervy professor and snapping at reporters. It hadn't exactly been a good day.

"Really. Just don't be super sleazy like your brother," Penny said.

"Hey!" said Rob. "I'm not sleazy. Horny, yes. Sleazy, no. I'll take care of your boyfriend. I won't let him do anything stupid."

"See," Penny said. "You're in good hands."

I wasn't sure that was true. But...she looked like she actually wanted me to go. And it had been forever since I'd caught up with Rob. We had a lot more to talk about. "If you're sure you're okay."

"I'm fine. You got me that huge T.V. I think I'll be plenty entertained."

"Awesome. Let's go," Rob said and walked past us.

As soon as Rob was out of the room, I leaned down and kissed Penny. She immediately melted into me.

What was I doing? She needed me right now. "I want to stay with you," I whispered against her lips.

"Yeah, me too. But I think maybe a night out with Rob will be good for you."

"I'm sorry that he's so...well, inappropriate."

"I think he's great. I mean, yes, super inappropriate. But I think he's just trying to be funny. I hope. I don't know, I like him. He's nice."

"Nice isn't exactly the word I'd use for him."

Penny shrugged. "So you're all about sex, huh?"

I ran my hand through my hair. "No. I mean, I told you about my past."

"Does Rob know about everything? He won't let you go...overboard?"

"Yeah, he knows." He'd been with me during a lot of my lowest lows. And it was one of the reasons why I'd invited him to stay while Penny and I were on a break. I'd needed him.

"So you're in good hands."

"I guess." I smiled down at her. "If he's ever bothering you, just let me know. He's all talk. He's harmless."

"He's fine. I'm getting used to taking care of myself."

I frowned. What did she mean by that? I was here to defend her. Always.

"I just mean I'm getting thicker skin. I didn't mean because you aren't taking care of me."

"Okay." But her words twisted around in my head. I tucked a loose strand of hair behind her ear. I needed to step up my game. "Tomorrow I'd like to go shopping for some stuff that will make our apartment more comfortable. Whatever you want. I want you to feel at home here."

"That sounds perfect."

I leaned down and kissed her again. "Try not to fight with the press while I'm gone."

"I'll be on my best behavior," she said with a smile.

"Me too. Text me if you need anything." I gave her one last kiss before pulling away from her.

"I will." She picked her pants up off the floor and folded them.

I smiled at her on my way out the door. But as soon as I was out of her line of sight, my smile dropped. I knew I'd told her I would be on my best behavior. But that was definitely a lie.

Penny said she'd gotten a thicker skin, but I didn't want her to need that. I was here to protect her now. And I knew exactly what I was going to do. Exactly what she'd asked me not to do. I was going to beat the shit out of Professor McCarty. No one touched my girl without consequences.

Chapter 23

Friday

"So you're really divorced?" Rob asked.

I nodded. "It's official. She finally signed the papers."

"Here's to the troll going back into her cave where she belongs." He tapped his beer against mine.

"Here's to that." I took a sip of my beer.

"So why exactly aren't we in that bar that we passed on Main Street?"

"I'm trying to keep a low profile." I wasn't happy about the way Joe had handled everything. But it didn't mean I wanted to give him more hell than he'd already gotten over this.

"Why? You've already been sacked."

"Technically I resigned. But you saw all the news vans. Everyone wants some salacious story, and I don't want to give it to them."

"Then you probably shouldn't have slept with a student," Rob said with a laugh. "But this bar is lame. There's literally a student reading in the corner."

I looked over to where he was pointing. There was a girl with brown hair staring at a textbook on the table. She was surrounded by her friends that were talking and laughing. I couldn't see her face, but she was completely immersed in whatever she was reading. I actually don't think I'd ever seen a student look that into a textbook before.

Another girl had just run over to her table, sliding into the booth next to the girl with brown hair. "Daphne!" she yelled and slammed the girl's book shut.

"Ah, shit," I said under my breath.

"What?" Rob asked.

"That girl that just sat down. She's the one I almost had to get a restraining order against." What were the odds that Kristen would come to *this* bar? Part of the reason I'd skipped the one on Main Street was to avoid her. "We have to go, unless you want to meet my stalker." I drained the rest of my beer.

"The one with the book?" Rob asked.

"No, the one that just sat down next to her."

Rob didn't say anything, but he stayed seated as I stood up.

"Come on, there's another bar down the street." Yes, I knew where every bar was in a five-mile radius from apartment. Because I had fucking issues. But my biggest issue right now was Kristen being at this bar. I didn't want her to see me. I really shouldn't have left the apartment.

Still Rob didn't move.

"Rob." I grabbed his arm and pulled him off the stool.

"Sorry," he said and looked over his shoulder once more at the table.

"Don't tell me you have the hots for my stalker," I said as I led him out of the bar.

"No." He didn't offer anything else. And he suddenly seemed...quiet. Which was something I wasn't used to him being.

"Well you could have fooled me," I said as we walked back outside.

"Did you see that girl reading?" he asked.

"The one you were just making fun of?"

"What? I wasn't making fun of her."

I just stared at him. "You said the bar was lame be-cause she was reading."

"That was before I got a good look at her. She was fucking gorgeous."

I'd never seen him look more serious.

"I think we should go back and you can wingman…"

"Definitely not. She's clearly friends with my stalker. I can't wingman in that mess."

"Yeah. Right." He looked over his shoulder again.

"You're acting weird."

He tried to laugh it off. "Sorry. It's just been a while since I've gotten laid by an American girl." But he looked over his shoulder again like he only wanted one American girl in particular.

At least he'd gotten his mind off of hitting on Penny. I opened the door to the next bar. We sat down and ordered some stronger drinks.

"So tell me everything I need to know about your new girlfriend," Rob said. "You said you met before classes started?"

A few girls started whispering down the bar from us, but I ignored them. I figured some people would recognize me. At least none of them were my stalker.

"We bumped into each other at a coffee shop on Main Street. Literally. I hit her with the door as I was walking in and she spilled her coffee all down the front of her shirt and then she fell into my arms." I smiled, remembering the feeling of touching her for the first time.

"And then you fucked?"

"What?" I laughed. "No. Nothing happened. I noticed she had a backpack. There were tons of students in the coffee shop. I just tried to forget I ever met her." *A miserable attempt.*

"Okay…"

"But then she showed up in my class the next day."

Rob smiled.

"We tiptoed around the line. Subtly flirting I class. And the way she looked at me..." I shook my head. "I couldn't get her out of my head."

"Yeah, I know how you get."

I finished my drink. He didn't need to elaborate. We both knew what he was talking about. "I really like her, man."

"I can tell."

"No, I mean...I *really* like her. I love her. I think I'm going to propose to her."

Rob laughed.

"I'm serious." I already had. But I'd made a mess of it. Penny deserved more than me just begging her in her dorm room while I was pissed off about another man touching her.

He finally stopped laughing. "James, you *just* got out of one marriage."

"A sham of a marriage. I could barely tolerate Isabella. It's been a really long time since I've felt like this about someone." For just a second I thought about high school, but I shook the thought away. "No, it's the *only* time I've ever felt this way. I know Penny's young. But I've never been more sure about something. I need everyone to know that she's mine."

A smile slowly spread across Rob's face as he stared at me. "Okay. How are we gonna do it?" He waved the bartender over for another round.

"You're not going to do anything. All you're going to do is stop flirting with her."

"Well that doesn't sound fun. How about this. I keep flirting with her. And I carve a hole in the ceiling of your bedroom and put..."

"No."

"But you didn't let me finish. We could put rose petals…"

"Absolutely not." I'd tried my best to stay out of Rob's pranks since high school. He tended to go way too far. And this sounded more like a prank than a proposal. Penny wanted something romantic, but that didn't mean over the top. I smiled to myself. I actually couldn't believe I was sitting here thinking about this right now. When a year ago I'd been thinking about ending my life.

"Well, what's your idea?" Rob asked.

"I haven't decided yet. But maybe I should propose where we first met. Because my life changed the moment I met her."

"That is the sappiest thing I've ever heard. I love it. Tell her exactly that. And I'll cut a hole in the floor and…"

"No. Definitely not."

"Boo." He finished his drink. "We need a picture. To remember this day. When we planned your proposal."

"When I planned my proposal which you're not a part of."

"Nah, what I said." He grabbed my phone from me and took a selfie of us. At the last second, he flipped the middle finger at the camera, and then he texted the picture to Penny.

"What the hell was that?" I asked with a laugh. "Why did you send her that?"

"To keep her on her toes. I gave her the finger so she won't expect what we're planning. It's the perfect plan within the plan."

"The plan within the plan." I nodded. "Oh, before I forget, we're invited to New York to catch up with Matt and Mason. Mason sent a fancy invitation and everything."

"To his sex club?"

"No, not to a sex club. It's just a bar."

"Boo," Rob said again as we finished our next round of drinks. "But yeah, I'm in. It's been forever since I've seen either of them."

"I know. It'll be good to catch up. Speaking of which...how was Costa Rica?"

"The prison part wasn't my favorite. But the rest was great. We gotta go there together sometime. Oh! Maybe for your bachelor party. Dude, we need to be celebrating right now!" Rob ordered another round of drinks and this time we cheered to proposals.

Shit, how many drinks was that? I'd been so good recently. I smiled to myself. But tonight wasn't about being good. And I felt in total control of what I was doing right now. "Wait. We need another plan."

"A second plan?"

"I need to beat the shit out of someone."

"Tell me more." He put his elbow on the bar top and placed his chin in his hand.

I couldn't help but laugh. "This sick professor made a pass at Penny today."

"What's he sick with? Is he dying or something?"

"No," I said with a laugh. He wasn't dead. *Yet.* "I just meant he's gross. He's all old and shit and a total perve. I can't believe he touched her."

"Oh, well if he's not sick, let's beat the shit out of him. I just would have felt weird about it if he was really sick, you know?"

"Yeah." I probably wouldn't have wanted to beat his face in if he was dying either. Even if he did deserve it.

"Here's to pervy professors," Rob said.

I tapped my glass against his.

He laughed. "We basically toasted to you there. Because you slept with one of your students."

"Penny's only seven years younger than me."

"So when you were seventeen she was ten, bro. That's sick."

"But I'm not seventeen and she's not ten, bro," I said back.

He laughed. "Shall we?"

"Shall we what?"

"Aren't we going to go beat up that ill professor?"

"He's not ill. But yes. Let's go do that." I wasn't sure what Dr. Clark would think of what I was about to do tonight. He probably wouldn't approve. And I knew for sure that Penny wouldn't approve because she'd told me explicitly not to do this. But sometimes I was right. And she needed to let me handle something for once.

"Do you know where he lives?"

"No. But Ian can tell us. One sec." I called Ian. He answered in one ring.

"Where are you right now?" Ian asked. "You forgot to clear your schedule with me again."

"Sorry, boss," I said.

Ian laughed. "Are you drunk?"

"No. I'm with Rob."

"So you are drunk?"

"Maybe?" *A little.* I'd definitely been drunker. "I need you to find the address of Professor McCarty for me."

There was a long pause. "Why?"

"He made a pass at Penny. And Rob and I are going to go pay him a visit."

"Do you really think that's a good idea?"

"No," I said. "I think it's a *great* idea. Someone needs to teach that asshole a lesson."

Ian laughed. "How about I come get you? And the three of us can go together."

Huh. Three was better than two. "Done." I gave him the name of the bar we were at and hung up. "Ian's going to help too."

"Fantastic," Rob said. "Wait. Or is he just going to try and talk us out of it?"

"Nah, he seemed into it. He likes Penny."

"But you haven't let the two of them meet."

"But he watches. He knows her."

Rob shook his head. "That's really fucking weird, man. How do you think Penny's going to react when she finds out about all that?"

"She's real kinky. I think she's going to be into it."

Rob whistled. "I figured she would be. She had that look, you know? And I mean…she did sleep with her professor."

"Yeah she did." I high-fived him.

"Maybe after we go beat up this professor we can go back to that first bar."

"I don't think so."

He groaned. "But I need to talk to that bookworm. All this talk about kinky girls has me all revved up. And you know that girls who read are the kinkiest ones."

I laughed.

"What? It's true."

"I was just thinking about that time in college when you and Matt visited for the weekend. And you made us go to a library to hit on girls instead of the awesome party the Griffin Club was throwing."

"In my defense, the girl at the library did know about that party. And also in my defense…you didn't tell me the party would be fun. Or that it was tops optional."

"It was a fun time."

Rob smiled. "One of the best."

Well, until it wasn't. But it was a lot more fun not to think about the bad times.

"So what exactly are the two of you planning?" Ian asked and slid into the bar stool next to mine.

"There's this really sick professor we're going to beat up," Rob said.

"Wait, he's sick?" Ian looked at me.

"In the head. He's not actually ill."

"Oh. Okay," Ian said. "So your plan it to go to his house at…" he glanced at his watch "…almost midnight and beat him up?"

"Yup," Rob said.

"What if he's sleeping?" Ian asked.

"Then we'll break through his window and then break his nose."

"And what if there's an alarm and the cops show up?"

"We'll beat them up too," Rob said.

"Solid plan," said Ian.

"Right?" Rob smiled.

"No, Rob. I was joking. You're going to get arrested. You're both lucky I'm here." Ian slid back off his stool.

Rob and I both stared at him.

"Aren't you coming?" he asked. "We have a professor to beat up."

"You're not going to talk us out of it?" Rob asked.

"My job is to protect James. That extends to Penny now. And no one messes with her."

I stood up and clapped him on the back. "Told you he liked her," I said to Rob.

"Oh I bet he does," Rob said. "Ian, where exactly can I see this super hot footage that James has been talking about?"

"He deleted it," I said.

"Yeah." Ian nodded. "I deleted it."

Well, that didn't sound sincere. Now I was a little concerned that Ian hadn't deleted the footage.

Rob looked back and forth between us. "You're both so full of shit. Luckily I have the rest of the night to convince Ian to give me whatever hard drive all those video files are on. I wasn't allowed to flirt with that beautiful bookworm, so you owe me."

I definitely did not owe him. And especially not that. We were about to go beat someone up for touching Penny. Did he seriously think I was about to let him watch her? That was basically the same thing.

We all climbed into Ian's new Tesla.

"And you thought my plan was bad?" Rob said and slammed the door closed. "This car is very conspicuous."

The plan probably was bad. And the car definitely stood out. But there was no way anyone was talking me out of defending Penny.

Chapter 24

Friday

"What about a bomb?" Rob said from the back seat as Ian drove us toward Professor McCarty's house.

"No," Ian said firmly and hit his turn signal.

"Boo, you whore."

"Did you just call me a whore?"

"If the shoe fits."

Ian laughed. "Think smaller."

"You're a teensy little baby whore."

"Wow. No. I meant about the bomb. Why are you being so mean?"

"Because you won't show me the footage of Penny!"

"Not happening," I said.

"Gah!"

"Just come up with a smaller prank," Ian said. "And I'll go along with it. I'm the only one that's not drunk so I have to give the okay."

"Fine. I'm thinking smaller. So…dynamite?"

Ian shook his head. "Smaller."

"A candle?"

"Let's forget about lighting anything on fire," I said. "I just want to kick his ass."

"No, we have to pull something epic." Rob poked his head through the gap in the front seats. "What if we get a chainsaw and…"

"We're not cutting anyone into pieces," Ian said. "Smaller, Rob."

"Ian always ruins all my fun. Can't we do this without him?"

"Ian's the only one sober enough to drive," I said. "Besides, he's great at secret missions. What do you think we should do, Ian?"

"I don't know. Something nondestructive that won't get us arrested."

"Here's the plan," Rob said. "We break into his house and fill his washing machine with way too much detergent so the bubbles…"

"Or we could not break in," Ian said. "Let's just toilet paper his house or something."

Rob nodded. "A classic. I like it. But maybe we can still break in after. Oh and back to the bomb thing…"

"No fires," Ian said.

"You didn't let me finish. If we put some dynamite in his pipes they'll explode. And then when the bubbles unleash from the washing machine they'll just keep growing and growing. He won't be able to see a damn thing. And the bubbles will get into his mouth. Which is good. Because he should wash his mouth out after being an ass and hitting on Penny."

"I kinda like that," I said.

Ian glanced at me for a second. "You want to put dynamite in the man's pipes? Where do you two even think you'd be able to get dynamite?"

"The grocery store?" Rob asked.

Ian laughed.

"What's funny?"

"Wow. When was the last time either of you went grocery shopping?"

I shrugged. "You know Ellen does that for me."

"Rich people," Ian said with a shake of his head. "You know what? If they have dynamite at the grocery store, I'll let you get it. This will be very entertaining for me."

"Score!" Rob lifted his hand for me.

I high-fived him and pulled up the directions to the closest grocery store that was still open. We pulled into the parking lot a few minutes later.

"Okay, so what do we need?" Rob asked. "Definitely a whole cart of laundry detergent. And toilet paper for Ian's lame plan." He grabbed a cart and climbed into it.

"Why are you getting into the cart?" Ian said. "You're not a baby."

"I want to rest my legs in case we have to run from the cops later."

Ian shook his head as I started pushing Rob into the grocery store. Tonight felt like I was in college again. And I couldn't wipe the smile off my face. I was still really upset about that pervy professor. But that didn't mean this couldn't be fun.

"Kind sir," Rob said and leaned out the side of the cart, almost knocking it over. "Where do you keep the dynamite?"

The guy just gave us a weird look and kept walking.

"He doesn't work here," Ian said.

"How do you know? He looks like a grocery store person to me."

"What does that even mean?"

"He had a vest on."

"Not with the store logo. It was just a normal vest."

Rob shrugged. "I don't know. I'm not a vest man myself. Hey you!" he yelled at someone else that wasn't an employee. "Do you have any firecrackers?"

Ian stepped in front of the cart. "Before you harass anyone else, I'm just going to cut to the chase. They don't sell dynamite or firecrackers in grocery stores. And I'm shocked that neither of you knew that. Just because you're rich doesn't mean you shouldn't know that grocery stores are for *groceries*. Think smaller, Rob."

"I have it!" Rob stood up in the cart. "Flaming poo."

I laughed.

Ian groaned.

"We have to," I said. "McCarty is a piece of shit."

"Yeah he is!" Rob yelled. "To the lighter aisle!"

I started running, pushing the cart and Rob toward a random aisle. Because I'd never been in this fucking store before. Which reminded me… "Rob," I said and took a sharp left turn, almost making him fly out and hit a shelf. "I have to take you to the dollar store."

"What is a dollar store?"

"A store where everything costs a dollar. It's crazy." We turned down another aisle.

"You're lying. That doesn't exist."

"I swear it's a thing. I found a piggy bank there. And a million other things. We'll go there after we light McCarty on fire."

"We're not lighting anything on fire!" Ian yelled after us. "Both of you stop it."

"Never!" yelled Rob at the top of his lungs.

***

We pulled to a stop a few houses down from the piece of shit.

"Who's going to poop in the grocery bag?" Rob asked.

"I don't have to go," Ian and I both said at the same time.

"Liars. You do it, Ian." Rob pulled the lighter out of the paper bag and then threw the empty bag at Ian.

"I seriously don't have to go." He pushed the bag back into Rob's hands.

"Well, fuck," Rob said. "I don't have to go either. We need tacos."

"Ground beef doesn't exactly look or smell like shit," I said.

"I know that! But they always go right through me. Hit the drive-thru, Ian."

"But we're already here…"

"Drive-thru, Ian! Stat! One of us needs to shit in this bag or I refuse to get out of the car."

Ian glanced at me. "It might be best if he stays in the car anyway."

"What?" Rob slapped the back of his head. "No man left behind. Drive-thru then we circle back and follow through with the plan."

I nodded my head.

"We're going to get arrested," Ian said and pulled away from the curb again. "And I call dibs on Ellen for my one call."

"It's fine, Penny will bail us out. Right, James? Because I can't go to prison again." He shuddered. "And we are doing this for her."

I wasn't so sure about that. Yes, I wanted to stand up for her. But I also just really wanted to kill McCarty.

*　*　*

"Don't look at me!" Rob yelled from the back seat.

"Do you really have to do that *in* my new car?" Ian asked.

"Do you want me to do it on the street? You said you *didn't* want to be arrested, smart ass."

"And you'd think you'd be able to shit better in public after being in Costa Rican prison."

I snickered.

"Just don't look at me. I'm a sensitive shitter." He groaned. "Fuck, it's still not coming. Taco me again." He put his hand up to the front.

I handed him yet another taco from the to-go bag. "Are you sure you want another one? You've already had five."

"I'm sacrificing my body for the sake of a perfect prank. Oh it's coming!"

Ian pretended to vomit and rolled down the windows.

"Luckily we bought all that toilet paper. Smart move, Ian." He grabbed a roll out of the packaging.

"Mhm," Ian said and stuck his head out the window.

"Should have bought wet wipes though. It's a little messy back here."

"I swear to God if you get it on my seats you have to pay for it to be detailed."

"Yeah, whatever, James will pay for it. But I'm done and I don't think it splooged out of the bag or anything. But the bag is a straight mess. The perfect consistency to really squish under a bare foot."

Ian gagged.

"McCarty is going to be smelling like my shit for days. High-five!" He put his hand through the seats.

"Nope," I said. I didn't want shit on my hand. "But thank you for doing it."

"Any time, man." He burped. "We might end up with two bags…"

"No, everyone out of the car," Ian said.

We all climbed out and grabbed as many rolls of toilet paper and laundry detergent as we could carry.

"I still don't think we should break into his house," Ian said.

"We gotta stick to the plan." Rob dropped everything in his hands onto the front lawn and tiptoed up to the window. He peered inside. "Oh. My. God. Jackpot."

"What?" I asked and walked over to the window too.

"He has a daughter." He pointed inside.

It was pretty dark inside, but the room had some spot-lighting over a framed family portrait. It looked like McCarty had a daughter about Penny's age. And that just made what he'd done a thousand times worse.

"She's pretty," Ian said.

Rob shrugged. "Eh. She's okay."

I stared back at Rob. The blonde in the picture was exactly Rob's type. Normally he'd be all over that. "She is pretty," I agreed.

"Eh," he said again. "She has nothing on that girl at the bar back there."

"The one reading?"

"Yeah." He sighed. "She was so fucking gorgeous. And smart too. This McCarty girl looks dumb. There aren't even any bookshelves in this room. Shame on that professor for raising an uneducated girl."

Um. Okay then. "So where do we start? The toilet paper or…"

"No," Rob said. "New twist. One of us has to step up and sleep with his daughter for revenge."

Ian laughed. "Have fun with that."

"Not me," Rob said. "I'm not attracted to her. It has to be one of you."

I held up my hands. "I'm with Penny."

"Great. Ian will do it. Fuck her real good and take a picture. We'll mail it to him later."

Ian laughed again. "No fucking way. You do it."

"I already forced this shit. I'm not forcing sexual chemistry too."

"Let's just forget about the daughter," I said. "We can leave her out of this."

Rob shook his head. "If you say so. But it would make him really mad."

Yeah, probably. But I didn't really want to make him mad. I wanted him to just stop being a creep. "Let's just focus on the plan." I grabbed the end of a roll of toilet paper and threw it over a nearby tree.

Ian followed my lead as Rob tried to open the window to break in.

"It's locked!" he said.

"Did you think it would be open?" I grabbed another roll of toilet paper off the grass.

"I thought it might be. Let's try the front door." He walked up and turned the door knob.

An alarm immediately started blaring inside the house.

"What the fuck?!" Ian hissed. "Abort mission! You guys are more wasted than I realized."

"I gotta leave the shit!" Rob pulled a lighter out of his pocket and tried to set the bag on fire.

A light upstairs turned on.

"We gotta go!" Ian yelled. "Now!"

"Not until I punch him," I said and stepped up beside Rob. Another light had turned on inside.

"What is wrong with you guys! You set off an alarm! The cops are probably already on the way!"

"Got it," Rob said and tossed the flaming bag of shit onto the doorstep right as the door opened.

McCarty stepped out. "What the hell is going on?!" He stared down at the fire and then started to stomp on it to put it out.

I smiled.

"Ah! What's that smell?!" he yelled and shook his foot as the blaze climbed up his pant leg. He screamed like a little girl.

"He's on fire!" Ian yelled.

"Yeah he is!" Rob cheered.

"Ahhh!" McCarty yelled. He tried to run forward, but his face found my fist.

"You piece of shit!" I said and punched him again. "If you touch Penny like that again, I'm going to fucking kill you. Or if you even say one fucking word to her."

"James? Is that you?" he asked as he slapped his pants. He normally wore glasses, but they weren't on his face.

"Burn in hell!" Rob yelled.

McCarty tried to stop drop and roll, but he just smothered his pants in shit.

I leaned down and punched him again. And again. And again. His pants finally stopped burning, but they were in tatters, hanging off his tighty-whities.

"Enough," Ian said and grabbed my arm before I could do any more damage to his ugly mug.

"Who are you people?" McCarty yelled. He still couldn't see anything and now there was blood smeared on his face.

"Your worst fucking nightmare," Rob said.

Sirens wailed in the distance.

"And if you tell anyone we were here, we're all going to take turns fucking your daughter."

"What the hell?!"

"And she'll be calling me daddy instead of you, you little bitch."

I couldn't help but laugh.

"We have to go!" Ian yelled.

But I didn't want McCarty to not know who had done this. I grabbed the front of his shirt and pulled him closer. "Can you see me now, you old prick?"

"James…"

"You heard me before, right? Don't ever talk to my girl again. Are we clear? Because this was nothing compared to what my crazy brother wanted to do. So if you so much as look at Penny again we'll be back."

He nodded.

"And don't creep on any other students either."

"You're one to talk," he said.

Okay, he had a death wish. I would have punched him again, but Rob threw one of the unused bottles of laundry detergent at him instead. Right in the groan.

McCarty wheezed and bent over. "Okay," he groaned. "Okay, just leave me alone."

"Take that!" Rob said. "And remember what I said! If the cops show up at our place your daughter will be choking on my cock tomorrow night!"

"That's enough," Ian said and grabbed our arms and pulled us off the front porch.

The sirens grew louder.

Rob tripped over one of the many bottles of laundry detergent we'd left scattered throughout the yard as we ran to the car. We all climbed in and Ian put his foot down on the gas.

"Damn it," Rob said. "We didn't get to turn his house into bubbles or blow it up. And Ian didn't even fuck his daughter."

"But his legs were completely covered in your shit," I said with a laugh. And I got to punch him several times. I cracked my knuckles.

Rob laughed. "Yeah. That was pretty epic. But he better keep his mouth shut, because I only want that bookworm from the bar to call me daddy."

Chapter 25

Friday

"No, that way," I said with a laugh and helped Rob toward the guest room. We were both still drunk and now Rob kept complaining about his upset stomach. I wasn't sure why that made him so bad at walking though. Or maybe I was the one that was bad at walking.

"But I want to sleep in your bed with Penny," he said.

"No." I wished Ian had come in to help me with Rob. But then Penny might have seen him and… *Shit, Penny.* "Shhhh," I hissed. "You're going to wake her up."

"Good. Then I can ask her for a cuddle and to rub my tummy."

"No," I said more firmly. "You can't cuddle Penny. She's mine."

"Well I wouldn't have to snuggle in your girlfriend's tits if you'd have let me speak to that beautiful angel at the bar."

I laughed. "Next time, man." I helped him sit down on the bed.

Rob burped really loudly.

"Do you need a trash can?" I asked. Not that I knew where one was in here.

"No." He shook his head. "I told you…tacos go right *through* me. Not out this end." He pointed to his mouth.

"Well the bathroom is right…"

"Penny showed me." He burped again and lay back. "I really like her."

Me too. I smiled. No, I didn't just like her. I loved that girl. "Just let me know if you need anything else," I said.

He yawned and closed his eyes. "I really missed you," he said. "I didn't like being cut out like that."

I swallowed hard. "I know, Rob." When I'd moved, I'd been so desperate for a fresh start that I iced out everyone. But I'd missed him and my other friends. I'd made a lot of mistakes in the past year, but losing touch with them was what I regretted most. Dr. Clark had even told me I shouldn't distance myself from everyone. But I'd just felt so…sick. Sick of myself. Sick in the head. Sick of living.

Rob started snoring.

"I'm sorry," I said, even though I knew he wasn't listening. "I'm just so fucking sorry about everything." Rob always had my back. And I should have had his. I'd abandoned all my friends and I was a prick.

I tried to turn the lights off and missed the switch. *I'm so plastered.* I tried again and successfully turned off the lights. *Take that, dumb lights.* I stumbled out into the hallway and closed the door quietly. *Sorry, Rob. About everything.*

It was like all I knew how to do was fuck everything up. Even tonight. Penny had specifically told me *not* to go see McCarty. And I'd done the exact opposite. I was a selfish asshole. All I ever did was hurt people. Dr. Clark had given me one task – to start talking things through as a team. And I couldn't even do that.

I opened the bedroom door. I just wanted to go to bed. I wanted Penny in my arms even though I'd never deserve her. I pulled off my shirt and stumbled a little to the side and started laughing. "Shit," I mumbled as I almost fell over. I tossed my shirt into the middle of the floor.

"Are you okay?" Penny asked.

I turned to see her climbing out of bed. A bit of moonlight was shining through the curtains and she was practically glowing. Yeah, I'd never fucking deserve her. But I wanted to. I so badly wanted to be better.

"Hey, baby." I smiled.

"Do you want some help?"

"God you're beautiful." I put my hand on the side of her face. "I missed you tonight."

"I missed you." She smiled up at me.

"You're really, really beautiful, Penny." All she was wearing was one of my old t-shirts and she looked like a goddess. I was scared to blink because I was worried she'd just disappear. Poof. Gone. Like anything good I was ever given.

"You've already said that."

Had I? God, I really was drunk. I laughed and then looked past her at the bed. "Oh, shit, did I wake you up? I thought I was being really quiet."

Penny laughed. "You weren't being quiet at all." She reached down and unhinged my belt for me and slowly pulled it out of my belt loops. "I heard you guys laughing. You scared me. I thought someone had broken in or something."

I couldn't help but laugh again. No one was ever breaking into this apartment again. It wasn't possible. "No. No, no, it's just me. It's just me, baby." My eyes dropped to her lips. "I'm glad you're awake, though."

She unbuttoned and unzipped my jeans for me. "You're drunk. You should probably get some sleep."

"I don't want to sleep. I missed you. I want you. I've been waiting to have you all day." All I wanted to do was touch her. Instead, I ran my fingers through my hair because I knew how much she liked it.

Her eyes followed the path of my hand. "It's the middle of the night," she said.

But I had her right where I wanted her. It was all over her face. I had all this guilt wrapped around my chest. And I just wanted to feel in control again.

"You told my brother that I like to spank you," I said. "But you didn't tell him how much you like it. How wet you get just thinking about it. You like getting punished. And if I recall, you were very, very bad today."

She grabbed the hem of her t-shirt and slowly peeled it off.

My eyes landed on her exposed breasts. But she immediately turned around, placed her hands on the mattress, and arched her back.

Good girl. She always knew how to give me exactly what I needed. I could have stood there all night staring at her in the moonlight. But her perfect ass was calling for my attention. I grabbed the sides of her underwear, pushed it down her thighs, and spanked her hard.

She moaned.

My chest still felt tight. "That was for going to your dorm room instead of coming to me when you were upset." I wasn't just angry at myself. I was angry at her too. She was just as bad at being a team as I was. She never fucking listened.

I spanked her even harder. "And for talking to the reporters."

She moaned again.

I spanked her again. "And for flirting with Rob."

"I wasn't flirting with Rob."

I spanked her again. "And for talking back." My red handprint on her ass and her wetness dripping down the inside of her thigh had me so fucking hard. I slipped two fingers into her tight pussy.

Her sharp inhale made me even harder.

"You're so wet. I think you like this even more than I do. And trust me, I'm enjoying myself." I leaned forward slightly, pressing my erection against her ass.

She moved her legs even farther apart, begging me to take her. "Professor Hunter, please."

"Fuck, I love when you call me that." I spanked her even harder than before. "And that was for rejecting my proposal."

"I do want to marry you. Ask me again right now. I'll say yes. A thousand times yes."

It was a little too late for that. She'd already said no. And there was the tightness in my chest again. I rubbed my palm gently across her sore ass cheek. "This is mine."

She shivered from my touch. "Of course."

"You said no to me." I kept my hand on her ass. "I don't like when you say no to me." I grabbed her hips and thrust my hard cock deep inside of her. I groaned and dug my fingers into her hips. "I really don't like when you say no to me," I said again.

"I'm sorry."

Me too, baby. For everything. I grabbed a fistful of her red hair and pulled her head back, making her arch her back even more. "God, you're so beautiful."

"You're so drunk," she said with a laugh. Her laughter made her cunt grip me even tighter.

"Fuck, that feels good."

"What?"

"When you laugh." I reached around her waist and tickled her stomach.

She started laughing again, clenching around me.

Fuck, Penny.

"James, stop. I can't breathe!" she said through her fits of laughter.

I groaned and pulled out of her. "I think I just found my new favorite punishment."

"No, please don't tickle me!" She laughed and climbed onto the bed, crawling away from me.

She knew perfectly well that I only liked it when she crawled toward me.

I climbed onto the bed after her. "I never realized how ticklish you were." I reached out for her.

She squealed and tried to move away from my hands. But I easily grabbed her ankle, holding her down as I climbed on top of her. I grabbed her hands and pinned them to the mattress above her head. Her chest heaved up and down, her nipples begging for my attention. Now *this* was how I preferred her. Completely at my mercy.

"Okay, you win!" she said. "I surrender."

I smiled down at her. Well, if she was surrendering… I let go of her hands and lifted her hips, sinking myself deep inside of her again. How was she still this fucking tight after I stretched her out?

"Professor Hunter," she moaned.

This is what made all the shit we'd been through the past few days worth it. The way she said my name. The way she touched me. The way she looked at me. The way she made me feel. I loved the way she made me feel. Like she worshipped me. Like I was everything to her. Like maybe I was good enough. Like I wasn't a complete fuckup.

I leaned over top of her and kissed her hard. I wanted to bruise her lips. Her neck. I wanted anyone who saw her to know that she belonged to me. And she didn't want my ring, so bruises would have to do. I pressed my lips against the side of her neck. But her skin was perfect. As flawless as the rest of her. I didn't want to keep hurting her. Why did I always do that?

I pulled back and moved my hips faster. Her long red hair was splayed across the pillow. "You're so beautiful."

She laughed again.

"Fuck, Penny. It's like you're trying to tease me." I grabbed her hands again, holding them in place with just one of mine. "Now you're going to get it." With my free hand I began to tickle her again.

She squirmed under my grip, laughing and clenching around my cock.

Jesus fucking Christ.

I slammed into her harder. Faster. And she kept gripping me as the laughter spread through her body. Tighter and tighter. Milking my cock like the perfect little slut she was.

"Professor Hunter!" she moaned as her orgasm crashed down on her.

Fuck. I pumped into her a few more times, filling her with my cum. I collapsed on top of her and buried my face in her lovely tits. "Please tell me that you liked that as much as me. Your heart's beating so fast."

She laughed and ran her fingers through my hair. "That's because it's hard to breathe when you're tickling me."

"Hmm." I kissed her neck.

"It felt really good, though."

"Hmm." I kissed her neck again.

"You're funny when you're drunk," she said.

"I'm not drunk," I mumbled into my neck. I laughed. "Maybe I'm a little drunk."

"You said I'm beautiful about a million times."

"That's because you are beautiful." I leaned down and kissed her clavicle so I wouldn't be tempted to mark her neck. "You're beautiful and you won't marry me." I sighed and placed my head on her breasts again. "It's okay. I understand."

"You understand what? I told you the reason why I said no. I just didn't want to go to Vegas." She ran her fingers through my hair again.

That feels good. "No. The real reasons." I yawned. "You don't need me."

"I always need you."

I sighed. "No. You don't need me. I can't even protect you. He touched you. I let that asshole touch you." *And then I didn't listen to you. I never listen. I'll never be good enough for you.*

"James." She put her hands on either side of my face, pulling me off her tits. "That wasn't your fault. You weren't even there. I do need you. You're all that I need."

I shook my head out of her hands and placed my head back down on her tits. "It's not just that. You don't love me."

"James, I do love you. I love you so much."

I yawned again. "No. No one loves me." *I abandoned all my friends. I'm a selfish asshole. And I keep letting you down. I'm not worthy of you.*

"James."

I yawned again.

"James."

I wasn't sure if she said my name again or that I just dreamed it. And I had the oddest sensation that I'd dreamed all of this. That Penny wasn't real. And that I was still staring out the window of my office in New York City contemplating whether or not to jump.

Chapter 26

Saturday

"Hey," Penny said softly and ran her fingers through my hair.

I slowly opened my eyes. My head was still resting against Penny's tits. I was clinging to her. Last night was foggy, but I'd had a terrible dream that she wasn't real. That I was still alone, drowning. But she was here. We were okay. I eased my grip around her waist.

She kept running her fingers through my hair.

I lifted my head off her chest and looked down at her. "Hey."

"How are you feeling? You were really drunk last night."

I laughed. That was nothing. She should have seen me when we'd been on a break. And if she was expecting me to have a hangover, it wasn't happening. My body had a very high tolerance level. But I kept all that information to myself. "I'm fine. Although I don't remember much about last night." My eyes scanned down her naked body and I smiled. "I remember that." I remembered my palm on her ass. Her laughter making her pussy grip my cock so tight.

She scrunched her mouth to the side as she stared at me. "Do you need some Advil or something?"

"No, I'm okay." My dream of her not being real was worse than any hint of a headache I had. But she was here. I reached out to touch her cheek.

"Oh my God, James." She sat up and grabbed my hand. "Your hand is bleeding. Why are you bleeding?!"

"Oh, shit." I ran my hands down my face as everything about last night fell into place. Rob. Ian. The flaming bag of shit. "Fuck. I remember that too." She was going to be so mad at me.

"What happened? James, you need to clean it. It's going to get infected or something." She grabbed my arm and pulled me toward the bathroom.

She looked frantic as she opened up a drawer in my vanity and then another.

And I found it incredibly adorable.

"Do you have peroxide?" she asked as she kept rummaging around in the drawer.

I'd been hurt plenty of times and no one had ever cared. Besides, she should have seen the other guy. Blood all over his face, rolling around in Rob's shit. I couldn't help but smile.

"Or Band-Aids or anything?" She pulled open another drawer.

"No. Penny, I'm fine. Really, it doesn't even hurt." I put my hand on her shoulder to stop her.

Her eyes met mine in the mirror, catching my smile. "This isn't funny. We were just in the hospital. I don't want to go back. Is Ellen here? Maybe she has something?"

"She doesn't work on the weekends. Penny, it's fine. See?" I closed my hand into a fist to show her I was okay, but the dried blood made the cuts on my knuckles resist the movement and I winced.

"Jesus, James." She turned on the water and grabbed the bar of soap. She grabbed my hand and put it underneath the faucet.

Ow, fuck. I exhaled sharpy and turned away from her in the mirror. I kept my head turned away from her as she gently washed away the blood on my knuckles. The water eventually stopped and she patted my hand with a towel.

Silence had always been comfortable between us. But right now it felt heavy. I could practically hear the questions running through her head. And I didn't want to answer any of them.

"James," she said, finally breaking the silence. "What did you do?"

"Thank you," I said, ignoring her question. "I'm sorry, I didn't know I was bleeding."

"James," she said more firmly.

I looked down at my hand and then back at her. I didn't want us to fight anymore. I'd done this for her. And yeah, maybe a little bit for me. But it was already done. "I wanted to fix it."

"Fix what?"

"He touched you. That asshole touched you."

"You didn't." The disappointment on her face made my stomach twist with guilt. "James, you promised me that you wouldn't hurt him."

"I didn't promise you that I wouldn't hurt him. I told you exactly what I was going to do. I said I was going to punch him in the face. And that's what I did." The toilet paper and the poop and setting him on fire didn't seem to be important to mention right now. At least none of us had slept with McCarty's daughter.

"You said you were going to call Joe. This wasn't the way to fix it."

Joe wasn't going to do anything. I had to take matters into my own hands. "He shouldn't have touched you."

"He's probably going to the dean right now. Or calling the cops on you."

"Trust me, he's not."

"What does that mean? Can he not move or something?"

James laughed. "No. I just made it very clear that I'd visit him again." And I was sure Rob's threats to make McCarty's daughter call him daddy had actually helped quite a bit in that department.

"You threatened him?" She was staring at me like I was a monster.

"You don't understand." *I did it for you.*

"Obviously. Because there was another way to handle this. So you're right, I don't understand why you got drunk and beat up another professor. Why would you do that?"

"Because I couldn't be there to protect you! Do you have any idea how that makes me feel?"

"Yes. Because you never let me protect you."

I ran my hand down my face. "That's different."

"It's not different. And I've never beat someone up because of it."

I forced myself not to laugh. I could not picture Penny hitting anyone. But she looked dead serious. I leaned against the sink. "I did what I needed to do. He's a freaking pervert. He deserved it."

"And that's how people see you. Because you won't defend yourself. And you won't let me try to protect you. I don't want people to see you like that. I want everyone to know how wonderful you are."

"But I'm not wonderful." She knew my demons. She knew what kind of man I was before we met. She knew. "I'm used to people saying bad things about me. I can handle it."

"You *are* wonderful." She put her hands on both sides of my face. "You're so wonderful. And smart, and funny, and sexy, and perfect." She was staring at me like she truly believed what she was saying.

But I wasn't perfect. Not even close. I was a fucking mess.

"Even when you get in fist fights you have good intentions," she added.

"I didn't have good intentions. I wanted to kill him."

She shook her head. "You can't convince me that you're a bad person. I don't know why you keep trying to do that. I love you."

"I'm not going to apologize for what I did. I'm still mad." I looked down at my hand. I would have kept hitting him until I broke my fist. I was lucky Ian was there to pull me back.

"If you're mad about what's going on, then maybe you should do something else about it."

"What else can I do?"

She just stared at me.

"What? Talk to the press? Penny, that really would just make it worse."

"Yes. Please. Please tell the real story."

I wanted to shut this conversation down. But I heard Dr. Clark's voice in the back of my head. We needed to talk these things through. And if this was what she wanted? How much could it really hurt? "Joe's going to be mad."

"I don't care. I don't want to go here anymore anyway."

Wait. What? "You don't?"

"No. I want to take the rest of the semester off. And try to enroll somewhere else in the spring. I want that fresh start you talked about."

I smiled. That was exactly what I wanted too. But she'd been so adamant about staying here. I thought... Well, I wasn't sure what I thought. But I knew what this meant. That she truly was all in. "You'd give up going here to be with me?"

"Yes. All that I care about is being with you."

I wanted to lift her up and twirl her around.

"I love you, James Hunter."

I smiled. I knew she loved me. But hearing her say she was willing to move? And start over somewhere new with me? Her actions aligning with her words made my heart beat easier. She was as far gone as I was.

"I love you with everything that I am," she said.

I grabbed her waist and kissed her. "I love you." I lifted her up onto the sink. "And it's rather convenient that you're already naked." Because I was about to show her how much I loved her too.

She laughed as I pressed my lips against hers again. I'd been barely holding on when I met her. But now it felt like I finally had everything figured out.

I'd thought a lot about my fresh start when I left New York. But it wasn't about moving to Delaware. It wasn't about being a professor. Those choices had just led me here. To her. Because she was the only person who could save me from myself. And she was the only thing I'd ever loved more than a vice.

Yes, I was still a mess. But I'd be better for her. Because she was fucking everything to me.

***

We finally emerged from our bedroom and Rob was in the kitchen with a knowing smirk on his face. Penny and I hadn't exactly been quiet this morning *or* last night.

"Good morning," Penny said to him.

"Well, you two look like you're in a good mood," he said as he opened up the fridge. "Must be all the sex." His head disappeared behind the fridge door.

Penny's face flushed and she looked up at me. "Could he hear us?" she whispered.

I leaned down so my lips brushed against her ear. "He might have been able to hear you. You're unbelievably responsive."

She pushed on my chest.

"I'm just kidding," I whispered. "I'm sure he couldn't hear us." But...it was a lie. Because she'd been very vocal when I ate her out this morning.

"Do either of you want some scrambled eggs?" Rob asked. "I assume you're both hungry after your double header."

"I would love some, but only because it's breakfast time and I have a normal person's hunger," Penny said and sat down at the kitchen counter.

Rob laughed. "Don't be shy now. You know, for such a nice place, the walls are kind of thin. Don't you think, *Professor Hunter*?"

"Shit," I mumbled. Rob was never going to let me live this down. But Penny had screamed my title several times this morning when my tongue was in her pussy.

"You don't have to be embarrassed. Penny already told me all about how kinky she is. I would have been surprised if she wasn't screaming Professor Hunter all night and morning."

I stifled my laugh only because Penny looked truly horrified.

"Please stop talking," I said.

"Besides," Rob continued. "We had to go on that top secret mission last night so I didn't end up getting laid. It was nice to have something to jerk off to."

Penny's mouth literally fell open as she gaped at him.

"Damn it, Rob, we've talked about this. Stop saying stuff like that around Penny. I don't want to have to kick you out."

Rob cracked an egg. "It's fine. Penny and I are cool."

"Actually, we're not cool," Penny said. "Because James told me all about your secret mission. And you told me that you wouldn't let him do anything stupid. Punching a professor in the face *is* something stupid. What is wrong with you?"

"I tried to stop him," Rob said.

Wow, he did not. He'd barely asked any questions about why I even wanted to do it. *And* he'd added on to the plan. I never had any intention of setting McCarty on fire. That was all Rob.

"Not well enough," Penny said.

"He's bigger than me." Rob shrugged and cracked another egg.

"You two must have been a disaster together growing up," Penny said.

"No, only me really. James is the perfect one. I'm a terrible influence on him." He pushed the eggs around the pan with a spatula.

"That's kind of what it seems like."

"Geez, you sound like my mom. What, you think I wanted to go kick some guy's ass last night? That was not how I saw last night going at all. That was all him." He pointed at me.

Penny just laughed and shook her head.

"So what are we doing today?" Rob asked. "Is there someone else we need to beat up?"

"Penny and I are going shopping," I said. "We need to pick up a few things for the apartment." I sat down next to her at the counter.

"I don't mind third wheeling." Rob put some of the scrambled eggs on plates and handed them out.

"Thanks, Rob, these look great," Penny said and took a bite.

"Actually, if it's alright, I was hoping to do something with just Penny. We'll only be gone for a few hours."

"Fine," said Rob. "I have some stuff I need to do too anyway."

"You do?" Penny asked. "What are you going to do? Nothing illegal I hope?"

"Very funny, Penny. No, I ordered an Xbox from this place down the street. I need to go get it and set it up."

"I can't even remember the last time I played video-games," I said. We used to play all the time with Mason and Matt.

"I know. It's going to be so much fun crushing you. I call dibs on James after your lunch date." He pointed his fork at Penny.

"I'm good at videogames," Penny said. "Maybe I can crush both of you."

I stared at her. I didn't know she liked videogames too. She really was full of surprises.

Rob laughed. "I seriously doubt that."

"I played tons of N64 growing up. I can beat anyone at Mario Kart."

Rob laughed again. "Yeah, this isn't N64. Xbox is for grownups."

"I'm sure it's not that different."

"Well, I guess we'll see later. Game on, Penny. Oh, and *Professor Hunter*, could you please pick me up some condoms? Like a huge box? Like all the condoms they have in the store."

"Please don't call me that," I said. "And there's some in my nightstand. You can have them."

"I think the two of you are going to need those."

"Yeah, we don't use them."

Penny's face turned completely scarlet.

"Fuck, I hate you," Rob said. "I hate both of you so much."

I laughed and grabbed Penny's hand, pulling her toward the elevator.

Chapter 27

Saturday

"What about something like this?" I stopped in front of a huge painting of the beach. There was a boardwalk that overlooked the sand and water. It made it feel like we were standing there together, even though we were standing in an art gallery.

"It reminds me of Rehoboth." She leaned her head against my shoulder.

"Me too. It's kind of perfect, right?" I wrapped my arm around her back.

"That's the day I fell in love with you, you know."

I kissed her temple. "You barely knew me." But fuck, I was already in love with her then. I hadn't admitted it to myself, but I couldn't get enough of her from the first moment I met her. I was pretty sure I fell in love with her the moment she first fell into my arms.

"I knew enough."

I turned back to the painting. "Let's get it."

"I thought you liked the idea of moving? Why are we buying stuff for a place we might leave?"

"We can bring it with us." I was trying not to put pressure on this conversation. I'd been hoping she wanted to move. And I was hoping she wanted to go to New York City. But we needed to come to that decision together. I cleared my throat. "Where do you think you want to go?"

"I don't know. Aren't you happiest in New York?"

"I'm happiest when I'm with you." I kissed her temple again. That was the truth. I'd be happy wherever we wound up. As long as we were together. But I really wanted a chance to repair the damage I'd made with my friends. I couldn't rewind time, but I could apologize. Maybe it could be like old times again one day. Well, old times plus Penny. They were all going to love her.

Penny smiled up at me "Maybe I should apply to some places and see if I can get in anywhere before we choose. I'm not sure how easy it's going to be. You said people might not think my grades are valid."

"You can get in wherever you want."

"What do you mean by that?'

"I'm more than willing to make a hefty donation to any university that you choose."

She laughed. "I don't want you to do that."

"How do you think I got Joe to change your incomplete to a withdrawal?"

"James. You're exasperating. I didn't ask you to do that. And now I'm going to drop out. That was a terrible investment."

"Eh. Maybe they'll name a lecture hall after me or something. You know, when things die down."

"I kind of doubt that."

"Then choose your next university wisely so I don't have to keep wasting money. Besides, I've always wanted a building named after me."

She laughed and looked back up at the painting. "I want you to decide where we go. I'm indecisive. You're better at making decisions than me."

"I'd rather make that decision together." I squeezed her shoulder. I meant it. I was going to be better at working together with her from here on out. "Until then, I definitely want this painting. You like it, right?"

"Yeah, I do."

"Okay. I'll be right back." I walked over to the art gallery manager. He seemed surprised that I didn't try to negotiate the price. But it was a lot cheaper than any art I'd ever bought before. And it was well worth the price. Wherever we ended up, I wanted a little bit of Rehoboth with us.

We walked back over to the painting and the manager pulled the canvas off the wall. "Let me package it up for you. I'll be right back."

When he was gone, Penny looked up at me. "James, could we maybe get the picture you sent me the other day printed out?"

"Of Rob giving you the middle finger? I'm sure we can get a better picture than that."

"It's the first picture you ever sent me of yourself. I like it. You look really happy. I even made it my background image." She handed me her phone. She'd cropped Rob out of it so that it was zoomed up on my face.

I did look happy. And I felt guilty that we'd fought so much. From here on out, I planned to only make her smile. "You're incredibly cute." I handed her the phone back. "Can it at least be smaller than the painting we just got?"

She laughed. "Yeah, that's fine. Just like a normal sized picture would be great."

"Okay." I wrapped my arm around her shoulders again. "So what else do cozy places have?" Because I literally had no idea. But I wanted everything to be perfect for her.

"James, I need to confess something."

Fuck. What now?

"It's not bad," she quickly said. "I just..." my voice trailed off. "When I told you I went to my dorm room after I was upset because it was cozy, that wasn't the whole truth. I was embarrassed. When you described what your brother was like, you said he wasn't independent. You made it seem like that was a bad thing. And I don't want you to think of me that way."

She went back to her dorm because she was embarrassed of not seeming independent? I didn't need her to be independent. I wanted her to depend on me.

"I wanted to prove to you that I could be strong and take care of myself. And I couldn't. I..."

"Penny, I want to take care of you." I kissed her forehead. It was wrong of me to say that about Rob. I was a shitty brother. And I never wanted her to ever doubt how I felt about her. I liked that she relied on me. "I want you to let me take care of you."

"I need you."

I lowered my eyebrows. I wasn't sure where all this was coming from. I remembered a lot of last night, but I was sure there were pieces missing. I wondered if I'd said something stupid. But...those words were exactly what I wanted to hear. I wanted her to need me. To need me just as much as she wanted me. Where need and want blurred because we were so attached to each other. "Penny, I need you too. You shouldn't be embarrassed about that."

"I know. But I told you I could handle it. I just wanted you to think I was strong. And I was embarrassed about how wrong I was about everything. Everyone was so horrible. I just felt..."

"Hey." I cupped her chin in my hand. "I do think you're strong. I think you're perfect. You don't need to prove anything to me."

She smiled up at me.

And anyone who thought she was weak just didn't know her. Penny was quiet and reserved. Loud people had a bad habit of associating volume with strength. But they could take their comments and shout them all day and they'd be dead wrong about my girl. "Does that mean my apartment is cozy enough already?"

She laughed. "It could be cozier."

"Mhm. So back to my original question. What else do we need?"

"A rug in the living room might be nice."

"Good thinking."

***

"What about L.A.?" I asked, as we pulled to a stop at an intersection. I'd asked her a few questions about where she wanted to move while we were shopping. But she wasn't giving me much back. She just seemed lost in thought. I knew she hadn't been many places. Maybe we needed to do a bit of traveling before we could really decide.

She bit her lip as she mulled it over. "I think I want to stay on the east coast."

"Finally, now we're getting somewhere." I turned to her and smiled. "North or south?"

"North. I think I'd miss the snow."

"Me too." I put my foot on the gas when the light turned green. "But I don't want to go too far north. Tons of snow would be worse than no snow."

"You're probably right." She pulled her legs up onto her seat.

New York City really did seem like a good fit. But...Penny had told me that she preferred a back yard with grass and friendly neighbors. Central Park was beautiful though. And we could get an apartment overlooking it. We could get any apartment she wanted. But I kept my mouth shut. I didn't want to pressure her.

"If we moved to New York, where would we live?" she asked.

I pictured my parents' mansion on the outskirts of the city. That wasn't the kind of life I wanted. Where there were so many rooms we never had to see each other. I wanted to be close to Penny. I could do cozy. "If we moved to New York, I think I'd like you to give the city a try. Maybe an apartment in Manhattan?" I tried to keep the hopefulness out of my tone. I was used to always getting what I wanted. But this wasn't just about me anymore. I wanted her to be happy.

"Would that be weird?" she asked. "You know so many people in the city. I wouldn't know anyone at all. Tyler said he was going to interview for a position where he'd have to move there, but that wouldn't be until after he graduates. And he might not even get it."

I forced myself to keep a straight face. When the fuck had she been talking to Tyler? He was such a piece of shit. *Breathe.* Of course Tyler was choosing to come to New York City after graduation. He was hellbent on messing with me. But the city was big. We'd never have to see him.

I took a deep breath. "You'd know me. Penny, if we moved to New York, I'd still be hanging out with you all the time. I prefer spending my time with you." And she'd like my friends. She already liked Rob.

She pressed her lips together as she stared at me.

I knew I was doing a bad job of hiding my intentions now. She must know that's where I wanted to move.

"You said you left New York because you needed a change. If you went back, do you think you'd be unhappy again?"

It was a valid concern. I had issues. I'd left NYC to help escape from them. And my brother had been here for less than 24 hours and I'd already drank more than she'd ever seen me drink. But things were different now. NYC wasn't the problem, I was. But I was doing so much fucking better. Because I had Penny now.

"I'm not sure I could possibly be unhappy as long as I have you," I said. But New York was my home. And I had this feeling in my gut that my friends needed me. For once I wanted to be there for them. I was stable enough to help them now. When the roles were reversed, they'd been there to help me. I owed them. But if we didn't move there, we could still visit. As long as I had Penny, everything was going to be okay.

Penny was quiet for a few seconds. "I think we should go to New York then."

I laughed because I wasn't expecting her to say those words. Especially because we hadn't talked about her main issue with NYC. "I thought you didn't like the city?"

"I liked it with you."

Yeah. Me too. I wouldn't have considered going back originally. But when we'd visited together? It felt like it used to when I was back in high school. Before everything broke. I put my hand on the center console and she quickly grabbed it. I ran my thumb across her knuckles. "Is that really what you want to do?"

"NYCU has a beautiful campus. And it's only a 15-minute subway ride from Manhattan."

I smiled and turned toward her. "You've been thinking about this for a while?"

She shrugged. "I did a little research. And wouldn't it be easier to start a company there? With all your connections and stuff?"

"Connections and stuff?" I laughed. "I don't need investors. I can start it anywhere. I was starting it here. But yes, I probably would have had to go to New York every now and then."

"So let's just go permanently."

I couldn't even hide my smile. "Is that really what you want to do?"

"Yes." She squeezed my hand.

"You're sure?" I was kind of waiting for her to say, "Just kidding."

"I'm positive."

I pulled to a stop outside my apartment building and leaned over and kissed her. I knew she was doing this for me. I'd tried to play it cool, but I was sure it was all over my face. She knew I wanted to move back to the city. And I needed to do something for her first. "So how about we tell the reporters what really happened?"

They were already rushing over to my car.

"You don't care about making Joe mad?" she asked.

"Nope. I care about making you happy." I kissed her again before stepping out of the car.

She opened up the door to follow me.

"James! Are the allegations true? Have you seduced several students at the University of New Castle?" A woman's microphone was already waving in front of my face.

God I hated these people. "No." I looked over at Penny and held out my hand.

She grabbed it and I pulled her beside me.

"Just Penny." I smiled down at her.

"How did your affair start?"

"It isn't an affair. I filed for divorce last year. My ex-wife and I have been separated since then." I tucked a loose strand of hair behind Penny's ear. We were in front of dozens of cameras, but it somehow seemed like we were alone. Penny had once told me that she was used to being invisible. But she really was the only person I ever saw in a crowd.

"How long has this been going on?"

"We met right before classes started."

"You met outside of class?" The woman looked surprised.

Penny turned toward the reporter. "Yes, we met in a coffee shop. Actually, we didn't really meet so much as he bumped into me and spilled coffee all over my shirt. He was really sweet; he let me borrow his sweater so I wouldn't have to walk around campus with a big coffee stain down the front of me. I thought he was just another student. I was shocked when I went to class the next day and found out he was a professor."

The woman smiled at us.

Another reporter stepped up with a microphone. "How many students did you have relationships with before Penny?" He was gruff and didn't seem touched at all by the story of how we met.

"None. Just Penny."

"And what about Blive Tech International? Did you make a habit of sleeping with your employees? Maybe your young interns?"

What the fuck? "No. All of my relationships at Blive Tech International were purely professional. I don't even think I ever met any of the interns."

"So what made you be unprofessional in your current position? What made you break the code of conduct at the University of New Castle?"

Do your research, asshole. "We didn't break any rules. Student-professor relationships aren't mentioned in the handbook. Given the fact that we didn't do anything wrong, I think we've both suffered enough backlash. I'm appalled by how the university has handled this situation. And I'm greatly disturbed by how the entire campus has reacted. By harassing Penny and me instead of trying to find the truth."

"Of course there's been backlash. Because the university has found the truth. There's evidence that you've had sexual relationships with several students in addition to her."

"Which isn't true. I get it, okay? It's their word against mine. But every girl that came forward was failing or almost failing one of my classes. With their testimony, their classes were canceled and they got As. They must have known what would happen. I don't think their motive could be any more obvious. The university should be punishing them, not us. Or at least trying to get to the bottom of what happened instead of pretending lies are the truth."

"Three young, innocent women with no priors are definitely trusted over a rich bachelor who didn't even need this job. Why did you even start teaching here? Was it just so you could sleep with your students?"

It was good that Penny was holding my hand, because I really wanted to punch this guy. "I was trying to give back to the community. And it's just one student. Just Penny. I had no idea when I accepted this job that I was going to fall in love."

"She's eight years younger than you."

"She's only seven years younger than me. You should really get your facts straight."

The reporter frowned.

"What made you pursue this relationship?" the first reporter asked, pushing herself back in front of the surly one. "Even when you knew what might happen if people found out?"

"Something happened to me when I met Penny." When she fell into my arms, it felt like I could breathe for the first time in years. "Everything just...nothing was..." My voice trailed off. "What no one seems to understand is that we're just two normal people who fell in love. Yes, the circumstances weren't ideal. But what we have is. I don't really care what people say about me. Spread all the rumors that you want. All I care about is Penny. All I care about is what we have."

"If you aren't guilty then why did you resign?" the rude reporter asked.

"I resigned because the dean told me that I couldn't keep working here if I continued my relationship with Penny. That was never an option. Like you said, I don't need this job. But I do need her."

"Did he sexually harass you, Penny? Did he force..."

"No." Penny stared at him like he was insane. "Haven't you been listening at all? Absolutely not. He resigned so he could be with me. Because he loves me. James is sweet and thoughtful. He's smart and kind and charming. He's always been such a gentleman. He never forced me to do anything. I'm so in love with him. I don't understand why you're choosing to vilify him. And I agree with James completely. Make up whatever you want about us. We're not going to let you affect our relationship. We're not going to let all this toxicity hurt us. That's why I'm done here. I'm not going to finish school at a university that clearly doesn't want me."

"Are you moving? Are you transferring to a different school?" the nicer reporter asked.

"Look, you're all going to need to find a new hobby," James said. "Because we're not going to be here for much longer. We don't want to be associated with a community that is filled with hate. I expected more from the students around campus. And I definitely expected more from the other professors at this institution. Maybe that's a story you should be chasing. Penny and I are going to try our luck somewhere else."

"Where are you moving?"

I did not want them following us to our new place. "We don't have any more comments at this time." I pulled Penny back to the car and opened the door for her. I walked around the back of the car to avoid the reporters and climbed into the driver's side. I took a deep breath. "You were right. That was a good idea. It was nice to finally say something bad about this ridiculous university."

"Yeah. Fuck them."

I laughed. "You're right. Fuck them."

Chapter 28

Saturday

Hey, guys!" Rob said as we stepped off the elevator. "Why won't you die?"

I looked over at him. He was sitting on the couch with a videogame controller in his hand. Sitting right next to him was…Brendan. I knew what he looked like because I'd lightly stalked him after Penny told me they'd kissed. And by I, I mean I'd had Ian do it and he sent me a whole background check on the guy. Fuck, I still needed to tell Penny about Ian. I blinked, hoping I was imagining Brendan sitting there. *What the fuck is Brendan doing in our apartment?*

"Boom, suck it!" Brendan stood up and made a rude gesture toward Rob.

Rob threw his game controller at him. "Suck that."

Brendan caught it in one hand and looked over at us. "Hey, Penny." He was smirking at her.

This pompous ass…

"Hi, Brendan," she said.

I tightened my grip around her waist. *Breathe.*

"Oh yeah, Penny, I ran into your friend in the elevator," Rob said. "If I had known he was so good at this game I never would have asked him to play, though."

"You're such a sore loser." Brendan tossed both controllers down on the couch and walked over to us. "Hey, man. We haven't officially met, but I've certainly heard a lot about you." He put his hand out for me. "I'm Brendan."

I took another deep breath. He was being nice. I could play nice too. I let go of Penny's waist and shook his hand. "I think I owe you a thank you for taking Penny to the hospital the other day."

"No problem."

"I'm glad to see you're still alive," Brendan said to her. "I've been waiting for your call all week." He leaned down and hugged her.

"Sorry," she said and awkwardly patted his back.

"Yeah, I'm thankful for what you did." I put my hand on Brendan's shoulder. "But I don't appreciate the fact that you made out with my girlfriend."

Brendan released Penny from his hug and laughed. "Oh. You know about that? Well, she wasn't exactly your girlfriend when that happened. Either time."

"Either time?" I said as calmly as I could. *Breathe.* What was this asshole talking about?

Rob laughed and ran over to us. "Seriously? You hooked up with Penny? This is just too good. Anyone want a beer?"

"What do you mean either time?" I asked again.

"The second time doesn't really count I guess," Brendan said and leaned against the kitchen counter. "I kissed her, she didn't kiss me back."

"When?" I turned to Penny.

"In the hospital," she said quietly.

I clenched my jaw. He'd been there with her before I even knew she'd been emitted. So they'd kissed before I showed up? I'd just thanked him for being there with her when I should have been wringing his neck.

"Don't get mad at her," Brendan said. "I'm pretty sure she was doped up on morphine and she still pushed me off. Clearly she chose you. I didn't even get a thank you for sending her flowers. I'm not used to losing. I'll have a beer," he said to Rob.

That didn't make it better at all. He'd kissed her when she was high. That was just as bad as what McCarty had done. And Tyler. *Freaking Tyler.*

"You got it." Rob slid a beer down the counter and Brendan picked it up.

"I do really appreciate the fact that you were there when Penny fainted," I said. "But I think it's probably best if we don't make it a habit to hang out here." *Fucking creep.*

"Calm down, James," Rob said. "Brendan's cool. He even apologized for hooking up with your girlfriend. That's a quality guy. Besides, you can't blame him for trying. That's the risk of having a hot girlfriend."

No, they were supposed to be terrified of hitting on her in front of me because I'd kick their asses. This was just another reason why I needed my ring on her finger. "I'm not sure I'm completely comfortable having two guys here hitting on her," I said.

"I'm not hitting on Penny," Rob said. "She's the one that clearly wants me." He winked at Penny. "Was she a good kisser, Brendan? I bet she was a good kisser."

"A great kisser." Brendan smiled at her.

"I knew it," Rob said.

This was fucking ridiculous. I was just about to open my mouth, but Penny beat me to it.

"Okay," she said. "Will you all just stop? Stop talking about me like I'm not standing right here. James." She turned to me. "Brendan's just a friend. I told you that."

True. But she was also just friends with Tyler Stevens and that guy definitely had ulterior motives. He'd given her roses for fuck's sake.

"And actually, you should be thanking him because I talked to him that afternoon when I left your place confused. And he told me to choose you. He was actually really nice and helpful."

"That's true," Brendan said. "She told me you were a better lay than Tyler, so I told her she should choose you."

I stifled a laugh.

"I didn't even hit on her. Or wait. Maybe I did. I think I probably said that if she really wanted to know what a good lay was she should call me."

Penny groaned. "I said stop talking. But yeah. See? He was just being a good friend. Despite that last part. And Rob," she said, turning to him. "I don't want to sleep with you. I'm in love with your brother. So please just stop saying super weird things to me. It's really inappropriate."

"I do like you," Rob said. "You're like a million times better than the troll. Feisty too. I like a girl that can stick up for herself."

"Oh my God. I asked you to stop."

Rob smiled at her. "Stopping." He pretended to lock his mouth and throw away the key. "And Brendan's not going to hit on Penny anymore either, right Brendan?"

I wasn't at all surprised that Rob had immediately started talking right after he had thrown away the key. He didn't know when to shut up. He never had. But I couldn't help but smile. Having him around really did feel like old times. Him being here plus me being so happy with Penny made me feel young again. It was hard to be upset about Brendan, or Tyler, or anyone else when I was so damn happy. I still preferred him not in my apartment though.

"Sure, I won't hit on her anymore," Brendan said. He took a sip of his beer.

"How about you two go hang out at Brendan's place?" I said.

"But I just set up the Xbox! Let's all play Golden Eye. We can shoot it out." Rob patted my chest and walked back toward the living room. "Besides, Penny promised to school us."

"I doubt that," Brendan said and followed him back to the T.V.

I sighed. "Of course Rob had to befriend Brendan," I whispered to Penny. "I don't like this at all. I want you all to myself."

She laughed. "James, they're just joking around. You do have me all to yourself."

"They're not joking around." I smiled down at her. "Even three men flirting with you isn't enough to make you realize how beautiful you are."

"You're the only man that makes me feel beautiful." She wrapped her hands behind my neck.

"Hey, love birds! It's game time!" Rob called over to us.

I leaned down and brushed my lips against her ear. "Let's take them down."

"Okay, partner." She reached down and squeezed my ass.

I laughed and grabbed her hand. "Rob is right. You are feisty. And all mine. I can't wait to move and have you all to myself again. There are so many things I'd rather be doing than playing videogames right now." My eyes fell to her tits. Yeah, I'd much rather be playing with them.

But I could behave myself for a few hours. I led her over to the couch and pulled her onto my lap as I sat down.

She laughed as I wrapped my arms around her.

"You guys can't seriously play like that. Come on, I need help killing Brendan." Rob handed us each a controller.

Instead of moving off of my lap, she looked down at the controller. "Wait, why are there two joysticks?"

"This is going to be hilarious," Rob said and restarted the game.

"Wait, you have to tell me how to use this."

I kissed the side of her neck. "So, the right joystick lets you move your view up and down. And the left one lets you move your guy around."

"Why did they make it more complicated? Aren't advancements in technology supposed to make things better, not worse?"

I laughed and kissed her neck again.

After we selected our characters, the screen split into four quadrants. I was pretty sure I knew which one Penny was…the girl continuously running into a wall. This was definitely a lot different than N64.

"Crap, why is this so hard?" She slid off my lap as she tried to focus. Her girl started running in circles, staring at her feet.

"Speaking of hard," Rob said. "Penny sitting on your lap got you a little excited there, James."

"What?" I looked down at my pants. "I don't have…"

Rob snuck up behind me in the game and shot me in the back of the head.

"Asshole." I reached around Penny and shoved his arm. "Game on. I'm going to kill you next."

"I have a better idea," said Brendan. "Let's see who can kill Penny first."

"No! Just give me a second to figure this out." She had just tilted her head back up when blood filled the screen.

"Gotcha!" Brendan said.

"Damn it, Brendan!"

He started laughing as Penny's character came back from the dead. Rob immediately shot her in the face and started laughing too.

"What is wrong with you guys? Just give me a minute to learn what to do."

I couldn't help it. I started laughing too. Why was she so terrible at this?

"Hey." She nudged my shoulder.

"I thought you said you were good at videogames," I said and smiled down at her.

"I am good at videogames! I don't know what this crap is." Her character reappeared on the screen again.

I lifted my gun to her face.

"Don't you dare, James."

I immediately shot her.

"James! You're supposed to be on my team!" She started laughing too.

"What?!" Rob yelled. "You're both supposed to be helping me kill Brendan!"

"I can't kill anyone, this game is impossible." She fired her gun at the floor.

"Maybe we should all play a different game?" Rob asked. "I know you're fond of pool, Penny."

I looked down to see Penny's cheeks flush.

"You're good at pool?" Brendan asked. "We could play that instead. It's too easy to beat everyone in this anyway." He shot Rob in the chest.

"Shit," Rob mumbled.

"No," Penny said. "Actually, I kind of suck at pool." She had finally gotten her character to run in a straight line. She hid behind a column.

Brendan's character was approaching her from the other side of the column.

I kept my mouth shut. I really wanted to see if she'd be able to kill him. He didn't seem to realize he was walking into a trap.

"Yeah, I guess not," Rob said. "If you were I wouldn't have found your underwear all over the pool table. James clearly demolished you."

Brendan started laughing. "Strip pool? Now that's a fun game."

I would have been annoyed, but I was very entertained by the fact that Penny was definitely about to kill Brendan.

He walked past her hiding spot and Penny fired her gun. Her first shot missed, but her second shot hit him in the side of the head. "Yes!" she screamed and stood up. "I just killed someone!"

"Shit, you just killed Brendan!" Rob said.

"Nice." I held up my hand and she high-fived me.

"See, I am good at videogames!" She high-fived Rob too.

"Yeah, I kind of thought you were lying," Rob said. "But you just killed the master himself." He looked over at her. "Why *are* you so good at videogames, Penny?"

"I was a very nerdy youth." She sat back down on the couch.

I wrapped my arm around her back. "You're ridiculously cute."

"I never would have guessed you were a nerd growing up," Rob said. "That probably explains why you're so kinky now though."

"Rob, come on," I said.

"Oh. Was that inappropriate too? I thought that was just a nice compliment. I guess I don't know where the line is."

"Obviously," I said with a laugh.

"Let's play a different map," Brendan said. "I'm demanding a rematch. I refuse to accept the fact that I just got beat by a girl who's never touched an Xbox before."

"You're just mad because she's touching an Xbox instead of you," Rob said and switched to a snowy mountainside.

Brendan laughed. "Fair enough."

"I'm so sorry," I whispered into Penny's ear.

"It's fine." She smiled up at me.

God, she really was ridiculously adorable. And even though Rob and Brendan were being terrible, I was glad that she liked hanging out with the guys. She was going to love Mason and Matt too. It was going to be just like old times when we moved to NYC.

***

After several rounds of Golden Eye, Brendan stood up and stretched. "I think I've redeemed myself."

"Yeah, whatever," Penny mumbled.

She had only gotten one kill since our first game. And it was because I'd let her kill me on purpose because I felt bad.

"Yeah," Rob said. "Clearly Penny just got lucky before. I think I'm done playing for the night. Who wants to go out?"

"I think I'm going to stay in tonight," I said and yawned. I didn't need to beat up any other professors. So I wanted to stay in with Penny. Besides, it was a lot easier to not do something stupid that would upset her when I was right next to her.

"Stop being lame." Rob stood up and stretched too.

"You can go," Penny said. "Melissa asked me if I'd come over and help her get ready for the Sigma Pi formal."

Oh. "Are you sure?" I ran my hand down the side of her neck.

"Yeah, go have fun." She smiled.

Well... "Actually, I do have a few things I need to get done," I said. I didn't want to go out drinking again. I had something better in mind.

Rob laughed. "Crap, do we have to go beat someone else up? That was fun and all, but I have some other things in mind for tonight."

"No, nothing like that." I gave Penny a mischievous smile.

"Why are you smiling like that? I'm with Rob on this one. Please stop beating people up."

I laughed. "I'm not going to beat anyone up. Do you want me to drop you off at your dorm?" Rob and Brendan had already started walking toward the elevator.

"No, I think I'd like some fresh air after sitting on the couch all day."

"Okay." I tucked a loose strand of hair behind her ear.

"Try to pace yourself tonight."

I knew I'd worried her this morning. She expected me to be hungover and I wasn't. Being with someone like me wasn't exactly easy. But she didn't have anything to worry about tonight. Or at all. I didn't need any vices when I had her. And last night I was in complete control. Alcohol had never really been my weakness anyway. Drugs were my real problem. Well, drugs and sex.

But I was fine. I was good. "You don't need to worry about me." I winked at her.

"What on earth are you planning to do? Now I'm more worried than before."

"There's nothing to worry about tonight." I kissed her cheek and got up off the couch. I was on a new mission, but this one wasn't going to upset her. At least, I hoped it wouldn't.

Chapter 29

Saturday

The leaves crunched under my feet. I took a deep breath. I used to get sad in the fall, remembering all the horrible stuff that happened my senior year of high school. I thought the fall would always feel suffocating.

But now?

I took another deep breath. Now the fall would always remind me of Penny. And new beginnings. I'd never been able to breathe easier.

"Why are you smiling like that?" Rob asked. "You look like a psychopath."

I laughed. "I'm just happy." We walked past the coffee shop where Penny and I first met. God I loved this fucking street. Even with all the shit that had gone down the last couple days, I loved this campus. I'd always love this place. Because it's where I'd met her.

"I'm going to be a lot happier when I get laid. Speaking of which...why are you suddenly fine with going to a bar right on campus?"

"We're not going to a bar," I said.

"Um...yes we are."

"Nope."

"I was kind of promised a drink," Brendan said.

Why is he even still here? This was strange to do with him. But I didn't really care. It was also strange that there was jewelry store on Main Street, but now I knew why it was here. Because I needed it. I stopped right in front of it. "You guys can go to a bar if you want. I need to go in here."

"Why do you need to go in there?" Rob asked.

"Because I need a ring."

He just stared at me.

"I told you last night that I was planning on proposing to Penny."

"Oh. Right. Honestly, I just assumed you were drunk. You were serious?"

"Of course I was serious. We had that whole conversation about proposals."

"Yeah, but you didn't like any of my ideas. So of course I couldn't take you seriously."

I shook my head. "I'm going to propose to her. Tomorrow." I nodded. "Yeah, tomorrow. If I can get everything done tonight."

"What else do you need to do?"

"Buy that coffee shop we just passed. It's where Penny and I first met and I don't want them to ever change anything inside. And that includes cutting any holes in the ceiling or floors." I glared at him.

"So controlling," Rob said and turned to Brendan. "This guy," he said and pointed at me.

Brendan cleared his throat. "Um. Maybe I'll just catch you guys later."

"Nonsense," Rob said. "We'll need your opinion. James has terrible taste."

"I do not have terrible taste."

"You do. Come on. We'll help." Rob opened the door and walked in.

Brendan shrugged and followed him into the jewelry store.

Yeah, this was really weird. But as long as I picked a good ring, I didn't care who was with me.

The guy working there was very nice, but I didn't exactly know what to tell him that I wanted. I'd know it when I saw it though. "I'm going to need it tonight," I said. "Is that possible? I'll pay in all cash."

"Oh. Um. Let me call my boss while the three of you look around."

I nodded and we started scanning the display cases. There weren't a ton of options, but they were all pretty.

"What about that one?" Brendan said and pointed to the one with the biggest diamond in it.

I smiled. He didn't know Penny at all. She didn't care about something huge and flashy. She'd want something elegant and sophisticated like her. "No," I said.

"The most expensive is usually the best," Rob said.

"It's not really about the price." Penny didn't care about that either. "Although, I'm willing to spend whatever it takes to find the perfect ring. It just has to be…her."

"What does that even mean? You want a ring that's a petite redhead with a kinky streak?"

I shook my head and moved to another display case.

"Speaking of which," Rob said. "Since Brendan kissed her, it's only fair that I get to too. I should probably do it before you propose. So maybe tonight?"

I hit the back of his head.

"Ow." He rubbed the spot. "So…is that a yes?"

Brendan laughed.

"The two of you aren't being helpful."

The man working there cleared his throat.

But I didn't look up. Because I'd found the ring. "That one," I said and pointed to the perfect one through the glass. It was simple and classy and elegant.

"That diamond is almost as big as the last one," Brendan said.

I ignored him.

"Excellent choice." The guy pulled it out of the display. "My boss is coming in. He'll be able to size any ring and place any diamond into the setting that you want. But it won't be ready until the morning."

"What time?" I asked.

"Six at the latest."

"That'll work." I had a few errands to run before I picked it up anyway. "Can I see the diamond options?" The one in the setting looked nice. But they usually kept the best cuts in the back.

"Of course." He disappeared into the back and reappeared with a locked case of diamonds. We sat down so I could look at all of them. But there were only a few that were the size of the one on display. It didn't take long to decide.

"And what size do you need it?" He was jotting down notes on the order form.

"Oh. Um…."

Rob laughed. "You don't know Penny's ring size?"

"Her hands are pretty small," Brendan said. "She's probably a size five or something."

I glared at him. I did not want his advice on this. But I did know who I could ask. "Give me one second," I said. I stood up, pulled out my phone, and called Melissa.

She answered after a few rings. "I heard you were kidnapping my best friend and taking her to New York."

Okay, this wasn't a great start. Why was she always so hostile with me? "Is that how Penny worded it?" I asked.

"No, that's not how she worded it."

"Well that's good to hear. Just so you know, I really didn't want to pull her away from school. I know how much you mean to her. And I know how well you know her. Speaking of which, are you with her right now?"

"Yeah, she's right next to me."

"Could you maybe step out of the room? I need to ask you something privately. It's important."

"Yeah, I guess. Hold on one sec." There were some mumbled voices and I assumed she had her hand over the speaker. A few seconds later she said, "Okay I'm alone."

"I need your help with something."

"Alright." She sounded very apprehensive. "But before you say anything, I don't know if moving really is the best option here. If one of Penny's professors is harassing her, can't you and Penny just go talk to the dean…"

"That won't be necessary. Her professor won't be doing that again."

There was a long pause.

"And why is that? Did you already talk to the dean?"

"No. But I took care of it."

"As in…"

"I punched him in the face. Several times."

Rob laughed beside me. Because we both knew it was a lot more than that. And we hadn't heard a peep from McCarty since. The combination of my threat to come back and Rob's threat to bang his daughter had seemed to work.

I was surprised when Melissa laughed too. "Good," she said. "That asshole deserved it."

He really did.

"So the move isn't really about that?" she asked.

"Partially about that. But more so that Penny and I need a fresh start. Where no one is judging us for being a professor and his student."

"That's exactly what she said."

I smiled. "I know it's all fast. But our whole relationship has been because I'm head over heels for her. Which is why I'm calling. I'm going to propose to her tomorrow. And I don't know her ring size."

"I'm sorry…did you just say you were going to propose to her?"

"She's the love of my life, Melissa. And I know I've fucked up. Several times. But I promise I will always have Penny's back. I will always put her first. And I…"

"I believe you," she said. "I do. I'm really bummed that you're stealing her away from me. But I want what's best for her. And that's you."

"Thanks, Melissa."

"She wears a five."

"Are you sure?" I was annoyed that Brendan was right about Penny's ring size.

"Positive," Melissa said.

"I picked out something pretty simple. But it's really beautiful. Can I send you a picture to see if you think she'll like it?"

Melissa laughed. "Yes, but there's really no need. From the sound of it, you nailed it."

I shot her a picture anyway.

"Oh my God. She's going to love it."

I couldn't stop smiling.

"But what should I tell her when I go back into our dorm? She's going to wonder why you called."

"Just say I butt dialed you."

"Seriously? That is definitely not going to work."

"Well, if she gets suspicious, tell her that I seemed wasted." I didn't think Penny had told Melissa about my addiction issues. But hearing that news would worry Penny. She was concerned about me this morning. I could just lean into that. She'd be so worried about me that she'd never see the proposal coming.

Melissa laughed. "Classic. I can do that."

"Thanks, Melissa." I hung up the phone and turned back to the guy working there. "She's a size five."

"I knew it," Brendan said.

I just shook my head.

"So who's Melissa?" Rob asked. "And is she hot?"

"It's Penny's best friend. But don't get any ideas. She has a boyfriend. And she's...a lot."

Rob laughed. "Exactly my type. Speaking of girls with boyfriends...I can't wait to kiss Penny tonight."

I was going to kill him. Luckily for him, I still had paperwork to fill out. I finished ordering the ring and we all headed outside. "I have another errand to run," I said. "Well, two. And we're going to need Ian's help." I shot Ian a text to come pick us up. We had a long night ahead of us.

Rob groaned. "But Ian didn't let us have any fun last night."

I laughed. "He didn't let us set McCarty's house on fire, but he did let us set McCarty on fire."

"I'm sorry, what the hell did the two of you do last night?" Brendan asked. "I overheard you punched some guy on the phone. But you set him on fire? And who's Ian?"

"Ian is James' bodyguard."

"That only answers a fraction of my questions..." Brendan's voice trailed off as my phone started to ring.

"Fuck," I said.

"Who is it?" Brendan peered over my shoulder.

"It's Penny. I can't talk to her. I'll give it all away."

"I'll gladly talk to her..."

"No," I said. Brendan seemed like a fun guy, but I didn't want him to be fun with Penny.

"Brother duties," Rob said and grabbed my phone. "So you said you wanted her to think we were wasted?"

I nodded.

"Done." He cracked his neck and hit speakerphone. "Hey, hot stuff."

"Umm...James?" Penny asked.

I tried not to laugh. Did she seriously think I'd answer the phone that way?

But Brendan tried and failed not to laugh. And for some reason, him laughing made me laugh too.

"Quit it," I mouthed silently at him.

"You quit it," he mouthed back.

"James?" Penny asked when Rob didn't respond.

I pushed on his arm and gestured to the phone.

"No, it's Rob. Do we sound the same on the phone?"

"Yes, you do."

Really? Weird.

"Damn it!" Rob said. "I should have convinced you to have phone sex or something. Can we rewind a couple seconds? Hey, Penny, it's Professor Hunter."

I started laughing again. I couldn't help it.

"Gross. Rob, can you please put your brother on the phone?"

Brendan elbowed me in the side so I'd stop laughing.

"Sorry, love, can't do that," Rob said.

"And why is that?"

"You're going to be mad at me."

"What are you guys doing?"

"We ran a few errands and then I finally convinced my tightly wound brother to go to a bar. But, we both know how he is..."

"Can you please just bring him home?" She sounded really worried. I felt a little bad about it, but the surprise would be worth it.

"In a bit."

"Rob, I'm serious. Bring him home right now." I'd never heard her talk so sternly before. It was kind of hot.

"Don't be such a party pooper, Penny. We're having fun! If he's too drunk to fuck you when we get home, I'll be happy to stand in. Don't you worry."

Seriously, Rob?

"Stop being gross. Just bring him home safely, okay?"

"You have my word, sugar tits."

Sugar tits? What the fuck was he doing? But I guess he did sound pretty wasted himself...

"You're drunk too, aren't you?"

"Mhm."

"You're impossible."

"You're impossible!" he mimicked back at her.

"And you're seriously not going to let me talk to James?"

"Professor Hunter is currently unavailable. Please leave a message at the beep." Rob made a farting noise and ended the call.

We all burst out laughing. "Epic, man," I said.

"You're a great actor," Brendan said. "I'm going to need to call you whenever I need to get out of a bad date now."

Rob looked very pleased with himself. "I'm definitely the go-to person for that. So which bar are we going to?"

"We're not," I said as Ian pulled up to the curb. "We're going for a drive."

"I feel like I'm about to get murdered," Brendan said.

Rob slapped him on the back. "Ian doesn't do that anymore. Right, James?" He opened up the back door.

I'd never asked Ian to kill anyone. But...yeah. I was sure he'd killed at least a few people in combat. I didn't really know. Ian didn't like to talk about it. All I really knew was that he had really bad PTSD.

"Where exactly are you going?" Brendan asked.

"I need to go ask Penny's father for permission to marry her."

"Yeah, okay. I think this is where I bow out. But tonight's been fun. We should all hang out again sometime."

I looked at Rob, waiting for him to bow out too and go hang out with Brendan.

"What are you looking at me like that for?" he asked. "There's no way I'm missing this. See you later, Brendan. We'll call you." He climbed into the car and slammed the door closed.

Would we though?

But Brendan put his hand out for me. "Despite all the joking around...I do think you and Penny make a good couple. I hope she says yes."

"Thanks, man." I shook his hand. Maybe Rob was right. Brendan wasn't so terrible.

Rob rolled down his window. "I can't wait to tell you all the details after I kiss Penny tonight."

Yeah...Brendan was fine. Rob was the terrible one. I climbed into the car.

"Where to?" Ian asked.

"Penny's parents' house." I quickly caught him up on the plan as we started driving.

"It's crazy, right?" Rob asked.

Ian shook his head. "No. I've seen the two of them together. They're a great couple."

"Seen? More like watched."

"Hilarious," Ian said. "You're just jealous because you're not allowed to watch the footage and I am."

"No one is allowed to watch any of the old footage," I clarified.

"No one is allowed to watch the super-hot footage," Rob mimicked.

And now I was wondering if he'd actually snuck a drink somewhere. Or maybe he was high...

"Do you think we should call Jen?" Ian asked.

I stared at him. "Why would we call Jen?"

He shrugged. "I don't know. Rob's part of this. I thought maybe you'd want to include your sister too."

Rob put his head between the front seats. "Ian, are you fucking our sister?"

"What?" Ian swerved the car and almost hit the curb.

I grabbed the wheel.

"No," he said with a laugh. "I'm not doing that." He laughed again, but it wasn't his normal laugh. It sounded a lot more nervous.

"Would you tell us if you were?" Rob asked.

"Um…yeah."

"I don't believe him," Rob said. "James, I think Ian's fucking Jen. Let's call her and ask."

"Don't call Jen!" Ian yelled.

"I thought you wanted us to call her…"

"Please stop," he said. His fingers were gripping the wheel so tightly that his knuckles were turning white.

Shit. I was pretty sure Ian was fucking my sister. Or if he wasn't, he definitely wanted to.

Chapter 30

Saturday

"Should we just stay in the car?" Ian asked.

"No, that would be super weird," Rob said. "We'll come in."

Honestly I wasn't sure which was less weird. But I didn't know how long this was going to take. And you weren't supposed to leave people in the car. Or was that animals? Or babies? Rob probably would cry like a little baby if I left him in the car with Ian. "Yeah, you guys can come in."

"Sweet." Rob climbed out of the car.

I quicky hurried after him. I really did not want him to just stroll right into Penny's childhood home uninvited. "Hold up." I grabbed his arm to stop him from turning the doorknob. "You can't just walk in."

"Why? Aren't they expecting us?"

"No."

He raised his eyebrows. "You didn't call them in advance?"

I shook my head. "Shit, should I have?"

"Probably. It's rude to show up uninvited, James. Especially when propositioning his daughter."

Well, fuck. It was too late now. But I wasn't propositioning Penny, so hopefully that would help.

"What if they're asleep?" Ian asked.

"It's only like 8 o'clock."

He shrugged. "Well it's really dark inside. Maybe they're not home."

"Only one way to find out." I rang the doorbell. And waited. And waited. We all looked at each other.

"I don't think they're home," said Rob. And then he knocked on the door super loudly.

No! Stop it!

But his knocking must have done the trick, because finally a light turned on and the curtains to the side of the window moved. The curtains fell back and the door opened.

"Oh, James," Mr. Taylor said. "What are you and these boys doing here so late?" He didn't open the door any further. Like he was worried we were about to jump him or something. Or…did he look kind of mad at me?

Crap, I really should have called.

"Did you say James?" Mrs. Taylor opened the door the rest of the way with a huge smile. "What a surprise. We were just watching a movie and we thought we heard the bell. But then we thought no one would be ringing at his hour. But then we heard the knock."

"Sorry," I said. "I didn't mean to disturb your movie."

"Good," Penny's dad said. "Because as my wife just said, we're busy watching a movie. See you boys later." He tried to close the door, but Mrs. Taylor stopped him.

"Nonsense. Come in, come in." She stepped to the side. "And who are your friends?"

I stepped inside. "This is my brother, Rob. And this is Ian."

"Nice to meet you, ma'am," Ian said and put his hand out for her.

"It's even nicer for me to meet you," Rob said and shook her hand next.

She laughed. The flush crossing her cheeks reminded me of Penny.

"It's a little late, James," Mr. Taylor said. "Was there something you boys needed?"

"They probably need something to drink," suggested Penny's mom. "Do you want some water? Or a soda? We also have some orange juice…"

"Thanks, but I'm not thirsty," I said. And why was Mr. Taylor being so curt? I thought we were okay after our last talk. I even thought he might like me.

"I could use some juice," Rob said.

I glared at him. Was he not reading the room right now?

But Mrs. Taylor seemed happy about it. "Come on into the kitchen and we'll fix you kids up something."

It was weird that she'd referred to us as kids. Especially because of why I was here. We all sat down. And I felt awkward. But Ian and Rob didn't seem to.

"So how did the two of you become friends?" Mrs. Taylor asked Ian.

"Well, I actually work for James," he said.

"Oh? Doing what?"

Fuck, I still needed to tell Penny. I'd tell her tomorrow. After I proposed. Right after.

"I run his security detail," Ian said.

Mr. Taylor took a sip of his juice. "Security detail? I didn't realize you needed one of those."

"I don't really," I said.

"I mean you kind of do," Ian said. "More so in New York City, of course. But just the other day Isa…"

"I really don't," I said more firmly. *Chill, Ian.* They didn't need to know that Isabella had broken into my apartment. Or that NYC was dangerous when I was planning on moving there with Penny. And Mr. Taylor already seemed upset about something. The last thing I wanted was for him to think I was putting his daughter in danger.

Ian cleared his throat. "I really don't do much. I just like...read magazines most of the time."

"Interesting," Penny's father said.

"Very interesting," Rob agreed. "I thought you preferred watching movies instead? Low budget stuff. And by that I mean..."

I cleared my throat. "Anyway, the reason I stopped by is because I needed to talk to you. Both of you."

"Is Penny okay?" her mom asked. "We haven't heard from her since your last visit. We've been worried sick."

Penny hadn't texted them since then? She hadn't told them anything at all? *Fuck.* "Oh. Well. A lot has happened actually. I resigned."

"Oh no," Mrs. Taylor said. "Why did..."

"I read the new article," Mr. Taylor said, cutting her off. "*Articles* actually. All of them."

Seriously, fuck.

"There were more articles?" Mrs. Taylor asked. "Why didn't you tell me? I'd like to read them too. Were any of them in today's paper? I have it in the other room."

"It wasn't favorable," he said. "It's probably better if you don't read it."

"Oh. Oh my," she said.

This was really not going well. "Mr. Taylor, whatever you read in the paper isn't true. I assured you last time I was here that Penny was the only student I've been involved with."

"That was before the investigation found..."

"What investigation?" Penny's mom asked. "There was an investigation?"

"It's bogus," Rob said through a mouthful of pretzels. Where had he gotten a snack from?

Rob kept munching. "The university just wanted to cover up the scandal as fast as possible. James didn't sleep with any other students, despite what those fuckers said."

And why was he cursing? *Stop it, Rob!*

"He's in love with Penny. I've seen it firsthand. They're smitten." He winked at me like he thought he was helping.

I wanted to slug him.

But Mr. Taylor somehow looked appeased by his explanation.

I breathed a sigh of relief.

Rob picked up another pretzel. "He's actually here to ask for your daughter's hand in marriage."

Seriously, what the fuck, Rob?!

"What?" Mrs. Taylor gasped.

Penny's parents both turned to me.

I cleared my throat. "I'm in love with your daughter. My brother's right, that's why we're here. And I'm sorry, I really should have called. But I wanted to do this in person. Mr. Taylor, I will do everything in my power to protect Penny. I'll take care of her. And I'll love her until my dying breath."

Mrs. Taylor was smiling so hard.

But I couldn't read Mr. Taylor at all.

"And if you'd give me your blessing...I want to propose to her. Tomorrow. It's been a crazy week. And I want her to know that it's the two of us against the world from here on out."

"Yes!" Mrs. Taylor said. "Of course, yes."

Mr. Taylor cleared his throat. "No."

Rob started choking on his pretzel.

Ian hit him on the back.

And I just sat there. Because I didn't know what else to say. Was this because of the bullshit investigation? Or was it something else? "Mr. Taylor, I promise that…"

He held up his hand. "I appreciate you coming, James. But you don't need my blessing. All you need is Penny's answer."

Did that mean he didn't want me to ask her? Or he didn't care? Or…what the hell? I came here for his blessing. And I wasn't leaving without it. "With all due respect, I know family means a lot to Penny. And I know that she'd want me to ask. That's why I'm here."

"I wasn't saying no to you," he said. "I'm just saying you don't need to ask. It's Penny's decision."

I opened my mouth and closed it again.

"But if you had to say yes or no," Rob said. "What would it be? I think my brother really wants to know."

"It's a yes," Mrs. Taylor said. "Right, Peter?" She turned toward her husband. When he didn't respond she put her hand on his shoulder. "Penny's happy. You saw how happy James makes her. And she'll be happy that he stopped by. Just give the boy your blessing."

Mr. Taylor sighed. "I just wanted him to know it's not my decision. It's Penny's."

"Of course it's Penny's decision. But Penny is going to say yes. So it's fine if you do too."

Mr. Taylor turned to me. "You swear you're only dating Penny? No other students?"

Jesus. "Of course. I'm obsessed with her." It was the truest thing I'd ever said.

"She's only twenty," he said. "It's pretty young to get married."

I knew that would probably be one of his concerns. But I wasn't in a rush for the ceremony. Her wearing my ring was enough for me for now. I just needed everyone to know she was mine. I needed Penny to know that we were a team. "I know she's only twenty. But I'll love her until she's ninety." If I was lucky enough to live that long.

He slowly nodded his head.

"Yes? It's a yes!" Rob yelled. "High-five." He put his hand up for Ian to high-five. "Mission complete."

Ian high-fived him unenthusiastically. Probably because Mr. Taylor's response had been so unenthusiastic.

Rob put his hand up for me too. And honestly? Even an unenthusiastic yes was still a yes. This was a win. And I understood why Penny's father had been hesitant. Those articles were pretty damning. I high-fived my brother.

"Pretzel?" he asked and offered me the bowl.

"I'm good," I said. And I was. I was really fucking good. I'd found the perfect ring. I'd gotten Penny's father's blessing. Now I only had two more things to do. Go to New York and get Penny a spot at NYCU for the spring semester. And call the coffee shop where we first met. I would have gone there after getting the ring, but they weren't open after dinner. Luckily Ian was great at finding whatever information I needed. He'd be able to find the owner's personal number.

I was done waiting. Originally I'd thought I'd had to wait two semesters to be with Penny. Back when I thought she was a senior. And then it became six semesters. But now? Our relationship was public. Penny was dropping out of the University of New Castle for me. And she was going to be my fiancée. There was no reason to postpone anything. I was going to propose and whisk her away to New York City for our fresh start. As long as she said yes to my proposal.

"So why exactly did you ask Bob and Eli to come with you for this?" Penny's father asked.

Bob and Eli?

"Don't be rude," Mrs. Taylor said. "It's lovely to have you boys here too. Anyone want another glass of juice?"

Rob looked very confused.

"Did you hear her, Bob?" Mr. Taylor asked. "She asked if you'd like another orange juice."

Rob looked around. "Are you talking to me?"

He nodded.

"My name is Rob. And that's Ian."

"Isn't that what I said?"

I held back my laugh. No. No it was not. And I still had no idea if he just kept messing up people's names to fuck with my head. Or maybe he was just fucking with Rob now. Because Rob looked very upset about being called Bob.

Chapter 31

Sunday

I thought I'd be tired as we pulled up in front of the jewelers, but I was full of energy. Nervous energy. But still.

The ring was even better with the diamond I'd picked out. I closed the box and thanked the owner for the quick turnaround.

I'd gotten everything ready. I'd gone over my proposal a hundred times. And a few times out loud to Rob and Ian. They both seemed to approve.

But yeah. I was really fucking nervous.

I was used to getting what I wanted. But this decision was entirely in Penny's hands. A simple yes or no was going to change my life forever. And I just really hoped it was a yes.

"Seriously, do I look like a Bob to you?" Rob asked as we stepped onto the elevator.

"He's just bad with names," I said. *I think*. We'd already been over this during the car ride home.

"I get if he messes up football players names," Rob said. "Especially since everyone on the Eagles is so forgettable. But he'd literally just learned my name. I think he was fucking with me."

"Ian and Eli aren't even close," Ian said.

"But at least Eli is a cool name. I mean...Bob? Bob?!"

I laughed.

"It's not funny. Do I look like I'm 70 years old with a beer belly?"

"I mean...you might look like that one day," I said.

"Never. I do too many sit-ups for that crap. Penny's father just hates me. I don't know what to do about this. Do I send him a fruit basket or something as a peace offering?"

"I don't think he hates you. He's just bad at names."

The elevator doors dinged.

"See you in a bit," Ian said. "Good luck with the proposal."

"Thanks, man." I stepped off the elevator and Rob followed me.

"Later, Bob," Ian added before the doors slid closed.

"Bob." Rob looked truly exasperated. "Bob!"

"Stop it, you're going to wake Penny." I gestured to where she was asleep on the couch. She must have fallen asleep waiting for me to come home. I smiled. There was something really nice about someone trying to wait up all night for me to come home. Growing up, no one had ever cared where I was. It made me feel...loved.

Rob shook his head. "I don't know how she's going to feel about her dad hating me," he whispered. "She might say no to your proposal now."

How was that even going to come up? "He doesn't hate you. But let's put a pin in it for later, okay?"

He sighed. "Fine. I'm doing the fruit basket thing though. I'll have Ellen arrange it." He grabbed my shoulders and leaned in a little too close for my liking. "Game face," he said. "Go get down on one knee and fuck our girl."

"My girl."

"Whatever. I'm taking a play from Mr. Taylor's playbook. Apparently you can say whatever you want now with zero consequences."

"Right."

He slapped both sides of my face. "I can't wait to hear all about it." He slapped my face again and yawned. "I need some sleep. I usually only pull all-nighters during threesomes. Two women are a lot to handle." He yawned again. "Sucks that you'll never get to do that again."

Yeah, I was good. "Good night, Rob."

He saluted me and wandered off toward the guest bedroom. But he stopped by the couch, leaned over, and pretended to motorboat Penny.

"Stop it," I hissed.

He did it again.

I was going to kill him. I took a step forward.

Rob immediately stood up and lifted his hands to his sides, like he was completely innocent.

"Go to bed," I mouthed silently at him.

He did this weird shimmy and waved his hand through the air like he was spanking someone. And then he pointed to Penny.

So I pointed to the hallway that led to his room.

And then he pointed to himself and Penny and then to his room.

No you can't take Penny to your room! That was definitely not what I was saying!

Rob laughed. And then threw his hand over his mouth when Penny stirred.

We were both completely still for a moment.

But Penny didn't open her eyes.

"Sorry," Rob whispered. "Good luck!" He finally went toward his bedroom.

I stared at Penny sleeping and took a deep breath. Penny and I had a lot to talk about. But all that mattered was that from here on out we made decisions together. Well…starting after she decided to say yes or no to my proposal.

Fuck, why was I so nervous? My palms were starting to feel sweaty. I wiped them off on my pants. I looked down at what I was wearing. The same outfit I'd worn last night. That definitely wasn't going to do. Penny had asked for romance. And a wrinkly shirt was hardly romantic.

I quickly changed and freshened up. I looked in the mirror and ran my fingers through my hair. I barely even recognized myself. Because even though I was nervous, I still had a smile permanently glued to my face. It has taken me 27 years, but I finally knew what I wanted. I finally knew what it felt like to be happy. And it didn't matter that I was Penny's professor or that she was seven years younger than me. Because she was made for me. I knew it in my gut. I nodded to myself and walked out of the bathroom.

Penny was still fast asleep on the couch. I took a moment to just stare at her. The freckles smattered beneath her eyes. Her red hair falling into her face. Her plump lips that looked best around my cock…

Breathe. I could have that later. I could have that forever. After she said yes.

I dropped onto one knee in front of the couch and put my phone on the ground. I ran my fingers along Penny's cheek. "Penny."

Her eyes flew open eyes. "You're okay?" She reached her hand out and ran it along the scruff on my jaw line. "Thank God you're okay."

"Of course I'm okay." I couldn't even try to hide the big smile on my face.

She looked down and saw that I was on one knee. Her eyes grew round and she pushed herself up into a seated position.

"Penny, I love you so much," I said.

She looked so damn excited. And my heart finally started beating normally again. She was going to say yes. When I *actually* proposed. But this definitely wasn't the moment. I just couldn't help messing with her though. I loved when her cheeks flushed.

"Why are you looking at me like that?" I asked. "Oh, you thought..." I laughed. "No." I laughed again. "I just dropped my cell phone." I picked it up off the ground and stood up. "I said it would be romantic. This is hardly romantic."

"Oh, no, I didn't think you were proposing."

There was that flush on her cheeks that I loved. She looked so embarrassed. And so damn cute.

"I was going to go get breakfast," I said. "I just wanted to see if there was something in particular that you wanted."

"I was worried about you."

"I know, I'm sorry. I should have called."

"And you shouldn't have let Rob answer your phone."

That had actually been pretty hilarious. Rob was great at pretending to be drunk. "Things got a little out of hand last night," I lied. I tucked a loose strand of hair behind her ear. "I'm sorry that I worried you, Penny."

"What time is it?" she asked.

"7:30."

"Can I come with you?"

"If you want."

She yawned and got up off the couch. "Just give me a minute." She hurried into the bedroom.

I took another deep breath. She was going to say yes. We were going to get our fresh start. I walked into the kitchen to wait for her. I slid my hand into my pocket and wrapped it around the ring box. She was going to say yes.

LOVED

Penny smiled shyly as she met me in the kitchen. And I wondered if she was still embarrassed that she'd thought I was about to propose. She wouldn't have to be embarrassed for long.

I wrapped my arms around her. "I missed you last night." I did. Normally hanging out with my friends would be a highlight. But all I ever seemed capable of now was thinking about her.

"I missed you too. What did you guys end up doing?"

"We went all over the place. Thanks for convincing me to go out. It's a lot of fun hanging out with Rob. And Brendan's actually alright."

"Why do you never seem like you're hungover?"

"I have a high tolerance to alcohol." That was the truth. But I also hadn't had anything to drink last night.

She bit her lip.

I forced myself not to groan. I really loved when she did that.

"When did you get home last night?" she asked. "I never heard you come in."

She really had been worried. I grabbed her hand and led her over to the elevator. "I only just got in. Which is why I so badly need some coffee."

"Or some sleep?"

"We got a hotel in New York. I'm not that tired. I just need some caffeine." I smiled at her. We hadn't gotten a wink of sleep. I'd just been practicing my proposal. But I truly wasn't tired. And I definitely didn't need caffeine. I'd already had a cup on the way home.

"Wait, you went to New York? Why?"

"I had some secret stuff to do."

She laughed. "Yeah, I got that." She looked up at me. "I like you when you're like this."

"Like what?"

"Playful. I think that maybe Rob is a good influence on you."

I don't think anyone had ever used those words to describe Rob before. "I've always thought he was a bad influence on me."

"Well, in a lot of ways he is. He drinks too much and he says awful stuff. Really, you do drink too much when you're with him."

"It won't happen again." I rubbed my thumb against her palm. She had nothing to worry about. All I needed was her.

"But you're happy when he's here. So in that way, he's the best possible influence." She looked down at the ground for a second and then back up at me. "Are you sure you want to move? Rob just got here and I don't want to make you leave if..."

"Penny. I was just thinking that I can't wait to move." I smiled at her. And odds were that Rob would follow us back to New York. That was his city too. I held her hand as we stepped off the elevator and led her toward the side exit of the parking garage. "And actually, I wanted to talk to you about that. The reason I went to New York was to talk to the dean at NYCU."

"About what?"

I rubbed my thumb along her palm again. "About you, of course."

"But I didn't even apply yet."

"I know. But I told her all about what happened. She seemed sympathetic. And impressed with your transcript. If you still want to go, you're in."

"Really?"

"Really. So, what do you say?"

She was quiet for a moment. I looked down at our intertwined fingers. And I realized that this was the first time we'd ever walked hand in hand on Main Street. There was no one around. It was the weekend before Halloween and it wasn't even 8 a.m. on a Sunday. No one would be up for hours. This is what I wanted. I wanted for us to be able to be us. That was only going to happen super early on the weekends if we stayed here. But New York was different. In New York we could be whatever we wanted to be. It was our fresh start. And I wanted that with her.

"Did you bribe her with lots of money?" she asked with a smile.

I laughed. "I didn't need to."

"So you didn't donate any money to the school?"

Well... "I didn't say that either." I gave her an innocent smile. The donation was trivial. Penny really did have good grades. And I could be very persuasive.

"You're infuriating."

"No, that's you." I squeezed her hand. "So, what do you say?"

"I say we should start packing."

"I was hoping that would be your answer. Maybe we can go back up in the next few days to look at apartments? Something cozy of course." I'd already lined up a real estate agent too.

"That sounds perfect."

"I guess there's just one last thing I need to do here." I stopped outside the coffee shop where we had first met.

"What, get a cup of coffee?"

Not exactly. I smiled at her and walked into the coffee shop, holding the door open for her.

Penny walked in and immediately froze. There were rose petals all over the floor and there had to be at least a hundred candles. The whole shop was empty except for us. The owners had set it up exactly as I requested.

"Penny." I grabbed her hand again and dropped to one knee.

She turned and the smile on her face made any nerves that were left go away.

"This wasn't just where I first met you. This is where I fell in love with you." I stared at the flush crossing her cheeks. "You took my breath away when you bumped into me. It was something that I've never experienced before. I've never been so attracted to someone in my life. It's very distracting when you blush."

My words made her blush even more.

Fuck, I was forgetting what I was going to say. I looked down for a second, took a deep breath, and then looked back up at her. "You made me realize that I hadn't been living. Really living. Because life without this feeling, the feeling that you give me, isn't a life that I'm interested in at all. You chose me even though I told you I wasn't good for you. You've always seen the good in me, which was something that I couldn't see in myself. You made me realize that it doesn't matter who I was before. It's about who I've become. Because of you."

"Yes."

I smiled up at her. "I have more to say."

"If you're asking me to marry you, the answer is yes."

I laughed and kissed each of her knuckles. I needed to get the rest of this out. I needed her to know how important she was to me. And how excited I was for our future. "I'm yours, Penny. I've always been yours. I love you with all that I am. And I don't want to go another day without knowing that you're mine. Not just for today and tomorrow and the next. I want you by my side forever and always. Penny Taylor, you are the love of my life."

I let go of her hand and pulled the ring box out of my pocket. "You asked me if I was a believer in fate. I am now. I don't know how I ended up as a professor in Delaware. But I know why I did. Because you were here. And my life would always be meaningless if I had never met you. Because without you, I'm not whole. Penny." I grabbed her hand again. "Will you marry me?"

"Yes!" She threw her arms around me.

I laughed and pulled her down into my arms.

"James, I love you so much." She put her hands on both sides of my face and kissed me.

I'd wanted to pull her into a kiss the morning we first met in this coffee shop. But everything we had been through, all the ups and downs, had led us to this moment. And this moment was perfect. I wouldn't have wanted to change a thing even if I could. I'd take all those moments of pain any day if they led me here.

"Don't you want to see your ring?" I asked.

"How did you do all this?" She turned and looked at the candles and rose petals. "How did you know no one would be here this morning?"

"It's closed today."

"I've been here on Sundays before."

"It's closed today because I bought it and I closed it." I smiled at her.

"You bought it?"

"I don't want anything to ever change about this place." The owners would stay on to keep the place running smoothly. But they couldn't make any changes without my permission. "I want to be able to come back here when we're old and gray and talk about how this is where we first met." I put my hand on the side of her face. "This place changed my life."

"So last night...you weren't out drinking?"

"No. I didn't even have one drink."

"But Melissa said..."

"What I told her to say. I knew you'd be totally consumed thinking that I was out getting wasted and never suspect that I was planning to propose. I told her to say she thought I was drunk if you started to get suspicious. Which I guess you did."

"You're such a jerk." But even as she said it she was smiling.

"I am sorry that I worried you. That wasn't my intention. I just really wanted to surprise you."

"You did surprise me. But wait, Rob was definitely drunk when I talked to him last night, though."

"No. Rob is great at pretending to be drunk. I had to make it seem like the story Melissa fed you was true. And Rob was definitely up to the challenge."

Penny laughed. "So you went to New York last night and got me into a new school. And bought a coffee shop. You've been busy." She couldn't stop smiling.

"And I went and talked to your parents."

"You did?"

"I wanted your father's blessing."

"Did you get it?"

I smiled at her. "Yes, I did." Rob, Ian, and I had somehow forced it out of him. "Although I still would have proposed without it."

"I love you so much."

"I also bought you a ring. Don't you want to see it?" I was still holding the box in my hand. She had launched herself at me before I'd gotten a chance to show it to her.

"Yes."

I opened up the box.

"James." She looked at the ring. And then back up at me. And then back down at the ring. She looked so damn happy. The same way she looked when I'd bought her all those clothes. She never asked me for anything. But I'd give her the whole world if I could.

"Do you like it?" I asked.

"It's beautiful."

I took the ring out of the box, grabbed her hand, and slid it onto her ring finger. It was the perfect fit. I took a deep breath and stared at my ring on her finger. "Now you're mine."

"I've always been yours." She looked back down at her hand and then smiled up at me. "So why did you call Melissa?"

"I wanted her help deciding what kind of ring you might like. And I wanted to run the proposal by her. She knows you best."

"You know me best."

I smiled. I wasn't sure when that had become true. But it was. And Penny knew me better than anyone else. She was the first person that I could be myself around. She loved every side of me. The good and the bad. And there was a lot of bad. But she was still all in.

I never thought I'd find someone who would love me. I didn't think that I was capable of being loved or loving someone. But as soon as she fell into my arms I was a goner. And now she was mine. I couldn't stop smiling. "I'm excited to introduce you to everyone as my fiancée." I ran the tip of my nose down the length of hers.

"I'm excited to introduce you to everyone as my fiancé."

"Hmm." I kissed the side of her neck and placed my lips next to my ear. "I still prefer when you call me Professor Hunter."

"You'll always be Professor Hunter to me."

Chapter 32

Wednesday

The next few days were full of celebrating and laughter and probably too much champagne for an addict and someone underage. But I was too happy to care. Ellen seemed the most excited. Followed by Dr. Clark. And I was pretty sure that Melissa was actually starting to not hate me. Everything seemed perfect. But...there was one tiny problem.

Today we were going to New York City to hunt for apartments. I wanted Ian to drive us. I was used to him driving me around. But I still hadn't told Penny about him. Or the cameras. I was most nervous about the cameras. I should have confessed everything before I asked her to marry me. But I'd done what I'd done and now I just needed to rip the Band-Aid off.

"Are we all ready to go?" Rob asked.

I still wasn't sure why he was coming with us. But...whatever. "Um, could you maybe give us a second alone?"

"Yeah, give us the room, Penny. James needs to talk to me bro-to-bro."

Penny laughed. "I think James was referring to me and him."

"Oh." Rob shrugged. "Sure. I'll just wait patiently on the couch."

He plopped down on the couch, where he could still clearly hear us from the kitchen. I shook my head. But it didn't matter, Rob already knew all this. And he'd just bug me for the details later anyway.

LOVED

"I need to tell you something," I said.

Penny leaned against the kitchen island. "Okay."

An awkward silence hung in the air between us.

"Are you going to tell me what it is?" she asked.

I laughed uneasily. "Of course." But still I didn't say it.

"This reminds me a lot of the time when you said we needed to talk. And I jumped to the conclusion that you were breaking up with me because I watch too much T.V. Is this one of those situations? Or not? Because the way you're looking at me makes it actually seem like whatever you're about to say is bad."

"It's not bad," I quickly said. Even though it actually was.

"You're kind of freaking me out. What's going on? Are you having cold-feet about NYC?"

"No. Definitely not."

"Okay..." she said again.

Fuck, how do I word this?

"James, just tell me."

"Remember when I told you about how the elevator has a camera in it?"

"Yeah."

Well...she didn't seem upset when I'd first told her. And she didn't seem upset now. *Just rip the Band-Aid off!* "The camera in the elevator wasn't set up by the apartment."

For a second she just looked confused. "Is there like a peeper problem in this apartment or something?"

Oh, fuck me. I'm the peeper problem.

Rob laughed.

Dude! I glared at him, but he was just looking at his phone, pretending not to listen.

"Should we call the cops or something?" Penny asked.

"Not unless you want me to go to jail."

"Wait, what?"

"I put the camera in the elevator. They're also all over the apartment. And a few scattered around campus. One might even be outside your dorm?" I said the last one like a question because each time I mentioned the location of cameras, her face looked paler and paler.

Rob laughed again.

Shut it, Rob!

Penny opened her mouth and then closed it again. "You've been watching me? The...the whole time?"

"No, not the whole time. It started at the country club..."

"You have cameras there too?!"

"For security reasons. I put them up purely for security reasons."

"So you put a camera outside my dorm for security reasons?"

"We were on a break and I was worried about you."

Her face softened. "James."

"Yes?"

She gave an exasperated sigh. "What the hell?"

"You know I was tinkering with starting a new tech company. This technology is the start of it. The cameras are virtually undetectable, but the live feed is still really clear. It's amazing quality."

"So you're watching me in high-def?"

"No. Well...yes." This wasn't coming out right. "Penny, I started working on it when we were dating. And then I got a little obsessed with it while we were on a break."

"Obsessed with playing around with the tech? Or obsessed with watching me?"

"Both?"

"James."

I tried to flash her that smile that she loved. "Penny."

"You can't get out of this by smiling at me like that."
She lightly hit my chest. "But at least you're not recording
it, right? You said it's just a live feed?"

"I mean...there is a record feature."

"Do you use it?"

I shrugged.

"James, do you use it?"

"It was never my intention to watch it back. But, Penny...I missed you."

She didn't look at all sympathetic.

"And...the footage is really hot."

Rob snickered from the couch again.

Dude, seriously, stop! You're not helping.

Penny opened her mouth and then closed it again. "Is
there a camera in the bedroom?" she whispered.

"Yes."

"Where else?" She looked up at the ceiling like she was
trying to find one.

But of course there wasn't one in the middle of the
ceiling. It was in the corner of the kitchen. "There's one or
two in every room. To see all the angles."

She just stared at me.

"And at the country club there was one in that private
room we dined in."

"You recorded our date?"

I knew what she was asking. Did I record her on her
knees with my cock down her throat. God, that footage
was my favorite. I nodded.

"But you're the only one watching it, right?" her voice
was hushed, but the words rushed out. She glanced at Rob
who was still staring at his phone but definitely eavesdropping.

Fuck. She seemed a little perturbed about the cameras.
But she seemed actually mad that someone else might be

watching. And no, Rob wasn't. But Ian definitely was. He was literally watching us right now and probably laughing his ass off.

"James," Penny said. "Please tell me you're the only one watching." She nodded her head toward Rob.

Rob laughed again.

"Are you listening to this whole conversation?" Penny asked him.

"Of course I am. This is wildly entertaining."

"Then if your brother can't answer the question, you answer it. Is he the only one watching the video footage?"

"I'd pay top dollar for that footage," Rob said.

Penny's face turned bright red. "Does that mean you *have* paid for it? James, are you selling sex tapes of us?!"

"What? No. Rob, cut it out."

"This isn't Rob's fault! He's not the one filming me."

"It's for security reasons…"

"James, you haven't answered my question. Are you the only one watching it?"

Rob laughed again. "You're in so much trouble, man."

Stop it! He was making this all sound so much worse than it was. I was about to open my mouth and tell her about Ian when a ring sounded through the apartment, letting me know we had a visitor. *Thank God.* I needed to figure out a better way to word this because she was clearly most upset about other people watching it.

"Saved by the bell," Rob said.

I opened up the elevator doors and Ian stepped out.

What the hell? Hadn't he been watching?! This wasn't exactly a good time.

"This is spectacular timing, Ian," Rob said. "Couldn't be better."

I looked over at Penny. Her cheeks were still flushed and she just looked…confused. Which made sense. Because this whole situation was fucked. "Um…hey, Ian," I said. "Despite what Rob just said, it's not a great time. We'll be down in a few minutes."

"I saw what was going on," he whispered. "I'm here to help."

How? "I don't think you can help with this. Just give me a minute to tell her about you."

He shook his head. "You're floundering. I've got this." He walked past me. "Hi, you must be Penny," Ian said and stuck his hand out for her. "I'm Ian."

"Hi," Penny said and shook his hand. "I'm sorry, you walked in at a really weird moment." She shook her head like she was trying to shake away all the questions she still had for me. "You said your name was Ian? How do you know James?"

"I was just about to tell you," I said. "Ian is…"

"I'm his driver," Ian said. "Just his driver. That's my job description."

Sorry…what?

"You're James' driver?" Penny looked back and forth between us.

"Yup," Ian said. "That's my job. I'm a normal driver person."

What the fuck is he doing?

"He's never mentioned having a driver," Penny said.

"Ah, yeah, well he didn't need my services since moving here. But he called me up and said that the two of you are moving to New York. So I came down for just the day to drive you two to the city…"

"And me," Rob said. "I'm coming too."

"To drive the *three* of you to the city, yeah."

Wow. Lies on top of lies. I was trying to be honest here…

IVY SMOAK

"So you worked for James while he was living in the city?" Penny asked. "And he just hired you back?"

"Yup. Because you'll need a driver again there. Trust me, navigating the subway or taxis is a nightmare."

She really shouldn't trust him because he was lying through his teeth.

"Oh, okay," Penny said. "Well, it's great to meet you."

"The pleasure is all mine. I've heard so much about you."

"Really?" Penny blushed again.

"Mhm. James talks about you all the time. I feel like I've known you for weeks."

Because you've been watching her...

Penny smiled. "Aw well that's really sweet." She turned her smile to me.

Wait, had Ian actually just gotten Penny to calm down about all this? But that didn't matter. Because Ian had just added on more lies and I was trying to come clean.

"Well this has been a very interesting turn of events." Rob got off the couch and joined us in the kitchen. "I'll roll with it. Ready to go apartment hunting?"

"You really don't have to come," I said.

"Of course I do. I need to make sure I like my room. I get the final say."

Was he being serious right now? We weren't picking a place based off of the guest room.

Penny just laughed. "Okay, yeah, let's go."

She really seemed good. And Penny wasn't great at hiding her emotions. Like when she'd basically yelled at me during one of her Comm speeches.

Rob escorted her toward the elevators.

Ian went to follow, but I put my hand on his shoulder.

"What the hell, man?" I said. "I was trying to come clean to her."

"I know. And you were doing a great job," he said sarcastically.

"And you think adding more lies on top of it makes it better?"

"She was already upset about the cameras. Imagine how she would have reacted when you told her a stranger was watching the live feed?"

I pressed my lips together.

"She's not used to this lifestyle, James. For right now, she doesn't need to know how much security is implemented into your everyday life. You don't want to freak her out. This is all a lot to get used to. Especially when you add a big move on top of it."

That was true… "So you want her to believe that you're just our driver?"

He smiled. "I've always wanted to do undercover work."

"I don't know, Ian. I think just telling her the truth might be better."

"Trust me on this. She'll be more comfortable thinking I'm just her driver. For now. You can come clean about all this later once you're settled into your new routine in NYC."

He did have a good point. I slowly nodded. "I guess so. You really think this is a good idea?"

"Yeah. I think it's for the best. Besides, I want her to like me. And if you immediately tell her I watch you guys have sex, it's a bad first impression."

He was probably right about that. I'd tell Penny eventually. After she calmed down about the cameras. Although…she already seemed pretty calm. She was laughing about something with Rob in front of the elevator. But she still probably had questions. I'd handle all this first and then tell Penny about Ian's actual job title.

The elevator doors opened and Penny smiled at me over her shoulder. "Are you guys coming?"

I felt like she was still going to give me hell. But I couldn't resist her when she smiled at me like that.

Chapter 33

Wednesday

I'd told the real estate agent that we needed a place that was cozy. But maybe the concept was as new to her as it was to me. Because the first apartment she brought us to was more rundown than cozy. And the abandoned couch in the center of the room did not look comfortable at all. It looked like it was filled with…

My train of thought ended when a cockroach ran across the floor and Penny jumped. Yup. The couch was definitely filled with cockroaches.

"No," I said firmly. "Next."

"But we haven't even seen the bedroom yet," Penny said.

Was she serious right now? She was glued to my side like she was worried the cockroaches would carry her away. "I know you saw that cockroach," I said.

She shrugged. "Isn't New York City filled with those? I figured I just had to get used to it. Like when you go to Disney World and there's all those little lizard things. Although…those are kind of cute."

Get *used* to cockroaches? *Fuck no.* "No, Penny. You don't have to get used to mouse-sized bugs. Or…lizards."

Rob tried to push the curtains to the side and the curtain rod fell and almost hit his head. He dodged it right in time and Ian laughed.

"Not funny," Rob said. "I was almost impaled! I don't think I've ever been on this side of town, and I'm always down for something shady. Where the fuck are we right now?"

That was a great question. I turned toward the real estate agent. "Evelyn, I'm so confused," I said. "You know my budget. There's no way that this place is anywhere close to that. And you sent me a couple listings. *This* is nothing like the ones you sent over."

"Oh. Well, Penny and I got to talking on our way to the car. She wanted something rent-controlled. And I kinda had to scramble because you can't really buy something rent-controlled if you don't have a family member already living there. And my boss said she probably meant a place like…this. I'm sorry."

I'd left them alone for literally one minute when we picked Evelyn up from her office. I turned to Penny. "Where did you even hear about rent-control?"

"Isn't that what all the best places have? Like in Friends?"

I just stared at her. What was she talking about? "Which one of your friends?" I didn't realize she knew anyone else in the city.

"The *show* Friends," she said with a laugh. "Monica has a rent-controlled apartment because it was her grandmother's. And it was so nice. I was kind of picturing a place like that."

Ian handed me his phone to show me a picture of the apartment from Friends. This apartment looked nothing like that.

I shook my head. "I think maybe we should stick to the list Evelyn put together in advance."

"I know this one was a bust, but let's try one more," Penny said. "Evelyn, can you take us to the nicest one you found for me?"

"Um…" She scanned her phone. "Yes?"

I didn't love the way she said it as a question. This next place was definitely not going to be better. But Penny was moving here for me. The least I could do was let her choose a few places to look at. Besides, she still wasn't yelling at me about the fact that I'd been recording her for weeks without her permission.

We all headed back to the car.

"No need to drive," Evelyn said. "The next place is in walking distance. Right this way."

Yeah, this next place was going to be shit too. I stared at the rat hanging out the side of a dumpster. Seriously…where the fuck were we?

"Penny," I said and grabbed her hand as we turned down a side street filled with more trash. "We don't need a rent-controlled apartment. Or whatever it is we're about to look at."

"I know you can afford anything you want."

"So…what are we doing here?" We were probably going to catch some kind of bug just standing here.

"If I'm going to pitch in with rent…"

"You're not."

"I might," she said.

"You're not," I said more firmly. This really wasn't up for negotiation. "You're going back to school. You can't have a job at the same time. I'd never get to see you."

"Well, I'm not supposed to start until the spring semester. What am I going to do all day until then?"

"Whatever you want."

"Except work?"

I smiled down at her. She was impossible. "I was kind of hoping to spend the fall hanging out just the two of us. Exploring the city together."

"What about your new business? I thought you wanted to move here to get things rolling?"

"Yeah, I'll be doing it on the side. Just like I've been doing now. But that doesn't take up much time. Spending time with you is my priority."

Her cheeks flushed. "Well, I'll still need something to do when you're working."

"I have an idea. Maybe you could sit in on a few classes? Get the feel for the campus."

"Hmm. Yeah, I guess that could work. I don't know though...you probably wouldn't be comfortable with me going to NYCU yet because you haven't had a chance to install any cameras." She tried to raise her eyebrow at me, like I so often did to her. But she wasn't very good at it.

I tried to hide my smile. "Don't worry. I can get Ian to install cameras there any time."

"Ian helps with the cameras?" She nervously glanced at him and then back at me.

Oh shit. I knew telling her the truth about Ian a little later was the right move. But I needed to be a little more careful about it.

"I thought you said he was your driver?" she asked.

"Yeah, but he's also kind of...an assistant. He helps with whatever I need."

"Why did you never mention him to me before?"

I shrugged. "It didn't come up." *I was trying not to freak you out. I'm still trying not to freak you out.*

She leaned a little closer to me. "Do we really need a driver though, James? I really can take the subway."

She was trying to make me live in a disgusting apartment with cockroaches and now she was trying to fire Ian? "He's been with me for years," I said. "Ellen and him are both like family."

"Oh, I didn't realize." She smiled up at me. "Okay. He seems nice."

"He is."

LOVED

"I might still ride the subway sometimes though."

"You're going to be the death of me," I said as Evelyn opened up the door of the next apartment complex. Just like the last one, there was no doorman and no concierge. And the elevator was broken.

The five of us walked up eight flights of stairs.

"Why is it so hot?" Rob asked as he pulled on the collar of his shirt.

"The heat is definitely on full blast for some reason," Evelyn said. "I'm sure that's not an all-the-time thing though."

Was she sure about that?

She opened up the door to the unit she wanted to show us and stepped to the side. This one was a lot nicer than the last. Although the view out the one window was of a graffitied wall. And it was even hotter in here than it was in the hallway. It was a pretty nice autumn day. There was no reason to have the heat on so high.

I wanted to love it for Penny's sake. But I couldn't live here. It wasn't cozy, it was fucking claustrophobic.

Rob tried to pull off his shirt, but it got stuck on his sweaty torso. He finally removed it and tossed it on the ground. "Throw some glitter on me, because I'm stripper-hot!"

What the fuck?

Penny laughed. "What on earth did you just say?"

Rob ran his hand down his sixpack. "Throw some glitter on me, because I'm stripper-hot." He thrust his hips toward her.

I glared at him.

"I heard you," Penny said. "But what the heck does that mean?"

"It could mean a lot of things. And I meant every single one of them."

"Like?"

"Well, I'm as hot as a stripper gets on stage under all those light, so you should throw some glitter on me. Or…I'm hot enough to be a stripper, so you should throw some glitter on me. Or… I'm just fucking really overheated because of the heater in this shit apartment and if you threw some glitter on me I'd look like a stripper, because it would definitely stick to my sweaty skin."

Penny burst out laughing. "Okay, you guys win. I don't want Rob to be stripper-hot. Let's go see one of the apartments you picked out before, Evelyn."

Thank God.

"You're welcome," Rob said and patted my back. "The thought of me covered in glitter made Penny want a nice place." He grabbed his shirt off the ground. "Let's get out of here, gorgeous," he said and linked arms with Penny.

She laughed.

"I kind of expected her to yell at you about the cameras," Ian whispered to me. "Or…do something. She's usually pretty fiery."

He would know. "I expected the same."

"Do you think she's waiting for the two of you to be alone to freak out?"

I shrugged. "I have no idea." I watched her laughing with Rob. "I think maybe she's just…happy." I found myself smiling too. What was there to be upset about? We were in New York. We were about to start fresh.

"Do you think she's like…into it?"

I really had no idea. I was kind of hoping she would be. She liked the idea of almost getting caught. A lot. And she really didn't seem upset. She'd just joked about it. "I guess we'll find out when we're alone."

"I guess we will," Ian said.

I shook my head and climbed back into the car, making sure to sit next to Penny. I didn't need her leading Evelyn astray anymore. Yes, Penny and I were a team. But I knew what kind of place I pictured. And it wasn't anything like what we'd already seen.

Rob vetoed the next place because it was too cold.

Penny agreed.

Although I was pretty sure they were talking about different kinds of cold. Penny thought the atmosphere was cold and lifeless. Rob was just upset he couldn't take his shirt off and talk about being a hot stripper.

Rob vetoed the next place too because the guest bedroom was too small.

"Rob," I said. "You can't just keep vetoing places. This isn't about you."

He pretended to look shocked. "I mean...it's a little about me."

"It's really not."

"Aren't I going to be living with the two of you?" he asked.

Wait...what?

He laughed. "I'm kidding. You should have seen your face." He laughed again. "But I will be staying with you frequently and giving you no advance notice."

That sounded accurate.

"And I need my room to be twice that size." He started walking toward the door.

"You mean the guest room," Penny called after him.

"No, I mean my room. I'm going to put my name on the door. And this door does not deserve my name. Which is Rob by the way. Not Bob. Never Bob."

Ian laughed.

Penny looked at me. "Why does Rob think I don't know his name?"

I'd never brought this up to Penny before. Because the whole thing was really awkward. "It's not about you. It's about your dad."

"What about my dad?"

"Penny, I think your father is really bad with names."

Penny laughed. "He absolutely is."

"Wait. You know that he is? Why didn't you warn me about it?"

"He got your name right."

"Yeah, but when we first met he was talking to me about football players and butchering all their names and I thought he was messing with me."

She laughed. "No, he's just bad at remembering names. Wait, and when did my dad meet Rob?"

"Rob and Ian were there when I got your dad's permission to propose."

"The three of you showed up to my parents' house together?" She laughed. "I wish I could have seen that. If only I had cameras all over my parents' house..." She attempted to raise her eyebrow at me again.

"Penny, I'm really sorry about the cameras. And for the life of me, I can't tell if you're upset or you just think it's funny. Are you mad? If you're mad, just tell me."

"I don't know..." she said playfully.

"Penny, just tell me."

She leaned closer to me. "You'll find out when we finally get some alone time. But I've always liked your eyes on me, Professor Hunter."

Fuck. Me.

She patted my chest. "Now let's go see the next place. Hopefully it has a room big enough for your brother and plenty of places for hidden cameras."

Chapter 34

Wednesday

All of the places we'd already seen were close to Penny's new campus. I thought it would be nice if she didn't have to sit in half hour traffic every time she went to class. And even though I was used to being on the Upper East Side, I didn't necessarily think it would be a good idea to live there again. I hadn't been my best self there. And I didn't want to ever slip into old habits. Besides, Isabella still lived there. I didn't want to run into her ever. This was Penny and my fresh start. Together. And that meant somewhere new for both of us.

But Rob had vetoed all of the nice places near NYCU. For a variety of reasons. One had a tub that was too small. He said the walls in one of the apartments were too smooth. Whatever the hell that meant. He didn't like the color granite in the kitchen of the next. He vetoed another because he wanted key cards instead of actual keys. And then he vetoed the next because he wanted actual keys instead of keycards. He couldn't make up his mind. He was…an annoying son of a bitch. And I could accurately say that because my mom was a bitch.

There was only one apartment left. Penny stared out the window as we drove farther north. Closer to Central Park. Closer to the New York City I was used to. And for some reason my heart started racing. We'd visited NYC once before. And I'd been fine. Happy. But I'd be lying if I said I wasn't a little concerned about my control slipping in this environment. Dr. Clark would probably tell me that avoidance wasn't helpful. Or something like that.

But I'd wanted Penny to choose something really close to campus. And honestly, I didn't even know if she'd liked any of the places because Rob's opinions were very loud.

Penny stepped out of the car before Ian or I had a chance to open her door for her. She still wasn't used to being taken care of the way I wanted to take care of her. I grabbed her hand.

"I'm sorry Rob hated all those places," I said. "I was really hoping for us to be close to campus so it would be an easy commute for you. If you liked any of them we could go back and look just the two of us…"

"I want your brother to want to visit. He makes you so happy."

I shrugged. I just wanted Penny to be happy.

"So where are we now?" she asked. "I'm all turned around."

"We're about halfway between campus and Central Park."

She smiled up at me. "Blive Tech was close to Central Park, right?"

I nodded.

"Do you think when you start your new company you'll want another office around there?"

"Maybe." It depended on a lot of things. How in-control I felt. How good I was. If I could convince Dr. Clark to move to New York. I had an idea for that. I wanted to offer him a permanent position at my new company. An on-site therapist. Mainly for my sake. But it would be a nice perk for employees. And he'd have a hard time turning it down because I was going to pay him whatever he wanted. In the meantime, I could talk to him on the phone. I'd been doing that a lot recently anyway.

LOVED

"Well, wouldn't a place in between campus and your new office be perfect then? Let's go see it." She intertwined her fingers with mine.

I always felt better when our skin touched. The concierge was nice at this one. And it had a garage beneath with direct access up to the penthouse apartment, just like back in Newark. In case I didn't want to see anyone. I rarely wanted to see anyone.

"Key cards," Rob said. "I like this place already. We're going to need three," he said to Evelyn.

"We don't know if we want this place yet," I said. "And we'll only need two keys."

"Three keys," Rob whispered to Evelyn, loudly enough for me to hear.

Rob could visit whenever he wanted. But no key. I didn't want him to walk in on me and Penny. I had a bad habit of taking Penny's clothes off as soon as we were alone. And Ian watching was one thing. Rob was another entirely.

We walked into the apartment. Light was actually filtering into the main living space. It had a view that overlooked several other buildings. It felt open and spacious. And I breathed a little easier when I wasn't staring at a wall outside my window.

"Wow," Penny said and looked up the stairs.

It wasn't quite a second story. There was only one bedroom up there. But it was nice to have the separation. There was an office. Two guest rooms. A place to put my pool table. And not a single cockroach. It was about the same size as my place in Newark. It felt...right.

We walked into the kitchen.

"Now this is more what I was expecting," Rob said and ran his hands along the granite.

Penny smiled as she turned around in a circle. She turned toward me and her face grew serious. "It's not *quite* cozy," she said.

Oh. I tried to hide the disappointment on my face. For a second, I'd thought she loved it too. I didn't really know what to say. We'd spent all day looking.

"But it will be," she said and her smile cracked through. "Once we decorate."

"Yeah? You like it?"

"I love it." She was practically beaming. "And it's perfect that it's right in between my school and your soon to be offices. Could we walk to Central Park do you think?"

"It's a couple miles away, but yeah. We could. Or we could get Ian to give us a lift."

She couldn't stop smiling.

So I couldn't stop smiling. "It's the one right?"

"If you love it," she said.

"I really do. But I only want it if you do too." It was close to her campus. And far enough away from the Upper East Side that I'd still be able to breathe easily. It was perfect. But only if she was all in.

"I love it too," she said and clasped her hands behind my neck.

I could feel the metal of her engagement ring against my skin. She was mine. I ran the tip of my nose down the length of hers.

"Don't you want to know what I think?" Rob asked.

"This really isn't about you, man," Ian said.

Rob sighed. "Bros before hoes, Ian."

I cleared my throat and glared at him.

Rob lifted his hands. "I wasn't calling Penny a hoe. You know what I meant."

Penny laughed. "It's fine. What do you think, Rob?"

"I think my bedroom is the perfect size for entertaining."

"No," I said firmly.

"We'll talk about it later," he said and winked at me before turning to Evelyn. "It's the one. We'll take it."

"How much is it a month?" Penny asked. She bit her lip as she braced herself to hear the amount.

But Penny was not working while she was in school. And she didn't need to know how much the place cost. I wanted to take care of her. We'd found a place we both loved. And I wanted to start our future right here.

Evelyn looked at her notes. "It's…"

"Rob's right," I said, cutting her off. "We'll take it."

Penny looked up at me. "James. I…"

"Just help me make it our home, Penny." I cradled her face in my hands. "It's us against the world now, baby."

Tears started welling her eyes. "I love you so much."

"I love *it* so much!" Rob yelled and hopped up on the kitchen counter.

"It's actually us and your brother against the world," Penny said. She laughed and I held her tighter.

The smell of her cherry perfume surrounded me. I never had to wake up another day without her by my side. I closed my eyes and breathed her in. I wasn't sure why I was so worried about being back in town. Penny grounded me. She was all I needed.

***

The next few days were a whirlwind of packing and goodbyes. Well, goodbyes for Penny. Everyone I knew was coming with me. Except Dr. Clark. I still hadn't convinced him yet. But he'd seemed intrigued when I offered him a permanent spot at my new company. Once everything was up and running, he wouldn't be able to resist.

But Penny's teary goodbyes with her friends made me nervous. What if she missed Melissa too much? What if NYC never felt quite like home?

"Take care of my girl," Melissa said and gave me a hug.

"I will. I promise."

She nodded like she believed me this time. She went back over to her boyfriend, Josh. He put his arm around her. She turned her head to hide her tears.

I felt like I was pulling Penny away from happiness. But we'd talked about it. We'd decided to move together. I tried to let go of the guilt gripping my chest.

Slow goodbyes were never a forte of mine. "Penny, we should go if we're going to beat traffic." Traffic was always bad. But it was especially bad this close to the weekend.

She nodded. "Just one more thing." She walked over to Tyler.

I tried not to eavesdrop on Penny saying goodbye to Tyler. But their hug lasted a beat too long for my liking. He kissed the side of her forehead and I turned away. I wanted to pull Penny over my shoulder, throw her in the tub, and scrub off any remnant of Tyler from her skin.

We waved goodbye and climbed into my car. Ian pulled away from the curb. Ellen would be meeting us in New York. She was just making sure everything was "packed right" by the service we hired. I had no idea what she meant by that. Weren't the guys we hired the experts? But she'd insisted.

"I'm going to miss everyone," Penny said.

"Melissa can visit whenever she wants."

"I know. And at least Tyler will be coming to New York after graduating," Penny said and rested her head on my shoulder.

Right. Oh joy. The little prick was not going to be hanging out one-on-one with Penny in NYC. Over my dead body. *Breathe.*

Rob turned around from the front seat. "It's weird that you're friends with a guy, Penny. Haven't you ever heard that guys and girls can't be just friends?"

Penny laughed. "You and I are just friends, Rob."

"*Are we though?*"

"Yes," she said firmly.

I tried not to laugh.

"Well, it's only because of bros before hoes," Rob said.

"Dude, stop saying that," Ian said as he hit his turn signal. "It's disrespectful."

"You know what's disrespectful? You hitting on our sister."

"I haven't been hitting on your sister."

"Mhm." Rob cleared his throat. "Oh, hey, Jen," Rob said in a very good impersonation of Ian. "Yeah, we're coming back to New York. So when you're in the city I can drive you around again. Or pick you up from the airport. Or anything else you *need*."

"How is that hitting on your sister? I always used to drive Jen around. I'm being helpful."

"Car sex is a thing," Rob said. "We've all done it. And you're car sexing our sister, Ian."

"I am not."

"I'm pretty sure you are." Rob cleared his throat again to impersonate Ian. "Jen, let me show you how to drive my stick."

"You're the disrespectful one," Ian said. "Talking about your sister like that. I'm sure Jen already knows how to drive stick *real* well."

"I'm going to kill you," Rob said.

Ian laughed. "I was just kidding."

Rob turned around to look at us. "Can you believe this guy? I think we should hire Brendan as your driver instead, James. Brendan gets me. And he only hits on Penny, not our sister."

"It's a pass from me," I said. I did not need Rob *and* Brendan around hitting on Penny all the time. "And if Ian says nothing is going on between him and Jen, I believe him."

"It's not," Ian said.

Rob shook his head. "Lies. I'm calling it. They're shagging."

I cleared my throat, trying to think of something to change the subject.

"Want to play a game?" Penny asked, helping me out.

I smiled down at her.

"Let's play I spy. I spy with my little eye...something...blue."

I stared into her blue eyes. I knew that wasn't the thing she was spying. But it was easy to pass the time staring into her eyes.

Chapter 35

Sunday

Penny finished unpacking the glasses into the kitchen cabinet. Ellen had tried to get her to stop unpacking stuff, but Penny refused. It was going to take Penny some time to get used to the extra help. But I knew she liked Ellen.

Penny put the last one in the cabinet and stared up at the corner of the room where you could just make out a camera if you were really looking for it. Penny had been quiet about the cameras ever since we'd talked about it the other day. She'd said we'd talk about it more when we had some alone time. But we'd been pretty busy planning the move, spending time with her friends before leaving, and packing.

She was staring at one of the cameras now though.

"I didn't realize you were going to install them here," she said and turned around.

"You said you weren't mad."

"I didn't say I wasn't mad."

Oh. Maybe she hadn't said that exactly. "I thought you've always liked my eyes on you?"

She pressed her lips together. "I *did* say that."

"So...what's the problem?"

"Can I maybe see one of the videos, James?"

"I can show you the live feed right now."

"No, I mean one of the...steamy ones. From before."

Please let this mean you want to reenact one. "We can do that." I tried to keep my voice even. I didn't want to get too excited, but I'd been having fantasies about this very moment ever since I'd told her about the cameras. "Come with me." I grabbed her hand and led her into my new office. There was still a lot to unpack, but my computer was already set up. It was the only thing on my desk. I turned it on and glanced at Penny out of the corner of my eye.

Her teeth had sunk into her lip. The combination of that and the fact that we were about to watch some of the footage together already had me growing hard.

I opened up the folder and clicked on my favorite clip. The one from the country club. I hit play.

I watched the screen. In the feed, I slowly unzipped my pants and undid my boxers, letting my erection spring free.

"Is there audio?" Penny asked.

I turned on the sound.

"I still need to remind you what the best thing that's ever been in your mouth is," I said in the video.

Penny dropped to her knees at my words. In the video. Not in real life. I stole another glance at her.

She wasn't on her knees. *Yet.* But her cheeks were flushed.

I hoped it was because she was turned on, and not because she was embarrassed. I looked back at the video. Penny's tongue traced up my length and around my tip. And then she went all the way down.

I loved the feeling of my cock against her throat. And I remembered this moment perfectly. She hadn't even flinched.

"Penny," I groaned as my fingers intertwined in her hair. I started to guide her mouth, setting the pace.

She bobbed her head up and down my shaft, letting me fuck her pretty little face. The skirt of her dress was riding up her thighs. So close to showing me what I wanted. The perfect tease. She moaned around my cock as my hips moved faster and my fingers tightened in her hair.

It was so fucking hot. And my erection was pressing against the front of my jeans now.

"Is this your favorite one?" she asked, her eyes glued to the screen.

"Yes." My voice was tight. I wanted her on her knees. There was no way she wasn't turned on by this. And if I didn't start reenacting this right now, I was going to cum in my pants. I was used to jerking off to this video. An instant release. I needed her. I slowly stepped behind her and pulled her back against my chest as we both faced the screen. I slipped my fingers under the waistband of her leggings and underneath her thong. I circled her clit.

She pressed her ass against me.

Fuck.

I slid my fingers lower as she moaned on the screen. As her greedy mouth sucked me off.

I groaned. She was fucking soaked. *My dirty girl.* I slid two fingers inside of her. I knew she'd be turned on watching this. I knew how to give her exactly what she liked. I pushed my fingers deeper as my thumb circled her clit. In a few seconds she'd be coming around my fingers. And then I was going to reenact fucking her face. I couldn't wait to bury my fingers in her hair. There was nothing better than Penny on her knees staring up at me with her innocent blue eyes.

She moaned again in the video and I watched her drink down every last drop of my cum. She pulled back and licked her lips.

And suddenly Penny's body got...stiff. Uncomfortable. Not at all turned on.

Shit.

It was one of my favorite parts of the video. But Penny didn't seem to agree, because she reached out and hit the pause button.

"Penny," I said and grabbed her hip, trying to keep her in place.

She moved away from me, like my touch scalded her.

But her wetness was literally dripping from my fingers. What the fuck was going on? "Tell me what you're thinking," I said. But I already knew what she was thinking. She was staring at me like I was sick in the head. Like I was a monster. "Penny," I said when she didn't respond." I tried to reach for her again.

But she stepped farther away. "I just..." her voice trailed off. She looked at the screen then back at me. "I just need a minute." She turned around and walked away, leaving me alone in my office, feeling like an idiot.

I'd thought she'd find it hot.

I stared at the screen. How did she not find that hot? I slid my fingers into my mouth to taste her. Maybe I was sick. She'd run away from me and I was fucking licking her juices off my fingers. I stared up at the camera in the corner of my office, knowing that Ian was probably laughing and eating popcorn again. I gave him the middle finger.

Fuck, what had I done? I should have told her about the cameras earlier. I never should have saved the footage. Penny had every right to be disgusted by me. I didn't know whether to try to go after her or give her space.

I ran my hand down my face. I'd fucked everything up. This was supposed to be our fresh start. And I literally had footage of our past. How were we supposed to move forward if I kept watching this shit?

I grabbed my mouse. It was time to delete it. I stared at the now-still image of Penny on her knees. She was so fucking perfect. I tried to take in every inch of her. I never wanted to forget this moment. But it would have to be a memory now. I was just about to click on the delete button when there was a knock on the door.

"Professor Hunter."

I turned to see Penny standing in the doorway in a schoolgirl outfit. A naughty schoolgirl outfit.

My eyes trailed down her body. Her collared shirt was tied at a knot on her stomach, showing off her midriff. And the plaid skirt was so short I knew her ass would be hanging out the back of it. And the stockings. The fucking stockings. My eyes drifted back to hers.

What the fuck is happening? I'd thought she was mad at me. But this felt more like a reward than a punishment.

"I thought you were upset, Penny," I said.

"I am, Professor Hunter. Because you changed my grade."

I stared at her as she strutted toward me. With her sky high heels on, her lips were almost at my ear when she leaned forward. "You taped so much. But I thought it was a shame that you didn't have footage of our first time."

"So you were just pretending to be pissed?"

"Did you not feel how wet I was for you?" She kissed my cheek. "I just wanted to surprise you." She kissed my cheek again and then pulled back. "How dare you change my grade?! Is this a game to you, Professor Hunter?" She slapped me hard across the face.

Fuck. I grabbed her wrist, digging my fingers into her skin. I didn't remember her doing that. But I did remember what happened next. And I was really loving this roleplay. Especially with her playing up the school girl part. She didn't care that I was a sick fuck. She was as kinky as me.

"You're infuriating," I whispered against her lips.

"Then punish me, Professor Hunter."

I grabbed her ass and lifted her legs around my waist. I slammed her back against the wall. "I told you to stop thinking about me."

"I couldn't possibly."

Me either, baby. I kissed the side of her neck hard. I loved my ring on her finger. But I still loved marking her too.

"I need you," she panted. "Please."

I moved her to my desk and sat her down on the edge of it. One taste of her from my fingers and I was desperate for more. I pushed her skirt up. Her pussy was already glistening. "No thong?" I asked and raised my eyebrow at her.

"I was already so wet." Her cheeks flushed.

Oh, Penny. I leaned down, spreading her thighs farther apart. I placed a slow stroke against her greedy pussy.

She moaned, lifting her hips to meet my mouth.

I thrust my tongue deeper. Penny was right, we really did need footage of this. I grabbed my laptop and spun it around so I could see the live feed. There was just one thing... I reached up and tore at her shirt. The buttons popped off. It stayed tied, but one of her breasts was exposed for the camera now. The angle was fucking perfect. Her legs spread wide, the pleasure written all over her face. One of her high heels dug into my back as I swirled my tongue around her wetness. *So fucking sweet.*

And she wasn't lying when she said she was turned on from the original footage. Because she came fast around my tongue. I groaned and lapped up her juices, making her body keep shaking. I remembered that first time. I'd been so desperate to taste her. I thought I could get one taste and move on. I was so fucking wrong. She finally stopped shaking.

My turn. And I remembered really liking what I was going to do next.

I grabbed her hips and spun her around. She slid toward me on the desk, knowing what was coming next. She let her head fall off the side of the desk. She licked her lips like in the video as she stared at me from upside down.

How did I get so lucky? I pressed my tip against her lips. She immediately opened her mouth and I thrust forward.

Fuck. There was something magical about her giving me head upside down. Her tongue on top of my length, licking me where she usually couldn't. The suction was different too. And I loved filling her slender neck with my cock.

"Look at you." I pulled the monitor closer so she could see. "Look at you choking on my cock, baby."

She moaned.

"Do you like that, dirty girl? You like when your professor fucks your face?"

She tilted her head farther back so I could press into her throat.

Jesus, Penny. My fingers tightened in her hair. I leaned forward and squeezed her perky breast with my free hand. I ran my thumb along her hard nipple and she moaned around my cock.

I didn't even know where to look. Her breasts? Where her skirt just covered the apex of her thighs? Her lips around my cock? Or the footage? The footage was so fucking hot. I leaned forward and pushed the hem of her skirt up to expose her pussy. It was still soaked. I gently ran my index finger along her wetness.

She moaned and took my cock farther down her throat.

She was going to make me cum. And I hadn't even spanked her yet. I thrust once more and slowly pulled out.

I grabbed her wrist and spun her back around. I pulled her off the edge of the desk.

"Turn around, Miss Taylor."

She immediately turned around and placed her hands on the desk.

Her skirt was shorter than the one she'd worn to my office that day, her ass completely exposed. I cupped one of her ass cheeks and squeezed it. She was a school girl porno brought to life. And she was letting me record the whole thing.

She turned to look at me over her shoulder. "Is it better if I look at the camera she asked?"

"Yes." *Wait, no.* Ian was watching. *Fuck.* But I'd already said what I said.

Penny looked past me at one of the cameras and bit her lip.

Fucking hell, Penny. Who cared if Ian watched for a few minutes? I'd get the footage for the rest of my life. Penny wanted to film this. She wanted to be bad. And I knew just how she liked to be punished. I spanked her hard.

Her body shifted forward. And she arched her back even more.

I spanked her harder, my palm leaving a red mark on her ass.

I watched a little of her juices spill down her inner thigh.

"You like being my dirty girl?" I asked as I massaged where I'd hurt her.

"Yes, Professor Hunter."

I groaned. "Do you want to ride my dick, you little slut?"

She arched her back.

Where the fuck had I found this girl? I grabbed her hips and slammed into her. My fingernails dug into her skin, marking her as I fucked her hard.

She moaned and pushed back on the desk, matching my thrusts.

I stared at the live feed. Her ass in the air. Her body glistening with sweat. Her little school girl skirt practically pushed to her waist now.

I turned back to the real thing as I moved my hips faster. I slid my hand along the arch of her back, dipping my thumb in the dimples right above her ass cheeks. She was fucking perfection. Every inch of her was made for me. And for my enjoyment later. Whenever I pleased. Because she loved being filmed. She loved how obsessed I was with her. She loved me despite my flaws.

"Stare at the camera as you come, dirty girl. Show me how much you love your professor's cock deep inside of you." I gripped her hips again.

She moaned and started to clench around me.

Fuck.

"Don't cum," she said as she moaned, pulsing around me.

"What?" How was she expecting me not to cum when she was gripping my cock from her own orgasm?

"Not yet." She kept milking my cock.

I gritted my teeth. I was seconds away from exploding inside of her. But she pushed on my hip, making me slide out of her.

She spun around and slowly untied the knot on her shirt. She let it fall to the ground. "You said the video we were watching earlier was your favorite." She dropped to her knees. "Let me give you what you like, Professor Hunter."

Jesus.

Her lips circled my cock and she went all the way down.

I grabbed a fistful of her hair and started guiding her. "Touch yourself, Penny. I know you want to."

Her hand slowly traced up her thigh.

"Show me how wet you are for your professor."

She moaned again as she slid one finger inside of her, swirling it around her wetness.

I glanced at the video feed. "Spread your legs wider, baby. Show the camera your greedy little pussy."

She spread her legs wider, pushing her skirt up higher. You could clearly see her fucking her fingers now.

It was so fucking hot. I knew she was expecting me to cum in her mouth like in the video from earlier. But there was one thing I loved doing more.

"I don't want to cum down your throat." I gripped her hair tighter. "I want to drench your pretty little face."

Her eyes grew round as she looked up at me.

"Would you like that, Miss Taylor?"

She moaned around my cock.

That was definitely a yes.

I felt the familiar pull in my stomach. *Fuck.* I pulled out of her warm mouth and grabbed the base of my cock. Two strokes and I exploded all over her face. Again. And again. And again.

My cum dripped down her chin, landing on her exposed tits.

I landed one last shot between her breasts. I watched my cum trace a path down her stomach, pooling in her bellybutton. So. Fucking. Perfect.

When we had sex in my office that first time, all I'd wanted to do was stay. I'd wanted to worship her body. I'd wanted to give her everything I had. Instead, I'd walked away. Leaving her naked and alone on my desk.

LOVED

But now? Now I could do what I should have done the first time. I dropped to my knees.

"You're so beautiful, Penny." I leaned forward and kissed her forehead. It was the only place I hadn't drenched.

"Covered in your cum?"

"I love you covered in my cum." I reached down and grabbed her wrist. "Now let me take care of you."

"You already have," she said with a smile. "Several times."

I pulled her fingers out of her pussy and slide them into my mouth.

Her chest rose and fell as she watched me lick her clean.

"Let me worship you, baby." I leaned down and traced gentle kisses up her inner thigh as I pushed up her skirt.

"I can't take anymore," she said. Her voice almost sounded pained.

"Remember what I told you after our date at the beach? You can handle more than you think." I buried my face in her pussy.

"Oh, God," she moaned.

Besides, she'd asked me to punish her. I lightly tugged on her clit with my teeth.

She gripped my hair.

I grabbed her ass, trying to get more leverage. I couldn't get enough of her. I thrust my tongue back into her wetness.

Her back started to arch.

I looked up at her as she came around my tongue. She was staring directly into the camera.

Good girl.

Chapter 36

Friday

"Are you sure it's okay if I come tonight?" Penny asked. "The invitation doesn't have my name on it." She was looking at the invitation that Mason had sent me.

I didn't even know why I'd mention the invitation to her. It didn't matter if her name was on it or not. I wanted her to come. I nodded. "It's fine. We're just catching up with some old friends. And I want them to meet you."

"Are you sure?" She waved the invitation in front of her.

But when she moved her arm, I was a little more focused on the way her tits moved in her dress. She looked like a goddess in her skin tight red dress.

"It seems...fancy," she said.

"Yeah." I ran my fingers through my hair. "I honestly have no idea why Mason is being so formal about it. He's not usually into all that. But I definitely want you to come."

"Well...okay. If you're sure. I really could just spend the night here. I still have a few things to unpack."

"Which Ellen will do."

Penny smiled. "I hid a few boxes from her so she wouldn't have to do any more work."

"You're ridiculously cute. But you're not staying here tonight." We'd been glued together all week. And I'd never felt so at peace in New York City before. Tonight I was heading into the belly of the beast. And I needed her beside me. She calmed me.

LOVED

I was nervous enough about going to the part of town I used to frequent. But I was also nervous about trying to clear the air with Mason and Matt. And I didn't like when I felt nervous. It made me feel out of control.

"Come here," I said to Penny.

She closed the distance between us and smiled up at me.

"I want you there. End of story." I tucked a strand of hair behind her ear. "Besides, you're already all dressed. And you're going to be the best surprise for them." My hands slid to her ass.

"Oh, no," Rob said and walked into our room unannounced.

I let get of Penny's ass. Couldn't he knock?

"Did you already tell Mason and Matt that you have a surprise for them? Because remember when you told me you had a surprise for me? And then showed me Penny? They're going to think she's a prostitute, man. That they get to share."

"I don't think Mason and Matt share women," I said. At least not that I remembered. "Besides, Mason has already met Penny. He knows she's my girlfriend."

"Well, there's a first time for everything. Penny is plenty sharable."

Penny frowned. "What does that mean?"

"That there's enough of you to go around," Rob said.

"Excuse me?"

"Chill," Rob said. "I'm not making a comment about your weight. But your tits." He groaned. "And your ass. It's enough to share is all I meant."

She picked up a pillow off the bed and threw it at him.

Rob caught it with one hand before it hit him. "If you want to hit me, I prefer you do it with your hands. Or your tits." He winked at her.

"Your brother is impossible," Penny said and turned to me.

"Rob, quit it."

"What did I do?" he asked.

"You know what you did."

"I do not."

I shook my head. "Be respectful of my fiancée."

"You know the rules, man. If there's only an engagement ring, a girl is still fair play."

"What happened to bros before hoes?"

Penny laughed. "The two of *you* are ridiculously cute. Now come on. If I'm crashing this little reunion party, I don't want to be late." She grabbed my hand.

***

The three of us were the first to arrive at the bar. We found a table in the back. I pulled out Penny's chair for her and then sat down before Rob could snake the seat next to her. The three of us had been out to eat a few times since moving here and Rob had a bad habit of always sitting between us.

"So what exactly happened between you guys and your friends? I feel like I'm in the dark. You mentioned a falling out?"

"Yeah, back in high school," Rob said.

"Oh." She turned to me. "I thought you said it was college?"

"It was college," I said and looked at Rob. What the fuck was he doing mentioning high school? He knew perfectly well we couldn't explain that mess to Penny. We'd promised Matt to never mention it again. And yes, I had talked about everything with Dr. Clark. But that was different.

"Oh yeah," Rob said and scratched the back of his neck. "Did I say high school? I meant college. We all just kinda drifted apart a bit. Well, James more than me. He fucking ghosted all of us for months when he moved to Delaware."

"We all still talk on occasion," I said. But Rob had kind of nailed it. I'd needed a fresh start. But I knew now that cutting out my friends wasn't the right move. They'd always been there for me when I needed them. When I *let* them be there, that was.

"When we ran into Mason when we visited New York, he didn't even know about your divorce," Penny said.

"Well, that's why we're here," I said. "To reconnect." I was back in New York for good this time. And I wanted my fresh start to include the Caldwells.

"I think that's great." Penny smiled up at me. "It'll be nice to have a few more friends. And maybe that will mean Rob has some other people to hang out with too."

"Don't pretend you're sick of me," Rob said. "I know which Hunter brother you truly prefer."

"Yeah. The one I'm engaged to." She flashed him her ring. "Are all your friends like Rob? Like when you tell them we're engaged are they going to hit on me?"

"Not unless they want to die." I was surprised by the words that tumbled out of my mouth. I cleared my throat and tried to laugh it off. "They're not like Rob."

"Well that's good."

"Penny, you have a very strange way of flirting," Rob said.

She laughed and rolled her eyes.

"They're pretty late," I said and glanced at my watch. "You'd think they'd be on time since this was their idea."

"I'm usually the late one," Rob said. "It's incredibly rude the other way around." He waved over a waitress and we ordered a round of drinks.

"I'm sure they'll be here any minute." Penny put her hand on my thigh and smiled. She looked so cute when she was nervous.

I grabbed her hand. "You're right."

"So the four of you kind of grew up together? What kinds of things did you used to do?"

"Gangbangs mostly," Rob said.

Penny's jaw actually dropped. "What?"

"Yeah." Rob shrugged. "One girl, four cocks. Do you think you could handle it?"

"Rob, I'm not going to tell you again," I said. "Stop it."

"But did you really?" Penny asked, her voice hushed. "Gangbang women together?"

"No. He's just winding you up. Ignore him."

Penny shook her head.

I really hoped my other friends would be more appropriate. But really...where the fuck were they? I glanced at my watch again.

A waitress walked over with our drinks. "And these arrived for you," she said. She pulled out two envelopes that matched the one Mason had sent. She placed them on the table and walked away. One had my name on it, and the other had Rob's.

"What the hell is this?" Rob asked and picked up the envelope addressed to him. "I swear, if Matt and Mason send us on some lame scavenger hunt I'm never speaking to them again."

Penny laughed. "I love scavenger hunts. Open them."

I grabbed mine too. Rob and I both opened them at the same time.

Inside of mine was a polaroid of Penny walking around campus back at the University of New Castle. I flipped it over. There was a note typed out on the back: "I can't wait to fuck Penny. I've always had a thing for red-heads. And when I'm done with her, I bet she'll go for a great price at my club. -Mason."

What. The. Fuck? My heart started racing. Seriously. What the fuck? I gripped my free hand into a fist. I was actually going to kill him. *Breathe.*

"What the fuck?" Rob said out loud.

I looked over at him. The picture on the front of his polaroid was a shot of the four of us from high school. We all looked…sad. Really fucking depressed. I was pretty sure it was taken shortly after the funeral.

"No one's laughing, Rob," Rob said as he read his note out loud. "If you ever see anyone laughing, they're laughing *at* you. Not *with* you. Because you've never been funny. -Matt."

Rob looked up at me. "What the fuck is Matt's problem?"

I clenched my jaw. What kind of sick game were Matt and Mason playing here?

"Maybe it's some kind of joke?" Penny said.

Rob shook his head. "This shit isn't funny. *I'm* funny."

I'd never seen Rob so offended before.

"I'm fucking funny, man," he said again. "What did Matt say to you?"

"Mine wasn't from Matt. It was from Mason." I pushed the picture back in the envelope. I could barely even think straight. All I could see was red. How dare Mason talk about Penny that way. He knew we were dating. He knew I was finally fucking happy. *Breathe.*

"What did it say?" Penny asked.

"Nothing." *Breathe.* But I was picturing Mason's filthy hands on my girl. And I couldn't fucking breathe.

"James. What did it say?" she asked again. She touched my wrist. Normally her skin on mine calmed me down. But my heart was racing too fast.

Rob grabbed my envelope out of my hand.

"Don't," I said but he'd already started reading the note out loud.

"I can't wait to fuck Penny. I've always had a thing for redheads. And when I'm done with her, I bet she'll go for…" his voice trailed off. "Those fuckers."

"Go for what?" Penny asked.

"Nothing," he said. He sounded as pissed as me.

Penny grabbed the picture from him. She stared at the image of her on campus and flipped it over. "I'll go for a great price at his club?" She shook her head. She looked…hurt. It wasn't like Rob joking around. She didn't know Mason. And this wasn't fucking funny, unlike my brother who was actually funny. Fuck the Caldwells.

"I'm going to kill him," I said.

"I'm going to kill both of them," Rob added.

"And you are funny," I said.

"I know I'm fucking funny!"

"One more thing," the waitress said. "I almost forgot that the person who left the notes also wanted you to have this." She placed a big bowl of chocolate pudding on the table. "And I was told to tell you that you've been served *The Thanksgiving Special*," she said. "Whatever that means." She shrugged and walked away.

Chocolate fucking pudding. Rob and I had played a prank on Thanksgiving my senior year of high school. It had involved way too much pudding. And it was what had actually led to my brother and me originally falling out with Caldwells. The prank went way too far. We'd fucked everything up. Nothing had ever been the same since. But I'd come tonight trying to put it all behind us. I'd wanted to move forward. And this is what they did?

"Cock suckers," Rob said.

"I'm so confused," Penny said. "What's *The Thanksgiving Special*? And who serves pudding at Thanksgiving?"

I couldn't talk about this right now. "We're going to Mason's." Matt moved around too much. I actually had no idea where he lived right now. And we could handle him calling Rob unfunny later. Right now I needed to beat the shit out of Mason.

Rob stood up too. He cracked his neck to the side. "Only brothers can joke about hooking up with their brother's fiancée. And the Caldwells will never be our fucking brothers again. I can't hang out with people with no sense of humor."

"Wait," Penny said and grabbed my hand. "I'm sure there's some kind of explanation…"

"He said he was going to touch you, Penny." She knew how I felt about that. She knew what I'd done to Professor McCarty after he'd laid hands on her. And Professor McCarty wasn't my fucking friend. This was a betrayal.

"But he hasn't. I'm sure there's a simple explanation…"

"Penny, not everyone is redeemable. The Caldwells are shit and they'll always be shit."

"What he said." Rob tapped my shoulder. "I wonder if Matt will think it's funny when I shove his head in a toilet."

"No one is shoving anyone's heads into toilets!" Penny said. "We're not in high school!"

Well apparently some of us were still stuck in high school. And if there's one thing I loved when I was a teenager, it was beating the shit out of someone. I stormed out of the bar.

"Can't we talk about this?" Penny said as she ran after me and Rob.

"You!" someone yelled from across the street.

I turned to see Matt and Mason standing outside another bar across the street. And they looked just as pissed off as us.

"I'm going to fucking kill you!" Matt yelled.

He could try. But I was going to be busy killing his brother.

Matt stepped into the street, ignoring the traffic. A car slammed on its brakes and stopped just in time. Matt hit his fist on the top of the car and ran toward me. And he didn't stop running when he reached the sidewalk. He slammed his shoulder into me, making my back collide with the brick wall behind me.

If he wanted a fight, I'd give him a fight. I pulled my elbow down. It collided hard with his shoulder.

Matt grunted and pulled back.

I immediately took a swing at him. My fist collided with his jaw.

"Stop it!" Penny yelled.

Matt swung back. And I wasn't quick enough to dodge it. I had just gotten rid of my black eye that Tyler freaking Stevens had given me. And now I was going to have another. I somehow managed to get Matt into a headlock as I gave myself a second to see straight.

"I'm funny, bitch!" Rob yelled.

I turned to see him punch Mason square in the nose. Mason's nose erupted with blood.

"You think my parents love you more?" Mason yelled at him as he grabbed his nose.

What was he talking about?

LOVED

"No one fucking loves you!" Mason forgot his bloody nose and lunged at Rob.

"Maybe no one likes you because you're a deranged pervert!" I yelled at Mason. I let go of Matt and slammed into Mason before he could hit Rob again. The two of us fell to the ground.

I grabbed the front of Mason's shirt. "If you ever touch my fiancée I will end you."

"As if I'd want anything a Hunter touched." He punched the side of my ribcage.

I winced and fell to the side. I could see Matt running over to us out of the corner of my eye. Rob jumped on his back to try and stall him. But it just made the two of them fall over.

"All of you, stop!" Penny screamed.

But I already had the taste of blood in my mouth. And I'd always loved fighting. Knocking someone out was the ultimate feeling of control.

I wasn't even sure who was winning. But all my swings landed. And I barely felt any pain.

Matt put his hand on the front of my throat. "Brooklyn loved you more?" His voice cracked.

What? I'd never said that.

There were tears in his eyes. And it wasn't from the cut on his cheek or his black eye. He tightened his fingers on my throat, like he actually wanted to kill me.

I felt bad about what happened back in high school. It haunted me. But I was a better man now. I'd worked hard to be better for Penny. And it didn't matter how bad I felt about my past. I wasn't going to let it ruin my future. And I didn't deserve to die for what I'd done when I was a teenager.

I lifted my knee, slamming it into Matt's junk.

Matt groaned and fell to the side.

I scrambled to my feet. I thought about what he'd just said. And what Mason had said. Something about his parents loving Rob more? What the fuck were they both talking about?

Penny stepped in front of me. Like she could protect me from the next blow. "Robert Hunter!" she yelled. "Stop it!"

A car's tires screeched. I turned to see Ian open the door from the inside.

I grabbed the back of Rob's shirt and pulled him to the car. We all climbed in.

Matt was just sitting on the sidewalk with his face in his hands. But Mason was still standing.

"You sick fucks!" Mason threw an envelope like the one he'd sent us at the windshield of the car. "You invited us here just to bring up Thanksgiving again? Go back to Delaware! No one wants you here!"

"I wonder what they were so upset about," Rob said as he wiped the blood off his mouth with the back of his hand.

Our car sped off.

I stared at Matt as our car passed him. There was a polaroid on the ground beside him in the street.

And I had a sinking feeling in my stomach. If Mason had an invitation… And Matt had a polaroid…

Fuck. I didn't think Mason had invited us out for drinks. Someone had set us up. Someone who knew enough about us to crawl under our skin. Someone who knew about the pudding prank. And there was only one person who remembered that night better than anyone. *Isabella.*

Chapter 37

Friday

"What the fuck?" Ian said as he sped down the street.

I didn't even know what to say.

"I know, right?" Rob said. "The Caldwells are a bunch of pussies. I think we should circle back and kick their asses a second time."

Penny shook her head and looked up at me. I was starting to get used to her looking at me with disappointment. Why did I keep fucking up so bad?

"I asked you to stop," she said. "Both of you," she added and gave Rob a death stare. "Why does no one ever listen to me?"

I pressed my lips together.

"Especially after what you both did to Professor McCarty? Don't either of you ever think before punching someone?"

Ian stayed quiet even though he'd been there with us when we visited Professor McCarty.

"I thought they were your best friends. Who punches their best friends?"

Rob turned around to look at us from the front seat. "You saw what they said. They're a sack of dicks."

"Maybe they were provoked by what you two said to them? Did you ever think about that?"

"I didn't say shit to them," Rob said.

"Well one of you did. Something about their parents hating them? Or...loving Brooklyn or something? I don't know. I'm so confused. I thought you guys grew up in Manhattan? Why did Matt say you loved Brooklyn more than him? At least, I think that was Matt. I didn't exactly get the introduction I was promised."

Rob and I glanced at each other.

"Great, you're not going to tell me." She threw up her hands. "Just keep me in the dark like always."

"Penny." I grabbed her hand but she pulled away from me. *Fair.* "I think maybe Isabella set us up."

"What?" Penny and Rob both said at the same time.

"That invitation always felt off. When I first got it, I was worried about it being from Isabella. But then I texted Mason and I thought he said it was from him." I shook my head. "But I don't know. Maybe he just said he was excited to see me too. Because he got an invitation from…me? I saw it in his hand. And I didn't fucking send it."

Penny just stared at me.

"And there was a polaroid on the ground next to Matt. I definitely didn't send that." And I was pretty sure I knew what it had said. That Brooklyn loved me more than him. *Fuck.* I never would have said that to him. "And Rob didn't send it." *I hope.* "Right, Rob?"

"No," he said. "Shit, are you serious right now? Isabella did this?"

"Isabella is the only one who knows the four of us well enough to get under our skin. And we played this dumb prank in high school one Thanksgiving involving chocolate pudding. She was there." The prank had been on Isabella. And she'd never gotten over it.

"So Isabella is the only one that knows the four you that well, huh?" Penny asked. Her voice was quiet. She sounded so hurt.

"That's not what I meant. She knew the four of us back then. I didn't mean anything by it."

"It's fine," Penny said. But she sure sounded upset.

"Penny…"

"I'm not an idiot, James. I know you were married to her. I know she knows you. All of you. I just..." her voice trailed off. "It doesn't matter. This is all such a mess. But if the two of you had listened to me and stopped fighting, maybe you could have figured this out together. And no one would have gotten hurt." She stared at my eye that I was sure was starting to turn purple.

Fuck. I wasn't used to being part of an us. I was used to doing whatever I wanted. Whenever I wanted. No matter how fucking stupid it was. But I wasn't single anymore. And I was trying to be less destructive.

What had I been thinking? I opened my mouth and closed it again. I didn't know what to say.

Penny folded her arms across her chest and stared out the window.

The rest of the ride home was silent.

I couldn't believe how stupid I'd been. I knew in my gut that something felt wrong about the invitation. I knew it and yet I hadn't followed up. I pulled out my phone and found the text exchanges between me and Mason. I'd asked him how he was. And he'd responded: "I'm good, man. Excited to see you in a couple weeks."

I'd never asked him about the fucking invitation. I'd been too distracted about my life blowing up around me. Which Isabella knew. Because she'd leaked the story to the press. She knew I'd be rattled. Off my game. That crazy bitch.

I took a deep breath and turned to Penny. And now I'd messed this up. Because I'd implied that Isabella knew me better than Penny did. And that couldn't be further from the truth.

Ian seemed eager to get away from the awkwardness, because as soon as we parked, he pretended to take a phone call. I knew it was a fake call. The only person that called him this late was me. And also his phone didn't ring.

So it was just Penny, Rob, and me on the elevator. The silent streak continued. I'd actually never seen Rob this quiet for this long.

Penny finally broke the silence when we stepped into the apartment. "Go sit down on the couch. Both of you."

Rob elbowed me in the side as we made our way to the couch. "I think we're in trouble."

"You think?" We both sat down.

Penny came over with peroxide and a box of Band-Aids. She'd probably picked some up after I beat the shit out of Professor McCarty.

She ignored me and started patching up Rob.

"I like when you take care of me," he said.

"Stop talking," she said and put a Band-Aid across his knuckles. And then she turned to me. She sighed and touched the side of my face. "What am I going to do with you?"

"Kiss me?"

"I need a kiss too," Rob said. "I got a booboo."

She sighed and cleaned the cut on my cheek. And then bandaged my hand for the second time in two weeks. She handed both Rob and me icepacks. Usually she sat next to me on the couch, but tonight she decided to sit in the chair across from us. Apparently so we could see the disappointment on her face.

I lowered the icepack from my eye. "I still have that piggy bank," I said. "But I'd prefer if you just told me what you were thinking." I thought she'd smile from the reference to a penny for her thoughts. But...she did not.

And Rob gave me a weird look. At least, I think he did. His face was half covered with an icepack too.

"What the hell are you talking about?" Rob asked. "Did Matt hit your head too hard against that brick wall?"

I ignored him and turned to Penny. "Please. Talk to me. Just tell me what you're thinking."

She pressed her lips together. "Well…it turns out I'm glad we have a driver. Because I can call him to save us when you two get into a street fight in the middle of the city."

I was wondering how Ian had known to show up at exactly the right time. "You called him tonight?"

She nodded. "At least one man in this city listens to me."

I deserved that.

"I told you to stop fighting a million times. After what just happened with Professor McCarty…I thought the two of you were done with this crap."

"I never promised to stop beating the shit out of people," Rob said. "It's one of my special talents."

"If you're staying in our apartment, you're not getting into fights," she said.

"But…"

"It's not up for negotiation, Rob. No fighting."

He sighed. "Fine, *Mom*."

Penny almost smiled at his comment. Almost.

"And you," she said and turned to me. "I don't like seeing you hurt."

"You should see the other guy," I said with a smile.

"Not funny." She got off her chair and sat next to me on the couch. "James, even if Mason had actually said those things about me? I wouldn't have wanted you to get in a fight. I don't want you to ever get hurt. You're the love of my life. I need you. Stop putting yourself in danger."

"James can take Mason in a fight," Rob said. "Mason may be built bigger, but he doesn't know what to do with his big dumb beef hands."

"Robert."

Rob laughed. "I like when you call me that. It's kinky as fuck."

Penny sighed and focused on me again. "I don't care if you have more experience fighting than Mason. He's built like a football player. Stop hitting people. Period."

"Okay," I said.

She grabbed the icepack out of my hand and put it back on my eye. "Promise me," she said.

"I promise, baby."

Her face finally cracked in a smile. I knew how much she liked when I called her that.

"Come here," I said and tried to pull her onto my lap.

"No," she said and swatted my hand away. "You two are both in trouble. I want you to sit here and silently think about what you've done."

"You're taking this mom thing too far," Rob said. "It's a fine line between sexy and demeaning."

"Phones," Penny said and held out her hand.

"Seriously? You're taking our phones?" Rob asked.

She kept her hand out.

"Gah. Fine." Rob handed her his phone and I did the same.

Penny got up off the couch and walked up the stairs to our bedroom.

"I really like her," Rob said and leaned back on the couch. "You've got a keeper there."

"I know." I kept my eyes trained on Penny until she disappeared into our bedroom and closed the door.

"My back hurts a bit. I think Matt karate chopped me or some weird shit. Do you think Penny can give me a massage?"

"Don't push it."

The elevators dinged and Ian walked in. He must have known Penny was out of the room.

"The front desk said this was delivered while we were out." He handed me an envelope that looked like the others.

I tore it open and read the note inside:

Hello Darling,

I hope you enjoyed the last gift you'll ever receive from me. The truth that you and all your friends all desperately needed to hear. Just facts. Hope I didn't cause a riff. Enjoy the rest of your terrible life without me.

XOXO,

Isabella Hunter

"I don't love how she signed her name," Rob said. "Is she seriously not changing her last name back to Pruitt?"

"Psycho," Ian said.

I didn't really care about that. I was fixated on the fact that she said enjoy the rest of my terrible life without her. I thought her parting gift was leaking all that fake shit to the news. But if she was telling me goodbye now? I'd take it.

Isabella was officially out of my life.

But she'd sure fucked up a bunch of stuff before leaving.

"I can't believe that after all these years, Isabella still doesn't think I'm funny." Rob shrugged. "What a troll."

She knew what would hurt Rob's feelings. She knew one of my friends saying they were going to bang Penny would make me furious. She knew Mason was struggling with his parents and feeling insecure. And Matt...she knew how to rip his heart out. And pinning it all on each other? Evil genius. She was definitely off her meds. But she wasn't my problem anymore. Hopefully her father would get her the help she needed. I just wanted to pretend the last few years with her had never happened. I was done punishing myself. And no one deserved living with Isabella as a punishment.

"Well, at least her retaliation is done," I said. I'd been a little worried about being back in the same city as Isabella. It was good to get whatever that was out of the way.

"It does seem like that's the end of it," Ian said.

Rob nodded. "She'll surely find someone else to sink her claws into."

Yeah. Hopefully. I felt bad for whoever her next victim was.

"Well that was another eventful evening," Ian said. "I think I'm going to cut out early."

"Good night, Ian."

As soon as he left, Rob shook his head. "I bet he's going to go bang our sister."

"Would you stop it? Ian's not sleeping with Jen."

Rob shrugged. "If you say so."

Penny's footsteps on the stairs made me look up. She'd changed out of her sexy red dress and into a tank top and a pair of yoga pants. She looked great. Especially because she was smiling now. But I would have rather peeled that red dress off her. I guess getting into a fight with my friends and not listening to her meant no sexy red dress.

She handed Rob and me our phones back and then plopped down onto the couch between us.

"Why do you look so happy?" I asked.

"No reason."

I stared at her.

"I get to pick the movie tonight, right? Because you two were both terrible?"

Rob groaned. "Not another rom-com. I'm all rom-commed out, Penny."

"Then next time don't punch your friend in the nose when he's clearly upset about his parents." She grabbed the remote and selected exactly what Rob didn't want.

He groaned again.

I spaced out during the beginning of the movie, trying to think of how I could possibly apologize to Matt and Mason. Yeah, I didn't send those notes. But we were all upset because clearly we believed we'd say this fucked up shit to each other. And I wasn't sure how we were going to move past it when we were all still fucked up from high school.

First I needed to fix things with Penny though. Despite what Rob said about the movie, he was totally engrossed.

"Come with me," I whispered in Penny's ear. "I need to show you something real quick." I grabbed her hand before she could protest, and led her up the stairs to our room.

"I got you something. Well, a few somethings."

"James. I told you to stop buying me things."

"These barely cost anything." I pulled out a box from under the bed and set it on the covers. "And one of them I didn't even buy." I opened my wallet and handed her a black Amex card with her name on it.

She stared at the card and then back at me. "What am I supposed to do with this?"

I laughed. "Buy whatever you want."

"I don't need anything."

"Well, we need to decorate our new apartment."

"Which we're going to do together." She tried to hand me the card back.

But I refused to take it.

"James, I don't want a credit card."

"But I want you to have it."

"You know...it is so tempting to go buy like...a big couch from Macy's or something to teach you a lesson."

"A couch, huh? From Macy's? That $1,000 will really set me back."

She shook her head.

"You can't even think of something more expensive than a couch, can you?"

"Well luckily for you I'm not an asshole that wants to spend all your money."

"One of the many reasons why I love you."

Her cheeks flushed. "I'm not going to use the card."

"Better to have it just in case. Now open the box."

She lifted the lid to the box and smiled. "You framed it." She grabbed the picture of me and Rob from the bar the other night. I had no idea why she wanted a framed photo where Rob was giving her the finger. But she'd asked for it, and she seemed very pleased.

"Penny?"

She looked up at me.

"I'm sorry I didn't listen to you tonight when you told me to stop. It won't happen again. And just for the record...you know me better than anyone else."

"Thanks, James." She held the picture to her chest. "That means a lot to me."

"And I like to think I know you better than anyone else. I know you had a lot of these on your bed back home." I gestured back to the box. "I know you can snuggle up to me now, but I wanted you to feel at home here too. With me."

She picked up the stuffed teddy bear. "You bought me a stuffed animal? So I'd feel at home in New York?"

I nodded.

She threw her arms around me.

I laughed and caught her before she knocked us both over.

"That is the sweetest thing, James." She smiled up at me. "I was worried about being homesick. But honestly? I haven't been at all. I love it here with you. Really, James. You're all I need."

I knew what she meant. She was home to me too.

"One moment you're hitting your friends and the next minute you're buying me a stuffed animal? Our life it going to be quite the rollercoaster, isn't it?"

I had a feeling that everything was going to be okay from here on out. Isabella was out of our lives. I'd figure out some way to make this all up to my friends. And most importantly…I had Penny. I pressed my lips against hers. Now I just needed to convince her to put her red dress back on so I could tear it off her with my teeth.

Chapter 38

Saturday

I reached out across the bed but all I felt were empty sheets. I slowly opened my eyes. Penny was nowhere in sight. I yawned and sat up.

Recently Penny and I had been sleeping in together. Enjoying these lazy mornings just the two of us. But I heard muffled voices downstairs. Her and Rob must have both already been up. And I could smell bacon in the air.

I pulled on a pair of pajama pants and headed downstairs. Penny, Mason, and Matt were all in the living room. *Wait. Mason and Matt?*

"If you don't clean it, you'll get an infection," Penny said as she blotted some peroxide over Mason's knuckles.

He winced. But only for a second. Penny finished bandaging him up. It looked like Matt had already been taken care of.

"Thanks, Penny," Mason said. He smiled at her. And not in a "I'm going to bang your girlfriend and then put her in a sex auction" way. It was a genuine smile.

But I was really confused about what Mason and Matt were doing here.

"You're welcome," Penny said. "Like I said last night, any friends of James' are friends of mine."

When had they talked last night? I was with her all night.

"Were you really his student?" Matt asked. "I saw the tabloids."

"Yeah. It's a long story. But we moved here for a fresh start. And I know James wants that fresh start to include the two of you. He mentioned that you guys all grew apart after college. But I know he misses you. You're his best friends."

I was pretty sure the rest of the apology had to come from me. I cleared my throat.

Penny turned toward me. "Surprise!"

I waited for either Mason or Matt to lunge at me like they had yesterday. But they just sat there.

"I explained everything to each of them last night," she said as she walked over to me.

"When?"

"When I made you and Rob give me your phones."

I shook my head, but I couldn't help but smile. My friends were sitting there. Not attacking me. "What exactly did you say to them?" Because I felt like I owed them apologies for the last few years.

"I explained the whole misunderstanding. Isabella's vengeance or whatever you want to call it. And they both agreed to bury the hatchet. As long as you do. I told them that they're your best friends. And that you want to move forward now that you're back here for good. The past is in the past, right?" She smiled up at me.

I nodded. "Thank you, Penny." This was better than any of the gifts I'd given her last night.

"And I invited them over for breakfast so the four of you could talk. Which I need to go finish cooking. How about you go talk to them. And please, please don't fight."

"I promised you I wouldn't."

She kissed my cheek and went into the kitchen.

I shoved my hands into my pockets. "So Penny told you what happened?"

"Yeah," Matt said. "The troll strikes again."

"I'm sorry about Isabella," I said.

"We should have known that you'd never say that shit," Mason said. "And as soon as I saw that fancy invitation for a bar hangout, I was wondering what the fuck happened to you."

I laughed. "I thought the same thing about you." I sat down next to Matt on the couch.

"I knew you guys thought I was funny!" Rob said as he walked into the room.

Mason laughed. "Annoying. Funny. Same difference."

"So does that mean we're cool again?" Rob asked. "Because I've missed the four of us hanging out. It's been a long time since we were all together."

I'd missed it too. We'd been inseparable growing up.

"Yeah," Matt said. "We're good."

Mason nodded. "And unlike what I said last night...I'm glad you're both back in New York. We've missed you too."

"I knew it!" Rob ran over to the couch and belly flopped on top of us.

Mason groaned.

I laughed.

Matt pushed him off onto the floor.

Rob got up off the ground and sat down on the couch too. "Just like old times. And I'm glad you don't actually want to fuck Penny, because then James never would have been able to invite you over."

Mason shrugged. "I mean, she is hot. And...*kind.*" He frowned and looked down at his bandaged knuckles.

"So she's from Delaware?" Matt asked.

I nodded.

"And she's your student?"

"She was."

He scratched the side of his jaw. "Does she know about Brooklyn?"

"No. I've done my best to keep my word to you. The only person I've ever talked about her to is my therapist. And I didn't use her real name. I know I've been a shit friend. But I'd never betray you, Matt. Never."

He nodded.

"And whenever you do want to talk about her...I'm here. And I'm not going anywhere this time."

"There isn't really anything to say, James."

I thought there was a lot to say. But I wasn't going to push it. Matt would talk to me when he was ready. And now that I was back in the city, I really would be here whenever that time came.

"I really am sorry about the past few years. I was in a dark place."

"Understandable," Mason said. "You married Isabel-la."

"Which we probably should have done more to prevent," Matt added. "But we were all fucked up."

"Except me," Rob said. "I've always been great."

"I wouldn't describe anything about you as great," Mason said.

"Well your parents would." Rob immediately lifted his hands to show his innocence. "Just kidding, man."

Mason shook his head.

"But seriously, guys," I said. I just needed to get this off my chest. "Penny probably said a bunch of embarrassing stuff about you guys being my best friends or whatever. Because I've told her a lot about you guys. So whatever she said to get you to come over today...it's all true."

"She told us that to make up for you being terrible the past few years, you want us to gangbang her in front of you," Rob said.

"Rob, I just promised Penny I wouldn't hit anyone today. So…stop."

"I mean…" Mason said. "We are here to make new memories and start fresh, right?"

"It would make up for those terrible things your ex-wife said to us," Matt agreed.

"Absolutely not," I said firmly. "Penny is my fiancée. Which means she's off-limits."

Rob shook his head. "How many times do I have to remind you that an engagement ring is more of a yield sign than a stop sign?"

"More like a green light really," Mason said. "The diamond is practically a beacon, calling out to get triple-teamed."

I rolled my eyes. I knew they were joking. But still.

Matt rubbed his hands together. "The only question is how we decide who goes where. I'm thinking we play rock, paper, scissors."

"I'm already rock hard just thinking about it," Mason said.

Penny sighed.

We all turned toward her.

"I just knew it," she said. "I knew you'd all be like Rob."

Mason laughed. "Like Rob? Never."

"A little like Rob," she said and set down a huge platter of waffles, eggs, and bacon. "Because you're all clearly joking around at my expense. Just like Rob." She gave Rob a fake stern look.

I was glad she wasn't actually upset. She knew it was just guy talk. And I was surprised how seamlessly she fit in with my friends. I shouldn't have been surprised though. Because she already got along great with Rob.

Mason grabbed a plate. "You seriously think we're just like Rob? That is the worst thing you could ever say to someone."

Rob elbowed his side and they both laughed.

It felt like old times. For real. The four of us. Well, the five of us now. I definitely preferred it the five of us.

I pulled Penny onto my lap. "Thank you for this, Penny."

"You're welcome, Professor Hunter," she whispered into my ear.

Matt choked on his waffle. "Did she just call you Professor Hunter?"

Ah, for fuck's sake. But it was strange. I didn't actually feel angry. I expected to. Normally I would have lashed out. But...I loved when Penny called me Professor Hunter. I loved the way we were together. And all I could do was smile. I didn't even have to remind myself to breathe.

I promised myself I'd be a better man for Penny. And I was better when I was around her. I was better when I was with my friends.

I'd put so much pressure on myself for as long as I could remember. Trying to please my parents. Trying to be something I wasn't meant to be. But really, life was simple when you really looked at it.

It wasn't about being a CEO. Or a perfect son. Or a great friend all the time. Or even about being a professor.

I was just a man. Who'd fallen in love with a beautiful woman. She knew all my demons. And she chose to love me back in spite of them.

I kissed the side of her neck. "I love you," I whispered.

She turned to look up at me. She looked so happy. So carefree. So fucking gorgeous.

"I love you," she said and pressed her lips against mine.

She wasn't asking me to be better. She wasn't asking anything of me at all. She just loved me. For me.

I guess even some monsters deserved to be loved.

What's Next?

Professor Hunter and Penny know how to melt a kindle.
And I can't stop writing about them!

To get your free copy of a steamy bonus scene about
James and Penny, go to:

www.ivysmoak.com/loved-pb

A Note From Ivy

The end? Nooooo. James Hunter will always have a piece of my heart. And it is so freaking hard to say good-bye to these characters!! I can't even.

Honestly, I can't even. That's why I'm writing the next generation. Gah but James!

I hope you loved his point-of-view just as much as Penny's. I hope you understand James better. Getting into his head was one of my favorite things. All that pain. And healing. No one deserves Isabella as punishment.

Also, if you have no idea who Brooklyn is or what really went down with James, Rob, Mason, and Matt in high school, then boy do I have a story for you!! Check out the Empire High series. Teenage James will steal your heart all over again.

I'm sitting here and I can't believe it's really over. I'm going to go cry now.

At least I know that James Hunter will always be loved. Not just by Penny and his friends. But by all of us. Because everyone deserves to be loved.

Ivy Smoak

Ivy Smoak
Wilmington, DE
www.ivysmoak.com

About the Author

Ivy Smoak is the USA Today and Wall Street Journal best-selling author of *The Hunted Series*. Her books have sold over 4 million copies worldwide.

When she's not writing, you can find Ivy binge watching too many TV shows, taking long walks, playing outside, and generally refusing to act like an adult. She lives with her husband in Delaware.

TikTok: @IvySmoak
Facebook: IvySmoakAuthor
Instagram: @IvySmoakAuthor
Goodreads: IvySmoak

Recommend *Loved* for your next book club!

Book club questions available at:
www.ivysmoak.com/bookclub

Printed in the USA
CPSIA information can be obtained
at www.ICGtesting.com
LVHW090402150224
771721LV00009B/897

9 781942 381587